YUREI

LEGEND OF THE SHADOW BLADE

MIKE BIDWELL

FLO LIFE PUBLISHING

Cover art and Illustration by Chris J'Tot
Formatting by Sienna Arts

ISBN 979-8-9907378-2-2

Published by FLO Life Publishing
Printed in the United States of America

First Edition 2025

Thank you for the gift of this book,
and for all that emerges through its existence.
May the Hum Resonate.

Contents

PROLOGUE

He looked up to the blue sky as he lay dying, the vast expanse above seeming to stretch into infinity. The sun's fading rays felt warm on his face, a stark contrast to the cold shadow that was now creeping through his body. He could feel the darkness pulling at his insides. He used his last bit of strength to touch the cold hand of his closest friend. This is how they would die, side by side, just as they had lived and fought.

"Wake up!" The voice was but a whisper. "Where am I?" He spoke, but with no words. "You were there, but you are now here. The space you exist in for now is neither here nor there but between life and death." The voice was soft, feminine, and familiar.

He could not hear or speak, but he was communicating with his thoughts.

"Who are you? Am I dead?"

"I am a Loa Spirit. I found you, and I can save you and help you seek revenge on those who have wronged you. I can be your guide." He listened. "If you wish to live, you must bind yourself to me and adhere to the path."

"What is the path?" he asked the spirit.

She whispered, "Follow me."

He opened his eyes and saw bright stars staring back at him. The air was cool and crisp as darkness blanketed the landscape. He felt an urge to stand up, but he could not move. "Where am I? Who am I?" he asked no one in particular.

She answered, "Your name is now Yurei. I chose this name for you. It means spirit or ghost, as you are now a shadow of your former self." The voice was not coming from outside of him but from inside his head. Yurei began to feel weak and hungry. But it wasn't a hunger for ordinary food. The voice spoke, "You must feed."

PART ONE

Chapter One

AWAKEN

He was sleeping when he heard his father announce his name from the fields, "Haruto! It's time to work!" He would be angry as they were already tending to the gardens. If he was late again, he would surely receive a lashing with a rice stalk.

The air was warm as the seasonal fog crawled its way across the landscape. The mountains in the distance stood silently, their imposing silhouettes acting as steadfast guardians of the village. Haruto was a farmer, but not by choice, rather by the traditions of his ancestors who had worked the land for generations.

Despite his acceptance of his families role, Haruto's heart yearned for a different path. He often dreamt of becoming a warrior, the feeling of the weight of a sword in his hand and the thrill of battle. But that dream remained distant and unattainable. His father would often remind him with a stern tone, "We are farmers, and we feed the warriors. Without us, everyone dies!" His father was a big strong formidable man, while Haruto was small for his age.

Haruto understood the important responsibility his family's work played in sustaining the village, but the repetitive toil of the fields left him feeling empty. Each day, he dragged his farm tools through the dirt. The rhythmic work felt like a chain binding him to a life he did not choose... or want.

As he worked, his mind would wander to visions of samurai warriors clad in armor, their swords brilliant and glowing in the sunlight. He imagined himself among them, his heart racing with the excitement of combat and the honor of defending his family and village. But for today, Haruto knew he must set aside his dreams. He would do as he was told and farm, the scraping of his tools against the soil a constant reminder of his duty to family first.

Haruto, whose name means "light," was born on an early morning as the sun peeked over the horizon, casting a golden glow across the land. From the moment he entered the world, he seemed to carry the serenity of dawn within him. As a baby, he was unusually quiet, his large, curious eyes taking in the world around him without a sound. Unlike other infants who wailed for attention, Haruto rarely cried, his silence a constant source of concern for his father.

He would sit with his face filled with frustration. "If my son cannot speak, how will his voice be heard?" He would plead to the empty room, his voice deep with worry. He feared that his silence might be a sign of some deeper issue, a barrier that would prevent him from finding his place in the world.

His mother, though equally concerned, took a more pragmatic view. "He is observing, learning in his own way," she would reassure him. Yet, even her calm words could not entirely dispel his fears. She would watch Haruto as he lay on his small tatami mat, his tiny fingers grasping at the air, his eyes following the movements of shadows and light with an intensity that seemed beyond his years.

As he grew, Haruto's quiet nature persisted. He preferred the company of nature, spending hours watching the way the leaves rustled in the wind or the way the sunlight slipped through the trees. His silence became a part of his identity, a tranquil presence that contrasted with the bustling energy of village life. His mother did not worry, she trusted in his unique nature and quiet demeanor, hoping that one day his inner light would shine as brightly as the dawn he was named after.

Even though words did not come easily for Haruto, his mind was always active, teeming with thoughts and observations. He was small and uncoordinated for his age but quick as a rabbit, he could dart from one spot to another, disappearing in a blur of motion. His speed was a source of amusement in the village, as he seemed to move like the wind, one moment here and the next gone.

Haruto's older brother, Daichi, whose name means "great first son," was three years his senior. Daichi was sturdy and dependable, embodying the strength and reliability expected of the firstborn. Despite their differences, the bond between the brothers was strong, marked by a mix of playful rivalry and genuine affection.

Often, Daichi would watch in awe as Haruto sprinted across the fields or wove through the trees with effortless grace. With a laugh, he would call out, "Be careful disappearing so quickly, Haruto! You might be mistaken for a shadow creature!" His teasing was gentle, a way to share in his brother's unique abilities and to warn him of the superstitions that lingered in their village.

Haruto, though often silent, would respond with a mischievous grin, his eyes twinkling with a silent challenge. He reveled in his ability to move unseen, becoming a fleeting shadow in the blink of an eye. Despite his skills, he was very careful not to show off or reveal too much.

Though typically reserved, there was a fierce intelligence in Haruto's eyes. He absorbed everything around him—the direction of the wind, the patterns of the clouds, the way the village elders spoke in hushed tones about ancient legends. His mind was a whirlwind of curiosity and understanding, even though his words were few.

As he grew, Haruto's quickness became both his signature and his shield, a testament to the vibrant life within him that sought expression in movement rather than speech. His mother began to see the depths of his perceptiveness and the strength in his silence. She knew the world would someday recognize the light that shone so brightly in her quiet, swift-footed son.

Haruto laughed and dashed around a corner, disappearing from sight. With a mischievous glint in his eye, he sneaked up behind Daichi, who was busy tending the animals.

"Get out of here, you little piglet!" Daichi exclaimed, playfully swatting at Haruto with a broom. "I don't need to catch you; Father will whip you if you don't hurry to the fields!"

Haruto, still grinning, quickly grabbed his tools and headed toward the fields. As he walked, he spotted his mother crouching in the garden, tugging at stubborn roots. She stood up and leaned on her walking stick. Her head was covered, and she wore a scarf over her face. She looked up and caught his eye, pulling down her scarf to reveal a warm smile that she quickly masked before his father could see.

The sight of his mother's fleeting smile gave Haruto a sense of comfort and encouragement. He hurried to his work, the weight of his tools barely noticeable as he thought about the morning's playful escape and his brother's teasing. He knew the work ahead would be hard, but the moments of lightheartedness with his mother and Daichi made the day more bearable.

The farm sat connected to a makeshift village that rested in the valley. Wooden houses sat in rows that were connected and heavily fortified by tall walls. Protection would come from the villagers. Additional security was offered (but seldom given) by the daimyo. The town would pay a rice tax to the warlord. This meant that nearly half of their annual rice yield went directly to the daimyo. In times of conflict, the daimyo could demand that young men take up arms in his service.

Providing food for an entire village placed great pressure on Haruto's family. While others also tended the fields, it was his father who oversaw the farming. A fourth-generation farmer, his father carried the weight of tradition and responsibility on his shoulders.

He had mastered his craft, but he knew that the will of the land was ever-changing. A season of too much rain, too little sun, or an untimely frost could spell ruin for all. As the years weighed on him, he understood that it would soon be his two sons who must have the strength to offer their devotion and seek favor from the harvest gods.

Haruto's father had always hoped for a larger family, more sons to help with the demanding farm work and to secure their future. However, fate had dealt them a harsh hand. Mother had endured the heartbreak of two additional pregnancies, both ending in tragedy. One baby passed away during birth, and another during pregnancy. On the third attempt, Haruto was born. Mother would often call him "her greatest miracle." After Haruto's birth she became infertile and could no longer bear children. Though Father longed for more children, he had to accept that her body could not endure another pregnancy.

Haruto enjoyed sitting by the communal fire, the warmth of the flames providing comfort as he listened to the elders speak. They would weave intricate tales of ghosts and blood-sucking demons, their voices filled with a mixture of reverence and caution. The elders' stories were not just for entertainment; they were filled with lessons and warnings. They spoke of vengeful spirits that roamed the forests, and demons that would punish young children who did not mind their parents. Haruto would sit wide-eyed, absorbing every word.

Haruto's favorite part of the day was when the work was done, and they could bathe in the river. While his father continued his labor, his mother would gather the boys and lead them to the river to be cleaned.

The journey was always a delightful break from the hard work in the fields. They followed a winding path through a vibrant field blanketed with flowers. The grass, lush and green, reached up to their chests, each stem crowned with delicate pink and purple blossoms that swayed gently in the breeze. The air was filled with the sweet fragrance of blooming flowers, a refreshing contrast to the smell of manure from working in the fields all day.

As they approached the village entrance, they passed between two imposing boulders that stood like natural guardians, marking the entrance of their village. Flanking the path on either side were large wooden gates, each adorned with intricate carvings that told the story of their ancestors. A guard stood watch, his posture firm and alert, gripping a long spear in his hands. His eyes briefly met those of Haruto's mother, and he gave a respectful nod. She returned the gesture with a modest nod of her own, her gaze quickly shifting away.

Daichi pointed to the guard with the spear and whispered, "That spear is silver-tipped to stop demons!" He then poked Haruto in the back, making him jump.

The sound of the river could now be heard in the distance, pouring down the mountainside. Mother moved slowly with what she called her "crooked walk." She had never shared with anyone why she walked that way and carried a stick to lean on. She always said, "It was just something she's had to live with." The boys moved faster, eventually breaking into a run as they neared the water. Mother smiled as she stepped into the shade to remove her head covering.

As the boys ran they pulled off their shirts and jumped right into the river. Haruto and Daichi popped their heads out of the water, spitting streams at each other. They laughed wildly as Mother shook her head in disapproval. When they submerged again, she couldn't help but smile to herself, a quiet giggle escaping her lips.

Mother would rub rich bran on the boys' bodies to loosen the dirt that had gathered from the fields. "Okay, stop, that's too hard!" Haruto would beg. Daichi laughed and dove back into the river.

Mother abruptly announced, "Okay boys, it is time for me to bathe. Go to the falls, but be back soon!" She pointed to a rock on top of the mountain. The boys knew that when the sun crossed the stone, they had to be home. At dark, the village gate closes and no one is to be let in or out. They loved to visit the falls, but mother would rarely let them go alone, so this was special.

Daichi looked at Haruto and pointed at his chest, "Stay with me and no disappearing!" He then grabbed Haruto by the back of his kimono and pushed him forward. "Walk in front of me so I can see you… you can be the samurai scout!" Haruto picked up a long tree limb, examined it, and nodded in approval. "You'll work just fine!"

He turned away from Daichi and advanced forward like a warrior entering the battlefield, weapon first. Daichi shook his head and laughed. They followed a winding dirt path that meandered through the fields and into a dense grove, eventually leading them to the base of the mountain. Here, a majestic waterfall cascaded down the rocks, its sparkling waters feeding into the clear, rushing river below. As they neared the water, two large white cranes took flight, their wings beating gracefully as they soared into the sky.

"Go in here!" Daichi instructed, pointing to a series of flat rocks that formed natural steps down into the water. "I'm going to jump in from the top," he insisted. Haruto watched as his brother climbed to a higher ledge, ready to leap into the deeper pool below. The rocks were slick with moss, but Daichi moved with the confidence of someone who had done this many times before. Haruto followed the steps, feeling the cool spray of the waterfall on his face, each step bringing him closer to the rushing water. Haruto was now in the water up to his torso. He then pointed to a rock that jutted out near the top of the waterfalls.

"Father said we should never jump off the top!"

Daichi responded, "It's not the top; it's the side." He was now making his way up the rocks. When he reached the top, he walked to the edge and looked up at the sun radiating through the rocks. He pointed his muscular arms upward and then jumped feet first. He went straight into the water like an arrow hitting a bullseye. When his head came up, Haruto jumped out of the water in excitement. Daichi pointed to the rocks above and demanded, "Your turn, little brother!" Haruto shook his head no. Daichi refused to accept it and said, "Do you wish to become a warrior or be a child forever?"

Haruto began climbing the rocks. He was quick but was known for his clumsiness. As he made his way forward, he refused to look back. The rocks beneath him were coming loose as he hurried his way up. Suddenly, as he reached for a higher boulder, a large foothold under his weight broke free. Haruto felt the stone shift, and in a terrifying instant, it dislodged completely. He could feel the rock scraping against his skin as it slipped away, tumbling downwards. Panic surged through him as he realized the large piece was falling directly towards Daichi, who was blissfully unaware in the water below.

In that moment, everything seemed to slow down. Haruto's heart pounded in his chest, the sound echoing in his ears like a drumbeat. Time itself seemed to shift into a surreal, almost dreamlike state. He could see every detail with crystal clarity: the sunlight reflecting off the falling rock, Daichi's carefree splashing in the water below, and the path of the rock as it hurtled towards his brother.

In one burst of energy, Haruto whispered, "Jump," and was instantly propelled through the air to Daichi, pushing him out of the way of the incoming boulder. They were now on the side of the river in waist-high water, with Haruto pinning his larger brother against the rocky riverbank. Daichi, who was unable to move, looked confused and said, "How did you do that?" Before he could answer, Haruto interrupted, saying, "The sun is disappearing; we must go!" Slowly, Haruto stood up, his legs wobbly from the jump.

When they arrived at the gate, mother was impatiently waiting as the last bit of sunlight was disappearing behind the mountains. The boys rushed through the gates with mother hurriedly pushing them along as the guard closed the wooden structure behind them. Haruto was able to avoid Daichi before bed and any possible questions about what had happened at the falls.

Haruto had never confided in anyone about his extraordinary experiences. Yet, he was certain his mother knew; her silent understanding acted as a shield to protect him. The villagers, steeped in superstition, would undoubtedly accuse him of being a demon. The emperor, on the other hand, might see him as a powerful weapon to be exploited. To prevent either fate, his mother kept his secret safe, never breathing a word to anyone, not even to her husband.

His mother had witnessed it for the first time when Haruto was just a baby. She had sat him on a tatami mat and turned her back for only a moment. Hearing him make a rare sound, she turned to look at him, and somehow, he had moved to the other side of the room. Her heart had skipped a beat, but she quickly composed herself, resolving to keep this secret for his sake. This incident was the first of many, each one more astounding than the last. As he grew, Haruto's ability became harder to conceal, but his mother remained vigilant in hiding it from everyone.

Haruto lay restlessly on his straw pillow, waiting for his family to quiet once and for all. The room was bathed in a cool, silvery glow as a trickle of moonlight crept through the small window. He listened intently as the sounds of the household slowly began to fade. Once the house was silent and still, Haruto rose quietly, careful not to disturb the delicate peacefulness of the night. He moved in total silence, his feet whispering against the wooden floor. He slipped out of the room and into the cool night air, his heart pounding with anticipation.

The path to their usual meeting spot was well-trodden, a secret trail known only to him and Rumiko. He moved swiftly through the shadows, the trickle of moonlight barely guiding his steps as he navigated through the dark village. The crisp night air invigorated him as he approached the clearing where they always met. Haruto walked slowly, his steps confident and unhurried. It was easy for him to quickly move from one spot to the next at an accelerated speed. He wasn't entirely sure how it worked; he simply pictured a place in his mind, imagined himself jumping forward, and he would jump through the air like a blur. The more familiar the place, the quicker he could jump to it.

At fifteen years old, this ability had been part of him for as long as he could remember. Over time, he had honed it, becoming more adept at controlling it. At least, that's what he believed.

The night sky was dark and silent, the village was bathed in shadows, the only light now was coming from a crackling fire in the open area between the houses. Its warm glow flickered against the walls. The fire was kept burning throughout the night to provide light for the guards, who stood watch until dawn.

He had heard the story many times. Two summers ago, three children had been mysteriously taken from their beds over three nights as they slept and were never seen again. There were no bodies or ransom demands. They simply disappeared. It was rumored that children from other villages had also vanished. Some warned it was an evil shapeshifter called the Kurokawa, which the elders often spoke of. Regardless, village life was never the same again after the disappearance of these children.

Haruto moved stealthily, his figure blending seamlessly with the shadows. He passed by the familiar wooden huts, their thatched roofs silhouetted against the night sky. The cool air whispered through the narrow streets. The village was in lockdown, its gates closed until the first light of day, a precaution against the dangers that lurked in the dark.

He paused for a moment, closing his eyes and visualizing his destination. In his mind, he saw the clearing where he and Rumiko always met. He could almost feel the soft grass underfoot and hear the gentle rustling of the leaves. Taking a deep breath, he concentrated, imagining the leap forward.

He whispered aloud, "Jump!" as if willing his body to move. In an instant, he hurtled through the air and was there. Haruto took a moment to steady himself, as he always felt slightly dizzy and wobbly after a jump.

He looked around, his eyes searching the shadows for any sign of Rumiko. This place, their secret haven, was where he felt truly at peace. Here, under the watchful gaze of the stars, he could forget the worries of the day and be himself. Haruto waited, knowing that Rumiko would soon join him, bringing with her the comfort and companionship he so dearly cherished.

As Haruto sat silently, he spotted Rumiko moving gracefully along the side of a house, her beautiful form blending effortlessly with the dark shadows. She wore a black kimono that hugged her slender figure, and a matching black scarf that concealed her face.

As Haruto approached, Rumiko turned and, with a deliberate slowness, unraveled the scarf from her face. The fabric slipped down, revealing her long, black hair cascading freely over her shoulders and down her back past her hips. In the soft glow of the night, her hair radiated like an endless silken waterfall. Haruto paused, taken aback by the sight. He wasn't accustomed to seeing her hair down and flowing. During the day, it was always meticulously styled in a traditional manner—neat and elegant. But now, under the cloak of night, with her hair loose and flowing, she seemed free and unrestrained.

Rumiko's eyes met Haruto's, and a shy smile played on her lips. "I wasn't sure you'd come," she whispered, her voice soft against the night sounds.

Haruto stepped closer, his heart pounding. "I'll always come for you," he replied softly, his gaze lingering on her transformed appearance. The nearby fire cast a gentle glow over them, creating an intimate nest of soft light. In that moment, the world outside their secret meeting spot faded away, leaving only the two of them crouching together in the quiet embrace of the night.

He quickly realized he was staring, and Rumiko blushed before turning away. They walked to a large boulder and huddled behind it. The two of them had been close friends since Rumiko arrived in the village to live with her grandmother when she was ten years old. Now sixteen, Rumiko was a year older than him. Haruto felt a deep connection to her but couldn't bear the thought of spending his entire life in this tiny village. He couldn't even tell Rumiko about his special ability; she might get scared and think he was a demon.

He looked directly into her dark eyes and, for the first time, realized how beautiful she really was. She looked away and pulled out a rice paper note that was rolled and tied with a flower stem. "Do not read this now," Rumiko said as she handed him the note. Haruto's mother had taught him the basics of reading and writing.

Their father thought it useless, but she would boldly state, "My sons will be better equipped when they can read and write." Haruto took the note and carefully tucked it into his kimono, feeling its weight against his chest. Rumiko leaned forward, her movements slow and purposeful, and for the first time, gently kissed Haruto on the cheek. Her lips were soft and warm, leaving a lingering sensation that made his heart race.

She then pointed toward the approaching guard and whispered urgently, "We must go now!" Haruto nodded, a smile spreading across his face as the orange coals of the nearby fire crackled, sending sparks dancing into the air. His heart beat like an untamed drum.

They both quietly slipped away in opposite directions, the silent agreement between them unspoken but deeply understood. Haruto, feeling the growing impatience gnawing at him, quickly ducked behind a large, old tree, its twisted roots anchoring it firmly to the earth. Hidden in its shadow, he pulled out Rumiko's note.

In the faint light, he carefully unfolded the paper. Her penmanship was exquisite, each stroke of the brush fluid and elegant, much like her long black hair that flowed down her body. The graceful characters conveyed not just her message, but a piece of her soul. As he read the note, the faint beam of moonlight filtering through the leaves above illuminated the delicate script. The words carried the promise of something more, a secret shared between them, and the possibility of a life together.

Dearest Haruto,

I can no longer wait to share my feelings with you. I know that you wish to become a

warrior, but I believe we could build a beautiful life together here in the village or leave

together under the cover of darkness. I cannot be the one to ask for your hand in

marriage. You must be the one to ask me.

Forever yours, Rumiko

Haruto's heart was now pounding like thunder in his chest. Overwhelmed by a sudden surge of emotion, he decided he would go back to her room to share his mutual affection and tell her that he would not leave her side. With a sense of urgency, he made his way through the darkened village. The familiar path to Rumiko's home seemed longer tonight, each step echoing with his racing heartbeat. Haruto was careful not to jump, as the guards seemed to be on high alert.

He was startled for a moment by the cry of a large dark bird perched on a nearby tree branch. Its outline was visible, sitting silently as it watched him. He stared back briefly before shifting his attention to Rumiko. As he approached her door, he paused to gather his thoughts and steady his breathing. With utmost care, he gently slid the wooden door open a sliver.

The room was softly lit by the orange glow of a single flickering candle. As Haruto's eyes adjusted to the faint light, he saw Rumiko standing by her mat, her back turned to the door. He paused, watching her from the shadows. She gathered her long black hair and swept it behind her, her movements graceful as she slowly loosened the obi cinched tightly around her waist. With a gentle shrug, she let her kimono slide off her shoulders and pool silently onto the wooden floorboards.

Haruto's heart pounded like thunder in his chest. He couldn't tear his gaze away as she stood there, her long black hair sweeping down her back, barely covering her buttocks. He was mesmerized by her body as the candlelight danced across her pearl skin, its soft, amber glow accentuating her curves. Haruto felt the blood rushing through his veins, only to be interrupted by a deep wave of guilt. *What am I doing?* he thought.

As Rumiko stood there, she was suddenly startled by a droplet of water that fell from the ceiling and landed on her head. She looked up just as a second drop fell, splashing onto her face. Haruto watched as she reached up and wiped the liquid away with her hand. She stared at her palm in confusion as the water turned to an oily black substance.

Dread washed over Haruto as he observed the liquid on her face transform into thin strands of black, weaving across her skin like a spider web. Rumiko began to panic, clutching at her neck in desperation, her fingers digging into her flesh as if trying to free herself from an invisible stranglehold. Her eyes were wide with terror, but no sound escaped her lips. Her mouth was completely covered by the thick black liquid. She then collapsed to her knees before falling backward onto the tatami mat.

Haruto stood frozen, knowing he had only moments before the darkness consumed her completely. Summoning every ounce of love he held for Rumiko, he cried out to himself, "Jump!" In a flash, he hurled himself onto her, shielding her with his body. Instantly, the black sludge dissolved into water, splashing across the wooden floor before vanishing.

Haruto was still on top of Rumiko, covered in water, when the door burst open. The guards pointed at Haruto and yelled, "Stop! Get off the girl now, you're killing her!" The men rushed forward and dragged the exhausted, wet Haruto away from Rumiko's naked body. Rumiko lay completely still, silent and motionless.

Her grandmother entered the room and let out a piercing scream, "Rumiko!" Rushing to her side, she draped a blanket over her. The guards pulled Haruto to the ground. Although Rumiko's heart was still beating, her eyes remained closed as if in a deep sleep. Two men dragged Haruto into the open area where a fire blazed.

A short, round guard with a large nose grabbed a stick and held it over the hot coals in the fire pit. "Hold him still!" he commanded the other men. Haruto didn't resist or speak. His strength was nearly gone, the jump leaving his body limp and weak. He sat on the ground, a guard gripping him by his shoulder-length hair, his face smeared with wet dirt. A small crowd of men had gathered, watching the scene unfold with tense anticipation. The tall guard brought the red-hot tip of the stick inches from Haruto's face, casting a fiery glow between his eyes. "What have you done to the girl, demon?"

"Stop!" Haruto's mother appeared, forcing herself between the scorching stick and her weakened son. "My son has done nothing wrong!"

Haruto lay weak and exhausted in a small cell. It consisted mainly of a hole in the ground with a wooden cover and door that acted as a ceiling. The enclosure hung low, preventing even a tall child from standing upright. He could barely summon the strength to move, let alone escape. Though awake and lucid, he was lost in his thoughts.

What had he done to Rumiko? Was she even alive? How did this all appear to everyone else? And what was it that consumed her? Had he summoned this darkness by spying on her and breaking her trust? The guilt he felt was overwhelming, a weight he could barely endure. What had he done? Desperately, he pleaded with the darkness that now enveloped him.

When the guards arrived, they found him on top of Rumiko's naked body. To their eyes, it looked as though he were mauling her. To them, he was an animal—or worse, a demon. Either way, the truth would not set him free.

He lay there for what felt like an eternity, drifting between sleep and wakefulness but never long enough to find peace. Reaching inside his kimono, he searched for his stone, but it wasn't there. The stone, a cherished gift from his mother, had always been with him. But now it was gone, just like everything else that mattered.

The cell was cold and damp, the only light coming from a small, barred window above his head. He could hear the occasional whisper of guards outside, but otherwise, it was silent. In the quiet, he found no peace, only remorse. "What had he done... what had he done," he repeated, the words echoing like the pulse of a dying heartbeat.

After what felt like an eternity, Haruto heard the door above him slowly creak open. Mud and water dripped onto his head as the guard pushed the heavy wooden door aside. "Hello there, boy! Come up now!" the guard's voice echoed into the dark chamber.

Haruto struggled to his feet and reached up through the opening. Two hands met his—one belonged to the guard, and the other felt familiar. As he climbed out of the hole, he saw that the other hand was his mother's. It was dark outside, with the only light coming from a nearby fire pit.

His mother wiped mud from his face and spoke, "My son! I am sorry for this. It is my fault, but we must act quick." Next to the guard was the *Doshin*. His mother knew this man well as it was her brother-in-law. He looked at Haruto's mother and said, "You only have a few minutes, so hurry." She grabbed Haruto by the wrist and led him to a shadowed area near the village walls. "My son, you must take these now; they will give you strength," she whispered urgently, pressing a small satchel into his hand. She then handed him a rolled-up note. "Take this, read it, and follow my instructions. It will keep you safe!"

Haruto looked at her, confused and anxious, as he accepted the note. His mother then gave him a pouch to store the note. Inside, she placed a dagger, a few other supplies, and a water skin. "Mother, what am I to do?"

She pointed to a guard who was discreetly signaling towards him. "Go now, I cannot explain!" she insisted, her voice filled with urgency. She looked Haruto in the eye as she squeezed his hand, "I will always be with you my son!"

Haruto opened the satchel and dumped the mixture of herbs into his mouth. He started to gag, but covered his mouth with his hand to stop himself from spitting. He swallowed the bitter concoction and ran to the man waiting for him. The man's face was covered by a black scarf as he directed Haruto to a small, hidden door on the village wall, concealed behind a flowering shrub. Many villages created secret passages for guards or villagers to use as escape routes if ever needed. The guard pointed downward as he pulled the tree back. Haruto saw the small door open. He knelt down and crawled through the opening.

Chapter Two

THE HIDDEN SELF

Yurei stood by the river, the setting sun casting a warped reflection on the water. He felt a deep hunger stirring in his core, a hunger that no ordinary food could satisfy. The Loa Spirit's voice echoed in his mind, calm and reassuring. "You must feed on blood. Your hunger is a part of you now. Control it, or it will control you."

"I don't want to hurt anyone," Yurei replied, his voice trembling.

"How can I live with this curse?"

"It is not a curse. You are more powerful than you can imagine," the Loa Spirit assured him "I do not control you. I am only here to answer your questions when you ask and guide you when you need it. Yurei, you're hungry, and you must eat."

He was standing by the river's edge, staring into the distance. His shoulder length black hair was down and blowing in the breeze. He wore a black kimono with dark baggy hakamas.

"I want you to listen for a heartbeat Yurei. When it gets louder, you will follow in that direction. It will lead you to food." Yurei felt warmth spread through his body, followed by a distant beating sound. When he turned his body in the direction of the sound, it got louder and more vibrant. "Feel the heartbeat of the forest, Yurei."

He began to walk towards the trees and into the coming night. As the pulse grew louder and faster, he could smell blood. "Yurei, you can start by feasting on animals. They won't give you complete power, but they will give you strength."

As he approached an opening in the darkening forest, Yurei's senses sharpened, picking up the subtle sounds of a struggle. Emerging from the underbrush, he saw a small, terrified young buck surrounded by a pack of wolves. The small animal was in a defensive stance, snorting loudly in fear, its head lowered and sharp antlers aimed at the predators. It was kicking at the dirt, creating small clouds of dust that swirled around its trembling legs.

The wolves, a mix of gray and tan coats, were pacing back and forth, their eyes locked onto the weakened prey. Their lips were curled back, revealing sharp, glistening teeth as they snarled and snapped at the air. "Yurei, attack the wolves now; they will give you power," the voice of the Loa Spirit, urging him into action.

In an instant, Yurei's instincts took over. He launched himself forward, his form a streak of motion as he closed the distance between himself and the struggling buck. He landed with a powerful thud on the young animal, pinning it to the ground. His crimson red eyes glowed brightly. The buck's struggles ceased as Yurei's fangs sank into its flesh, its warm blood pouring from the wound.

The wolves, caught off guard by Yurei's sudden appearance, paused in their tracks. They cowered, lowering their heads in submission before disappearing into the woods. Yurei, now standing alone in the clearing with the lifeless buck at his feet, felt a surge of power course through him. The blood of the animal invigorated him, heightening his senses and building his strength. He wiped his mouth, his eyes gradually dimming as he regained control over his vampiric instincts.

The Loa Spirit asked, "Why did you take the weak animal when you could have feasted on the entire pack?" Yurei said nothing as he wiped blood from his face. The Loa Spirit pleaded, "You need to feed regularly. Animals will give you temporary energy, but only for a short time. You can also feed on humans if you need to."

Yurei spoke, "I am not a demon who slaughters the innocent." He licked the blood from his hands as he stood over the empty carcass. Feeling energized but not full, Yurei asked, "What happens if I feed on a human?"

The Spirit continued, its voice resonating: "You can drain them fully and they will die. You also have the power to transform someone into a vampire. However, the process is not without its darkness. You would need to drain them completely, bringing them to the brink of death, and then share your blood to bind their soul to you." The Loa Spirit paused before adding, "There are different breeds of vampires. Some can even make union with humans, but there is a risk that a half-breed child could be born. However, these creatures rarely survive."

Yurei's face contorted with a mixture of revulsion and contemplation. His thoughts raced as he imagined the gravity of such an act, the weight of transforming another human being into a vampire. "Are there things I need to avoid?" he asked, his voice laced with both hope and despair.

The Loa Spirit responded, "You have a sensitivity to sunlight; and it's best you stay in the shadows when you can. Too much sunlight could destroy you."

"Why can't I remember who I was as a human?" The Spirit paused before continuing. "Because your humanity has left your body, you are no longer that person. That is why you cannot recall memories of the man you once were. Everything that made you who you were as a human is now gone. You even look different than your former self. But I will help you uncover your past. It is your fate to become one with who you are now and who you once were."

Yurei continued his questions with a sense of desperation. "Will I live forever like this?""Vampires can live forever, but they need to feed on human souls to do so. For every soul consumed, a vampire adds years to their life. Without human blood, they will eventually die naturally. But remember, you have the power to exist in both the human and Astral realms. This is not a curse but a powerful gift."

"How can I be destroyed?" Yurei asked with a hint of fear. "You can be destroyed by ignoring your hunger, over-exposure to the sun or a silver tipped weapon piercing through your body! But you now have greater strength and agility and are not easily defeated. But your greatest strengths are yet to reveal themselves."

"I have one last question."

The Loa Spirit responded with a soft whisper, "Yes, Yurei?"

"Why did you make me a vampire?"

"More will be revealed as your journey progresses. For now, you should leave this area and move on." The sky was a brushstroke of orangish-red as the sun receded over the horizon. It would be dark soon, so he began to walk.

The darkness felt different, vibrant, and alive. He could feel the energy stirring within every shadow and inch of the landscape. The world was awake. Yurei walked aimlessly through the forest for many days, staying in the shadows during the daylight and walking the landscape at night. His mind was constantly racing with thoughts of what he had become."What am I? What is my purpose here now?" he wondered aloud.

The Spirit's voice would remind him, "Yurei, I promise that all your questions will be answered in time." However, he was growing impatient with his new existence. After many long nights he stumbled upon a clearing, illuminated by the full moon. In the center stood a woman in a flowing black robe, a black scarf covered her face and drifted down her back, a hood covering her head. She was surrounded by a circle of candles, and in her hands, she held a staff adorned with charms and talismans. At the very top of the thick wooden stick hung a small animals head surrounded by bright feathers.

The woman's presence was commanding, and Yurei felt an inexplicable pull towards her. He stepped into the clearing, and she turned to face him. Her eyes were dark and piercing, filled with curiosity and caution.

"Who are you?" she asked, as she pulled her hood back.

"I am Yurei," he replied. "And who might you be?"

"I am Aiko, I commune with the spirits of nature, harnessing their energies to help others. What brings you to this place?" Yurei hesitated, unsure of how much to reveal. "I am lost," he said simply. "And searching for answers." Aiko studied him for a moment, before unraveling her scarf. "You carry a dark presence with you, Yurei. One that is both ancient and powerful. The spirits whisper of your arrival."

Yurei felt drawn closer to her. "You can hear them too?"

Aiko's expression softened slightly. "The spirits speak to those who listen." She then motioned Yurei to come sit by the fire and talk.

In his head he heard the Loa Spirit whisper, "Listen to the girl..." Yurei sat with Aiko, listening quietly, saying nothing of his vampiric nature. He didn't want to frighten her, though he wondered if she sensed it. Her pale skin stood in stark contrast to her short, jet-black hair, and her piercing, dark eyes resembled polished onyx. His gaze was drawn to the rhythmic pulse in her neck, the veins subtly visible as she spoke, stirring his thirst. She then exclaimed with excitement, "Come with me, I can help you!" Yurei stared at her with a hint of distrust. She stood up, pointing as she added, "I promise I can help." The Loa Spirit whispered to Yurei, "Follow the girl."

Aiko instructed Yurei, "I'll follow the path, and you should stay in the shadows along the sides." She then pulled her black hood over her head, wrapped her scarf around her face, and began to walk, stick in hand. Yurei moved alongside the path, camouflaged by the trees.

They walked for some time before they came upon three men sitting on the side of the path passing a gourd flask of sake back and forth. A short man with a round belly and bald head stood and pointed at Aiko. "Hey you girl, get over here!" Aiko turned her head towards the ground and said, "I don't want any trouble." The man responded with a slurred voice, "It won't be any trouble!"

The Loa Spirit spoke to Yurei, "Stay in the shadows, do not advance!" Yurei paused and crouched near some underbrush. The moon was reflecting off the mans head. His drinking buddies were laughing at him. He began to walk towards Aiko. She turned towards him and held her staff in front of her body and calmly demanded, "Stay as you are or you will pay!"

The man looked at his friends and nervously laughed, "Pay? I'm not paying you anything little girl!" He then advanced towards her reaching awkwardly at her neck. Aiko stepped out of the way and smacked the man in the back of his head with her staff. He fell forward to his knees, hitting his head on the loose dirt. The other two men stood and began circling Aiko.

Yurei's anxiety grew, his hunger swelling within him. The Loa Spirit's voice echoed in his mind, quickly reminding him, "Stand down, Yurei. She will be fine." He crouched low, his crimson eyes peeking through the trees, watching intently.

A tall man with an overgrown beard charged at Aiko, aiming to tackle her. She turned her staff, trapping his neck like a guillotine as he wrapped his arms around her legs. He attempted to charge forward but was halted by Aiko's stranglehold. She began choking the man with her stick as she backpedaled, then dropped him to the ground. The second man put his arms in the air and began walking backwards. "I don't want no problems with you girl!"

Aiko stepped forward, drove the man to the ground with her staff, and pressed her split-toed boot against his throat. "Don't ever give anyone trouble again!" The man was gurgling and spitting blood as she released the hold. She then pulled her hood up over her head and motioned to her rear, "Come on Yurei!"

Her small stone house was covered in moss, nestled deep within the woods, almost entirely invisible among the trees. All four sides were purposely camouflaged by thick foliage and shrubbery. The structure looked ancient, with thick, uneven stones that had weathered the elements of time. A narrow, crooked chimney poked out from the roof. The large wooden door, reinforced with iron bands, was the only entry, as there were no windows to offer a glimpse inside.

As they approached the house, Aiko knelt beside the door and pushed a small, hidden lever concealed by a cluster of moss-covered stones at ground level. With a soft click, the heavy door creaked open.

When they stepped inside, the house revealed itself as a treasure trove of curiosities. The walls were lined with sturdy wooden shelves, each meticulously arranged with small ceramic containers. Each held a different item, creating a mosaic of preserved wonders spilling from the top. Others contained strange artifacts, glistening stones, and various trinkets. While Yurei studied the walls, Aiko started a fire.

Among the more interesting contents were animal body parts: claws, feathers, eyes, beaks, small organs, and even tiny bones. These containers sat alongside cups of vibrant-colored powders and dried flowers. A faint, earthy aroma of dried herbs, ancient wood, and incense filled the small room. In one corner, a low table was cluttered with open books, scrolls, and candles, their wax melted and hardened into a web of intricate patterns. Aiko bent down and lit a candle with a torch from the fireplace. The flickering candlelight illuminated the space.

Aiko noticed Yurei curiously examining the various artifacts. "Those are for my practice," she explained, her voice soft but filled with conviction. "Each item has a purpose; I use them to perform rituals." She walked over to a shelf and gently picked up a covered glass containing a luminous, swirling liquid. "This, for instance, is an essence distilled from moonlight. It enhances clarity and intuition," she explained, holding it up to the candlelight. The yellow glow inside seemed to move like a vortex, swirling, twisting, and dancing about.

Turning to Yurei, she placed a reassuring hand on his cold arm. "I can help you understand who you are and make you stronger," she promised, her eyes reflecting a deep well of knowledge and empathy. "With the right spells and guidance, you will uncover your past and harness your true potential. Trust in my practice, and together we will unlock the secrets that lie within you."

Yurei looked at the girl and nodded. She was captivated by his deep-black eyes, which held a subtle hint of red as they stared back at her intently. After a moment, she broke her gaze as if waking from a trance. "Would you like to rest?" she asked softly. Yurei smiled, "I don't sleep much these days." The girl smiled, "I understand." They sat together and talked late into the night, Aiko's voice gradually growing softer until she finally succumbed to sleep. The dim light from the fire flickered, creating an ambient glow. Yurei, however, remained wide awake. He sat in a corner, his eyes fixed on Aiko as she slept peacefully on a mat by the hearth.

The room was filled with a quiet stillness, broken only by the gentle crackling of the fire and the rhythmic sound of Aiko's breathing. Yurei became entranced by the steady beat of her heart, each thump resonating in his ears and drawing him in deeper. The sound grew louder and louder. He placed his hand on his own chest and listened, but there was no sound. A sense of sadness began to overtake him, a hollow ache growing where his heartbeat should have been.

The Loa Spirit's voice pierced through the confusion, a whisper in his mind. "You must eat, Yurei." The voice persisted, becoming more insistent. "Your strength wanes, and with it, your purpose. Feed, or risk fading into the shadows forever."

Yurei closed his eyes, torn between the hunger gnawing at him and the part of him that wished to be human. He knew he could not ignore the insistent pang of hunger that had been growing within. The warmth of the fire did little to stave off the cold ache in his core. He clenched his fists, fighting the urge as he watched Aiko's chest rise and fall, her heartbeat a tempting rhythm that tested his hunger.

He made his way outside the small one-room structure and into the darkness of the woods. The moon hung low in the sky, leaving a glow on the landscape. The air was cold and still. He moved quickly, his senses heightened, every sound and scent guiding him through the trees.

He listened intently, his ears picking up the faint footsteps of a deer. He followed the sound, his movements silent and precise, until he spotted the large deer grazing in a moonlit clearing. He could hear its heartbeat, a harsh reminder of the emptiness that lurked within his core. With the precision of a predator, he pounced, his strength overpowering the animal quickly and efficiently.

Yurei feasted, the rich, warm blood quenching the hunger that had been consuming him. When he was finished, he wiped the blood from his body, using the nearby leaves and moss to cleanse himself. He took a moment to breathe in the cool night air, feeling a surge of renewed energy.

He made his way back to the cabin, the forest now quiet and still. As he stepped inside, the soft glow of the dying fire welcomed him. He carefully cleaned any remaining traces of blood from his hands and face, ensuring there was no sign of his late-night hunt. Then he settled into a corner, his eyes on Aiko, waiting patiently for her to awaken. The anticipation of their next steps together filled his mind.

Aiko's home became a sanctuary for Yurei, a place where he could explore the depths of his new existence without fear. Over the next few weeks, they developed a routine. During the day, Aiko taught Yurei the fundamental principles of casting spells. At night, he would go to the forest and secretly feast.

She also introduced him to meditation techniques that helped him to quietly control his bloodlust and harness his newfound strength. The Loa

Spirit would encourage Yurei to listen to Aiko and follow her teachings as she represented the hands that the Spirit did not have.

They sat outside her cabin on a tree stump turned on its side, the cool evening air carrying the scent of moist earth. Aiko, her face partially illuminated by the fading sunlight on the horizon, turned to Yurei, who sat in the shadows. "I have to be honest about something, Yurei," she began, her voice with a hint of apprehension. "I attracted you to my circle that first night."

Yurei, intrigued, looked at Aiko, who was now staring into the distance, her gaze fixed on a point beyond the horizon. "What do you mean?" he asked, his curiosity aroused.

Aiko took a deep breath, her eyes reflecting a hint of regret. "There is a being called the Kurokawa that is stealing children from their beds. It is a dark force, growing stronger with each child it takes. I fear for the safety of the children." She paused, collecting her thoughts. "I cast a spell to summon protection, to bring forth a guardian who could help me fight this evil. And then, you came."

Yurei's eyes widened as he absorbed her words. The revelation hung heavy in the air, the weight of his unexpected role settling on his shoulders. "So, I was brought here by your spell?" Aiko nodded, her expression a blend of hope and determination. "Yes, Yurei. You are meant to help me combat this darkness. I believe you have the strength and the will to face the Kurokawa. Will you stand with me?"

Yurei quietly laughed to himself at his secret and thought, *I am a vampire, not a savior.* The magnitude of the situation settled in, and Yurei slowly felt a newfound sense of purpose. He looked into Aiko's eyes, seeing the trust and faith she had placed in him. "Yes," he said, his voice firm. "I will help you, but I must share something about myself."

Aiko smiled and placed her hand on Yurei's cold arm. "I know, you're a vampire."

Yurei smiled. "Is it that obvious?"

Aiko laughed. "To me it is. But I think I can help you discover your true nature, Yurei."

Yurei looked at Aiko and asked, "Were you not afraid of me?"

Without a hint of hesitation, Aiko responded, "Not at all." Yurei, I can see something in you that others cannot. I know you will not hurt me. If you were going to, you would have done it by now." Yurei smiled, "Thank you for trusting me, Aiko." She smiled back, "Yurei, there is more to you than being a vampire, and together we will uncover who you really are and your role in stopping the Kurokawa."

Yurei often found himself watching Aiko as she slept, captivated by her strength, power, and beauty. The steady rise and fall of her chest entranced him. Each beat of her heart was a subtle rhythm that echoed in his ears. He could feel the pulse of her blood flowing through her veins, a tantalizing reminder of his hunger. But his attraction to her was far deeper than just food.

Feeling trapped in frustration, Yurei ventured deep into the woods to hunt. In these moments of solitude, he attuned himself to the heartbeat of the forest. He wasn't sure if the Loa Spirit had truly fallen silent or if it was merely granting him a reprieve, but he didn't question it. He listened to the pulse of the forest, yet wondered where his own heartbeat was hidden. Seeking solace, he climbed to the highest branches of a towering tree, where he could sit alone with his thoughts.

Perched high above the ground, he would close his eyes and attempt to summon fragments of his past, but his memories remained frustratingly elusive. The gentle sway of the branches and the rustling of the leaves provided a meditative backdrop, but never answers.

One night, as he sat surrounded by the tranquility of the forest canopy, the Loa Spirit's voice broke through the silence. "Yurei, I want to take you somewhere," it whispered with an inviting tone. "You have become increasingly connected to the forest," the Spirit continued. "Follow the pulse of darkness, Yurei. There is a place where shadows gather and secrets are traded."

Intrigued, Yurei followed the spirit's guidance, moving farther into the woods than he had ever gone before. Eventually, a faint, flickering light appeared in the distance. In a large clearing, illuminated by torches and lanterns, sat a group of tents. It was some sort of bazaar bustling with activity, despite the late hour. Yurei pulled his black hood over his head to hide his identity and slowly walked into the market.

The air was thick with incense, exotic spices, and sweat. Strange creatures roamed about as the sounds of low conversations, bartering, and the occasional laugh filled the atmosphere. Shadows danced along the ground, blending and shifting in the light, adding to the unsettling ambiance of the market.

The bazaar was frequented by a variety of beings. There were oni, demons with red skin and sharp horns, yokai with their bushy brows and large pointy teeth, and humans who had fallen into dark practices. Each being seemed to have its own agenda in a hidden world far away from prying eyes. For a brief time, the veil grew thin here, and beings could pass freely between bordering realms.

As Yurei made his way through the maze of tents filled with herbs, talismans, and magic potions, he saw a large pavilion in the center filled with various cages. When he entered, he was greeted with rows of enclosures both big and small.

A voice came from a small glass tank filled with cloudy greenish water. "Pretty boy, wanna swim with me?" In the tank swam a half-woman, half-fish. A small wooden sign hanging below the tank read: "Ningyo the fish girl." Her face was delicate and young, like a village girl's. Her long hair flowed down her body and over her iridescent scales and fins. Her teeth were dangerously sharp.

"Come closer," Ningyo purred, her voice a tantalizing mix of innocence and seduction. "I promise, I won't bite... much." Her smile, revealing those razor-sharp teeth, was both inviting and terrifying.

A short, bald man with a bamboo tobacco pipe perched from his lower lip approached Yurei. He lowered his pipe and spoke in a deep growl. "Don't worry about those teeth, she's got a blowhole in the back if you know what I mean..." He began to laugh, which quickly turned into a cough. He spit on the ground, and a small slimy creature appeared, slopped it up, and then disappeared.

In another cage sat a man in a chair with his back turned. A small sign attached to the enclosure read, "Noppera-bo, the faceless man." Yurei couldn't take his eyes off the figure. The man sat unnervingly still, his posture rigid and unmoving. The only sound was the faint creak of the wooden chair as it subtly shifted under the man's weight. As if sensing Yurei's gaze, the man began to turn his head slowly. The motion was almost mechanical. Yurei let out a small gasp as the man's face came into view to reveal a smooth, featureless expanse of skin where eyes, nose, and mouth should have been.

Yurei stared in a mixture of fascination and horror. The Noppera-bo's face was like a blank canvas, devoid of any features or expressions. The skin was unnaturally smooth, reflecting the faint light in an almost glossy sheen.

He continued walking and was drawn to a glass case with orbs of dancing lights. The hovering spheres of fire cast a heavenly glow as they moved about. They would brighten for a moment and then quickly dim.

Yurei cleared his throat, the proprietor still following, and asked, "What are they?"

"They are hitodama, souls of the dead. I gotta warn ya though, these are old souls, so I can't guarantee them." The man leaned into Yurei, picked at his nose, and inspected his fingers before continuing in a low whisper, "I know where to get your hands on young souls, if you're into that sort of thing."

Yurei spoke in a low, raspy voice, "Where do you get them from?"

"Naw, I can't tell you my connections, then you'll be my competition!"

Yurei did not move. "I am only interested in where you get them from."

The Loa Spirit whispered, "Look him in the eyes, he is weak." Yurei pulled his hood back and stared intently into the man's eyes. He paused and did not move. "I'll ask again, where do you get these souls from?" Yurei's eyes turned from a midnight black to a crimson red in an instant.

The man stared blankly at Yurei before robotically responding and pointing, "Talk to the yokai." A group of short creatures stood in a huddle. They wore robes that covered their torsos. They had red skin with bushy white eyebrows and black hair. Their large sharp teeth hung from their upper gums as they spoke quietly.

Yurei did not need to get close to hear them speak. One ability that had advanced since his meditation practice was his ability to easily hear lower-level beings from great distances. Yurei stood beside a blue and white striped tent selling enchanting weapons and listened to the yokai. They spoke of the recent disappearances of children from the physical realm.

Behind them stood a large black tent, guarded by a tall figure draped in a black robe and hood. The creature's smooth, black hands emerged from the robe's sleeves, its fingers long and gangly, stretching unnervingly from beneath the wide cuffs. Its fingernails were long, serrated, and razor-sharp. The face was hidden deep within the shadow of the hood, entirely concealed. Yurei whispered to himself, "I wonder what's in that tent?"

A tall, slender man emerged from the tent. A wide-brimmed black straw kasa shaded his face, the brim dipping low so only the faintest outline of his jaw could be seen. He approached the yokai, speaking softly. Yurei could not decipher his words, so he quietly followed him, staying in the shadows. The Loa Spirit whispered, "Yes, Yurei, follow the man."

As the man walked down a dark path, Yurei pursued him from the shadows. When the man was finally alone, Yurei swiftly appeared before him, seized him by the neck, and demanded, "Tell me what's in that tent!"

Holding the man's throat with one hand and gripping his black kimono with the other, Yurei slowly lifted him off the ground. The wide straw hat partially covered the man's face.

The man looked up from the ground, his hat slightly tilted and said, "Why should I tell you anything?" Yurei set the man down, pulled back his hood to reveal his crimson eyes, "Because if you don't, I will destroy you!" Yurei released the man from his hold briefly and let the man speak. "They gamble with and trade young souls in that tent. That's all I know."

Yurei squeezed the man tighter and spoke,

"Tell me everything you know about who controls the Kurokawa."

"I do not know for certain," the man sputtered. "This place is a front to lure only the wealthiest. There's talk of an abandoned shrine in the mountains. That's where he conducts his rituals. He's building an army. The souls of the children are just the beginning. He is summoning a great darkness!"

Yurei grabbed the mans neck tighter, "I'll only ask one more time. Who is in control of Kurokawa?" The man gagged as Yurei loosened his grip, "He never shows his face, nobody knows... He always wears an oni mask!"

Yurei waited until morning to share what he had gathered with Aiko. "I must share something with you." She could sense the serious tone in his voice,

"What is wrong Yurei?"

"I think I know how to track and locate the Kurokawa," Yurei whispered.

"It's time, Aiko, for us to prepare."

They spent weeks honing their weapons and perfecting their spells for the fateful encounter. Yurei and Aiko moved silently through the thick shrubs, their senses heightened. Yurei had been tracking the shadow creature for weeks, honing his power to listen to the pulse of darkness. He could hear the rhythm of the darkness beating like a drum in his head. The

Loa Spirit encouraged him, "Listen and follow it, Yurei. Connect to it, feel its essence."

Yurei closed his eyes for a moment, attuning his senses to the faint, rhythmic pulse that resonated through the forest. It was a sensation he had learned to recognize, a subtle vibration that hinted at the presence of something dark. Each beat was like a distant echo, guiding him toward the source of the darkness.

Aiko followed closely, her eyes scanning the surroundings with complete focus. Together, they formed a seamless team, each movement synchronized as they pressed forward through the woods. As they approached a clearing, Yurei halted abruptly, his eyes turning to a bright crimson. "We're close," he whispered. His long black robe was blowing behind him as the wind began to stir. His dark shoulder-length hair was pulled back into a top knot.

Aiko nodded. "I can sense its presence." Yurei glanced up as a black raven let out a piercing shriek, circling just above the treetops. "We need to move quickly," Yurei said, his voice barely above a whisper. "The Kurokawa is close."

They moved fast, with Yurei leading the way. Shadows seemed to shift and dance around them, as if the forest itself was alive with dark energy. As they neared the edge of the clearing, Yurei signaled for Aiko to stop. She began to chant softly, invoking protective wards to shield them from the energy surrounding them. Suddenly, the ground trembled, and dark figures emerged from the shadows, their forms shifting and contorting.

A black, gurgling form began to slowly move toward them.

"This is the Kurokawa!" Yurei yelled.

Aiko nodded, "We must stop them, Yurei. But be careful."

The dark beings moved with a fluid, almost otherworldly grace, their shadows blending seamlessly with the night. Yurei engaged the creatures with his sword, circling and slicing in every direction. His crimson eyes glowed brighter with each movement of his weapon.

Aiko chanted an incantation, summoning protective wards around her body as she stood alone and now surrounded. "Stay within the circle!" he urged her. Aiko nodded, as she slowly moved in a circle. The creatures hissed and recoiled as they encountered the barrier. Yurei was in his own battle as three creatures began to engage him.

Aiko continued circling with her knees bent, her staff pointed toward the outer ring. "Hold steady, Aiko." Her black scarf was wrapped around her face, revealing only her midnight eyes. The tail end of the scarf danced wildly behind her as the wind increased.

The creatures were now advancing from every direction, their black forms slithering across the ground. "I cannot hold them much longer, Yurei!" He turned in her direction and watched in horror as the creatures broke the circle and engulfed Aiko. The black liquid snaked around her body as she fell to the ground. The creatures swarmed over her, converging into a coiled mass of darkness, and began to drag her away. Her arms clawed at the dirt as they pulled her towards a dark corner of the woods.

Yurei watched as Aiko was swallowed by the encroaching shadows. The Loa Spirit spoke with urgency, "Yurei, go to her immediately and cover her body!" Yurei sprinted to Aiko. In an instant, he was lying on top of the black creature. He covered Aiko's body, and the sea of black sludge transformed into a watery liquid and flowed away. Yurei found himself straddling Aiko as she coughed up water. Her eyes opened for a moment, and she looked up, whispering, "Yurei..." before falling unconscious.

Aiko would sleep for days before finally awakening in her cabin with Yurei at her side. With the help of the Loa Spirit, he was able to tend to her wounds and provide her with sustenance. During her sleep, Yurei meditated, seeking guidance and strength, knowing that their battle was far from over.

When Aiko finally opened her eyes, she saw Yurei watching over her, a look of relief in his

eyes. "You saved me," she whispered weakly.

Yurei smiled and said, "It's good to hear your voice."

Aiko coughed and then whispered, "Yurei I need to show you something."

When she was finally able to walk and move freely, she approached Yurei. "I miscalculated, and I almost paid for it with my life. We cannot stop the darkness alone. It is time to learn who you were before you became Yurei. It is the only way we can stop the Kurokawa." As twilight descended, Aiko and Yurei prepared for the ceremony that would unlock the secrets of Yurei's past. The thick forest around them was shrouded in mist, the air heavy with anticipation. Aiko led the way, her footsteps barely making a sound on the forest floor, while Yurei followed closely behind.

They reached a secluded area, where tall pine trees formed a natural circle around a clearing bathed in moonlight. At the center of the open field lay a flat stone altar, covered in intricate carvings and surrounded by glowing crystals. Aiko had spent days preparing the site, gathering the necessary elements for the ritual.

At the center of the altar sat a bowl filled with ground brown herbs. Yurei and Aiko stood before it, Aiko holding a gold-colored ceramic bowl in her hands. She wore a black kimono and black hakama pants, her short midnight hair slicked back tightly against her head. "Yurei, I will light the herbs in the bowl, and I need you to inhale the smoke three times. You'll want to stop at two, but you must take all three breaths."

Yurei wore a black robe that brushed the ground, his hair tied back. His unshaven face reflected the firelight from the torch in Aiko's hand. She touched the fire to the bowl, igniting the mixture and sending a plume of brown smoke into the air. "Breathe it in now, Yurei!" Aiko commanded. As Yurei inhaled, the smoke climbed up his face, swirled around his head, and entered his nostrils. He held the smoke in his lungs before releasing it in a deep exhale.

A surge of energy coursed through his body. "Again, Yurei!" He inhaled a second time, then a third, before collapsing to the ground. As he looked up at Aiko, she reassured him, "You're safe, Yurei. Don't fight it."

The Loa Spirit whispered softly, "Let go of your body, Yurei." Yurei closed his eyes and felt his body become weightless, as if it were dissolving into the ground below him. In his mind, a kaleidoscope of vibrant fractals burst into existence, each one a dazzling array of colors and intricate shapes. The fractals multiplied and fragmented, breaking into smaller and smaller pieces with breathtaking speed. The images expanded and shifted, morphing into new patterns before dissolving into an ever-changing cascade of light and color.

He could feel himself moving forward at an unprecedented speed through a tunnel. Everything became a blur as each fractal continued to split into smaller and more intricate patterns, their vivid hues blending and fading until they finally fell beneath him and vanished. As the last fragments disappeared, Yurei found himself in a void of profound calm and clarity, a tranquil silence that filled his mind and spirit. The space around him was a blend of white and gray, slowly shifting from a blur into focus.

The space before him was an open field of tall grass and wildflowers. This place felt familiar, like home. Suddenly a whispering soft voice echoed through the air repeatedly, "Ha-ruto, Haruto! Wake up!"

CHAPTER THREE

WARRIOR PATH

"Wake up," the voice rang through his head. Then he opened his eyes and spoke, "Mother?" He looked up at the warm morning sun. He was laying on a grassy knoll. His mother was nowhere in sight. "It must have been a dream," he whispered. Then he remembered that his mother had given him a small satchel the previous day when he left the village. He had walked in the darkness of the night, with only the light from the stars guiding him. He finally stopped on a grassy embankment near a creek to sleep. The soothing sound of the water flowing over stones provided a calming lullaby for the exhausted Haruto.

He sat up in his grassy bed, wiping the last bits of sleep from his eyes. His fingers were trembling as he fumbled for his bag. Inside, he found a stone wrapped in a cord and the note his mother had given him. He carefully unrolled the letter. Upon seeing his mother's beautiful handwriting, a tear formed in his eye. Even in a rush, she could create script that was a work of art, each character flowing gracefully into the next.

Dearest Haruto,

You must leave the village and never come back. Follow this map and you can stay with a trusted old friend. His name is Kenji and he will give you shelter, guidance and protection.

This black stone will protect you, I put a cord around it so you can keep it close to your

heart. I promise that I will look after Rumiko and remember I will always be with you.

-Mother

Haruto felt more alone than ever. His tears fell onto the note, mingling with the ink of his mother's beautiful script. He held the black opal in his hand; it was cool to the touch. His mother had woven a cord around the stone to hold it in place, creating a necklace. As he held the stone in the sunlight, its dark surface shifted subtly to a deep green. Haruto gently placed the cord around his neck, the stone weighing heavily against his heart.

He looked around, the once-familiar landscape now feeling foreign and unfriendly. He remembered the promise his mother had made to him when he was just a young boy. She would always say, as she covered Haruto's eyes with her hands, "No matter where you are, Haruto, I am always with you. Even when you can't see me." She would then whisper in his ear, "Reach inside your kimono, Haruto." Suddenly, he could feel a small stone pressed against his chest.

His mother had always given him different stones to hold onto ever since he was a small child. She would often say, "Haruto, hold this stone; it will calm you and guard you, my son."

Many times, Haruto had trouble remembering where he put his stones and would end up losing them. His mother, however, was clever and would always slip him a new stone when he wasn't looking. Sometimes they would appear at his bedside, in his kimono, or just about anywhere. Haruto would even pretend to lose his stones just to get more and stash them away. It was a playful, back-and-forth game they shared for as long as he could remember.

Haruto held the black opal in his hand as it hung from his neck. "I promise I won't lose you!" he whispered. He then looked over the map his mother had drawn on the note. Carefully, he folded it and tucked it into his kimono jacket. Wiping the tears from his eyes, he surveyed the land around him.

He then took stock of his very minimal supplies, which consisted of nothing more than the clothes on his back, a dagger his mother had given him, a flint stone, a water skin and a small iron striker for making fire. Desperation and survival instinct kicked in as he realized he needed to find additional sustenance. He scanned the immediate area and spotted a cluster of bushes with small, glistening berries. He approached them cautiously, recognizing them as safe to eat from his mother's teachings. He picked a handful, the sweet and slightly tart flavor a welcome distraction from his thoughts.

He began to think about Rumiko and his promise to protect her. The only way to ensure her safety, however, was to leave her in his mother's care. Deep down, he knew he had to distance himself from the village and from Rumiko to keep them both safe. The villagers' fear and suspicion of him would only bring danger to those he cared about most.

He was also deeply troubled by the dark substance that had tried to claim Rumiko's life. *Was that the Kurokawa, the entity that had taken children from their beds? Why was it now targeting Rumiko? Had he somehow called this darkness into existence by secretly betraying her trust by watching her undress?* These questions consumed his mind, refusing to let him rest.

Haruto walked to the rushing creek, bent down, and scooped up two handfuls of water. He drank quickly, the excess trickling down his chin and onto his black kimono. After filling his water skin, he wiped his wet hands across his face and ran them through his shoulder-length black hair. Looking up at the sun, he wiped his chin and said to no one in particular, "I guess we have to go find this Kenji."

With his meager supplies gathered he pointed himself in front of his first landmark on his journey, a tall mountain far in the distance and began to walk. As he hiked alongside the river he thought, *It sure would be easier if I could just jump to Kenji's house, but since I've never been there and its too far, I cannot.* Haruto had only ever been able to jump short, familiar distances. Anything further either failed completely or left him utterly exhausted.

The walk for Haruto began easily enough as he made his way across the grassy flatlands, the warm heat from the sun surrounding him like a familiar embrace. The sky was a clear, endless expanse of blue, and the gentle rustling of the grass was the only sound accompanying his footsteps. This part of the journey was straightforward, but he knew it would grow more challenging as he progressed through various terrains over the next 2-3 days. Despite the calmness of the initial journey, Haruto's heart was heavy. He was leaving behind his home and everyone he cared about, venturing into the unknown. Doubts plagued his mind—was he making the right choice? Yet, he trusted his mother above all others, and her guidance was his steadfast compass.

As the hours passed, the weight of his minimal supplies became more apparent. His food and water dwindled faster than expected, breaking one of his mother's cardinal rules. She would often remind him during their foraging trips, "Never run out of essentials. Food, water and shelter are a must." He cursed his oversight, realizing he had underestimated the journey's demands.

The sun began to lower in the sky, painting the horizon in hues of orange and pink. His stomach growled, reminding him that he needed more than just berries to sustain himself. He needed meat. But for that, he would also need a fire. He began by gathering materials, moving quickly and efficiently. Leaping from one area to the next, Haruto collected what he needed with precision. With each movement, he nodded and shouted, "Jump!" as he seamlessly launched his body forward from spot to spot.

He scoured the forest floor for dry grass, leaves, and bark to form a tinder bundle for starting a fire.

Haruto had lived his whole life in secret when it came to jumping, his extraordinary ability hidden from the world by both him and his mother. But out here, in the isolation of the forest, he felt untethered—free to be his true self without fear of judgment or discovery. Nobody would see the way his body defied normal limits, moving through the air like a shadow, and for once, the burden of secrecy was lifted from his shoulders.

Haruto ventured into the forest, scanning the underbrush for the materials he needed to construct a rabbit snare. He jumped from spot to spot gathering supplies. He found flexible young saplings, which he cut into lengths to form the snare's frame. He also gathered some sturdy vines to use as cord, ensuring they were strong enough to hold a rabbit.

He then selected a spot near the edge of the woods were rabbits would surely gather as the day came to a close. He had watched his brother Daichi do this a hundred times and had memorized the steps.

He secured it with a trigger mechanism he fashioned from a forked stick. He then constructed a loop from the vine, attaching it to the bent sapling and positioning it near the woods. Once a rabbit passed through and disturbed the trigger, the sapling would snap upright, tightening the loop around the rabbit and trapping it securely. Now he just had to wait for dinner to arrive.

As the sun began its descent, Haruto decided it was time to start his fire. The evening chill was already creeping in, and he knew that a warm fire would provide much-needed comfort through the night. But he had to be careful not to attract any unwanted attention with the smoke from his fire. With a sense of purpose, he returned to his campsite by the creek, the gentle sound of flowing water calming his anxious mind.

He had to work quickly, arranging the dry tinder and kindling he had gathered earlier. He held the flint securely in one hand and began to strike it at an angle with the iron striker in the other, sending sparks onto the tinder, hoping for a small ember to catch. He had done this time after time with his mother and Daichi.

After repeated attempts, Haruto's determination paid off as smoke began to rise from the tinder bundle. A few gentle breaths, and it caught flame, the small fire growing steadily as he fed it twigs and branches. As the flames crackled and danced, Haruto felt a wave of relief and satisfaction. The warmth spread, driving away the coming chill. He glanced toward the rabbit snare he had set earlier, hoping that it would yield a catch before nightfall. With a little luck, he would not only be warm but also have a full stomach.

As he sat staring at the crackling fire, his thoughts raced with old memories. The flames flickered hypnotically, casting dark shadows across Haruto's face. His mind wandered back to his village, and the faces of those he had left behind danced in his head like fleeting whispers.

He thought of Rumiko, her gentle smile and the way her long black hair reflected the sun and moon. He remembered the secret notes they shared and the whispered conversations at their secret meet ups. The memory of her kiss, soft and unexpected, stirred a deep longing within him. His thoughts drifted to the moments before her life was almost taken. He saw her standing there, her long black hair spilling down her back, just barely brushing against her hips.

Suddenly, an intense pain welled up within him, shattering the vision and engulfing him in guilt. He told himself, *No, you don't deserve these thoughts. You must never see her in that light again.* He had promised to protect her, to return one day when the darkness that threatened them all was vanquished, and to prove his worth to her. These secret visions had no place in his heart.

His thoughts shifted to his mother—her wise eyes and the comforting warmth of her embrace. She had always been his guiding star, teaching him the ways of the world and the importance of resilience and survival. She was a strong woman with an even stronger heart. If anyone could help Rumiko, it was her. Her belief in him had never faltered, even when he doubted himself. But he couldn't help but wonder, *was Rumiko even alive?*

Without warning a sharp snap broke the stillness of the night, followed by a loud squealing sound. His heart leapt into his throat as he turned quickly toward the source of the noise. His eyes darted to his snare, which was now trembling with movement. The moonlight provided just enough illumination for him to see that the trap had been triggered.

Haruto immediately rose, moving toward the snare with a mixture of anticipation and caution. As he approached, he saw a white rabbit caught in the loop, struggling against the vine that held it tight. The animal's frantic movements caused the snare to shake, and its squeals echoed in the quiet night.

This was the part Haruto always struggled with: killing the animal. He remembered the time Daichi shot a similar rabbit with his slingshot. They had been walking down the path near the river that led to the waterfalls, the sound of rushing water in the distance a comforting rhythm. The sun was high, seeping flecks of light through the leaves and warming the cool forest air. Daichi, always the more observant and patient of the two, suddenly halted and raised his hand.

"Silence, little brother," Daichi whispered. He began to crouch, his movements slow and steady, signaling Haruto to do the same. "There's a rabbit over there," Daichi said, pointing to a grassy spot near the edge of the woods. Haruto followed his brother's gaze and saw it—a large white rabbit, its fur almost glowing in the sunlight. The rabbit grazed quietly, unaware of their presence, its pink nose twitching as it nibbled on the tender green shoots of grass. Daichi reached to load a stone into his sling but realized he didn't have one. "Little brother, hand me a stone quickly."

Haruto glanced around but couldn't find a suitable stone. Frustration began to set in, but then he remembered the small gift his mother had given him. He reached inside his kimono and felt the smooth surface of the stone resting against the fabric. Carefully, he pulled out the perfectly round black obsidian stone, its glossy surface reflecting the sunlight. Haruto hesitated, holding the stone up to his face to see his reflection before handing it to Daichi.

Daichi loaded the smooth, round black stone into the leather pouch, and pulled back the silk cord with precision. He took aim, his eyes slightly squinting as he focused on the animal. Haruto held his breath, feeling the tension in the air.

With a soft thwack, the dark stone whizzed through the air, finding its mark with perfect accuracy. The rabbit fell, and the sudden silence that followed was filled with a sacred stillness. Daichi approached the animal, his steps no longer cautious but respectful. Haruto followed, his heart pounding in his chest. The white rabbit lay on its side its eyes still fluttering with a hint of life. A small red patch of blood was expanding on the animals fur.

Daichi pulled out a knife and said, "You must finish it now little brother. Do not let it suffer!" Haruto stepped back and said, "I cannot!" Daichi pushed the knife handle at Haruto and said, "You must!" He cried as he took the knife from him. Haruto heard Daichi's voice in his head, "Quickly slice his throat Haruto!"

Haruto snapped back to the present as he gently but firmly grasped the animal by the throat. His heart ached for the creature, but he knew what had to be done. In one brisk, decisive motion, he sliced through the rabbit's neck. Warm blood poured from the wound, soaking his hands and the ground beneath. The rabbit's struggles ceased almost immediately, and Haruto felt a mixture of relief and sadness. He thought, *Daichi would be proud.*

The night sky had arrived and Haruto had a full stomach and was ready for sleep. As he settled beside the dying fire, its embers casting a soft, reddish glow, he felt exhaustion pull him into a light, restless sleep. The rhythmic sounds of the creek and the forest's nighttime symphony provided a temporary sense of security. Just as he began to drift off, an eerie stillness fell over the forest, as if every creature had suddenly fell silent.

He immediately sensed a presence nearby. The hairs on the back of his neck stood on end as a wave of unease washed over him. His eyes darted to the edge of the woods, searching for any signs of movement. His heart skipped a beat as he caught a glimpse of a dark shadow disappearing into the trees. It reappeared briefly before moving rapidly across the ground and climbing a tree. A chill ran down his spine, and the temperature plummeted, leaving him shivering uncontrollably.

Haruto held the stone his mother had given him tightly against his heart. He began to recite a spell she had taught him, his voice just a whisper. The words flowed from his lips, weaving a protective barrier around him.

"From the earth and sky, I call upon the light,

Guard me now, shield my heart from the night.

With this stone in hand, I summon the grace,

Protect me from the shadows, in this sacred space."

He closed his eyes, focusing on the spell, willing it to take effect. The chill in the air seemed to intensify, and he could feel the presence drawing closer, a dark force lurking just beyond the edge of the firelight. As he chanted, a soft glow emanated from his hands, the spell taking hold and enveloping him in a shroud of white light. He imagined Rumiko, and his heart began to fill with the warmth of her love. The shivering subsided, and he felt a surge of strength and courage. He then opened his eyes. The creatures were gone, and the pulse of the forest had returned. The world seemed to breathe again, its natural sounds slowly returning with a gust of warm air.

He awoke the next morning with a renewed sense of urgency, the memories of the shadow creatures spurring him to reach Kenji as fast as he could. Haruto quickly gathered his few belongings. He pulled out the map his mother had provided, tracing the route with his finger. *With a little luck, I could be there by day's end!* he thought enthusiastically, feeling a wave of hope.

Haruto removed all signs of his presence from the campsite. The shadow creatures were aware of his location, so he could not risk being followed. The elders had always said that they could only travel in the darkness of the night. So, for now at least, he was safe.

Haruto took a moment to survey the landscape, knowing that the journey ahead would involve steep inclines and rugged terrain. He needed a walking stick to help him navigate the climb. As he scanned the area, his eyes fell upon a long, sturdy stick resting near a fallen tree. Its surface was smooth and free of knots, making it an ideal choice.

"This will do just fine," he whispered to himself, testing the stick's strength with a few firm taps against the ground. With the steep inclines, it was difficult for Haruto to jump through the air, as it required a lot of energy. He told himself that for this leg of the journey, he would have to rely on his own two legs.

With the walking stick in hand, Haruto took one last look around the campsite, ensuring he hadn't left anything behind. His thoughts turned to Daichi, his mother, and Rumiko. He remembered Daichi's guidance, his mother's wisdom and support, and Rumiko's enduring love. Each memory fueled his strength, reminding him why he was on this journey.

As the hours passed, Haruto's legs began to cramp and ache. He found a stream of water traveling down the mountainside. Crouching along some rocks, he put his hands under the ice-cold water, feeling sharp prickles as it ran between his fingers.

Carefully, Haruto loosened the straps of his waraji, the traditional straw sandals that had carried him many miles through the countryside. He slid the sandals from his feet and placed them gently on a rock. These were his only foot coverings and he could not afford to lose them.

Haruto lay back and placed his legs under the ice-cold water. He let out a long, deep breath as the water poured over his sore legs.

As he lay there, his mind raced back to Rumiko. He remembered the day she first arrived in the village. She was ten years old, and her arrival had stirred whispers among the villagers of a terrible tragedy that had befallen her parents. Two men on horseback had brought her to the village and handed her over to her grandmother. Rumiko had arrived with little more than a small, tattered bag and her Ichimatsu doll—the last gift her mother had given her before they were separated.

Her grandmother had sent her out to play, hoping she would make friends. Rumiko, nervous but obedient, clutched her beloved doll close to her chest as she stepped into the village square. The doll was dressed in a delicate kimono, hand-sewn by Rumiko's mother. Some of the older girls noticed her and pointed at the doll. Their curious glances quickly turned into sly smiles. A tall girl stepped forward and pointed at the doll with a smirk.

"What's that?" the girl asked, her voice filled with mockery. Without waiting for an answer, another girl stepped forward and grabbed the doll from Rumiko's hands.

"Stop!" Rumiko cried, her voice trembling as she reached for the doll. The girls only laughed, tossing it between themselves as if it were a toy to be fought over. Rumiko's heart pounded in her chest as she pleaded, "Give it back!"

Haruto, standing nearby and watching this unfold, felt his anger begin to boil over. He approached the bigger girls, his expression firm. Reaching for the doll, he demanded, "Hey, give me that back!"

The taller girl, taken aback by Haruto's sudden intervention, hesitated for a moment. But before she could respond, Rumiko stepped forward and grabbed the doll back from the girl's hands, clutching it tightly to her chest.

The other girls, startled by Rumiko's unexpected defiance, exchanged shocked glances and muttered to each other as they backed away in a group. The wood from their sandals clicked in unison, like the rhythm of a woodpecker, as they retreated. Haruto stood beside Rumiko, silently watching them disappear into the distance. Rumiko looked up from her doll at Haruto, "Thank you, but I didn't need your help!" For a moment, he stood in silence, searching for the right words. "I'm sorry," he said softly, his voice full of sincerity. "I only wanted to help." After a pause, she sighed and met his eyes again. "I just... I didn't want them to think I'm weak," she admitted, her voice quieter now. Haruto nodded in understanding. "You're not weak. Standing up to them like that? That took a lot of strength." He smiled slightly, trying to ease the tension. "Besides, we all need a little help sometimes."

Rumiko's defenses melted a little more, and for the first time that day, she allowed herself a small smile. "Maybe," she said softly, still clutching the doll but no longer out of fear. "But next time, I'll handle it."

"Deal," Haruto said, grinning, glad to see her spirit wasn't crushed. As he reflected on his memories of Rumiko, he was reminded of her incredible mental strength. If anyone could survive this ordeal, it was her.

Haruto climbed for several more hours, each step more strenuous than the last, before finally reaching the top of the steep hill. His muscles burned with exertion, and sweat dripped from his brow, but the thought of reaching his destination spurred him on. As he cleared the last cluster of rocks, he could feel a surge of energy swell within him, a renewed sense of purpose driving him forward. He knew he was close now; he could almost sense Kenji's presence in the air.

When he stood up, the sight before him took his breath away. Below him stretched the most beautiful green valley he had ever seen. The landscape was a lush tapestry of vibrant hues, with rolling meadows dotted with wildflowers in every color imaginable. A river wound its way through the valley, its waters sparkling in the sunlight.

Nestled amidst this natural splendor was a small, rustic wooden cabin, its thatched roof blending seamlessly with the surrounding landscape. Smoke gently lifted from the stone chimney. Haruto could see a neatly tended garden beside the cabin, bursting with vegetables and herbs, and an old stone path leading to the front door.

His attention was drawn to three large hawks circling the landscape, their powerful wings cutting through the air with effortless grace. It was as if they were announcing his presence, heralding his arrival in this sacred place. Their sharp cries echoed across the valley, blending with the gentle flowing of the river.

Haruto was thankful that climbing down was always easier than climbing up. He carefully navigated his way down the grassy hillside, each step more stable and assured. The grass was soft underfoot, cushioning his descent and adding a spring to his steps. As he descended, the scent of wildflowers filled the air, mingling with the earthy aroma of the forest and the crisp freshness of the mountain breeze.

He took in every detail as he made his way down—the delicate petals of the wildflowers swaying in the breeze, the vibrant green of the grass stretching endlessly, and the occasional flutter of butterflies and insects dancing from blossom to blossom.

The meadow below was a patchwork of color and life. He felt a deep appreciation for the beauty and serenity of his new home. With the valley floor now within reach, Haruto's excitement grew.

As he approached the stone pathway, the wooden door of the cabin slowly creaked open. Standing in the doorway was a very tall, dark-skinned man with a commanding presence and an ebony complexion. His face was square and sturdy, with high cheekbones and a strong jawline. His muscular arms, visible beneath the rolled-up sleeves of his simple gray robe, spoke of years of physical training and hard work.

His hair was styled in short dreadlocks, and his thin beard was more white than black. His deep-set eyes, lined with wisdom and experience, revealed his age and the many stories he carried. The man nodded at Haruto and spoke in a voice that was both gentle and authoritative. "I am Kenji."

Haruto felt relief wash over him. He had finally reached his destination and was standing before the man who could change the course of his life. Kenji looked up to the sky just as the three hawks began their descent, their powerful wings beating the air as they approached. Haruto watched in amazement as Kenji extended his arm in front of him with the grace of someone who had done this many times before. Kenji wore a thick leather glove to protect his skin from the hawk's talons, which gripped firmly but gently.

The bird's keen eyes locked onto Haruto, as if sizing him up. The two other hawks stood

guard, perching themselves on the edge of the small home's roof.

Haruto nervously spoke, "My mother sent me."

Kenji, still focused on the hawk perched on his arm, responded,

"Yes, I know your mother well." He then whispered something to the bird and gently released it into the air, watching as it soared away. Turning to Haruto, Kenji gestured toward the entrance and said, "Come inside my home."

With a hint of trepidation, Haruto slowly followed Kenji into the cabin. Inside the home, the air was cool and earthy, with a hint of incense lingering in the background. Haruto's attention was immediately drawn to a polished katana prominently displayed on the wall, its brilliant blade reflecting the sunlight streaming through the open door. The handle of the katana was intricately wrapped in black and gold silk, with a tiger's eye stone embedded at the base of the hilt. The stone glistened with a warm, amber glow.

Below it sat a set of samurai armor. Though aged, the armor was meticulously maintained and stood as a testament to Kenji's former life as a warrior. Each piece was arranged with precision, ready for use at a moment's notice.

A small, well-worn tatami mat lay on the earthen floor, serving as both a sleeping area and a place for meditation. The wooden walls of the cabin were adorned with intricate carvings.

Furs hung, providing both insulation and a touch of warmth. The furs varied in color and texture, hinting at Kenji's skill as a hunter. A low wooden table sat in the center of the room, cluttered with various tools and artifacts, including a mortar and pestle, bundles of dried herbs, and small, delicately carved figurines.

On the opposite wall, a small stone fireplace provided both heat and a place for cooking. The hearth was neatly arranged with firewood, and a blackened kettle hung above the flames, ready for brewing tea or preparing a meal.

Kenji spoke, "Are you hungry?"

Haruto cleared his throat and bowed before answering,

"Yes, Kenji-sama."

Kenji smiled and replied, "Just call me Kenji."

He walked over to the kettle and said,

"I will prepare us a meal and tea."

Then, handing Haruto the large black kettle, he added,

"Now, go and fetch water from the river!"

CHAPTER FOUR

WITHIN THE VALLEY

Life for Haruto in the valley began quietly. Kenji rarely spoke to him, except to give instructions on the chores that needed to be done around the small farm. The work was simple but constant, grounding Haruto in a routine that left little room for idle thoughts. He promised himself he would not dwell on the world he had left behind, nor would he ever "jump" again. Haruto decided it was best to fit in, avoiding any trouble or unnecessary attention.

Kenji's small garden was meticulously maintained, bursting with a variety of vegetables and fruits. Haruto tended to rows of cucumbers and beans, as well as plum trees that bore sweet, juicy fruit. The rich, healthy soil of the valley seemed to nourish everything with ease, making the garden a bountiful source of food.

A black horse with a white circle like the moon on her rear, named Tsuki, lived in a small barn at the back of the house. Several chickens clucked around the coop, their constant pecking yielding a steady supply of fresh eggs. Each day, Haruto carefully collected the eggs.

A single cow that Kenji called Ushi-ko roamed a small fenced area. Her name meant "little cow." She was Haruto's only friend. He brushed her coat and ensured she always had fresh water from the nearby river, which also supplied the farm with all its irrigation needs. The river's gentle surge was a constant companion, its clear, icy waters a lifeline for the farm.

Haruto would watch Kenji as he playfully interacted with his animals as if they were his own children. One afternoon, as Haruto was tending to Tsuki, he overheard Kenji playfully joking with Ushi-ko, the cow.

"Hey, Ushi-ko, are you trying to steal Haruto's attention with those big eyes of yours?" Kenji chuckled, gently patting the cow's side. Ushi-ko responded with a low, contented moo, and Kenji continued, "You know, Haruto, I think Ushi-ko believes she's the queen of this valley."

Haruto smiled, feeling a warmth from seeing this softer side of Kenji. "Well, she does have a rather pleasant personality," he replied, laughing.

Kenji nodded, his eyes twinkling with amusement. "Indeed she does. And don't let her fool you; she's quite the mischief-maker when no one's looking. Isn't that right, Ushi-ko?"

Haruto was also introduced to Kenji's three hawks, each with a unique presence. The mother hawk, Hikari, exuded a commanding and graceful aura. Haruto felt a special connection to her, as both of their names meant "light."

The first son, Yume, whose name meant "dream," had a softer, more delicate quality. His feathers shimmered in the sunlight, and his movements were almost dreamlike as he glided effortlessly through the air. Her second son, Kaze, whose name meant "wind," was swift and agile. His name reflected his speed and his ability to navigate the skies with quiet precision. Kaze's sharp, piercing gaze and quick movements made him an invaluable scout and messenger, always ready to respond to Kenji's commands.

Each day, Kenji would release the hawks into the sky, and they would always return to the large bamboo enclosure that Kenji had built for them behind the cabin. On some occasions, they would be gone for long periods, soaring high above the valley and beyond, their watchful eyes scanning the landscape.

Kenji would often stand outside, watching the sky with a calm, patient expression, waiting for their return. When the hawks finally reappeared, they would descend gracefully, landing softly on Kenji's outstretched arm, each one bringing with it a sense of reassurance and vital information.

"Welcome back, Hikari," Kenji would say softly, stroking the mother hawk's feathers. "What news do you bring me today?"

With all these resources, they had everything needed to live a quiet, self-sufficient life. And with Kenji, it was very quiet. The old man moved with a quiet calmness, his actions efficient and his words few. Haruto often found himself working side by side with Kenji in silence.

As Haruto was working in the barn near the horse Tsuki, Kenji approached. "Today, Haruto," Kenji began, "I want to show you a different way to connect with Tsuki. It's not about riding or commands. It's about understanding and feeling her heartbeat, her life force."

They stood near Tsuki, the black mare with a white circle on her rear. Kenji spoke, "Her name means moon, as the circle looks like a full moon against a night sky." Kenji grasped Haruto's hand and placed it on Tsuki's neck. "Close your eyes, and focus on the rhythm of Tsuki's pulse. Feel it beat against your fingers."

Haruto closed his eyes, concentrating on the steady thump of Tsuki's heartbeat. As he tuned into the rhythm, he felt a warm connection spreading through his fingertips.

"Now, try to match your own breathing to Tsuki's heartbeat," Kenji instructed gently. "Breathe in time with her. Feel the connection between you."

Haruto took deep breaths, aligning his inhales and exhales with the rhythm of Tsuki's pulse. With each breath, he felt more in tune with the horse, sensing a calmness and strength flowing from Tsuki into himself.

"This is the essence of our bond with animals," Kenji explained softly. "When you can feel Tsuki's life force, you understand her better. You become one with her." Haruto continued to breathe in sync with Tsuki, feeling a profound sense of unity with the animal. He sensed her calmness, strength, and presence in a way he never had before. It was as if her heart was speaking to his, sharing a silent, powerful language.

After a few moments, Haruto opened his eyes, still keeping his hand on Tsuki's neck. He looked at Kenji with newfound understanding. "I can feel it," Haruto said quietly. "It's like I can hear her heart speaking to mine."

Kenji nodded, a proud smile on his face. "Remember this feeling, Haruto. This connection will guide you in all your interactions with Tsuki."

Though life was simple and quiet on the farm, one mystery occupied Haruto's mind. While gardening behind the cabin, he had noticed a camouflaged door built into the hillside. The door seemed so out of place in the open landscape of the farm. His curiosity grew with each passing day, but he was too afraid to ask Kenji.

One evening, just as the sun dipped below the horizon, Haruto saw Kenji heading toward the hillside. Kenji moved with a sense of purpose, carrying a bundle of items wrapped in cloth. He wore a long black robe with a hood pulled over his head. Haruto's heart quickened; this might be his chance to uncover the secret of the hidden room.

He followed Kenji from a safe distance staying hidden in the shadows. He watched as Kenji approached the door and, with a swift motion, removed the vines covering it. Kenji took a key from his robe and unlocked the door, which creaked open, revealing a flickering red light from within. Kenji stepped inside, and the door closed behind him.

Haruto waited a few moments before creeping closer. His hands trembled with anticipation as he pressed his ear against the door, trying to catch any sound from within. The door was open a small crack. He could hear the sound of Kenji chanting and making strange sounds. Haruto's curiosity got the better of him, and he slowly pushed the door open just enough to peer inside.

The small room was dimly lit by red, flickering candles arranged in a circle. In front of Kenji stood an altar covered with various objects: bowls of herbs, small figurines, and a small skull that seemed to watch over the proceedings. The walls were adorned with strange symbols, and the floor was a rocky formation with painted drawings. Kenji sat on his knees, tucked in the center of the circle. In his hand, he held a small object, his eyelids tightly closed, eyes darting beneath.

A small bowl of burning herbs sat before him, a thin trail of smoke rising into the air, drifting into Kenji's nostrils. As he inhaled, he chanted, "Ya-su-ko..." over and over, as if in a desperate plea. Haruto stared in awe and fear, unable to look away. He had heard stories of voodoo rituals but had never witnessed anything like this. Kenji's presence was commanding, and the air seemed to vibrate with energy.

Overwhelmed by what he had witnessed, Haruto felt a rush of fear grip his heart. He turned and bolted back to the house, his footsteps echoing in the quiet night. His breath came in short, panicked bursts as he sprinted towards the safety of the cabin. Once inside, he quickly crawled under his covering, pulling it tightly around himself in a desperate attempt to find comfort.

His heart pounded loudly in his chest, and he tried to steady his breathing. He closed his eyes and pretended to be asleep, hoping that Kenji wouldn't find out about his intrusion. The flickering shadows from the fireplace danced across the walls, but Haruto kept his eyes shut tight, trying to calm the panic that had overtaken his mind.

As he lay there, his thoughts raced. The images of the ritual and Kenji's commanding presence swirled in his head. Despite his fear, a part of him was undeniably curious about the secrets Kenji was keeping and what they meant for his own journey. But for now, he tried to focus on slowing his breathing and quieting his heart, seeking the comfort of sleep.

Haruto was too afraid to confront Kenji about the secret room. The images of the strange symbols and the dark rituals haunted his thoughts. He was paralyzed by fear and couldn't bring himself to ask Kenji directly. Days passed in silence, the unspoken tension hanging heavily between them.

On the fifth day, as the sun began to set, they sat together for their evening meal. The quiet was punctuated only by the gentle clicking of chopsticks against bowls. Kenji's face was calm, but there was a hint of something deeper in his eyes.

As Haruto lifted a bite of rice to his mouth, Kenji finally broke the silence. "Haruto," he began, his voice steady but carrying a weight of sincerity, "we cannot keep secrets from one another."

Haruto looked up from his rice bowl, startled. His eyes met Kenji's, and he saw a reflection of his own apprehension mirrored in them. The room seemed to hold its breath, the usual background noises of the farm fading into silence.

Kenji continued, "I know you've discovered the room in the hillside. You saw more than you were meant to without explanation. And for that, I am sorry. But it is time that you understand."

Haruto's heart pounded in his chest. He set his bowl down, his appetite forgotten. "What... what is that place?" he asked, his voice trembling slightly.

Kenji sighed and leaned back, his expression thoughtful. "That room is a sanctuary of sorts, a place where I perform rituals to protect this valley and those within it. It's a practice passed down through generations, meant to guard against the darkness that threatens us."

"The Kurokawa?," Haruto whispered, feeling a cold chill run down his spine.

"Yes," Kenji affirmed. "The Kurokawa is a powerful force of darkness. The rituals I perform are meant to counteract its influence, to keep it at bay. It's a practice that I inherited, and one I take very seriously. It is the only way for us to be safe here."

Haruto felt a sense of relief and anxiety. "Why didn't you tell me?" he asked, his voice filled with hurt.

Kenji's gaze softened. "I wanted to protect you, to prepare you before burdening you with such knowledge. But you have proven yourself strong and capable. It's time you know the truth."

The silence that followed was different, charged with understanding rather than fear. Haruto nodded slowly, accepting the importance of Kenji's words. "I'm ready to learn," he said quietly.

Kenji smiled, a rare but genuine expression of approval. "Good. We will start tomorrow. There is much to teach, and much for you to understand. Together, we will protect this valley." As they resumed their meal, the air felt lighter, the bond between them strengthening.

The small cabin was filled with a strong aroma of burning sage and incense. Kenji laid out an assortment of items on a low wooden table: a piece of polished jade, a small bundle of dried herbs, a vial of sacred oil, and a length of red silk thread. Each item had been meticulously chosen for its spiritual significance and power.

Haruto knelt beside him watching Kenji carefully prepare the items. "Today, we will craft a talisman," Kenji began, his deep voice resonating with authority. "This talisman will serve as both a protective shield and a source of strength for you Haruto."

Haruto watched intently as Kenji picked up the piece of jade. "This jade symbolizes purity and protection. It will be the heart of your talisman," he explained, handing the stone to Haruto. The jade was cool and smooth in Haruto's palm, its green surface reflecting the candlelight.

Kenji then took the bundle of dried herbs and began to chant softly, invoking the spirits of the earth and air. He passed the herbs over the flame of a candle, the smoke curling and wafting through the air. "These herbs are for cleansing and protection," Kenji said, placing the bundle beside the jade.

Next, he opened the vial of sacred oil, the scent filling the room. He dabbed a few drops onto the jade, rubbing it gently with his fingers. "This oil will help to seal the energy within the talisman," Kenji explained.

Finally, Kenji picked up the length of red silk thread. "Red is the color of life and vitality. It will bind the elements of your talisman together," he said, threading the silk through a small hole in the jade and tying it securely.

Kenji placed the assembled talisman on a small, intricately carved wooden altar. He motioned for Haruto to join him, and together they knelt before the altar. Kenji began to chant, his voice rising and falling in a melodic incantation. Haruto felt a surge of energy in the room, a presence that seemed to flow through Kenji and into the talisman.

"Place your hands over the talisman, Haruto," Kenji instructed. Haruto did as he was told, feeling the warmth and vibration of the jade beneath his palms. "Focus your mind and your spirit. Visualize the energy flowing from you into the talisman. This is your protection, your strength."

Haruto closed his eyes, concentrating on the image of light and energy flowing from his body into the talisman. He felt a connection, a bond forming between him and the jade. After a few minutes, Kenji placed his hands over Haruto's. "It is done," he said softly. "This talisman is now charged with your energy and the blessings of the spirits. Keep it with you always."

Haruto stepped outside the cabin and was immediately struck by a breeze of cold air that quickly shifted into a warm, comforting embrace. The transition felt almost magical, as if the air itself acknowledged the presence of his newly crafted talisman. He took the talisman from his hand and placed it around his neck, feeling the cool jade stone rest against his chest. He glanced down at the black opal necklace his mother had given him, now resting beside the talisman. He smiled and whispered, "I guess both of you can watch over me!"

Kenji and Haruto began a daily practice of learning, each session filled with new teachings and deeper understandings. Every morning, as the first light of dawn broke over the valley, they would start their day with meditation. Sitting cross-legged on the tatami mats, Kenji would guide him through chants and incantations, grounding themselves and opening their minds to the spiritual energies around them.

After meditation, Kenji would take Haruto through various rituals and practices. One day, they might work with herbs and plants, learning how to identify, harvest, and prepare them for potions and elixirs. Kenji showed Haruto how to crush dried herbs with a mortar and pestle, releasing their potent aromas and preparing them for use in healing salves.

On other days, Kenji would take Haruto to the small room built into the hillside. There, they practiced drawing ancient symbols, each stroke of soft stone on the earthen floor charged with intention and focus. Kenji explained the significance of each symbol, how they interacted with the natural and spiritual worlds to create barriers of protection or channels for energy.

"These symbols are ancient and powerful," Kenji would say, his voice filled with reverence. "They connect us to the spirits and to the earth. When you draw them, you must do so with clarity and purpose."

Haruto, curious yet hesitant, looked at Kenji and quietly asked,

"Where did you learn these secrets?"

Kenji paused, after a long moment, he finally spoke,

"In my village, my mother was a healer, a keeper of the old ways. She taught me these symbols and their meanings, passed down through generations. They were more than just marks on the ground—they were a way to commune with forces greater than ourselves. She believed that by respecting the spirits and the earth, we could harness their power to protect and guide us."

At the end of each day, between his rigorous training sessions with Kenji and the demanding daily chores on the farm, Haruto was exhausted when he reached his mat. His muscles ached from the physical exertion, and his mind buzzed with the new knowledge and skills he had absorbed, leaving him both physically and mentally drained.

As he lay in the darkened room with the faint glow of the fire's dying embers glowing, Haruto's mind often drifted back to the village. The warmth of the fire couldn't dispel the ache of homesickness that settled deep in his chest. He missed his mother and Rumiko more than ever, their faces and voices a constant presence in his thoughts. Despite his eagerness to learn from Kenji and the fulfillment he found in his training, the longing for home and the familiarity of his loved ones never fully left him.

Haruto was brushing Ushi-ko, her tail flipping from side to side like a hand swatting at the persistent flies. "Okay girl, we are almost done," he said soothingly, passing his hand over her back with a brush one last time.

Just then, Kenji approached with his usual quiet intensity. "Boy, you are small and weak,"Kenji stated bluntly, his eyes assessing Haruto with a critical gaze. Haruto's shoulders slumped, and he dropped his head in embarrassment, the harsh words stinging. Kenji continued, his firm tone. "I can teach you magic, and I will. But you are a boy living in a human body. The magic will not help if you cannot even win a fight against another boy your age. Strength and skill are your foundation. Without them, the magic is useless."

Haruto felt a surge of determination mingled with his embarrassment. He looked up at Kenji, meeting his look with newfound determination. "I understand, Kenji," he replied quietly. "I will work harder. I'll become stronger." Kenji nodded, a faint smile playing at the corners of his mouth. "Good. We will begin physical training tomorrow at dawn. It is time to strengthen your body as well as your mind."

The next morning, Haruto woke up before the sun even rose, eager to get an early start on his chores. The sky was still a deep shade of indigo, the stars just beginning to fade. He quickly completed his tasks, his anticipation growing with each passing moment.

"Okay, Haruto, let's go to the forest and train," Kenji called out as he approached. Kenji wore a light gray kimono that was loosely open in the front, revealing his powerful, well-defined dark muscles. His pants were wide gray hakamas that flowed with his movements, allowing him to move with grace and precision.

Haruto followed Kenji into the cool morning forest. As they walked they were greeted by the vibrant smell of pine and earth. Kenji stood nearby, his watchful eyes never leaving Haruto. He pointed to a boulder laying alone on the ground. "Lift the stone, Haruto," he commanded, his voice firm but encouraging.

Haruto stood before the massive boulder, its surface rough and unyielding. His hands were calloused from days of chores and farm work. With a deep breath, he summoned all his strength and heaved. The boulder barely moved.

"You can do it, Haruto," Kenji urged. "Focus on your breath. Use your entire body, not just your arms." Haruto tried again, his muscles straining under the effort. Sweat poured down his face, stinging his eyes and blurring his vision. He managed to lift the boulder a few inches off the ground before his strength gave out. The stone fell back with a thud, and Haruto stumbled backwards, falling to his backside in exhaustion.

"I'm too weak," he muttered under his breath. "I can't do it."

Kenji approached, his expression stern and demanding. "Stand up," he ordered.

Haruto shook his head, there were tears of frustration mingling with the sweat on his cheeks. "I can't," he repeated, his voice breaking. "I'm too weak."

Haruto's mind drifted to when he was nine years old, standing in the village square on a bright autumn morning. The villagers had gathered for the annual harvest festival, a time when everyone came together to celebrate the bounty of the fields. Children ran around, laughing and playing games, while adults prepared food and shared stories.

In the center of the village sat a large bag of rice, drawing the attention of a growing crowd. A round man with a small mustache stood beside it, announcing to the gathering crowd of adults and children, "Whoever can move this bag will win a prize of fresh produce and a fine jug of sake!"

The crowd buzzed with excitement, and several teens stepped forward, eager to take on the challenge. Haruto watched from the edge of the square, his heart pounding. He knew his father would want him to try and prove his strength to the villagers.

The round man continued, "This bag of rice is no easy feat. It weighs as much as a full-grown man! Do we have any volunteers?" His eyes scanned the crowd, searching for the bravest and strongest among them. Haruto's father stepped forward, his broad shoulders and muscular frame cutting an imposing figure. The round man spoke, "No, you're too big good sir. This is a game for the young men!"

Fine, "My son, Haruto, will attempt it," he declared, pushing him forward.

Haruto's stomach tightened with nerves. He looked at the heavy sack of rice, then back at his father, whose stern gaze left no room for an argument. "Father, please don't." Haruto said quietly, stepping behind his fathers large frame. He grabbed Haruto by the arm and pushed him onto the bag of rice. Haruto stood up and looked back at his father who nodded.

The villagers' murmurs grew louder, with some whispering words of encouragement and others expressing doubt. Haruto bent down, wrapped his arms around the sack, and tried to lift it. The weight was immense, far more than he could manage. He strained even harder, his face turning bright red, but the sack never budged.

The round man with the mustache called out with a laugh, "Come on, young Haruto, show us your strength!" Haruto tried again, his legs trembling with the strain. The sack stood firm, and it was clear he couldn't lift it. The crowd's whispers turned to laughter, and Haruto's cheeks burned red with shame.

He looked at his father whose face was darkened with disappointment. "You're weak, Haruto," he said loudly, his voice echoing over the laughter. "How can you call yourself my son when you cannot lift a bag of rice an inch?" His father then turned and walked away.

As the memory faded, Haruto found himself sitting on the forest bed in front of Kenji, feeling the weight of his past.

Kenji noticed the distant look in Haruto's eyes and asked,

"Are you alright?"

Haruto nodded, a determined look growing on his face.

"I'm fine," he said, as he made his way to his feet.

For a moment, the forest was silent except for the sound of Haruto's labored breathing. Then, a soft breeze rustled the leaves, and Haruto closed his eyes, feeling the cool air on his face. In the whisper of the wind, he heard a familiar voice, gentle yet firm. "Ha-ruto," she said slowly, her tone filled with warmth and encouragement. It was his mother's voice filling his head. "You are more powerful than you think. Your strength comes from your heart, my son. Seek love and you will find strength."

Haruto's heart swelled with emotion. He could see his mother's face in his mind, her kind eyes and comforting smile. She had always believed in him, even when he doubted himself. Her words uplifted him, pushing him to rise above his fear and doubt.

Haruto wiped his tears and stood up. He looked at Kenji, who nodded silently, understanding the change that had come over his student. Haruto turned back to the boulder, feeling a newfound strength surging through his veins.

He took a deep breath, focused his mind, and gripped the boulder once more. This time, he felt his entire body working in unison—his legs, his back, his arms, and his heart—all contributing to the effort. With a mighty heave, he lifted the stone off the ground, holding it there for several moments before gently lowering it back down.

Kenji's eyes widened with pride. "Well done, Haruto," he said quietly. "Remember this moment." Kenji pointed to his heart. "Your greatest strength comes from here." Haruto nodded, his chest heavy with exertion but his heart light with triumph.

Kenji continued to push Haruto every day with rigorous physical training. Each dawn, they ventured deeper into the forest, where Kenji devised increasingly challenging exercises to test Haruto's endurance, strength, and agility. They climbed steep hills, carried heavy logs, and sprinted through the forest.

Kenji would take Haruto to a part of the river where the current was strong and powerful, rushing over and around jagged rocks that jutted out menacingly. The water roared as it cascaded downstream, echoing through the surrounding forest. "Get in the water, Haruto!" Kenji commanded, his voice low and firm.

Haruto felt a surge of fear creeping into his growing frame. He had swum in shallow waters before, where he could touch the bottom and feel safe, but this was something entirely different. The river here was wild and untamed, its current threatening to sweep away anything in its path. He glanced at Kenji, whose intense expression left no room for questioning.

Kenji pointed to the middle of the river. "Come on Haruto, go now and stand your ground!" Taking a deep breath, Haruto slowly climbed into the rushing river. The cold water stung his skin like a thousand tiny needles, and the force of the current tugged at his legs, pulling him towards the sharp rocks that lined the riverbed. Each step was a battle to maintain his footing, the icy water making his muscles ache and his heart race.

"Feel the water, Haruto," Kenji called out over the roar of the river. "Do not meet resistance with more resistance. Haruto, become one with the water." Haruto closed his eyes, relaxed his legs, and let his arms lay at his sides, his breath now in sync with the river. He could feel the water's power surging around him, but instead of fighting it, he began to move with it, finding a rhythm in the chaos.

Kenji watched intently, his eyes never leaving Haruto. He observed the boy's determination, the way he adjusted to the river's relentless fury, and the subtle shifts in his movements. "Good," Kenji whispered to himself. "He's learning."

As the water crashed against Haruto, he instinctively turned his body sideways, flowing with the current instead of fighting it. A flicker of pride crossed Kenji's face as a small smile tugged at the corner of his mouth, only to fade as he quickly returned to his stern demeanor.

Haruto climbed out of the rushing river. He jumped up and down and began to shake out his wet clothing. Kenji approached him, a look of approval on his face. "You did well, Haruto," he said, his voice filled with a rare warmth. "The river is a powerful teacher. It shows us that strength is not just about force, but about understanding and adapting to the challenges we face."

Haruto nodded, his body aching but his spirit more alive than ever. He looked back at the rushing river, its waters glistening in the morning light. The fear that had gripped him earlier was gone, replaced by a newfound sense of inner strength. He felt as though he had conquered not just the river, but a part of himself that had doubted his own capabilities. "Thank you, Kenji," Haruto said, his voice calm despite his exhaustion. "I won't forget this lesson."

Kenji looked back at Haruto, who was now a few paces behind, and gave him an approving nod. "Good," Kenji said, a hint of a smile playing on his lips. "Next will be your hand-to-hand combat and weapons training!"

As they walked back to the cabin, Haruto's mind was already racing with thoughts of the new techniques and skills he would learn. He envisioned himself mastering the art of combat, moving with the same grace and precision as Kenji. The path ahead was daunting, but he felt ready to embrace it.

Today was the day that Kenji had promised they would begin Haruto's combat training. As Kenji walked out of the cabin, Haruto noticed he was carrying his bow and arrows. Circling above him was Hikari, the mother hawk, her sharp eyes scanning the valley below.

Haruto felt a surge of disappointment when he realized they would not be starting his combat training. As he prepared to depart, his tall, sturdy frame silhouetted against the morning light, Kenji adjusted the bow strapped securely to his back. The bow, crafted from polished wood and strung with a taut, sinewy cord, was a testament to his skill as a craftsman.

"Haruto, I want you to tend to the farm today while I am out hunting. Specifically, I would like you to clean Hikari and her sons' enclosure," Kenji instructed, his voice clear and commanding.

Haruto nodded, his posture straightening with determination. "Yes, Kenji" he replied, ready to take on the responsibility. However, a flicker of disappointment crossed his face. He had been eagerly anticipating the start of his combat training, the next step in his journey to becoming a warrior. He watched as Kenji, with Hikari perched on his arm, disappeared into the forest. Her two sons circled the sky overhead.

Haruto walked into the hawks' enclosure and surveyed the job at hand. The area was scattered with feathers, droppings, and remnants of the hawks' meals. He set down a wooden pail filled with water, a straw brush, and a wooden scraper, ready to begin cleaning.

As he knelt to start scraping away the grime from the wooden perches, his mind wandered. *I want to learn to fight more than anything*, he thought to himself, frustration bubbling under the surface. *I can run fast, and I am stronger, but I've never been able to fight. How can I learn to fight if I'm just cleaning bird droppings?*

Haruto's thoughts drifted to his secret ability. *I surely can't reveal my 'jumping' secret to Kenji*, he mused. *What would he think? Would he even understand?*

As he continued to clean, his mind drifted to the one and only time he had been in a fight. Haruto had always been smaller than the other village kids. Even the younger children were often taller and more muscular than he was, and it was not uncommon for people to mistake him for being much younger than his actual age. On occasion, his long hair and small frame even led to him being mistaken for a girl, which was a constant source of embarrassment for Haruto.

Father would exclaim to Haruto's mother almost daily. He would throw his hands in the air, frustration written across his face. "How will my son be a farmer if he cannot lift a sack of rice?" Then, he would storm out of the room, leaving Haruto feeling small and inadequate. His mother would always come to his side, offering her love and support. In frustration, she would say aloud, "My son, you're special in ways he cannot understand."

In these moments Haruto would go outside and distance himself from his father. As Haruto walked, lost in his thoughts, he suddenly heard a voice calling behind him, "Hey, baby Haruto! Why don't you go play with the girls?" It was one of the older village boys taunting him. The voice was filled with ridicule, drawing the attention of the other children nearby.

The older boy, a head taller and much stronger, came up behind Haruto and shoved him. Haruto stumbled forward before regaining his footing, his cheeks burning with humiliation. A surge of anger built within him, quickly reaching a boiling point. Suddenly, without thinking, he turned and ran at the boy, swinging wildly. His fists flailed in the air, each punch fueled by a mix of frustration and desperation.

The older boy easily sidestepped Haruto's awkward attack, and with a swift motion, extended his leg, causing Haruto to trip and fall to the ground. The impact knocked the wind out of him, and he lay on the ground sobbing. The boy stood over Haruto, a cruel smile spreading across his face. "See? You are a weakling!" he taunted, his laughter ringing in Haruto's ears.

Haruto snapped back to the present moment as he continued to clean the cage. He vowed to himself that he would not let that moment of humiliation define him. He had come a long way from the scared, small boy who was taunted by the village children. Under Kenji's tutelage, he had grown stronger, both in body and spirit. Each chore, each lesson was a step towards becoming the warrior he aspired to be.

Suddenly he could hear mothers voice in his head, "Haruto these challenges were not meant to break you, but to build your resolve and allow you to be the warrior you are destined to become. Let go of the pain, Haruto."

Haruto smiled and whispered, "Thank you Mother." Haruto took a deep breath, feeling the crisp morning air fill his lungs. He could sense the strength he had gained through his training, the resilience that had been forged in the fires of his past challenges. He did not have to become those trials, but could learn from them. *I have proven myself worthy to Kenji,* Haruto thought with a sense of pride. *I am ready for whatever lies ahead.*

Kenji returned at dusk with the day's hunt, his silhouette emerging from the shadows of the forest as the last light was disappearing over the clearing. His steps were strong and purposeful. He carried a large, freshly killed deer slung over his broad shoulders, its antlers reflecting the last bits of sunlight. Kenji's face, though marked by lines of age and experience, radiated a quiet satisfaction. The hunt had been successful, and the bounty he brought back would sustain them for weeks.

Haruto, who had been waiting by the cabin, immediately noticed the impressive catch. The deer's coat was a rich brown, its body muscular and heavy with a trail of blood going down its side. Overhead Hikari, Yume and Kaze circled the sky.

"I've returned, Haruto," Kenji called out as he approached, his voice deep and resonant. "Today's hunt will provide us with plenty of meat. Tomorrow, we will begin your hand-to-hand combat training," he added. Haruto smiled and nodded, feeling a burst of excitement.

Kenji and Haruto woke before the first crack of sunlight. The air was still and cool, the silence of the pre-dawn hours amplifying the sounds of their movements as they prepared for the day. They moved with purpose, dressing quickly and gathering their supplies.

They walked through the dew-covered grass, the moisture seeping into their sandals and chilling their feet. The ground beneath them was soft and slightly muddy, the dew creating a thin layer of moisture over the earth.

Kenji led the way into the forest, with Haruto following closely, his heart pounding with anticipation. They ventured deep into the woods until they arrived at a small clearing where Kenji had set up a training station. Hanging from a sturdy tree limb was a large woven rice bag filled with straw and sand. The makeshift striking bag swayed slightly in the breeze, its rough surface illuminated by the first hints of dawn.

Kenji stood in front of the training bag and spoke, "I will start by showing you the three fighting ranges." He stepped back, lifted his leg effortlessly, and kicked the bag. "This is called long range. Here, I can kick you." He then took one step closer. "Here we have mid range. I can still kick, but now I can strike with my hands as well." Kenji threw four rapid-fire punches followed by a front kick. Finally, Kenji stepped forward, locked his arms around the bag, and said, "This is close range. Here, I can elbow, knee, and seize and throw you to the ground." He threw two knees followed by two elbow strikes to the head of the bag.

Haruto listened carefully and followed Kenji's instructions, his eyes focused and attentive. He mimicked Kenji's movements with complete effort and intensity. His body had become bigger and stronger through the rigorous training, and it showed in the fluidity and power of his movements.

After days of practicing on the striking bag, Haruto was ready to give his bruised limbs a rest. The relentless training had left his knuckles raw and his muscles aching, but he felt stronger and more prepared than ever. As he stood catching his breath, Kenji walked up to him, holding two long strips of cloth.

"Let me see your hands," Kenji instructed. Haruto extended his arms forward, his palms facing up. Kenji took Haruto's hands gently and began to wrap the cloth around them. His movements were precise, ensuring that the wraps were snug but not too tight. After several passes, he tied the ends securely around Haruto's wrists.

Kenji smiled as he finished, his eyes filled with anticipation. "Today we will spar!" Haruto felt a surge of excitement mixed with a bit of apprehension. Sparring with Kenji was a significant step in his training. He had seen Kenji's fighting prowess and knew that this would be a true test of his skills.

Kenji walked into the middle of a dirt-covered clearing. He removed his grey kimono top, the fabric sliding off his broad shoulders and falling to the ground in a heap. Veins bulged prominently along his muscular arms. Several large, healed scars crisscrossed his shoulders and ran down his back, telling silent stories of past struggles and hard-fought encounters.

Kenji pointed to Haruto, his eyes filled with intensity. "Come on, boy, let's fight!" he shouted, his voice a low, commanding growl. The challenge hung in the air, heavy with anticipation. Haruto nodded, stepping forward into the makeshift arena, ready to face his mentor in combat.

Haruto slowly made his way to Kenji, stepping his foot back and placing his arms awkwardly in front of his head. His stance was hesitant, lacking the confidence that Kenji demonstrated. Kenji snickered and motioned for Haruto to come forward, a mocking glint in his eyes. Haruto began circling Kenji, looking for an opening, his eyes never leaving his mentor's. Then, without warning, he ran at Kenji, throwing two well-executed front kicks. Kenji easily anticipated the barrage and stepped aside with the grace of a seasoned warrior, causing

Haruto to fall forward. As Haruto stumbled, trying to regain his balance, Kenji began to taunt him, "You can't hit what isn't there!" This taunt irritated Haruto even more, and he pursued Kenji with increased aggression. His movements became more erratic and forceful, driven by his growing frustration. Kenji simply smiled, a calm and calculated expression, and countered each move by effortlessly stepping out of the way. Haruto's punches and kicks met only air, further fueling his frustration.

Kenji watched Haruto closely, sensing the growing irritation. He decided it was time for a lesson beyond physical training. He stopped the match and walked over to Haruto, who was panting and visibly upset. Kenji poked him in the chest with his finger, his expression serious. "Anger and frustration will not help you in a fight," Kenji said firmly.

Haruto's eyes widened, and he looked down, feeling the impact of Kenji's words.

"But I want to win," Haruto muttered, his voice filled with desperation.

Kenji placed a hand on Haruto's shoulder, his grip firm yet reassuring.

"Haruto, I know you have a big heart," he said, his voice softer now, filled with a teacher's patience. "Heart alone is not enough. You must use your intelligence, your strategy. A true warrior fights with his mind as much as with his body. You must build a bridge between your heart and mind."

Haruto nodded slowly, absorbing Kenji's words. He realized that his anger had clouded his judgment, making him predictable and easy to counter. He took a deep breath, calming his racing heart, and looked up at Kenji with renewed determination. Haruto began to circle Kenji, his eyes focused. He threw a punch-kick combination, but both strikes missed their mark. Desperate to gain an advantage, he lunged forward and grabbed onto Kenji's neck and arm.

However, before he could regain his balance, Kenji swiftly turned his hip and lifted Haruto into the air, flipping him over his head and onto the ground with a resounding thud. Dirt kicked up around Haruto as he hit the earth, the impact jarring him.

Before Haruto could react to the hard fall, Kenji was already on him. In one fluid motion, Kenji straddled Haruto's chest, secured his arm, and spun toward his head, locking Haruto's arm in place. As Kenji fell backward, he slowly raised his hips, increasing the leverage on Haruto's elbow. The pressure was immediate, forcing Haruto to cry out, "Stop! Stop!"

Kenji immediately released the pressure and stood up, offering a hand to help Haruto to his feet. Haruto's chest rose and fell rapidly as he caught his breath, his body aching from the throw and the arm lock. "Do you see now, Haruto?" Kenji said, his voice firm. "It's not just about strength. Technique, strategy, and a clear mind are what win fights. You must anticipate your opponent's moves and stay calm under pressure." Kenji pointed at Haruto's chest. "Use your heart," he then pointed at his head with a laugh, "but use your head too!"

Haruto nodded, his sore arm a reminder of the lesson learned. He realized how important it was to maintain composure and use his mind as much as his heart in combat. He took a deep breath and straightened up, ready to continue learning.

Kenji patted Haruto on the back. "Good. Let's try again. This time, remember what you've learned. Use your mind, not just your muscles." Haruto took his stance once more, his determination renewed. He knew he had a long way to go, but with each lesson, he was becoming stronger and wiser.

For many weeks, Haruto and Kenji practiced with discipline and purpose. Each day began before the sun rose, the misty morning air filled with the sounds of their training. Haruto's movements became more precise, his strikes more powerful, as he absorbed the lessons Kenji imparted. The forest clearing where they trained became a well-trodden sanctuary of learning and growth.

Kenji expanded the teachings to include weapons training. He introduced Haruto to the bo staff, a long, sturdy piece of wood that required both strength and coordination to wield effectively. To build his strength Kenji had him carry pails of water on each side of the wooden staff while keeping it balanced on his shoulders. Keeping it steady without spilling it was very challenging. As Haruto grew more accustomed to the routine, Kenji added another layer to the training.

He instructed Haruto to stand still with the water pails swaying from side to side and practice throwing kicks into the air. Every movement had to be precise, or the delicate balance would be lost, and water would spill. Each kick required Haruto to focus on maintaining control, his muscles straining to keep the staff level while still executing the technique with proper form.

Haruto learned to spin and strike with the bo staff, his muscles burning as he mastered the intricate techniques. Kenji would demonstrate complex moves, and Haruto would mimic them, his skills growing with each lesson.

"Grip it firmly, but don't let your hands become rigid," Kenji advised, demonstrating a swift, fluid strike with the bo staff. Haruto followed suit, feeling the weight and balance of the weapon as he executed a series of strikes. The staff whistled through the air, connecting with imagined targets as Haruto's confidence strengthened.

As the weeks passed, Kenji taught Haruto that weapons were not just for combat but for hunting as well. One morning, while Haruto was still asleep on his tatami mat, he felt an insistent poking at his side, followed by a familiar voice. "Wake up, boy!"

Haruto rolled over to see Kenji standing above him, holding a long hollow bamboo rod in one hand. In the other, he held a set of sharp, slender metal blades, each catching the faint glow of the morning light. The sight of the bamboo blowpipe and blades aroused Haruto's curiosity, signaling that today's lesson would be unlike any he'd experienced before. "Come on, Haruto, today we hunt!"

After a quick meal, Kenji announced, "Now that your spirit has awakened, it's time to learn to hunt in complete silence." As they approached the edge of the woods, Kenji's movements slowed, becoming controlled and stealthy, like a predator in search of prey.

He quietly removed his sandals, and Haruto followed suit. Kenji's toes pointed and slid effortlessly into the tall grass, each step gentle and precise, as if he were gliding on air. It was as though he had become one with the forest, fitting perfectly into the landscape, moving like the wind through the blades of grass.

Kenji glanced back at Haruto, moving his body into a low crouch as he motioned for him to follow. "You must become one with your surroundings," Kenji's voice silent like a gentle breeze. "Engage all of your senses. What do you see, hear, smell, taste, touch? Feel the forest around you, become part of it. You are it, and it is you. Let every breath and every movement connect you to this moment."

Kenji's words were not just instructions but a guiding philosophy, a way of life that demanded complete presence. Haruto tried to absorb each lesson, feeling the cool earth beneath his fingertips as he moved across the forest floor on his hands and knees. He could taste the damp moisture in the air, the earthy scent of moss filling his senses as if it were growing inside him. The forest seemed alive, and Haruto could feel its pulse, a deep and rhythmic beat that connected with his own.

As Kenji moved through the thick trees, his body seemed to become one with the landscape, flowing as a single unit in perfect sync with his surroundings. Haruto followed as best he could, though his movements occasionally disrupted the delicate harmony with awkward, clumsy steps.

Whenever Haruto faltered, Kenji would pause and motion him closer, whispering, "Do not just move through the forest; become one with it. Feel the rhythm around you and let it guide your steps. That is the rhythm you seek."

Kenji's presence was like a shadow, fading effortlessly into the surroundings, while Haruto struggled to find any sense of balance. He watched with frustration as his mentor seemed to blend into the trees, only to suddenly reappear moments later as if he were part of the forest itself. It was a sight Haruto had witnessed countless times since his arrival. One moment he would be standing alone, and the next, Kenji would materialize beside him as if by magic.

Kenji had mastered the art of moving through the world unseen, blending so completely with his surroundings that he seemed more specter than man.

As they moved through the forest floor, Kenji suddenly paused near a clearing and motioned for Haruto to come closer. Kenji pointed to a wild boar feeding in the open area. It had a large, round, robust black body with streaks of gray running through its coarse fur. Short, bristly hairs were scattered like the teeth of a comb. The boar's head was lowered, chewing on loose acorns on the ground. Protruding from its chin were two large ivory tusks that curved outward.

Kenji crouched low in the shrubs with Haruto by his side. He pulled out his bamboo blowpipe and quietly slid a long sharp metal projectile into the opening. Kenji then removed the dagger strapped to his leg and handed it to Haruto. "I will distract the beast. Once it's stunned, you must climb on its back and cut the animal's throat."

This was the part that Haruto hated the most—killing the animal. But he knew it had to be done to put the creature out of its misery. He also knew that with Kenji, no part of the animal would go to waste. His heart pounded as he clutched the dagger tightly to his chest, preparing himself for what was to come. Kenji raised the bamboo blowpipe to his mouth, his movements slow and silent. He carefully aimed at the unsuspecting boar, its head buried in the pile of acorns.

With a powerful breath, Kenji launched the projectile through the clearing. It sliced through the damp forest air, striking the boar in the neck. The creature snorted loudly, shaking its head from side to side as it stomped its hooves, kicking up clouds of dust into the air. Haruto dashed into the open, dagger in hand, and leapt onto the back of the thrashing boar.

The animal bucked wildly, and Haruto was immediately thrown off, landing hard on the ground as a cloud of dust billowed beneath him. Kenji, now standing, pointed at Haruto, urging him to get back on the boar.

Haruto slowly stood up, wiped his brow, then ran forward and leapt onto the boar's back once more.

With one hand, he held the animal around its back, he could see the thin blade still hanging from the animals neck. As the boar bucked and thrashed, the blade came loose and fell to the ground. Haruto could see blood coming from the open wound. He then raised his hand into the air and with a swift motion thrusted the dagger into the animals wound. The boar stopped in its tracks, throwing Haruto from its back as it collapsed to the ground.

Kenji slowly walked over to the animal, knelt down, and placed his hand on its silent heart. He closed his eyes and quietly chanted. Haruto lay nearby, watching silently through a cloud of dust.

With deep respect, Haruto approached Kenji.

"What was the weapon you used to shoot the projectile?" Kenji turned to Haruto.

"It's called a fukiya, something I learned in my travels."

Haruto hesitated before asking,

"Did someone teach you how to use it?"

Kenji looked down at the fallen boar.

"There was someone I once learned many things from, but he betrayed me deeply."

Haruto asked, "Who is this person?"

Kenji stood up quickly. "I don't speak his name. He will continue to exist as long as his

name is spoken, and I put an end to that a long time ago."

Haruto often wondered where Kenji had come from. He had never seen a man with such dark skin and thick hair before. How was he connected to his mother? He had so many questions he wanted to ask, but Kenji rarely spoke about his past—it was as if he truly were a ghost.

As the weeks passed, Kenji introduced the katana, a revered weapon that demanded respect and precision. The weapons blade glowed brightly in the sunlight, its sharp edge a constant reminder of its lethal potential. Kenji's movements with the katana were a blend of grace and deadly accuracy, and Haruto watched in awe as his teacher demonstrated various techniques.

"Every movement with the katana must be intentional," Kenji explained as he handed Haruto a wooden practice sword called a bokken. "It's not just about cutting; it's about understanding the flow and purpose of each strike." Kenji positioned himself in front of Haruto, demonstrating a few fluid movements with his own bokken. "Watch closely," he said. "Notice how the body moves in harmony with the weapon. The feet, the hips, the shoulders—all must work together in unison."

Haruto watched intently as Kenji performed a series of strikes and parries, his movements almost a dance. "My teacher, Master Takeda taught me many great lessons," Kenji continued. "He would often say that mastering the katana is not just about physical prowess but also about mental clarity. A warrior's mind must be as sharp as his blade."

Haruto practiced diligently, the weight of the katana unfamiliar at first, but soon it felt like an extension of his own arm. He learned the proper stances, the precise angles of attack, and the disciplined focus required to wield the sword effectively. Kenji would correct his posture, guide his hands, and push him to perfect each technique.

"Focus, Haruto," Kenji would remind him. "The katana demands your full attention. Every strike must be precise, every movement deliberate." Kenji taught that mastering evasion was as crucial as mastering the art of striking. To teach Haruto the importance of agility and quick reflexes, he introduced a series of evasion drills. One particularly intense drill involved Kenji pursuing Haruto with a wooden sword, forcing him to move out of the way before being hit.

"Evasion is not just about dodging," Kenji explained. "It's about reading your opponent's movements, anticipating their next strike, and positioning yourself advantageously. You must become a shadow, always just out of reach." They began the exercise in the familiar forest clearing. Kenji, holding a wooden sword, stood at one end, while Haruto, with a determined look on his face, stood at the other. The wooden sword, though not lethal, would still deliver a painful reminder if Haruto responded incorrectly.

Kenji swung the wooden sword with speed and accuracy. Haruto anticipated each move, ducking, jumping, and sliding out of the way with increasing confidence. They moved together with the fluidity of a dance. The sounds of their breath and the swish of the wooden sword slicing through the air filled the clearing.

Kenji paused, his eyes assessing Haruto's progress. Haruto's chest gasped with exertion, but his focus remained sharp. Kenji placed the wooden sword against a nearby boulder. He then turned and selected the razor-sharp katana.

Haruto stepped away from Kenji as he examined the weapon, his eyes tracing the intricate details of the katana's hilt with a tigers eye stone mounted securely. As he turned it over, the light caught the blade, reflecting a brilliant sheen.

Kenji, observing Haruto's reverence for the weapon, crouched and pulled a green leaf from a nearby plant. The leaf was vibrant and fresh, its veins intricate against the sunlight. Kenji stood up and held the leaf delicately between his fingers, positioning it above the katana.

"Watch closely, Haruto," Kenji said, low like a whisper. Haruto's eyes were focused on the blade as Kenji gently ran the leaf along its edge. The steel sliced through the leaf effortlessly, as if it wasn't even there. The two halves of the leaf fluttered to the ground, severed with a precision that spoke to the katana's sharpness and quality.

"This weapon was given to me by my teacher, Takeda. It holds great power. Her name is Tora Katana, the Tiger Sword. This blade embodies the energy and precision of the tiger, swift and unyielding. To those who can wield her, she grants immense strength. But first, you must prove yourself by evading her strikes, for she does not yield to just anyone."

Kenji walked to the center of the dirt-covered ground, which had been worn from their many practice sessions. He held the katana in one hand, the blade pointed at the ground. With a calm and deliberate motion, he signaled Haruto to step forward. Haruto took a deep breath, feeling a mix of anticipation and determination. He stepped into Kenji's range, his stance steady and his eyes locked on his mentor. In one hand, Haruto held a katana. Kenji pointed at Haruto's weapon and spoke, his voice firm. "Place your weapon on the ground, you do not need it."

Haruto hesitated for a moment, then carefully placed the katana on the dirt-covered ground, its blade resting gently on the worn earth. He straightened up, his heart pounding as he faced Kenji unarmed. Without warning, Kenji rapidly advanced on Haruto, swinging the Tora Katana at Haruto's head. The movement was swift and precise, a blur of motion. "Now move, Haruto!" Kenji commanded, his voice sharp.

Haruto's instincts kicked in, and he ducked just in time, feeling the rush of air as Kenji's blade passed over his head. He rolled to the side, springing back to his feet with a newfound urgency. His mind raced, recalling all the evasion techniques he had practiced. Kenji pressed the attack, his strikes coming fast and furious. Haruto's eyes darted, tracking the movements of the Tora Katana. He twisted and turned, narrowly avoiding each swing. The adrenaline pulsing through his veins heightened his senses, his body moving with a fluidity. "Good, Haruto," Kenji shouted between strikes. "Use your surroundings. Stay light on your feet!"

Haruto's gaze shifted to the trees and rocks around them. He began to incorporate the environment into his movements, using a tree branch to shield himself from a downward slash and leaping over a moss covered boulder to avoid a strike. Haruto's mind and body worked in perfect unison to outmaneuver Kenji's relentless assault. Despite the intense pressure, Haruto felt a growing confidence. He was no longer the hesitant boy who had arrived at Kenji's doorstep; he was becoming a true warrior, agile and strategic.

Kenji began to breathe heavily, his chest rising and falling as he lowered the Tora Katana to his side. "Haruto, that was good," he said, a proud yet challenging spark in his eyes. "But you have one final test." Kenji walked to the center of the dirt-covered training area, the ground worn smooth from their rigorous sessions. With his foot, he drew a body-sized circle that would serve as the setting for Haruto's ultimate trial. Pointing to the center, he said, "You will sit in a meditative position on your knees with your eyes closed. Do not open your eyes! At some point, I will come behind you and strike down upon your head without hesitation with Tora Katana. She will show no remorse. You must connect to her and escape, or you will die!"

Haruto's heart pounded in his chest as he walked toward the circle. He understood the seriousness of the test before him. It was not only a measure of his physical agility but also his ability to sense and anticipate danger without the use of his eyes. It had been well over a year since he first arrived at Kenji's. He was no longer a boy but a trained warrior. He had to trust in his training and the skills he had developed under Kenji's guidance.

He slowly stepped into the circle, the boundary feeling both comforting and daunting. Haruto knelt down and settled into a meditative position. He rested his hands on his knees, palms up, and closed his eyes. The world around him faded, leaving only the sounds of the forest and his own steady breathing. Kenji walked behind Haruto and tied a thick black scarf around his eyes, completely covering them and shutting him off from the visual world.

The sun was beginning to set. The temperature dropped slightly, and a chill breeze rustled through the trees, the leaves whispering secrets of the approaching night. Haruto could hear the sounds of the forest around him change from the lively chirps of daytime creatures to the calls of nocturnal ones.

A distant owl hooted while the rustle of unseen animals moved through the foliage. Haruto could not see anything as his eyes were closed and covered, and he dared not look per Kenji's instructions. The light continued to fade through his eyelids, and the forest seemed to close in around Haruto, the shadows growing deeper, darker, and more silent.

Haruto focused on his breathing, trying to calm his nerves. He could feel the cool, damp earth beneath him, the sensation grounding him as the darkness pressed in. The sounds of the forest were no longer just background noise; they felt vibrant and alive. He had never felt so alone amidst so much.

The night seemed to march on at a snail's pace, each minute stretching into an eternity. Without the use of his eyes, Haruto's other senses became heightened, taking in every detail of the forest around him. The world of darkness was a symphony of sounds and scents that called for his attention, each one more distinct and urgent than the last.

The rustling of leaves overhead sounded like whispers from unseen spirits, their voices blending with the night breeze. Haruto could hear the soft flutter of bat wings as they darted through the air, hunting for insects. The distant call of a wolf echoed through the trees, a haunting reminder of the predators lurking in the shadows.

Haruto's sense of smell was equally acute. The scent of damp leaves filled the air, grounding him in the natural world around him. Occasionally, a faint whiff of something more pungent, perhaps a passing animal, caught his attention. Every touch of the cool night air on his skin seemed amplified, the slightest breeze sending shivers down his spine. He felt the rough texture of the earth beneath his knees, each grain of dirt pressing against his skin. His legs were numb, and his back was aching. The air was filled with the cool humidity that clung to his skin and clothes.

Haruto's hearing became his primary guide, picking up even the faintest of sounds. The soft crunch of a twig underfoot or the distant rustle of an animal in the underbrush called his attention. Many hours had passed, and Haruto was beginning to tire. His eyelids grew heavy, and he would start to nod off, only to be jolted awake by his mother's voice echoing through his mind, "Ha-ruto... Wake up!" Each time, his body would pop upright, and he would begin his focused breathing all over again.

In his head, he repeated, *In breath, out breath...* but then his internal voice would scream, *Shut up! You won't hear Kenji!* Haruto was becoming delusional; the strain of maintaining his heightened awareness was taking its toll.

He suddenly felt a slight tickling at his neck as small red ants began crawling upward. Haruto tilted his head from side to side, then scrunched his shoulder against his neck, trying to dislodge them. He was careful not to move too much or make unnecessary noise. But the sensation became unbearable, and he finally swatted at his neck, causing the ants to fall to the ground... only to start their journey all over again.

The night seemed endless, the darkness pressing in on him from all sides. The temperature had dropped further, the cold seeping into his bones. Haruto could feel the exhaustion tugging at his consciousness, his body aching from the tension and the stillness. Each time he started to drift off, his mother's voice would bring him back, like a lifeline pulling him from the brink of sleep.

In the early morning hours, Haruto felt a sudden flood of energy course through his body, demanding his immediate attention. An image of Rumiko appeared in his mind. *It's her,* he thought, *my sole reason for living.* Suddenly everything seemed to move in slow motion. Rumiko smiled and whispered, "Jump, Haruto. Jump." Her words echoed in his mind, cutting through the fog of his thoughts like a beacon.

Haruto's instincts took over. The world around him seemed to hold its breath, the sounds of the forest fading into a muffled hum. He could feel the presence of Kenji behind him, the sharp intent of the impending strike looming closer.

In a split second, Haruto's vision tunneled. He saw Kenji's silhouette and the sheen of the Tora Katana. The blade was aimed directly at the back of Haruto's head, poised to deliver a lethal blow. Haruto could feel himself connecting to the incoming weapon. He could feel the heartbeat of the sword synchronize with his own. Time slowed even further, each fraction of a second stretching into an eternity.

In front of him, a tunnel of swirling, vibrant fractals appeared, each one brighter than the last. They spun at an unparalleled pace, shifting, turning, and transforming. Haruto felt himself being pulled into the vortex. Then, with a sudden burst, he vanished.

One moment he was kneeling in the circle, and the next, he was gone—his body disappearing from the spot as if he had never been there. The katana sliced through the empty air where Haruto's head had been, the force of the swing sending a gust of wind rippling through the leaves and driving the weapon deep into the earth.

Haruto reappeared several feet away, his heart pounding and his breath coming in labored gasps. He could only hear a gentle hum vibrating in his head. He stumbled slightly, the sudden movement disorienting him for a brief moment. His surroundings snapped back into focus, the slow motion lifting as reality reasserted itself. The forest was alive again.

Kenji turned and looked at Haruto with astonishment, his eyes wide with disbelief. He took a step forward, his katana still lowered, as he struggled to find the words.

"Haruto... how did you...?" Kenji began, his voice trailing off as he tried to comprehend

what had just happened.

Haruto smiled and said, "I jumped!"

Kenji responded immediately, "That wasn't a jump, you disappeared and reappeared!"

Haruto laughed, "I call it jumping. But it has never happened like that before. Usually I

hurtle through the air like a jump. But this time I vanished and reappeared here."

Haruto was pointing at the ground as Kenji stared in disbelief.

Chapter Five

EMBRACE THE PAST

The sun was setting behind the mountains as Haruto emerged from the woods with a large buck strapped to the back of Tsuki, its antlers holding the fading sunlight. Seven years had passed since Haruto left the village and began his new life as Kenji's student. He had not heard a word from his mother or Rumiko. Haruto was sure they had moved on or worse. But he had to block them from his head and heart if he was going to go on.

The transformation in him however was profound; he had grown from a small, timid boy into a skilled and confident young man. He had taken on most of the chores on the farm, handling them with ease and efficiency. He had become adept at tending to the horses, chickens, and Ushi-ko the cow, who had grown quite fond of him.

Haruto had also developed a deep connection with Kenji's horse, Tsuki. He would often tend to her needs and give her the special herbs that Kenji claimed, "Keep our girl younger than the rest of us!" Kenji had concocted a special mixture of herbs for all his animals to protect them and keep them young and healthy. Haruto's bond with the animals was a testament to his nurturing nature and the discipline instilled in him by Kenji.

Haruto had also taken over the care of the hawks... Hikari, the mother, and her two sons, Yume and Kaze. He had learned to release them into the sky each day, watching as they soared with grace and precision, only to return to their large bamboo enclosure behind the cabin at dusk. He had developed a deep respect for these magnificent birds, understanding their role in Kenji's practice and their watchful eyes that keep them safe.

Kenji, on the other hand, was showing signs of age. His once powerful frame had become leaner, and the lines on his face had deepened. His once dark dreadlocks were now longer and filled with hints of white. The years of training, battles, and the harshness of life had taken their toll on his body, but his spirit remained unyielding. He still trained Haruto with the same intensity and dedication, pushing him to master every skill and technique.

Haruto had noticed Kenji grimacing more frequently, especially after their strenuous training sessions. He would often see Kenji soaking in the icy river in the evenings, trying to alleviate the pain that had become a constant companion. Despite his physical decline, Kenji's wisdom and strategic mind were sharper than ever. He continued to impart invaluable lessons on Haruto. He would often remind Haruto in his raspy voice, "There is no mastery, you must always be willing to learn more!"

One evening, as they sat by the fire, Kenji spoke, his voice carrying the weight of years gone by. "Haruto, you have grown strong and capable. You have taken on the responsibilities of this farm and more. But there is something we need to discuss."

Haruto looked at his mentor, sensing the gravity of the moment.

"What is it, Kenji?"

Kenji took a deep breath, his eyes reflecting the flickering flames.

"I am not as young as I used to be. My body is failing me, and there will come a time when I

can no longer guide you."

Haruto briefly interrupted his mentor,

"Kenji you're very strong!"

Kenji smiled, "It is time that I shared my whole story with you."

He looked at Haruto, who listened with complete attention, his eyes wide with curiosity and respect. "I was born far to the west, across the great ocean," Kenji began, his voice carrying the weight of many untold stories. "My people live by the coast, where the sun burns fiercely and the sea roars. My father was a respected warrior and navigator, known not only for his skill in combat but for his ability to read the stars and guide us through the endless waters beyond the horizon." Haruto leaned in closer, eager to absorb every word. Kenji's past had always been a mystery, and now, the pieces were starting to come together.

"My childhood was filled with stories of great battles and voyages," Kenji continued. "Our tribe lived close to the coast, and my father often took me to the shores to teach me the ways of the sea. He taught me how to fish, how to sail, and most importantly, how to survive."

Haruto's eyes widened, picturing a younger Kenji standing on the shores in a far off land. "My mother," Kenji paused for a moment, "was a powerful medicine woman. She knew the secrets of the earth—how to heal, how to commune with the spirits, and how to protect our people. She taught me many things, more than just healing wounds. She showed me how to call upon the spirits for guidance and how to use the land's gifts to maintain balance and harmony."

Kenji paused, his eyes distant as he recalled the memories. "One day, when I was much younger, our village was attacked by foreign invaders from across the sea. They came in large, strange ships, armed with weapons unlike any we had ever seen. Despite our best efforts to defend ourselves, we were overwhelmed. My father fought bravely, but he and my mother were killed. I was taken captive and forced aboard one of their ships, bound for a land I did not know."

Haruto's heart sank at the thought of Kenji enduring such hardship. "What happened next?" he asked, his voice barely a whisper.

"Life on the ship was very difficult," Kenji said, his tone somber. "We were packed tightly in the hold, treated like cargo. At night, I was chained to a railing. During the daylight hours, I was allowed on deck to help navigate the ship. The captain saw my skills, inherited from my father, and allowed me to be free of the chains and shackles during the day." Haruto's eyes widened in admiration.

Kenji nodded. "I used that time to learn as much as I could, to prove my worth and gain more freedom. The captain was a harsh man, but he valued skill. I became a navigator, using the stars and the winds to guide the ship. It was a difficult time, filled with backbreaking work and constant fear, but it gave me a purpose and kept me alive."

Kenji's expression grew darker as he continued. "After many months on the ship, several of the other men became sick and died. The cramped, dirty conditions took their toll. Disease spread quickly, and the air below deck was thick with the stench of vomit and urine. Every day, I watched as more and more of my fellow captives succumbed to illness. Their bodies thrown overboard."

"I was fortunate," Kenji replied. "Being allowed to work on deck gave me access to fresh air and some degree of cleanliness. I also drew strength from my father and mother's teachings and my determination to survive. I knew that giving in to despair would mean certain death." Kenji took a deep breath, steadying himself before continuing. "After a long time at sea, we encountered a fierce storm that drove the ship off course. The vessel eventually wrecked near a group of islands not far from the mainland." Kenji continued his story with Haruto's complete attention.

He was lying on the sandy beach, the coarse grains clinging to his skin, when he felt a sharp poke in his side. Groggy and disoriented, he struggled to open his eyes, the bright sunlight glaring off the water blinding him momentarily. As his vision cleared, he felt another, more insistent poke, this time sharper and more powerful.

Blinking rapidly, he finally managed to focus on the figure towering above him. It was an elderly man, his weathered face framed by a large, round straw hat that shaded his eyes. The man held a long bamboo fishing pole, which he was using to prod at his ribs. His expression was a mix of curiosity and concern, his eyes narrowing as he studied the unfamiliar dark figure washed ashore.

"*Hey,*" the man said in a language he didn't understand, his voice gruff yet carrying a hint of compassion. He poked him again, this time with less force. He spoke again in words he couldn't understand.

He groaned and shifted, the effort causing a jolt of pain to shoot through his body. Every muscle ached, and his throat was parched from the saltwater and sand. He tried to push himself up but his limbs felt heavy, almost foreign. The man crouched down, setting aside his fishing pole, and offered an open hand.

Grasping it, he felt a burst of relief. He allowed the man to help him sit up, the world tilting precariously as he did. The man muttered something under his breath, then pointed to himself and said, "*Saitō!*" He then pointed his finger and asked in his language, "*Name?*" Before he could respond, the fisherman exclaimed, "*Kenji!*" He made a gesture indicating someone big and tall with his arms, then smiled and contentedly repeated, "*Kenji!*"

He nodded weakly to the small man, not understanding the words but recognizing the intent. With the old fisherman's help, he rose unsteadily to his feet, swaying as he tried to regain his balance. The man wrapped a supportive arm around his waist and began to lead him toward a small hut. As they trudged across the beach, Kenji glanced back at the wreckage of the ship. Broken timbers and scattered debris were strewn across the shore, a grim testament to the violent storm that had brought him here. He doubted anyone else had survived.

Saitō gave Kenji a robe to wrap his body in as they walked. Although it was small, it was dry and would do for now. The robe was made of coarse, woven fabric, its edges frayed from years of use. Kenji's broad, dark shoulders strained against the tight fit, but the warmth it provided was a welcome relief from the chill of the ocean. The robe clung to his damp skin, absorbing the remaining moisture and gradually bringing a sense of comfort to his exhausted body.

Saitō, noticing Kenji's discomfort, patted him on the back gently and smiled. Kenji nodded gratefully, his teeth still chattering from the cold as he tried to pull the robe tighter around his broad frame. The fisherman motioned for Kenji to follow him. They made their way further along the beach, the sand crunching underfoot, towards a small, makeshift shelter constructed from driftwood and palm leafs. Inside, a modest fire crackled. The heat from the fire was a comforting relief for the shivering Kenji.

The old man rolled out a tattered, worn tatami mat onto the sand and motioned for Kenji to sleep. The mat, though frayed at the edges, still held a semblance of comfort. Kenji nodded, laid his exhausted head on the mat, and immediately fell asleep.

He awoke to the harsh sensation of a straw waraji striking his side. Groaning, he slowly opened his eyes. Two men in black lacquered armor loomed over him, their faces stern and unreadable. Kenji's heart raced as he tried to make sense of the scene. His gaze shifted to the side, where he saw Saitō, the fisherman who had helped him, standing near another man. This man was dressed in fine robes, his clothing exuding authority and wealth. In his hand, he held a small leather pouch, which he was in the process of handing over to Saitō.

The pouch made a clinking sound as Saitō accepted the bounty. His expression was a mix of regret and resolve, his eyes avoiding Kenji's as he quickly counted the gold pieces. One of the armored men grabbed Kenji by the arm and yanked him to his feet. "GRRR!" he growled. Kenji stumbled, still disoriented from sleep and the sudden rough treatment. The man's grip was ironclad, leaving no room for resistance.

The man in fine robes stepped forward, his eyes scrutinizing Kenji. He spoke in a language that Kenji did not understand. *"You will come with us,*" he said, his tone devoid of empathy. Kenji clenched his fists, his mind whirling with anger and fear. But he knew he was exhausted, battered, outnumbered and outmatched. For now, he had no choice but to comply. He cast one last, sorrowful glance at Saitō before allowing himself to be led away by the armored men.

Kenji brought his thoughts back to the present moment as he paused and looked directly at Haruto. There was a brief moment of silence before Kenji cleared his throat and continued his story. As Haruto listened to his mentor share his treacherous ordeal, he had to fight the emotions building inside.

The men brought Kenji to a horse, their movements brisk and aggressive. They bound his hands tightly behind his back with coarse rope, the fibers digging into his wrists, and hoisted him onto the horse's saddle. The horse snorted and shifted under the unfamiliar weight, but the men quickly steadied it and mounted their own horses. With a sharp command, the group set off across the countryside. The rhythmic clatter of hooves on the dirt path echoed in the morning air. As the hours passed, the towering walls of a grand castle came into view. The massive estate stood atop a steep hill, its imposing presence a testament to its power and influence.

The closer they got, the more details Kenji could make out: the intricate carvings on the stone walls, the flags bearing the family crest fluttering in the breeze. A kanji on the flag read: *Akurosai Family.* Kenji would later learn that the Akurosai were a noble family. In the hierarchy of feudal Japan, the emperor held the highest authority, while the shogun acted as the military dictator. Below the shogun were the daimyos, powerful feudal lords who controlled large estates and commanded their own armies of samurai. The samurai, in turn, served the daimyos.

Additionally, there were noble and aristocratic families who served at the Imperial Court. These families played a crucial role in maintaining courtly and religious duties. Noble families, like the Akurosai, were integral to the social and military fabric of Japan. They shaped the country's history through their actions and legacies, wielding significant influence.

The men rode their horses to the gate of the stone castle. The large estate was neatly manicured, with meticulously trimmed hedges and a pristine garden that spoke of wealth and power. The imposing castle stood at the heart of the estate, its stone walls towering over the surrounding landscape.

As they approached, Kenji could see two large iron gates that served as the main entrance to the estate. Each gate was adorned with intricate designs and family crests, showcasing the rich heritage and power of the Akurosai family. At the very center of each gate was a dragon etched into the surface, its menacing eyes shifting from black to red to green.

Guarding the gates were two large men in full black samurai armor. Each held a long spear with a sharp, silver-pointed tip. The guards stood at attention, their expressions stern and disciplined. As the men reached the gates, one of the guards stepped forward, inspecting the newcomers with a piercing gaze.

After a brief exchange of words, the gates creaked open, allowing the men to pass through. The sound of hooves echoed on the cobblestone path as they rode into the courtyard, which was equally well-kept, with carefully arranged flowerbeds and perfectly manicured trees.

As Kenji lay on the horse, his hands bound tightly he took in his surroundings with a sense of awe and apprehension. As they dismounted and led him further into the castle grounds, Kenji's thoughts raced, trying to understand the fate that awaited him within these walls.

The men rode their horses to an open area within the confines of the massive estate. The courtyard was expansive, with meticulously maintained cobblestones that formed intricate patterns. Ornamental bonsai trees and flowering plants lined the perimeter.

As the men dismounted their horses, they pulled Kenji roughly to the ground. The impact jarred him, but he quickly regained his footing, his hands still bound behind his back. The commotion attracted the attention of the estate's inhabitants, and a crowd began to gather.

Servants paused in their tasks, whispering among themselves as they watched the scene unfold. Their curious and anxious gazes shifted between Kenji and the armored men. Among them were members of the noble household wearing fine silk garments.

Children peeked out from behind their mothers, their eyes wide with fear and fascination. Some clutched their mothers' kimonos tightly, while others whispered to each other, their curiosity barely contained. A few guards, intrigued by the unusual sight, walked over to Kenji and began poking him, their fingers prodding his arms and shoulders. Their expressions were filled with curiosity, as many had never seen a man with dark skin before. The guards exchanged glances and spoke among themselves, their fascination mingling with a sense of unease at this unfamiliar-looking man.

The men took Kenji to a cold, damp room below the main level of the castle, where they kept prisoners. The air was thick with the smell of mold, and the orange and red light from a few torches cast shadows on the stone walls. The room was filled with bamboo cages suspended from the ceiling by metal chains. The guards called them "kakebako," or hanging boxes. Inside the small bamboo cages were the remnants of former prisoners. Several cages held piles of rotting flesh and bones, another contained a thin man, his face filled with fear and despair. His frail arms dangled through the openings of the bamboo slats.

The cages swayed gently with every movement in the room, the metal chains creaking ominously under the weight. One of the enclosures began to rock back and forth more violently. A guard grabbed a large metal pole and stood under the cage with caution.

The guard began poking the creature with the pole, provoking a loud hissing sound. The creature's eyes turned bright red as it recoiled and lashed out, its movements growing more erratic with each jab. The guard, finding perverse pleasure in the torment, continued to poke and prod relentlessly. Suddenly, the creature let out a loud gurgling sound and spewed slimy green and yellow bile onto the guard below. The guard recoiled in disgust, wiping the foul substance from his face and armor. The other guards laughed, mocking his misfortune.

They dragged Kenji to a bamboo cage resting on the ground with a chain suspending it from the ceiling rafters. He was exhausted and weak, wearing only the small robe that the fisherman Saitō had given him. They pushed Kenji into the cramped enclosure, the bamboo floor unforgivingly pressing against his aching muscles. With a loud thud, the guard closed the door and tied a rope around the opening to keep it secure.

The kakebako began to lift off the floor as two other guards rotated a large metal wheel that tightened the chain. Kenji's cage slowly ascended, swaying slightly as it rose. The confined space made every movement painful. The guards watched with satisfaction as the cage reached its designated height, leaving Kenji suspended in mid-air. The creaking of the chains echoed through the room, a constant reminder of his precarious situation.

Kenji tried to find a more comfortable position, but the small enclosure offered no relief. His muscles ached, and the cold air chilled him to the bone. The mental torment of being so exposed and helpless was almost as unbearable as the physical discomfort. As the hours passed, Kenji's mind wandered, grappling with the hopelessness of his predicament and the faint glimmer of hope that somehow, he might escape this living nightmare.

After a few days, Kenji's isolation was interrupted by the sound of footsteps echoing through the damp, cold space. The door creaked open, and a tall man accompanied by a teenage boy entered the room. Their presence brought a slight shift in the oppressive atmosphere, yet Kenji remained wary.

Below his cage, Kenji saw a tall man carrying a walking stick. The long stick had a dragon mounted on the top, its tail wrapped around the handle with red gems for eyes. The man moved with an air of authority, his dark eyes scanning the room before settling on Kenji in the kakebako. The man's face was stern, his features hardened by years of experience and command.

Beside him, the teenage boy watched with a mixture of curiosity and caution. He wore a finely crafted kimono, his long black hair neatly tied back. His posture was erect and composed, mirroring the disciplined stance of his elder. The tall man tapped his walking stick on the ground, the sound resonating in the confined space. "*This is the one,*" he said in a foreign tongue, his voice deep and commanding as he pointed to Kenji's enclosure dangling above his head.

Two guards approached the large round wheel and began rotating it, slowly lowering Kenji's enclosure to the ground. The guard approached the cage and began untying the complicated knot. The rope fell away, and with a creak, the bamboo door swung open. He motioned for Kenji to come out. Kenji moved cautiously, his muscles stiff from days of confinement. He extended one leg out of the cramped cage, feeling the cold, damp floor beneath his bare foot. He shifted his weight, his joints protesting as he slowly stood up. The sudden freedom of movement felt strange, almost surreal.

The guard stepped back, giving Kenji space but keeping a watchful eye on him. He made a grunting sound and began waving his hand in a gesture of impatience. Kenji took a tentative step forward, then another, stretching his limbs as much as the narrow space allowed. He glanced around the dimly lit room, taking in the details he had missed while confined. The guard gestured toward the door at the far end of the room. "*Follow me,*" he ordered in a language Kenji could not understand. Kenji met the guard's gaze and nodded in acknowledgment before falling into step behind him, his bare feet making soft, splashing sounds on the cold, damp floor.

They passed through several doors, each one creaking as it swung open. Guards stationed at various points watched them pass, their expressions curious but guarded. The castle's architecture felt oppressive in the low light. Finally, they emerged into a larger, more brightly lit chamber. The walls were adorned with vividly colored images. Each finely woven tapestry depicted not just the physical world, but realms beyond it—dimensions layered atop one another, overlapping in intricate patterns. Some showed warriors descending to earthly realm, others depicted bridges of light stretching between worlds. The guard led Kenji to the center of the room and then stepped aside, allowing him a moment to take in his new surroundings.

Kenji paused for a moment as he came back to the present. Haruto sat absolutely silent, his eyes wide and unblinking, as he took in every detail of Kenji's story. The glowing light from the fire danced across Haruto's face, reflecting the turmoil of emotions stirring within him. His heart ached for every moment of suffering and hardship his mentor had endured.

Kenji sipped some cold water and began again, "I could not speak or understand the language. But I was a strong young man and they would use me for their hunts."

Kenji would later learn that the father was called Lord Akurosai, a man of great honor and strength. His teenage son, Ryuji, carried a name meaning "second dragon." Ryuji had been a twin, born alongside another boy named Ryuichi, whose name meant "first dragon." The twins were a symbol of hope and legacy for Lord Akurosai's family, a chance for two possible heirs.

Which meant they would maintain control of the Akurosai estate if he were to pass. The birth, however, was tumultuous and fraught with unforeseen complications. Tragically, both Ryuichi and their mother did not survive, leaving Lord Akurosai to raise Ryuji alone. The loss of Ryuichi and his mother cast a long shadow over the household.

Throughout his childhood, Ryuji often felt the weight of his father's grief and resentment. There were many times when Lord Akurosai, in his moments of sorrow and anger, blamed Ryuji for the death of his twin and mother. These accusations and the lingering pain of loss created a strained and challenging relationship between father and son.

Despite the emotional turmoil, Ryuji was a diligent student of combat and strategy. He dedicated himself to his training with a desire to prove his worth to his father and honor the memory of his lost family members. His instructors often praised his determination and his ability to learn quickly. However, Ryuji frequently found himself falling just short of the achievements of those around him.

This constant struggle to measure up only intensified the pressure he felt. Ryuji's self-doubt was compounded by his father's high expectations and occasional outbursts of disappointment. When he was eleven years old, Ryuji faced one of his greatest challenges: competing in the family martial arts tournament for the first time. This annual event was a prestigious occasion, drawing skilled fighters from across the region, all eager to demonstrate their prowess and earn the respect of their peers and elders. For Ryuji, the tournament was more than just a competition; it was a chance to prove his worth to his father.

In the weeks leading up to the tournament, Ryuji trained tirelessly. He woke up before dawn to practice his throws and spent long hours refining his techniques under the watchful eyes of his instructors. Despite his dedication, he couldn't shake the feeling of deep inadequacy. His father's critical gaze seemed to follow him everywhere, a constant reminder of the high stakes he faced.

During the final round of the competition, the combatants faced each other, and the first to take their opponent to the ground and pin them was awarded a point. This required both strength and balance. In the opening rounds, Ryuji did well against kids his age, even dominating some matches. In the final round, Ryuji faced his toughest opponent yet, a boy two years his senior with a reputation for being unbeatable. The match was intense, with both fighters displaying impressive skill. Despite his best efforts, Ryuji found himself struggling to keep up. In a moment of desperation, Ryuji made a bold move, hoping to catch his opponent off guard. As they circled each other, Ryuji dove for the boy's legs. However, his opponent anticipated the attack, grabbed hold of Ryuji, turned his hips, and easily threw him to the ground, pinning him and winning the match. Ryuji's father walked over, his face full of disappointment, and said, "Your brother would not have lost if he had lived!"

Lord Akurosai's intention with Kenji was more than just to have a servant. He saw Kenji as an opportunity for Ryuji to have a companion who was tougher and could push Ryuji to his limits. After some time, they began to trust Kenji even more and gave him a small room to live in, free of chains. Kenji was also provided with a single black kimono and a pair of pants. They ensured he had access to clean water and plenty of food, as it was in their best interest for him to be strong and healthy. The room was modest but comfortable, with a tatami mat for sleeping and a small wooden table where Kenji could sit and eat. This newfound freedom and care indicated their growing reliance on his skills and strength.

Kenji was fast asleep on his tatami mat when he heard a light tapping sound. He suspiciously opened his eyes and saw Ryuji quietly walking towards his mat. Kenji sat up and nodded, acknowledging the boy's presence. Even though Kenji couldn't fully understand the language, he and Ryuji were able to communicate on a basic level.

Ryuji gestured for Kenji to follow him, his eyes wide with urgency. Kenji rose silently, careful not to make a sound, and followed Ryuji out of the room. Despite the language barrier, Kenji had developed a sense of understanding with Ryuji, recognizing the subtle cues and gestures the boy used to convey his thoughts.

Over time, the two became close, and Ryuji began to teach Kenji how to speak his language. Their bond grew stronger with each passing day, and they developed a mutual respect and understanding. They would secretly meet in a quiet corner of the garden, hidden behind tall bamboo and lush greenery. Here, they felt safe and could converse without fear of interruption.

Ryuji brought small scrolls and writing tools, patiently explaining the characters and their meanings. Kenji, eager to learn, practiced diligently, repeating phrases and writing characters in the dirt with a stick. Ryuji would correct his pronunciation and stroke order, encouraging him with a smile. Over time, Kenji's communication skills improved rapidly. He began to understand the nuances of the language, picking up on the subtleties of tone and context. This newfound ability to communicate opened up a world of possibilities, allowing Kenji to integrate more fully into the household and gain a deeper insight into the family's dynamics.

Ryuji often brought a small torch, as their secret lessons frequently extended into the night. The serene sounds of the garden, with its trickling stream, provided a peaceful backdrop to their studies. During these sessions, Kenji also shared stories of his homeland, describing the vast landscapes, the rich culture, and the challenges he had faced. Ryuji listened intently, fascinated by the world beyond his own.

In return, Ryuji confided in Kenji about his life, his responsibilities as the sole heir to the Akurosai family, and his dreams for the future. He shared how his brother who was older by one minute had passed when they were born. He spoke of the intense guilt he felt for the deaths of his brother and mother, a burden that weighed heavily on his heart.

As their bond grew stronger, Ryuji felt a sense of relief in being able to express his innermost thoughts and feelings to someone who understood duty and loss. The weight of his guilt seemed lighter with each conversation, as Kenji's wisdom and empathy provided a new perspective on his path forward. Their secret meetings were not just about learning and teaching; they became a sanctuary where both could escape the pressures of their respective lives and find solace in each other's company.

It was a rare afternoon of leisure at the estate, and Lord Akurosai had allowed Ryuji some time to enjoy the nearby river. The cool waters were filled with fallen leaves from the nearby trees. Ryuji, eager to escape the confines of the estate, quickly changed into a simple loincloth and dashed towards the river. Kenji was assigned to accompany him and be aware of any signs of danger. As they reached the riverbank, Ryuji turned to Kenji with a mischievous grin. "Kenji, watch this!" he called out, running and jumping into the river with a splash. He disappeared under the water before reappearing much further out.

Kenji watched with a mixture of amusement and concern. Though Ryuji was a strong swimmer, the river's current could be unpredictable. He stayed close to the bank, ready to intervene if necessary. Ryuji swam further out, practicing his strokes as he pushed himself further and further. However, as he ventured into the deeper part of the river, he underestimated the strength of the current. It began to pull him downstream, faster than he could swim against it. Panic set in as Ryuji realized he was in trouble. He tried to call out, but water filled his mouth, and he started to flail, struggling to keep his head above the surface.

Kenji's sharp eyes caught the moment Ryuji began to struggle. Without a second thought, he sprinted to the riverbank and dove into the water. The cold shock of the river barely registered as he swam with powerful strokes towards his friend. Ryuji's vision blurred as he fought against the current, his strength waning. Just as his body threatened to give in to exhaustion, he felt a strong hand grab his arm. Kenji's grip was firm and powerful as he pulled Ryuji with ease.

Kenji wrapped an arm around Ryuji's chest, securing him, and began to swim back towards the shore. With a final push, Kenji reached the shallower waters, where the current was less forceful. He guided Ryuji to his feet, supporting him as they stumbled onto the riverbank. Ryuji collapsed onto the grass, coughing and gasping for air.

Kenji knelt beside him, his breathing heavy but controlled.

"Ryuji, are you alright?" he asked, his voice filled with concern.

Ryuji nodded weakly, still catching his breath.

"You saved my life, Kenji!" he exclaimed, his voice trembling with emotion.

Kenji placed a reassuring hand on Ryuji's shoulder.

"You're safe now. Just rest for a moment."

As Ryuji's breathing steadied, he looked up at Kenji with newfound respect and gratitude.

"I... I didn't think... I thought I was done for," he managed to say between gasps.

Kenji shook his head, offering a gentle smile.

"Ryuji. We're friends. Friends look out for each other."

Lord Akurosai sat at the head of a long lacquered table in the main hall of his estate, his expression stern as he reviewed a set of parchment scrolls. The room was filled with the subtle light of lanterns, which created shadows on the silk wall hangings. Ryuji, wrapped in a warm robe after his near-drowning incident, stood before his father, gathering his courage to speak.

"Father," Ryuji began, his voice filled with emotion.

"I need to tell you about what happened today at the river."

Lord Akurosai looked up from his scrolls, his eyes narrowing slightly.

"Go on," he said, his tone laced with concern.

Ryuji took a deep breath. "I went swimming, as you know, but I underestimated the current.

It was much stronger than I anticipated, and it pulled me under. I couldn't fight it, and I was

sure I was going to drown."

Lord Akurosai looked up from his papers, his eyes widened slightly, his stern façade

cracking with a hint of worry. "And then what happened?"

"Kenji," Ryuji continued, "he saw me struggling and didn't hesitate for a second. He dove into the river, fought the current, and pulled me out. If it weren't for him, I wouldn't be standing here now." Lord Akurosai's gaze shifted to Kenji, who stood quietly in the background, his demeanor respectful but confident. The room fell silent as the weight of Ryuji's words settled. "You saved my son's life," Lord Akurosai said, his voice solemn. "For that, you have my deepest gratitude, Kenji."

Kenji bowed deeply. "It was my honor, Lord Akurosai."

Ryuji stepped closer to his father, his eyes deep with determination.

"Father, Kenji has proven his loyalty and bravery time and again. He possesses remarkable

skills and strength. I believe he has the potential to be much more than a servant. I propose

that we train him as a warrior."

Lord Akurosai leaned back in his chair, considering his son's words.

"You propose to train him as a warrior, Ryuji?"

"Yes, Father," Ryuji replied. "He has the heart of a warrior and has already shown that he is

willing to risk his life for our family. With proper training, he could become a valuable asset

to this entire estate."

Lord Akurosai studied Kenji for a long moment, weighing the proposal. "Very well," he finally said. "Kenji, you have saved my son's life and earned our respect. From this day forward, you will be trained as a warrior under Ryuji's guidance. Prove yourself worthy of this honor, and you will find a place of great value in this household." Kenji bowed again, a sense of gratitude and determination washing over him. "Thank you, Lord Akurosai. I will not disappoint you."

Kenji broke from his story to adjust his aching body and clear his throat. The memories, though years old, still weighed heavily on him. Haruto, who had been holding onto every word with rapt attention, leaned forward eagerly. "So this is how you became a warrior?" he asked, his voice filled with awe and a swell of pride building in his body as he spoke. Kenji nodded, "It was more than just training, we developed a brotherhood."

As the sun dipped below the horizon and the sky transformed into night the bustling activity of the Akurosai estate would slowly quiet down. The evenings brought a sense of calm and introspection, and it was during these tranquil moments that Kenji and Ryuji would engage in another form of training—one that connected them to the vast universe above. After their intense physical training sessions, Kenji and Ryuji would often find themselves sitting on the grassy hill behind the estate, overlooking the tranquil expanse of the countryside.

"Tonight, I will teach you how to read the stars," Kenji said one evening, pointing towards the sky. "These are lessons I learned from my father, a revered warrior and navigator in my homeland." Ryuji's eyes widened with interest.

"Your father taught you this?"

Kenji nodded, a hint of nostalgia in his voice.

"Yes. He believed that the night sky held many secrets and could guide us through the

darkest of times."

Kenji began by identifying the major constellations visible in the sky.

"Look there," he said, pointing to a cluster of stars.

"That is Sah, the great hunter. The three stars in his belt are easy to recognize and can

guide you."

Ryuji looked at Kenji, his expression unusually serious. "Have you ever experienced love?" he asked, his voice carrying an unexpected weight. Kenji, caught off guard by the question, tilted his head in confusion. "What is love?" he asked, genuinely puzzled.

Ryuji sighed, his gaze drifting away as if searching for the right words. "Love is... complex," he began, his tone softer than usual. "It's a feeling that binds you to someone else, stronger than any force you've ever known. It can lift you up, give you strength, and make you feel invincible. But it can also bring you to your knees, make you vulnerable, and tear you apart from the inside."

Kenji looked down at the ground, feeling both confused and embarrassed by the question. Ryuji noticed his discomfort and continued, "Kenji, love is what you might feel for a girl. Is there anyone on the estate you've noticed who has caught your eye?" Ryuji pointed to his face as he spoke. Kenji laughed a bit awkwardly. "There is one I've seen who looked at me with a special look." Ryuji raised an eyebrow, intrigued. "Special?"

Kenji smiled shyly, then used his index fingers to poke at the sides of his cheeks, trying to mimic dimples as he awkwardly grinned. Ryuji burst into laughter. "I don't think that's exactly how she looked!" Kenji shook his head with a grin, acknowledging the silliness of his gesture. Ryuji, still chuckling, said, "Are you saying she had ekubo when she smiled?" He pointed to the sides of his mouth to demonstrate dimples.

Kenji laughed out loud, "Yes, ekubo!"

Ryuji's amusement lingered as he asked,

"What's the girl's name?"

Kenji responded, "I do not know."

Ryuji shook his head in disagreement.

"My brother, you must learn her name. Do not miss this chance for love!"

He continued, "Do you know that when you find love, that love can create a child?"

Kenji looked down at the ground. "How do you know these things?"

"When I was a child, my Oba-san told me that babies are created through the union of love." Kenji hesitated, then asked, "What happens when a union is made without love, and a child is born?" Ryuji paused, taking a deep breath. "Maybe that child then lacks love," he replied. "I've wondered this about my parents—perhaps they didn't share love, and maybe a seed of darkness grew within my mother. Maybe that's why they passed."

Kenji quickly responded, "You cannot blame yourself."

Ryuji's voice grew pleading. "But what if I carry this seed of darkness within me?"

Kenji looked up from the ground at Ryuji. "We all have seeds of darkness; it's how we face

them that matters."

Ryuji and Kenji talked and trained together every day, forging a bond that grew stronger with each passing session. Ryuji, driven by a desire to prove himself to his father and repay Kenji's steadfast loyalty, shared everything he knew about combat, horses, weapons, and strategy. Their training sessions became a blend of intense physical challenges and thoughtful discussions about strategy and philosophy.

"Watch your footwork, Kenji," Ryuji would say, his voice echoing in the quiet dojo. "A strong stance is the foundation of any good fighter." Kenji absorbed each lesson with keen interest, replicating Ryuji's moves with precision. He practiced tirelessly, perfecting each strike and counter until they became second nature. Their sparring matches were fierce but respectful, each pushing the other to improve.

The Akurosai estate employed numerous skilled warriors and trainers, each a master in their own right. When Ryuji encountered something he couldn't teach, he sought the advice of these experts. "Today, we'll learn from Master Takeda—he's a sword master," Ryuji said, a mixture of reverence and excitement in his voice. Kenji noticed that Ryuji had two swords, one strapped to each side of his body.

"Brother," Kenji asked, "why do you always carry two long swords?"

Ryuji looked down at his weapons.

"I call them my twin swords. I carry one for myself and the other for my brother, who will

never have the chance to strike down an enemy." Kenji nodded silently.

Ryuji led them through the meticulously maintained garden of the Akurosai estate to a secluded training area. There, a powerful older man with a commanding presence stood silently, his posture exuding an air of discipline. Master Takeda was dressed in a black kimono and wide hakama pants, his razor-sharp katana resting confidently at his side.

The katana itself was a masterpiece. Its handle was wrapped in gold and black silk, intricately woven to provide a secure grip. At the base of the handle was a tiger's eye stone that shimmered with a golden-brown hue. Master Takeda explained that this stone represented the warrior's focus and courage. The tiger's eye was believed to bring protection and insight, qualities that Master Takeda valued deeply.

He acknowledged their presence with a slight nod and then, without a word, began to demonstrate the finer points of wielding the katana. His movements were fluid and precise, each swing of his weapon was executed with the grace and efficiency of a true master. The katana was like an extension of his arm, moving with a perfect balance and coordination.

Kenji watched intently, his eyes following every nuanced motion. Master Takeda explained the importance of grip, stance, and the seamless transition between offense and defense. He emphasized the katana's unique balance and reach, showing how to maximize its potential through careful control and focused intent.

Kenji began to mimic Master Takeda's movements, his initial attempts were clumsy and awkward. But under the watchful eye of Takeda, he quickly adjusted, refining his technique with each lesson. His silent approval and occasional corrections guided Kenji towards mastering the weapon's intricate dynamics. "Feel the weight of the blade," Master Takeda would say, his voice calm and authoritative. "Let it become an extension of your spirit. Only then can you wield it with true power."

Ryuji stood to the side, watching his mentor and friend. He was struck by the transformation he saw in Kenji—each movement becoming more confident and fluid. The connection between Kenji and the katana grew stronger as time passed, the weapon becoming a natural part of his combat repertoire.

Master Takeda led Kenji and Ryuji to a nearby river, where a long log stretched from one side to the other, serving as a bridge. The bark had been completely stripped away, revealing a smooth brown surface with a few short, broken limbs protruding from its sides. Above the bridge stood a large persimmon tree, its trunk rising along the shoreline and stretching over the log like a giant canopy. Large orange fruits hung from the branches in every direction, like ornaments. Deep below the makeshift bridge, a rushing river carved its way through the landscape, jagged rocks shooting out in all directions.

Kenji and Ryuji stood silently, staring at the river, cautiously wondering what Master Takeda had planned. Takeda walked to the edge of the wet log, drew his katana, and raised it into the air. He then carefully stepped onto the log and made his way to the center.

Despite the slippery surface, he maintained a firm stance as he sliced his sword through the air, cutting a small branch that held a fist-sized, orange persimmon. The vibrant orange fruit dropped toward him; in one smooth motion, he pivoted and caught it gracefully in his free hand. He then tossed it into the air and sliced it into halves that fell into the river below.

He then walked to the edge of the log and motioned for Ryuji to grab the katana sticking into the ground near the log bridge. Ryuji stepped forward and pulled the weapon from the earth. He then slid his index finger along the blade, wiping the mud and dirt away. He gazed at the blade for a moment, noticing his own distorted reflection staring back.

Master Takeda was now standing near Kenji as he pointed to Ryuji, signaling him to walk onto the log. He then turned and leaned into Kenji and spoke in a low whisper, "I want you to climb to the branch hanging over the log and await my instructions." Kenji slowly walked to the tree, removed his sandals, and pulled himself up to the second branch. He looked at Ryuji, who was now standing in the middle of the wet log.

Kenji climbed all the way up to a large branch hanging directly over Ryuji. Master Takeda's loud voice echoed over the rushing river: "Kenji, I want you to shake the branch. When the fruit falls, Ryuji, you must slice through them before they hit you or fall past you."

Ryuji held his sword at the ready, his face filled with determination despite his knees slightly shaking. Master Takeda nodded at Kenji to begin. Kenji sat on top of the long branch, his legs securely crossed underneath him. He looked down at Ryuji before reluctantly shaking the branch. A few fruits fell, and Ryuji easily sliced them in half with his katana.

Master Takeda shouted, "Harder, Kenji!" Kenji shook the branch even harder, causing a hailstorm of fruit to fall onto Ryuji, making him drop his sword into the river below. As he watched the sword disappear into the rocks, a large orange fruit struck him directly on the head, causing him to slip on the log. Kenji watched in horror as Ryuji tumbled onto the wooden beam. Instinctively, Ryuji grabbed a small, forearm-sized branch jutting out from the side of the log bridge. He was now hanging by one arm from the side of the bridge.

Ryuji looked up at Kenji, pleading for help. "Brother, don't let me fall!" Kenji turned his head toward Master Takeda, unsure of what to do. Takeda held up his sword, its tiger's-eye stone now glowing. He then launched the katana into the air. It arched high before falling toward Kenji. He reached out his free hand, and the sword landed in his grip. The stone now glowed a bright golden brown, gently humming like vibrating metal.

Kenji pointed the sword at the log below and leaped off the tree branch. He landed with the blade embedded deep into the wet log, his hand still gripping the weapon firmly. Straddling the log, he reached down to Ryuji, who was barely holding on. With one swift pull and a deep grunt, Kenji hauled Ryuji to safety.

The two men sat on the log in a deep embrace. Ryuji whispered in Kenji's ear, "You saved me once again." Kenji simply nodded as he stared at the tiger's-eye stone mounted on the sword's handle as it slowly dimmed and the humming faded. Master Takeda stood silently with his arms crossed, chin tucked, and a slight smile tempting his disciplined facade.

The following day, Master Takeda decided it was time to present Kenji with his own sword. In a private ceremony held in the estate's serene garden, Takeda wore an all-white kimono and white hakama pants. He approached Kenji with a look of respect. Ryuji stood nearby with his hands resting at his side, head pointed at the ground.

"Kenji," he began, his voice filled with pride, "you have shown remarkable dedication and skill. It is now time for you to bear a weapon that reflects your growth and potential." He carefully unwrapped a beautifully crafted katana, its handle adorned with intricate black and gold silk, and a lustrous tiger's eye stone embedded at the base, shimmering with a deep, rich golden-brown. It was Master Takeda's prized sword, the very one Kenji had used to save Ryuji's life.

"I think you will remember this weapon. The sword is named 'Tora Katana,' which means Tiger Sword. It has been passed down through generations of skilled warriors. It represents not only your proficiency, but also the focus and determined spirit that a true samurai must embody. This sword is for you to protect Ryuji and this estate. Wield it with honor and wisdom." As Master Takeda handed Kenji the sword, the tiger's-eye stone began to glow with a soft, amber hue. Kenji accepted the katana with deep reverence, bowing respectfully to his master.

Ryuji approached Kenji and smiled, "I must thank you my brother. But twice now I've been seized by the grasp of death and twice now it was your hands that saved me. If there were to be a third time, it would bring dishonor to us both." Ryuji bowed, turned and quietly walked away.

Haruto interrupted Kenji's story. "Was Ryuji angry that you saved his life?" Kenji leaned forward and looked Haruto directly in the eyes. Haruto pulled back slightly, somewhat regretting his intrusive question. Kenji cleared his throat. "I think he felt shame for not being able to save himself and having to rely on me."

Haruto quickly interjected, "But you saved his life twice—once when he nearly drowned in the river, and now this. He should be thankful." Kenji paused before continuing. "Sometimes, when faced with shame, we overlook the good intentions of others, only to drown in our own self-judgment."

Ryuji was awakened by a servant who instructed him to report to Lord Akurosai's chambers immediately and to bring Kenji with him. Groggy but alert, Ryuji quickly roused Kenji, and together they made their way through the dark corridors of the estate. When they arrived at Lord Akurosai's chambers, they found him standing with a stern expression, accompanied by a messenger dressed in full armor. The messenger, carrying a katana at his side, exuded an aura of urgency. Lord Akurosai turned to face Ryuji and Kenji as they entered.

"We have received word that there has been an attack on our family."

Ryuji stood up abruptly. "Father, what has happened?"

"My brother Hirokazu has been killed. Master Takeda is away traveling, so I need you and Kenji to take some men and investigate what has happened," Lord Akurosai said, his voice heavy with grief.

"We will leave at once, Father," Ryuji replied, his voice calm despite the questions that burned within. "We will find out who is responsible and bring them to justice." Lord Akurosai placed his hands on Ryuji's shoulders and looked him directly in the eyes. "Be careful, my son. The enemy we face is cunning and ruthless."

With that, Ryuji and Kenji bowed and left the chamber, their minds already focused on the task ahead. They gathered men, supplies, and saddled the horses. They would ride through the night to Hirokazu's castle. Kenji secured the Tora Katana, the Tiger Sword, to his back. The weapon's black and gold handle, adorned with a tiger's eye stone at its base, glowed subtly. Ryuji, on the other hand, carried a katana with a silver-tipped blade, specially given to him by his father for this mission.

Before they left, Lord Akurosai called Ryuji aside for a private conversation. The weight in his father's eyes was unmistakable as he handed Ryuji the katana. "My son, I want you to take this sword," he said, his voice filled with concern. "The tip is infused with silver. If you face an enemy that consumes the blood of men, you must use this weapon to pierce through its body!"

Ryuji's eyes widened slightly as he realized the implication of his father's words. "Vampires?" he asked, his voice barely a whisper. Lord Akurosai nodded solemnly. "We have received reports that such creatures might be involved. They are formidable and dangerous, but silver can harm them where other weapons fail. Keep this katana close, do not tell Kenji of this conversation, and trust no one."

Ryuji bowed to his father, a deep, respectful gesture that conveyed both his obedience and the heavy burden he now carried. He carefully placed the katana securely in a side pocket attached to the saddle of his horse. The pocket was lined with soft leather to protect the blade, and Ryuji ensured that the weapon was easily accessible for the journey ahead. He patted the horse's backside, feeling the tension in the air as the animal seemed to sense the severity of the mission.

Kenji approached Ryuji, his expression serious as he confronted him about the conversation with his father. Ryuji, unaware that Kenji had been nearby, was caught off guard "Brother, I do not mean to intrude on your business," Kenji began, his voice laced with concern. "But I overheard your conversation with Lord Akurosai. He mentioned giving you a silver-tipped katana. Is there something more you need to share with me?" Ryuji ran his hand along the leather case that held the sword, his expression calm. "No, this is just a personal katana that has been in our family. It holds no power that you couldn't harness yourself."

Kenji's eyes lingered on Ryuji's hand before he looked up, a trace of doubt forming in his eyes. "My weapon, though a treasured gift from Master Takeda, does not have a silver tip. Will I be able to face the enemies who took Hirokazu's life?" Without hesitation, Ryuji placed his hand on Kenji's arm. "Brother, you are a brave warrior, and there is no enemy who can stand against you and not feel your wrath!"

Kenji and Ryuji would ride with two armored guards, both seasoned warriors who had proven their loyalty time and again. The guards, clad in traditional samurai armor, were armed with katanas and bows, ready for whatever dangers might lie ahead. The path to Lord Hirokazu's castle twisted and turned through thick, overgrown forests and along steep, narrow mountain passes, ideal places where enemies might lurk within the shadows. Perched atop a hill, the large, formidable castle loomed ominous-ly, its towering silhouette outlined against the dark sky. The moon, only a sliver, hung like the blade of a sickle.

Upon arriving inside the castle, they dismounted their horses, their bodies stiff and weary from the long journey. They handed the reins over to the young attendants who eagerly led the horses away to the stables. There, the horses would be generously fed, and given a well-deserved rest. The travelers, relieved to be on solid ground, then turned their attention to the imposing archway that served as the gateway into the heart of the castle.

They were promptly met by two guards, their imposing figures armed with long, sharp, silver-tipped spears. As they approached the main house, the heavy wooden doors creaked open slowly, revealing a short man dressed in a long, flowing robe. His head was completely shaved, and his thin mustache extended down each side of his face, past the corners of his mouth. His demeanor was calm and his eyes sharp, observing them with a critical gaze as he stepped forward to greet them. This man was the house steward, the key holder to all things on the estate.

They would learn that the man's name was Isamu. For many years, he had served as a trusted ally and confidant to Lord Hirokazu and his family. Known for his wisdom and discretion, Isamu had been integral in managing the estate's affairs and safeguarding the family's secrets. As the travelers stood before him, they understood the importance of earning his trust and cooperation in uncovering the truth behind the tragic events that had brought them there.

Isamu eyed Kenji with a mixture of apprehension and distrust. Sensing this, Ryuji spoke up abruptly, "This is my servant Kenji, a strong and trusted member of our household." In response, Isamu offered Kenji a half bow, his gesture showing his lingering distrust for the unfamiliar looking man with dark skin. Kenji stared at Ryuji with a look of frustration and contempt. He would later take the opportunity to privately confront Ryuji about his remarks. They were waiting to speak with Lord Hirokazu's wife when Kenji decided to voice his concerns. "I don't understand why you called me your servant and not the warrior brother you claim I am?"

Ryuji looked up at Kenji, who was now standing imposingly in front of him. "We are brothers, Kenji. We do not look alike and others do not always understand our bond, and I want to protect our friendship." Ryuji stood and extended his hand in a gesture of solidarity. "Do not worry, we are brothers for life!" he affirmed, his voice deep and strong.

Just then, Isamu reappeared, ushering Hirokazu's wife, Keiko, into the room. She was a petite woman with long black hair pulled tightly back from her face. She was dressed in a traditional black kimono with a white under layer, customary during mourning. The deep black fabric created a stark contrast to her pale skin, while the black obi cinching her waist subtly accentuated her delicate frame.

As she entered, she shyly turned her head downward, a gesture of humility and respect, as she bowed to the men. Ryuji approached his aunt and tentatively smiled, offering a semblance of comfort amidst the tension. "Obasan," he began, his voice soft yet filled with earnest sympathy, "I am sorry for this terrible tragedy. What happened to Ojisan?"

Keiko looked down as she spoke, her voice trembling with the weight of her words. "Something terrible came here in the night and drained the blood from my lord." Her eyes welled up with tears, and she broke down, sobbing as she struggled to continue. The room fell into a heavy silence, punctuated only by her quiet cries. Kenji stood silently, his expression one of shock and disbelief, his mind racing to comprehend the horror of what Keiko had described. Ryuji gently interrupted, "Were there any witnesses?"

Keiko, still looking at the ground and wiping tears from her cheeks, continued with difficulty. "His concubine was in his chambers, but she escaped unharmed." Ryuji asked, "Where is she now? Can we speak to her?" Keiko turned to Isamu, who was standing behind her, and nodded. Isamu bowed and took two steps backward before disappearing. Moments later, he returned with a tall, thin woman at his side.

Ryuji and Kenji bowed in unison as the woman bowed in return. Ryuji looked at Keiko and Isamu and asked, "May we speak to her privately?" Keiko and Isamu exchanged a brief look before giving a nod of approval. With a gentle yet firm gesture, they encouraged the woman to step forward, allowing her to move closer to Ryuji and Kenji.

Ryuji looked the girl in the eyes and introduced himself, "I am Ryuji, nephew to Hirokazu. I am here to help." The girl glanced up, her long black hair partially obscuring her face. "I am Sakura," she replied softly. She wore a long black kimono tied with a deep crimson obi that hugged her body tightly. Ryuji smiled warmly. "Would you walk with us?" he asked, gesturing toward a long hallway. Sakura began to walk, with Kenji following a few steps behind.

As they headed down the long, open passageway, Ryuji began to question Sakura. "I know this is difficult, but can you tell me what happened to Hirokazu?" Sakura paused, her head bowed, eyes fixed on the ground. "I was alone with him, and we were together in union when this creature appeared," she said, her voice trembling. Ryuji pulled a cloth from his kimono and handed it to Sakura as she began to weep. "The creature pulled me away from his body and threw me to the floor. Then it attacked my lord. I couldn't stop it. The creature made it so I couldn't move." Ryuji's voice was gentle but probing. "How?" Sakura took a deep breath before continuing. "It cast a spell on me, binding my body so I couldn't move."

At that moment, Isamu reappeared with the two guards who had accompanied Ryuji and Kenji. Isamu bowed and spoke, "Another body has been found." Ryuji turned to Kenji. "Stay here and talk to Sakura. I will look into this further." Kenji nodded as Ryuji disappeared down the passageway with the guards and Isamu.

Kenji and Sakura were left alone in the tall, dark hallway. A single candle mounted on the wall flickered, casting shadows that danced along the cold stone floor. The air was thick with tension as the silence pressed in around them. Kenji cleared his throat, breaking the stillness and spoke softly. "Sakura, what happened to Hirokazu when you were on the floor?"

Sakura wiped the tears from her face with the cloth Ryuji had given her. "I watched as it drank the blood from him," she whispered, her voice trembling with the memory. "I couldn't move, couldn't scream, couldn't make a sound." Kenji placed a comforting hand on Sakura's shoulder, his voice gentle but insistent. "Did the creature approach you? How were you unharmed?"

Sakura's eyes filled with fear as she recalled the events. "I can only remember it crawling on top of me," she said, her voice just a whisper. "Then everything went dark. When I awoke, the guards were in the room." Her voice trembled as she continued, her eyes pleading with Kenji. "Please, do not tell anyone the creature was on top of me. If they think it made union with me, they'll kill me. I promise you, I am still pure." Her hands shook as she clutched Ryuji's cloth, the weight of her fear filling every word. "I don't know what happened after I fell into sleep, but I swear, I am telling the truth. I beg you, Kenji-sama, please protect me from their judgment."

Kenji looked into her tear-filled eyes, seeing the desperation that lay behind them. He could sense the depth of her fear, not just from the creature, but from the potential wrath of those who might misunderstand her situation.

Just then, the guards reappeared, urgency in their voices.

"Master Kenji, Ryuji needs you right away!"

Kenji turned back to Sakura, placing a reassuring hand on her shoulder.

"Is there anything else you can tell me about the intruder?"

Sakura paused before responding, "On his hand, I saw a ring."

Kenji nodded. "Is that all?"

Sakura looked Kenji in the eyes. "That is all." He bowed slightly, his voice calm but firm.

"You have my discretion. I promise you that."

With that, Kenji hurried after the guards. When he arrived in the garden, he was struck by the horrific scene before him. Ryuji stood over the remains of a man, his face locked in fear. The man's body lay torn open at the neck, his skin stark white from the blood that had been completely drained from him. His face was sunken in, like a flower petal pressed to a wet stone. Kenji crouched beside Ryuji, his eyes scanning the lifeless body. "Who is he?" he asked quietly, his voice filled with shock.

Ryuji didn't look up, his eyes fixed on the ghastly wound. "He was one of the household servants," Ryuji replied. "I don't think this is the same creature that took Hirokazu's life. His body was totally in tact, other than the blood taken from him. This man..." Ryuji pointed to the body, "has been torn apart by a demonic creature." Kenji stood up, his voice filled with both confusion and concern. "What could have done this?"

Ryuji met Kenji's gaze, his expression grave. With a serious tone, he began to speak, the weight of his words heavy in the air. "There are things I must share with you, Kenji, things I have kept hidden for too long. My family has been at war with a darkness for a very long time." Kenji's eyes widened, but he remained silent, listening intently as Ryuji continued. "The vampires," Ryuji said, his voice filled with anger, "they have long sought to control the Shadow Blade, a weapon of great power. The blade is no ordinary sword—it is forged from the darkest of magics and holds the ability to harness and command the spirits of the dead. Whoever wields it can control the balance between the living and the dead, between our world and theirs." Kenji's heart raced as he processed this revelation. "Why would they want it? What do they hope to achieve?" Ryuji's eyes darkened, and he took a deep breath before answering.

"The vampires believe that with the Shadow Blade in their possession, they can cut into and gain access to the other realms. They would use the blade to bend both the living and the dead to their will, enslaving all who oppose them. My family has been the guardians of the blade for some time, protecting it from falling into the wrong hands. But now it seems they have grown bolder and more desperate. The Shadow Blade has been safely hidden by my family."

Kenji nodded slowly, the pieces of the puzzle beginning to come together in his mind. "So this creature... it must be one of their agents, sent to retrieve the blade." Ryuji's jaw tightened as he nodded in agreement. "Yes, and it will stop at nothing to achieve its goal. The attack on Hirokazu was no coincidence. They believe he knew the whereabouts of the blade, and they will continue to hunt down anyone they think holds that knowledge."

Kenji looked back at the lifeless body on the ground, his mind racing with the implications of what he had just learned. The stakes were higher than he had imagined, and the danger more imminent. Ryuji met Kenji's eyes, his expression grim. "I believe Hirokazu was killed by a vampire, but this man was taken by a half-vampire, half-beast creature. The vampires sometimes crossbreed wild animals with vampiric blood, creating these monstrous hybrids. This man was attacked by the companion of whoever killed my Ojisan."

When they arrived back at the Akurosai estate, Kenji felt a growing urgency to share his own secret with Ryuji. As they walked away from the stables, the cool evening air settling around them like a shroud, Kenji placed a firm hand on Ryuji's shoulder and spoke with a tone of quiet intensity. "My brother, there is something I must share with you." Ryuji stopped in his tracks, turning to face Kenji. Curiosity filled his eyes as he looked into his friend's face. "What is it, Kenji?" he asked, his voice edged with anticipation.

Kenji took a deep breath, gathering his thoughts before continuing. "When I lived back in my homeland, my family practiced an ancient tradition," he began, his voice filled with reverence and a touch of hesitation. "These traditions are not mere rituals—they involve summoning spirits, guardians of protection, who can be called upon in times of dire need." Ryuji's eyes widened slightly, his interest sparked. "Spirits? Guardians?" he echoed.

Kenji nodded, his expression serious. "Yes. These are powerful entities, not to be taken lightly. They are protectors, bound to our family by ancient pacts, and they can be summoned to defend against great threats. I have been trained in these arts, and I possess the knowledge and skill to invoke them. If necessary, I can use these abilities to protect this estate and your family." Ryuji remained silent for a moment, his mind racing as he processed Kenji's words. "Will you teach me and let me be your student?"

Kenji could not shake the fact that Ryuji had saved his life. He had provided food, a home, a language and a new life for Kenji. Yet, he was conflicted. The rituals and practices he carried out were deeply personal, rooted in the traditions of his ancestors that had been passed down through generations. Sharing this part of his life meant revealing secrets that he had guarded closely, secrets that held great power and responsibility. Kenji turned to Ryuji, seeing the earnest curiosity in his eyes. Kenji felt a sense of trust with Ryuji. He had proven himself time and again, showing not only skill and bravery but true friendship. Kenji looked Ryuji directly in the eyes, "Let's begin tomorrow night!"

As the stars began to emerge, Kenji and Ryuji made their way to the secluded clearing in the forest. The path was lined with trees whose leaves danced softly in the night breeze. Kenji had set up the small, makeshift altar earlier in the day, preparing for the evening's lesson. The altar, decorated with an array of crystals and herbs, stood as the centerpiece of their rituals. A single candle was flickering as the temperature began to drop.

Kenji and Ryuji knelt before the altar, the soft glow of the candle dancing in the breeze, as if tempted to blow out. Kenji glanced at Ryuji, a wave of gratitude washing over him. He constantly reminded himself of the sacrifices Ryuji had made for him, as well as the trust and loyalty he had shown. "Ryuji," Kenji began, his voice soft and calm, "these rituals are more than just actions. They are a connection to my ancestors, a way to honor their wisdom and seek guidance from the spiritual world." Ryuji nodded, his eyes wide with anticipation and respect. "I understand, Kenji. I am ready to learn." Over time, their evening meet-ups became a cherished routine. Each night, Kenji would introduce a new ritual or share a different aspect of his spiritual practices. They performed healing rituals, calling upon the spirits to mend wounds and soothe the pain of the villagers. They invoked protection, ensuring the safety of their loved ones and the estate against dark forces.

Kenji's teachings were meticulous, his instructions clear and patient. He constantly reminded himself of the bond they shared, the trust Ryuji had earned through his friendship. After weeks of sharing his rituals with Ryuji, Kenji was surprised one morning with a special gift from his friend. Kenji was tending to the animals in the estate barn when Ryuji approached him.

"My friend Kenji, you have been kind enough to share so much with me, so I have brought you a special gift!" Ryuji said with enthusiasm. Kenji smiled as he stood up in the barn stall. "Ryuji, you have provided a life for me. There is nothing you owe me." Ryuji led Kenji to the stables, where a magnificent horse awaited them. The horse was a striking black mare with a distinctive white circle on her rear, resembling the full moon against the night sky. "This is Tsuki," Ryuji said with a smile. "Her name means moon because of the unique marking on her. She has been raised here with great care and has shown exceptional strength and intelligence. I trust she will serve you well."

Kenji reached out to gently stroke Tsuki's sleek coat, feeling a deep connection with the beautiful creature. He looked at Ryuji, gratitude shining in his eyes. "Thank you, Ryuji," Kenji said, his voice filled with emotion. "Tsuki is a beautiful and noble gift. I will honor her and the trust you have placed in me." Ryuji nodded, his expression one of mutual respect and friendship.

As time went on, Kenji had grown much bigger and stronger. The grueling physical training sessions with Ryuji, combined with the daily demands of helping on the estate, had transformed Kenji into a towering force to reckon with. His once slender frame was now muscular and imposing, his movements strong and powerful.

The sun was high in the sky, casting a warm glow over the meticulously maintained training grounds of the Akurosai estate. Kenji and Ryuji stood in the center of the open space, hands protecting their faces as they prepared to spar. Unbeknownst to them, Lord Akurosai had come to observe the session. He stood quietly on the side, his stern vision fixed on the two young warriors. His presence commanded respect, and the guards and servants in the vicinity bowed deeply as he passed.

Kenji saw the change in Ryuji's demeanor and prepared himself. As Ryuji's fists flew towards him, Kenji lowered his body, ducking under the oncoming barrage. In a swift and calculated move, he locked his arms around Ryuji's legs, lifting him off the ground with a powerful tackle. The force of the maneuver sent both of them crashing to the ground, dust swirling up around them. Before Ryuji could react, Kenji climbed on top of him, using his weight to pin him down. He secured Ryuji's extended arm, spinning on his body to apply an arm lock. The pressure was immediate and intense, and Ryuji cried out in pain, "Stop, stop, stop!" Kenji released the hold instantly, rolling off Ryuji and helping him to his feet. Ryuji rubbed his arm, wincing slightly but giving Kenji a nod of respect.

As Ryuji stood up, he noticed his father, was standing at the edge of the training ground. His unrelenting stare was fixed on Ryuji, a look of disapproval formed in his eyes. Without a word, Lord Akurosai turned and walked away, leaving Ryuji with a sinking feeling in his chest.

Seeing the disappointment in Ryuji's eyes, Kenji placed a reassuring arm around his shoulders. "We are both warriors, my brother," he said, his voice filled with genuine respect and camaraderie. "Strength and skill come with time. You have the heart of a warrior, and that is what matters most." Ryuji looked up, his expression softening as he met Kenji's gaze. "Thank you, Kenji. Sometimes it's hard to remember that." Kenji smiled, his eyes reflecting the bond they shared. "We push each other to be better. That is how we grow. Together, we will achieve greatness."

The Akurosai estate buzzed with excitement as the annual archery contest approached. Nobles and samurai from neighboring estates gathered to witness the event, a time-honored tradition that tested skill, precision, and honor. Lord Akurosai stood at the forefront, his focused stare sweeping over the contestants. By his side stood his son, Ryuji, along with Kenji, his protégé.

Ryuji felt the weight of his father's expectations bearing down on him. He was determined to win, not just for the glory, but to earn his father's approval and prove himself worthy. Kenji, on the other hand, was calm and focused, ready to demonstrate the skills he had honed under Ryuji's guidance. The targets were set up at varying distances, and each contestant was given three arrows. The rules were simple: the archer with the most accurate shots would be declared the winner. The tension in the air was overpowering as the contestants took their positions.

Ryuji's heart pounded in his chest. He had practiced diligently, but he knew Kenji was a formidable opponent. As he watched Kenji draw his bow with confidence, a seed of doubt sprouted in Ryuji's mind. He couldn't afford to lose, not today. Kenji was the first to shoot. He took a deep breath, drew his bowstring back smoothly, and confidently released the arrow. It sailed through the air with a quiet whoosh and struck the target dead center. The crowd cheered in approval.

Ryuji stepped up next. He took his time, trying to calm his nerves. He released his arrow, and it hit the target, but not as accurately as Kenji's shot. Frustration ate at him, and he felt his father's eyes on him. As the contest progressed, Kenji continued to perform flawlessly, hitting the center of the target with each arrow. Ryuji couldn't match Kenji's precision. He glanced at his father, who stood silently, his facial expressions completely still.

Desperation crept into Ryuji's mind. He needed an edge, something to turn the tide in his favor. As the final round approached, Ryuji's eyes landed on Kenji's arrow case. An idea began to form. During a brief break, Ryuji approached Kenji with a forced smile. "Kenji, let's make this interesting. Why don't we exchange arrows for the last round? It'll test our adaptability."

Kenji, always up for a challenge and trusting Ryuji, agreed without hesitation. "Alright, Ryuji. May the best archer win." Kenji took his case holding his arrows and handed it to Ryuji. Unbeknownst to Kenji, Ryuji had subtly tampered with one of the arrows in his own set. He had carefully loosened the feathers, making the arrow unstable. He handed his collection of arrows to Kenji, hiding a hint of guilt.

As the final round began, Kenji took his position, not suspecting a thing. He drew an arrow from Ryuji's case, unaware of its defect. He took aim and released the arrow, watching in confusion as it veered off course, missing the target entirely. The crowd gasped, and Ryuji seized the moment. With complete focus, he drew an arrow from Kenji's case and released it. The arrow flew straight, striking the target near the center. The audience erupted in applause.

Lord Akurosai stepped forward, a rare smile on his face. "Well done, Ryuji. You have proven your skill today." Ryuji's heart swelled with pride, but a shadow of guilt loomed over him. He had won his father's approval, but at what cost? He glanced at Kenji, who was retrieving his arrows, his expression unreadable. Kenji approached Ryuji. "Congratulations, Ryuji. You shot well." Ryuji nodded, unable to meet Kenji's eyes. "Thank you, Kenji. You were a worthy opponent."

Later that evening, as Kenji examined the arrows, he noticed the tampered feather. The realization hit him hard, and he felt a wave of disappointment. He understood now why his shot had gone awry. Ryuji had cheated. Kenji stood silently, weighing his options. Confronting Ryuji could ruin their friendship and strain the bond they had built. He decided to keep his discovery to himself, hoping that Ryuji would come to realize the severity of his actions on his own.

As they resumed their training, Kenji silently vowed to guide Ryuji not just in combat, but in honor and integrity. The path to redemption was still open, and Kenji hoped that, in time, Ryuji would choose to walk it. Ryuji secretly felt guilty for cheating at the archery contest and offered to take Kenji on a special training trip. He approached Kenji's modest living quarters and knocked on the door. Kenji slid it open. "What is it, brother?"

Ryuji was holding two hollowed bamboo reeds in one hand. Strapped across his chest was a leather satchel containing a set of thin, sharp blades. "Today, I want to teach you a new weapon," he said, lifting one of the hollow reeds to his mouth. He pointed it at Kenji's chest and blew out a large breath of air through the tube. Then, he ran at Kenji, poked him in the chest with his finger, and announced, "You're dead!"

They left the estate and headed toward the nearby woods. Kenji walked alongside Ryuji, towering over his shorter, broader counterpart. Kenji wore a gray kimono with the sleeves rolled up, revealing his dark, muscular arms. His thick dreadlocked black hair was tied back behind his head. When they reached the edge of the forest, Ryuji stopped and removed his sandals. He looked at Kenji, gesturing toward his feet. "Brother, we do not need coverings. Let's travel barefoot. We can move like the creatures of the forest." Kenji slid off his waraji and nodded back at Ryuji.

Kenji followed Ryuji to an open area surrounded by tall oak trees. Ryuji opened his leather satchel and pulled out several fukibari projectiles. With a swift motion, he stuck two of them into a nearby tree stump, their sharp tips embedded deep in the wood. He then carefully loaded another into his bamboo blowpipe, raising it to his mouth. "Watch this, Kenji!" Ryuji said. With a deep exhalation, he launched the projectile across the clearing, sending it through an oak leaf and into the tree. The leaf now dangled, pierced by the blade.

Kenji looked at Ryuji with a deep smile, "What is this weapon?" Ryuji motioned for Kenji to follow him to the tree to fetch the projectile. As they walked Ryuji spoke, "This is a weapon used by hunters and spies, it is called a fukiya. It can take down a large animal, or quietly execute a human target." Ryuji pulled the sharp projectile from the tree and handed it to Kenji, "It is your turn brother."

Kenji placed the fukibari into the bamboo blowpipe, raised it to his mouth, and quickly turned his body in the opposite direction and took a knee. With a powerful breath, he shot the projectile across the clearing, sending it through a ripe orange persimmon hanging from a branch before it landed in a large tree. Ryuji stared at Kenji, wide-eyed. "Are you sure you've never used this weapon before?" Kenji laughed. "Never."

They spent the day with Ryuji teaching Kenji how to move silently and blend seamlessly into his surroundings. Ryuji spoke at length about the interplay of light and shadow, explaining how to position oneself in the darker areas to remain hidden from view. He demonstrated how the forest could be an ally, using its natural sounds to mask his footsteps. Ryuji assigned Kenji a series of tasks to complete with the fukiya. Kenji was a natural, mastering the new weapon with ease.

Kenji was walking back from the nearby river after filling his water skin when he noticed Ryuji sitting in the tall grass, leaning against a tree with his eyes closed. As Kenji drew closer, something caught his eye, causing him to freeze in his tracks. Next to Ryuji's hand, he saw movement—a mamushi, the Japanese pit viper. A deadly snake known for its potent venom.

Kenji stood motionless, watching as the snake slithered dangerously close to Ryuji's hand. The thick snake was reddish-brown with a black zigzag pattern running down its back. Ryuji remained completely still and unaware of the snake as he slept. Kenji crouched down on one knee, slid a projectile into the bamboo fukiya, and lifted it to his mouth. He turned his head slightly, feeling the cool breeze brush past his face. As Ryuji moved his hand, the snake coiled up, lifting its head from the ground, now within striking distance of Ryuji's neck.

Kenji took aim, steadying his breath. With a deep exhale, the blade shot from the blowpipe. It flew across the clearing, its thin metal form cutting through the air toward the snake. The projectile pierced the snake's neck, pinning it straight into the tree behind Ryuji's head. Startled by the sudden movement, Ryuji jerked his head just in time, narrowly avoiding the blade as it embedded itself in the bark. His eyes shot open in shock as he turned to see the snake, limp and lifeless, hanging from the tree. Kenji rushed to Ryuji's side. "Are you okay? That snake was about to strike!" Ryuji sat up, staring at the snake in disbelief. "How did you know I would move? That fukibari could have killed me!" Kenji extended his hand to help Ryuji up. "The snake would have killed you first." Ryuji, now standing, met Kenji's eyes. "That's the third time you've saved my life. Let's not tell my father about this incident. Perhaps next time, I'll be the one saving you." Kenji nodded, but as they began walking back toward the estate, he couldn't stop thinking about the moment with the fukibari. Ryuji was right, he could have easily killed him. The weight of that realization settled heavily on his mind. He recalled his conversation with Ryuji about love, and how each of them held both seeds of light and darkness. He remembered his own advice to Ryuji: *that it was how they faced those seeds that mattered.*

Had his intuition truly guided him to take the shot because he somehow knew Ryuji would move in time? Was that a seed of light? Or was there something deeper, something more unsettling beneath the surface? The more Kenji dwelled on it, the more uncomfortable he became. It wasn't just about the shot; it was about something deeper, something Kenji wasn't sure he was ready to confront.

As time passed, the once inseparable bond between Kenji and Ryuji began to fray. The friendship that had been forged through countless hours of training felt different. The mutual respect they had built now felt strained by unspoken tensions and unresolved conflicts. The changes were subtle at first. Kenji noticed that Ryuji started slowly withdrawing. The shared conversations, which used to flow effortlessly, were now punctuated by awkward silences. Ryuji's laughter, once a familiar sound, became increasingly rare. Kenji continued to dedicate himself to his duties on the estate, maintaining the gardens, tending to his horse Tsuki, and ensuring that everything ran smoothly. He found solace in the routine, but he couldn't shake the feeling that something fundamental had shifted between him and Ryuji.

Ryuji's growing obsession with magic led him to withdraw more and more from the daily life of the estate. He stopped participating in the daily activities that had once been routine. Where he used to help with the training of the warriors, oversee the running of the household, and partake in family meals, now he was conspicuously absent. Often, Ryuji missed meals entirely, leaving his place at the dining table empty. The servants and staff, who had always respected and admired Ryuji, began to whisper among themselves, noting his increasing detachment.

In the corridors and courtyards, Ryuji was rarely seen. When he did appear, it was only briefly, moving swiftly and silently like a shadow. He avoided eye contact, his stare often fixed on the ground as he moved. The staff's attempts to engage him were met with short replies or complete silence. The dark circles under Ryuji's eyes told a story of sleepless nights spent practicing forbidden arts. His once vibrant and energetic demeanor had faded, replaced by a gaunt, haunted look. The servants noted the changes with fear. They whispered about the strange sounds they heard at night coming from his chambers.

Ryuji's appearance also began to change. His clothes, once impeccably maintained, now hung loosely on his frame. His hair, usually neatly tied, often appeared disheveled and oily. The transformation was alarming to those who had known him well. Amidst Ryuji's descent into darkness, another shadow loomed over the estate: the illness of Lord Akurosai. The once formidable and imposing leader had grown frail. He spent most of his days confined to his chambers. The Lords sudden illness added to the growing tension within the estate. His weakened state left a power vacuum, and many looked to Ryuji to step up and fill the void. However, Ryuji's increasing detachment and secretive behavior did little to inspire confidence among the staff.

Kenji's duties had taken him away from the estate for extended periods. As one of the most skilled hunters, he was often sent on missions to secure food and resources for the Akurosai clan. These hunts took him deep into the surrounding forests and mountains, far from the watchful eyes of the estate. The long absences were both a relief and a burden for Kenji. He enjoyed the solitude of the wild, the thrill of the hunt, and the feeling of peace that it brought him. However, each return to the estate filled him with a sense of dread, as he feared what changes he might find upon his arrival.

Kenji entered the main hall, his presence commanding attention. The servants and guards greeted him with a mix of relief and apprehension, their eyes nodding toward the direction of Ryuji's quarters. Kenji's heart sank as he made his way through the estate, each step heavy with anticipation. He found Ryuji in his private chambers, the room dimly lit by flickering candles. The air was thick with the scent of strange herbs, mingling with an undercurrent of something darker. As Kenji stepped inside, his eyes adjusted to the low light, and he saw his old friend sitting at a small table surrounded by scrolls. Ryuji looked up, and Kenji was taken aback by the sight before him. The once vibrant and energetic young man was now gaunt and hollow-eyed. Dark circles marred his complexion, and his eyes glowed with an unsettling intensity. His clothes hung loosely on his frame, and his hands trembled slightly as he set down the scroll he had been reading.

"Ryuji..." Kenji's voice trailed off, unable to hide his shock and concern.

Ryuji's lips curled into a faint, humorless smile.

"Kenji, you're back. I didn't expect you so soon."

Kenji took a step closer, his eyes fixed on his friend's emaciated form.

"What has happened to you? You look... different."

Ryuji's smile faded, replaced by a look of frustration.

"I've been busy, Kenji. There's much to do, much to learn."

Kenji's eyes scanned the room, taking in the various ritual items and the strange looking scrolls scattered across the desk. "This isn't learning, Ryuji. This is obsession. You're destroying yourself. This isn't what I taught you... This is a darkness!" Ryuji stood abruptly, his chair scraping against the floor. "You don't understand, Kenji. This power—it's necessary. For the estate, for our future." Kenji shook his head, his heart aching for his friend. "At what cost, Ryuji? Look at yourself. This isn't the way."

Kenji's frustration had reached its breaking point. The sight of Ryuji's gaunt, haunted appearance and his friend's stubborn refusal to abandon the dark arts filled Kenji with a sense of helplessness. He couldn't stand by and watch Ryuji destroy himself and those around him. As he stormed out of Ryuji's quarters, the echo of his footsteps resounded through the quiet corridor. "This is madness!" Kenji yelled, his voice reverberating against the stone walls.

As Kenji rounded a corner, he nearly collided with a woman. Her eyes were wide with fear, and her hands trembled as she reached out to steady herself. She grabbed Kenji by the arm with her thin strong hand, squeezing with all her might. Kenji paused, his anger momentarily tempered by concern for her obvious distress.

"Kenji-sama," she began, her voice barely above a whisper. "Lord Akurosai has fallen ill, and the staff... they are scared. A darkness has fallen over the land." The woman bowed her head, "I am Yasuko." She smiled revealing her dimples. Kenji smiled and nodded. "I know who you are; you are the head of the house for the estate." Yasuko, a petite young woman with a delicate smile and a strong will, stood before him. Small dimples appeared when she smiled, something Kenji had privately noticed before. She carried herself with a quiet confidence that commanded respect.

As the head housekeeper for the estate, Yasuko was known for her meticulous attention to detail and dedication to her duties. She managed the household staff with a firm but fair hand, ensuring that every task was completed to the highest standard. Her sharp eye missed nothing—whether it was a speck of dust out of place or a subtle shift in the household's daily rhythm.

Kenji had been so consumed with Ryuji's descent into darkness that he hadn't fully grasped the impact it was having on the estate. Yasuko's eyes filled with tears as she continued. "Some children from the village... they've vanished without a trace. Parents are desperate, and fear is spreading. They say the darkness is connected to the Akurosai estate. People are beginning to whisper about the return of the Kurokawa." Kenji looked Yasuko in the eye and said, "You have my word, I will make sure everyone is safe."

Yasuko pleaded, "Kenji-sama, I have been following Master Ryuji, and he is the cause of Lord Akurosai's illness. He has been doing something to his tea... my Lord is always in a deep sleep after they have tea. I watched him perform rituals in his chamber and go through his belongings." Kenji bent down to her level and asked, "What happened when you followed him?" Yasuko paused before sharing her story with Kenji. "I became suspicious because Master Ryuji suddenly asked to prepare Lord Akurosai's tea. So I waited and silently watched from the shadows."

Ryuji had been having tea with his father every week for as long as he could remember. The ritual was a cherished tradition, a time when the world seemed to pause, and the worries of their responsibilities could be set aside. It was a moment of peace and connection, a shared sanctuary in their otherwise busy lives. Recently, however, Ryuji began to use these sessions for more nefarious reasons.

Ryuji went to the kitchen area to prepare the tea for himself and Lord Akurosai. He gathered the finest tea leaves, carefully measuring them out with precision. He paused, glancing around to ensure he was alone. From a hidden compartment in his robe, he produced a small vial containing a slow-acting poison. With a deep breath, he added a few drops to his father's tea, watching as the clear liquid blended seamlessly with the brew.

Ryuji carried the tray of tea to Lord Akurosai's chambers where he awaited him. He handed his father the cup with a deceptive smile, masking his true intentions. As they sipped their tea, Ryuji engaged his father in conversation, discussing the affairs of the estate. Lord Akurosai, unaware of the treachery in his son's heart, praised Ryuji for his dedication and wisdom.

Yasuko stood silently in the shadows observing.

"Father, I have many more ideas that could help the estate, and I would like to share them

with you," Ryuji said.

Lord Akurosai coughed slightly.

"For now, I make the decisions for this family!"

Ryuji lowered his gaze to the ground.

"I understand, Father. Let's enjoy our tea and put these matters to rest for now."

As they drank, Lord Akurosai had became weakened by the poison in his tea. His hand trembled as he set the cup down, and moments later, his eyes fluttered closed as he succumbed to the effects. The once formidable lord slumped into his chair, unconscious.

Ryuji pulled a long black stick of incense from his bag. This was no ordinary incense but one specially crafted to reveal hidden truths and guide the seeker to what they most desired. Ryuji placed the stick over the burning candle that flickered on Lord Akurosai's side table. The flame caught the tip of the incense, releasing a thick, curling stream of dark smoke. The smoke did not rise straight up but instead twisted and swirled, as if guided by an unseen hand. It moved with a life of its own, coiling through the air like a serpent.

Ryuji's pulse raced as he watched the smoke. He knew the incense was working, guiding him to the secrets that had been hidden from him for so long. The smoke drifted away from the table, slowly moving across the room toward Lord Akurosai. It curled up near his body, swirling around his nose before slipping into his nostrils, only to drift out the other side moments later. Ryuji followed the smoke as it guided him to a corner of the room where a shoji screen partially concealed a small alcove. There, in the shadows stood the shrine dedicated to his fathers deceased wife and son. The smoke thickened as it gathered around the shrine, hovering over the altar as if pointing the way.

Ryuji knelt before the shrine, his eyes fixed on the items that held so much meaning. He stared at the brush, still tangled with strands of his mother's hair, and next to it, pressed in wax, lay a single small black hair that belonged to his brother. The smoke seemed to pulse, urging him to look closer. Ryuji waved his hand over a small shelf, but nothing happened. The smoke then circled around the lower shelf, drawing his attention. He reached under the ledge and felt a button hidden from plain view. Ryuji pressed the button, and with a soft click, a hidden panel in the base of the altar slid open, revealing a small compartment. Inside, wrapped in a piece of silk embroidered with the family crest, lay a key.

Yasuko followed Ryuji as he took the key to his father's study, where the families hidden chamber was kept. The study was dimly lit, its shelves lined with scrolls that seemed to hold the weight of generations. Ryuji walked purposefully to a small room hidden at the back of the study, a place he remembered well from his childhood.

He made his way to the very back, where a small, inconspicuous lever was cleverly concealed within the wood paneling of the wall. Pulling the lever, he revealed a hidden door with a keyhole at its center. He took a deep breath, steadying his trembling hands, before carefully inserting the key into the lock. The key slid in smoothly, almost as if it had been waiting for this very moment. With two deliberate turns, a click echoed through the quiet room as the door yielded, revealing the chamber within. The heavy door creaked open, revealing a small silver box. He carefully slid the box onto the ledge, the sound of metal scraping against wood echoing softly in the silent room.

As his hands settled on the box, Ryuji felt an unexpected warmth radiating from it, a subtle but steady heat that seemed to pulse with life. A low vibrating sound, filled the air, resonating through his fingertips and up his arms. After a moment's hesitation, Ryuji carefully lifted the lid. As it opened, the vibration grew stronger, and the warmth intensified. Inside, nestled within a bed of dark silk, sat a small black stone. The stone was unlike anything he had ever seen before—its surface smooth and polished, yet it seemed to absorb the light around it, creating an almost void-like effect.

Ryuji stared at the stone, a sense of awe and unease washing over him. Suddenly, the stone moved. Startled, Ryuji placed it in his hand. The stone began to pulse, as if directing him to move his body in certain directions. As he stared at the stone, he heard a sound at the doorway. He looked up and saw a small woman staring at him before quickly vanishing. He did not know it was Yasuko as she vanished before he could see her face.

Kenji's resolve to stay at the Akurosai estate and protect Ryuji grew stronger each day. After what Yasuko had shared with him, he knew he couldn't abandon his friend in such a vulnerable state. Kenji took it upon himself to keep a vigilant eye on Ryuji, determined to steer him away from the dark path he had embarked on.

Kenji sat silently in the darkened corridor, his back against the cold stone wall. The moonlight filtered through the small windows. His eyes were fixed on Ryuji's door, his mind racing with thoughts of what his friend might be up to. Suddenly, late into the night, Kenji heard the faint creak of Ryuji's door sliding open. He held his breath, straining to hear every sound. The door opened slowly, and Ryuji stepped out, his movements slow and cautious. Kenji's heart pounded in his chest as he watched his friend look both ways down the corridor before starting to walk.

Ryuji moved quietly, almost stealthily, down the dark corridor. Kenji waited a moment, ensuring he wouldn't be seen, then rose to his feet and followed. He stayed close to the walls, slipping from shadow to shadow, his training with Ryuji serving him well in his silent pursuit. The corridor was quiet, the only sound being the soft footsteps of Ryuji. Kenji's senses were heightened; he could feel the cool draft of the night air and smell the faint scent of burning incense wafting through the halls. As they moved further away from the main quarters, the estate seemed to grow colder and darker.

Kenji followed Ryuji as he walked down a stairwell that he had never seen before. The stone steps were narrow and steep, descending into the darkness. Kenji followed quietly, careful to avoid making any noise that might alert Ryuji to his presence. The air grew colder and damper as they descended. At the bottom of the stairs, Ryuji walked through a long, narrow passageway lined with iron-barred cells. The cells were empty, but the scent of death still lingered in the air. He continued through the dark hallway until he finally stopped in front of a heavy wooden door. Kenji remained hidden in the shadows.

Ryuji took a key from around his neck and inserted it into the lock. The door creaked open, revealing a small, darkened room with a wooden table. Ryuji lit the candle with his striker. Kenji's breath caught in his throat as he saw what lay on the altar: the Shadow Blade, its dark surface absorbing the candlelight. This was the weapon Ryuji had spoken of, the one hidden away to keep it from falling into the wrong hands. And here it was now under Ryuji's control.

Ryuji began to chant softly, his voice filled with reverence. The words seemed to hang in the air, heavy with dark power. Kenji watched closely as his friend's hands moved aside, revealing a small, ornate box from within the folds of his kimono. Inside was a small black stone. The stone was unlike any other, seeming to pulse with an eerie, almost sentient life. Ryuji then took the black stone and placed it into the hilt of the Shadow Blade. As it locked into the handle of the weapon the black stone began to glow.

Tiny, bright lights spiraled out of the stone. They fluttered about like trapped fireflies before being pulled towards the Shadow Blade. Kenji's eyes widened in shock and realization—these were not just lights, but souls. The souls began to swirl faster, their light growing brighter and more frantic as if reacting to the dark energy emanating from the blade. Just as Ryuji's voice trailed off, they swirled in the air, forming a mesmerizing dance of glowing orbs. The lights then coalesced into a single, radiant line of light that snaked through the air and into the blade of the sword. The surface of the blade began to glow white.

Kenji watched in shock as Ryuji touched the blade of the sword with both hands. His muscles tensed and bulged, his veins standing out against his skin like dark, twisted ropes. His once familiar features became distorted, twisted by the power of the Shadow Blade. His cheekbones sharpened, and his skin took on an unnatural sheen, almost as if it were glowing from within.

Then, just as suddenly as it began, the light disappeared. Ryuji stood there, transformed. He looked different, his appearance was younger, more virile. His hair seemed fuller and darker, his body stronger and more muscular. His eyes took on a crimson hue, and then suddenly transformed back to their original color.

Kenji slowly and quietly made his way out of the dark chamber, his footsteps barely making a sound on the cold stone floor. His mind raced with thoughts of what he had just witnessed and the implications it held. He decided that he needed to get to the council and report what he had seen. They needed to know about the Shadow Blade and the dark transformation taking hold of Ryuji.

Kenji's heart raced as he took in the sight of his transformed friend. The air in the chamber felt thick with dark energy, and the weight of what he had witnessed pressed down on him like a slab of stone. He knew he couldn't leave Ryuji to face this alone, but he also knew that he needed help—this power was beyond anything he could confront on his own.

Kenji knew he needed to get to the council right away, but before he left, he wanted to check on Lord Akurosai to ensure he was okay. Kenji went to Yasuko to ask her to accompany him to the Lords chamber. When they arrived at his room, they found two women quietly tending to him as he slept. The room was mostly dark, with only the soft glow of a nearby lantern lighting the large open space. Yasuko entered the room first, her presence commanding but gentle as she dismissed the attendants with a quiet nod. The women bowed respectfully and quietly left the room, leaving the three of them in silence.

Kenji stepped forward, his heart heavy with concern, and approached Lord Akurosai's tatami mat. He knelt down beside him, his eyes tracing the frail form of the once-powerful lord, a man who had commanded respect and fear throughout the land. Now, this illness had reduced him to a shadow of his former self. "My lord, can you hear me? It is Kenji," he whispered softly, his voice filled with urgency and a deep sense of loyalty.

Kenji leaned in closer, desperately hoping for a sign of recognition, any indication that Lord Akurosai was still aware, still fighting against the darkness that had taken hold of him. Gently, Kenji placed his hand over Lord Akurosai's heart and closed his eyes, concentrating on the faint, weakening pulse beneath his fingertips. Just as a sense of despair began to creep in, he heard a raspy voice, faint but unmistakable: "Kenji…"

Kenji's eyes flew open, and he saw Lord Akurosai looking at him. "My Lord," Kenji said, his voice trembling with relief, "your son Ryuji has control of the Shadow Blade." Lord Akurosai gave a slow, deliberate nod. "I know…" he whispered. His hand trembled as he raised it, pointing weakly to a plain silver ring on his finger. "Take my ring… to… Master Takeda," he instructed, each word a struggle against the weakness overtaking him.

Kenji reached for the ring, carefully sliding it off Lord Akurosai's thin finger. The cool metal warmed quickly in his hand before suddenly transforming into a glowing jade. Just as he secured the ring, Lord Akurosai was seized by a violent coughing fit, his frail body trembling with the effort. When the coughing subsided, his eyes fluttered closed, his strength depleted. His chest rose and fell steadily as he drifted back into a deep sleep.

Kenji remained kneeling by his side, clutching the jade ring tightly in his palm. He knew that time was running out, not just for Lord Akurosai, but for the entire estate. He turned to Yasuko and looked her in the eye. "I need to go to the Council of Elders immediately and report what has happened." He then grabbed her small, powerful hand and placed the ring in it and closed her hand. "Take this ring to Master Takeda right away; he will know what to do!" Yasuko looked Kenji in the eyes and faintly smiled, her small dimples appearing at the corners of her mouth. "You can trust me, Kenji-sama. We are in this together." Kenji squeezed her hand and smiled, "Thank you, Yasuko."

The Council of Elders is a revered assembly within the community, composed of the wisest and most respected individuals. Their primary role is to oversee the welfare of the community, make critical decisions, and provide guidance on matters that affect the collective well-being. As he emerged from the dungeon into the cool night air, Kenji took a deep breath, trying to steady his nerves. The estate was quiet, the usual nighttime sounds muffled as if the very atmosphere had been tainted by the darkness that had arrived.

Kenji entered his small room and quickly gathered his supplies. He grabbed his bow and case of arrows, a small bag of food, and a water flask. He also took a long cloak to guard against the chill of the night and shield himself from curious eyes. He strapped the Tora Katana to his side, feeling the comforting weight of his weapon. His mind was focused, and his determination unshakable.

Kenji led his horse Tsuki, out of the stable. He took a moment to brush her coat and whisper calming words, feeling the tension in the air. Tsuki snorted softly, sensing her master's urgency. Kenji saddled Tsuki and checked the reins, ensuring everything was secure for the long ride ahead. He placed his supplies in the saddlebag and mounted the horse. The night was still dark, but the first light of dawn would soon be on the horizon.

Kenji pushed Tsuki forward, the sound of hooves echoing softly in the stillness. He kept a vigilant eye on his surroundings to ensure he wasn't followed. As they passed through the estate gates, Kenji glanced back at the dark silhouette of the castle. The council needed to know the truth, and he was the only one who could deliver the message.

The journey to the council's castle was long and arduous, taking Kenji through thick forests and over rugged hills. Kenji rode tirelessly, only stopping briefly to rest Tsuki and give her water. His thoughts were consumed with the dark ritual and the transformation he had witnessed. The image of Ryuji, bathed in the eerie red glow, haunted his every thought. He could not escape the guilt of feeling like he had caused this change in his friend. He kept asking himself, *Why did I share these secrets unchecked with him?*

The landscape changed with the light of dawn, the shadows retreating as the sun began to rise. Birds started their morning songs, and the new day slowly came to life around him. After hours of relentless riding, Kenji finally saw the stone walls of the council's fortress in the distance. Relief washed over him, but he knew his journey was far from over. He pushed Tsuki onward, determined to reach the gates as quickly as possible.

As Kenji approached, the tall stone walls and fortified gates loomed before him. The guards at the gate recognized him immediately and quickly opened the heavy doors. Kenji rode through, the sound of Tsuki's hooves echoing off the stone walls. He dismounted, his legs stiff and sore from the long ride. Kenji removed his bow and arrows and placed them safely against the wall. He then handed Tsuki's reins to a stable hand and took a moment to steady himself before making his way toward the council chambers.

Kenji pushed open the large wooden doors of the council chambers, his heart pounding in his chest. As he walked inside, he was shocked to see that all the members of the council were present. The room was filled with a tense, expectant silence. Sitting at the head of the long table was Ryuji. His face looked young and full of life, a striking contrast to the weary, hollow-eyed man Kenji had seen just a day before. But beneath the surface, Kenji could sense something far more sinister. There was an unnatural glint in Ryuji's eyes, a darkness that created a knot in Kenji's gut.

On the table before Ryuji were several of Kenji's personal items: a bundle of herbs, a talisman, scrolls, and a small human skull. The sight of these items laid out so deliberately filled Kenji with a sense of dread. He had a sinking feeling that this was not a coincidence. Ryuji stood up, a smug smile playing at the corners of his mouth. He raised his hand and pointed directly at Kenji. "Our traitor has arrived!" he announced, his voice echoing through the chamber. The council members turned to look at Kenji, their expressions filled with shock and suspicion.

Kenji's heart raced as he struggled to comprehend what was happening. "Ryuji, what are you talking about?" he demanded, stepping forward. "I came here to warn the council about the Shadow Blade and the danger it poses to all of us." Ryuji laughed, a cold, hollow sound that tightened the knot in Kenji's gut. "Oh, I'm sure you did," he sneered. "Shadow Blade? Pure myth! But the truth is, you've been practicing dark arts right under our noses. These items," he gestured to the table, "are proof of your treachery."

Ryuji picked up the small skull and held it in the air,

"Is this not a child's skull?"

Ryuji was speaking even louder, "We cannot trust this foreigner whose skin is as dark as

the arts he practices. He is not one of us!"

"Kenji I will ask you once, are these your personal items?"

Kenji responded by saying, "Yes, but..."

Kenji's heart sank as two guards stepped forward and grabbed his arms and removed his katana. "You're making a mistake," he pleaded, but his words fell on deaf ears. The guards led him away, the heavy wooden doors closing behind them with a resounding thud. The guards took Kenji out of the council chambers and through the courtyard. As they approached the stables, Kenji saw Tsuki, his loyal horse, being prepared for the journey. But instead of being given the reins, he was hoisted onto the back of another horse, his wrists bound tightly behind his back. The guards mounted their own horses, and with a nod from their leader, they set off toward the Akurosai estate.

Kenji's mind raced with thoughts of betrayal and despair. Kenji could not believe his fate. Here he was again being taken back into the Akurosai estate as a prisoner. Kenji's imprisonment was under the direct oversight of Ryuji, who had been given the task of ensuring his former friend's captivity. Ryuji's face, once familiar and full of life, now bore a cold, calculating expression. The red gleam hidden in his eyes hinted at the dark power that had taken hold of him.

Ryuji approached Kenji whose hands were bound behind his back. "Kenji, you have brought this upon yourself. The council will decide your fate if you survive that long, but until then, you are my responsibility." Kenji met Ryuji's gaze, his own eyes filled with sorrow. "Ryuji, you know this isn't right. The darkness is consuming you. You need to fight it."

The dungeon was empty with Kenji's voice echoing off the walls. Three bamboo cages sat empty, their doors hanging ajar, while the chains that had suspended them lay coiled on the floor nearby. Another cage hung in the air, tipping to one side, its door also hanging open. Dark water dripped from within, pooling on the floor below.

The air was thick with the lingering scent of decay, mingling with the dampness that permeated the stone walls. Kenji's heart ached as he looked back at Ryuji, seeing the man he once knew slipping further into the abyss.

Ryuji pointed to the two guards who were holding Kenji by his arms, "Put him in the kakebako now!" A third guard standing at the crank-wheel began to turn it, the gears grinding loudly in the otherwise silent chamber. The cage, suspended by thick chains, began to lower slowly to the damp, cold floor. The metal creaked under the strain, and the sound echoed off the stone walls.

As the cage crashed to the floor, its door flung completely open. The guards approached the bamboo structure and lowered Kenji's head before shoving him inside. He closed the door and tied the rope into a tight knot. Kenji looked at Ryuji, the man who called him brother, as the two guards began to turn the crank-wheel, lifting the kakebako off the floor.

Kenji gripped the bamboo slats tightly as the cage began to ascend, the tension causing his knuckles to tense and strain. He braced himself as the enclosure swayed from side to side. As it lifted off the ground, black colored liquid dripped from the bottom. When the cage reached its intended height, the chain made a loud clicking sound before locking into place. Ryuji looked up at Kenji one last time before abruptly exiting the dungeon, his footsteps echoing through the hallway.

Kenji lay in the cold, damp cage for two days before he heard Yasuko's whispering voice. "Kenji-sama, it is me, Yasuko. I am here to help." Kenji blinked, his weary eyes searching for the source of the voice. He carefully shifted his position, peeking through the narrow bamboo slats of the cage.

His breath caught in his throat as he saw Yasuko's familiar figure, her face partially obscured by the shadows. "Yasuko..." he whispered back.

He could see her blurry figure below, holding a long stick. "Kenji, I've attached a small bag of rice and a water skin for you. I'll lift it up to you." Yasuko gripped the long pole with both hands and carefully lifted it over her head. The pole swayed from side to side before leaning against Kenji's enclosure.

"Kenji-sama, reach through and get the food. You need to eat quickly." With the last of his strength, Kenji reached through the bamboo slats and pulled the bag of food and water skin into the cage. He shoved the rice into his mouth, small pieces falling to the floor as he devoured it. Yasuko lowered the pole again, retrieving the now-empty bag and water skin. "Kenji-sama, I will come back soon. You must regain your energy so I can help you escape."

Kenji reached his arm through the slats to let Yasuko know he had heard her message. He then closed his eyes and fell asleep. In his slumber, Kenji would return to his childhood home, the memories of his family and the lessons his father had imparted upon him providing a comforting escape.

He envisioned himself at the bank of the river, fishing with his father. Kenji's father stood beside him, a tall and imposing figure with a kind smile. "Patience, son" his father would say, his voice calm and reassuring. "Fishing is not just about catching fish; it's about understanding the river and becoming one with it." Kenji would feel the cool water rushing over his feet, the sensation grounding him in the memory. He could see the fish swimming just below the surface, their scales glimmering in the sunlight. His father would cast his line with mastery, the fishing rod an extension of his arm.

"See how the river flows," his father would continue. "It is powerful and relentless, but it also knows when to be gentle. You must learn to be like the river my son. Strong, yet adaptable." Kenji would awaken from these dreams with a deeper sense of purpose. The lessons from his father, the strength of his family, and the serene beauty of his homeland gave him the resilience to endure his captivity.

After a few days Yasuko returned to check on Kenji. "Kenji-sama," she whispered urgently, "I have heard troubling things. Ryuji... he is not the same. Dark forces are at work again. The villagers are terrified, and more children have gone missing from their beds. The families are outside the estate, holding signs with drawn pictures of their missing children. They carry torches and spears. I fear for everyone's safety."

Kenji could barely summon a response, his voice a hoarse whisper. "Where is Ryuji?" Yasuko glanced around nervously, ensuring no one was nearby. "He has disappeared. I will return later tonight and help you escape. Eat the food so you have the energy." With that, Yasuko raised the pole to Kenji, offering a small bag of rice and a water skin.

Kenji's heart raced as he processed Yasuko's words. He ate the rice and drank the water, feeling his strength slowly return. With renewed energy, he managed to whisper, "Thank you, Yasuko," his eyes filled with gratitude. As Yasuko slipped away into the shadows, Kenji could hear the sounds of the restless villagers outside the castle. Kenji's mind raced with thoughts of the past few weeks, the darkness that had enveloped Ryuji, and the strange power of the Shadow Blade. He knew he had to find a way to stop the madness, to save the children and protect the estate from the encroaching evil.

But amidst the turmoil, Kenji's thoughts kept returning to Yasuko. Her kindness had been a beacon of light in the darkest of times, a reminder that not all was lost. He thought of her smile, a smile that touched him in a way no other woman's had before. It wasn't just the warmth of her actions, but something deeper—a connection he hadn't felt before. He wondered what would become of them, of her, once this was all over. Would there be a future where they could share a peaceful life, free from the shadows that now threatened to engulf them all? Or was this fleeting moment of connection all they would ever have? For now he knew that they needed to survive this ordeal and bring light to the darkness.

Hours seemed to stretch into eternity as Kenji waited in the dark dungeon. Finally, the faint sound of footsteps reached his ears. Yasuko had returned with Master Takeda. Yasuko stood beneath the kakebako. "Kenji-sama, we must hurry," she whispered urgently. Master Takeda rushed to the crank-wheel, unlatching the locking gear before turning it with all his strength. The enclosure rocked from side to side as it descended to the ground, the chains rattling with each movement.

As soon as the cage touched the floor, Yasuko ran to the bamboo door and quickly unraveled the knot, pulling it open. Kenji, weak from his imprisonment, stumbled forward, and Yasuko caught him, wrapping her arms around him in a firm embrace. "Kenji-sama, we must leave the estate immediately," she whispered, her voice filled with urgency. "It's not just the villagers."

Kenji interrupted her. "Is it Ryuji?" Yasuko shook her head. "No, Ryuji has escaped. But the villagers... they've attracted demons to the estate." Kenji's breath caught in his throat as the weight of her words sank in. The situation was far worse than he had imagined. The darkness that had taken hold of Ryuji had now drawn even more sinister forces to their doorstep. Master Takeda was standing next to Yasuko holding a long case in his hands as he bowed, "Kenji," he began, "Ryuji has escaped with the Shadow Blade. Lord Akurosai entrusted me with its counterbalance, the Jade Sword."

"I have been secretly watching over this weapon for many years, knowing that one day it might be needed. The Jade Sword is the only force capable of stopping the Shadow Blade, but it must never fall into Ryuji's hands. If he were to gain control of both, he would wield absolute power over light and darkness, plunging us all into an unimaginable abyss."

Master Takeda then revealed the jade ring, which had been given to them by Lord Akurosai, its color shifting from silver to green. "This ring represents the transfer of guardianship over the Jade Sword," he explained, his voice deep with urgency. "By placing this ring upon your finger, you accept the responsibility that Lord Akurosai has bestowed upon you. You are to guard the Jade Sword until the One comes forward who is worthy of its power."

Still weak from his ordeal, Kenji straightened his body and held out his hand to accept the ring. "How will I know who the One is?" he asked. Master Takeda pulled the weapon's handle from its case and pointed to the faded jade stone embedded in it. "This stone will glow brightly when the One holds it, granting the bearer absolute power and control of the Jade Sword." He replied.

Kenji took the jade ring and looked at it intently, understanding the weight it carried. He then slid the ring onto his finger. As the ring reached his first knuckle, it suddenly became stuck. Kenji frowned, applying more pressure in an attempt to push it further, but the ring refused to budge. Just as he was about to pull the ring back, it seemed to respond on its own. The metal expanded slightly, as if guided by an unseen force, and smoothly slid past his knuckle, settling perfectly into place. Kenji felt a strange warmth emanate from the ring, spreading through his hand and up his arm. It was as if the ring had recognized him as the guardian of the Jade Sword.

Master Takeda observed the process with a knowing nod. "The ring has chosen you, Kenji." He said quietly. "It is now your duty to protect the Jade Sword and await the One who is destined to wield its power." Kenji flexed his fingers, feeling the ring's presence as a part of him. He then placed the Jade Sword, now tightly secured in its leather case, over his shoulder and onto his back. The strap, adorned with ornately carved symbols, pressed firmly against his chest. Yasuko grabbed Kenji by the arm, "We must leave now. I know a secret way out. I have your horse waiting for you."

As they made their way through the darkened hallways, a distant roar reached their ears. Yasuko's face went pale as she realized what it was. "The villagers," she whispered, "they've set the castle on fire." Kenji's heart pounded as they quickened their pace. Master Takeda looked at them one last time. "Kenji, I must go and ensure that Lord Akurosai has found refuge. You must leave the estate, take the sword into hiding, and wait for the One." With these final words, Master Takeda bowed and quickly disappeared into the darkness. The flickering light from the flames cast a glow through the windows, illuminating their path with an ominous orange hue. The heat intensified as Kenji and Yasuko neared the upper levels, the smell of smoke thick in the air.

Yasuko led Kenji through the winding hallways, avoiding the guards who were frantically trying to control the spreading fire. They reached a small, hidden passageway that opened out into the courtyard. The sight that greeted them was one of chaos. The villagers had breached the gates, their torches and spears raised high as they stormed the burning estate.

With a loud screech a monstrous figure leapt from the top of the stone wall, its eyes glowing with evil intent. The creature had horns protruding from its head. Its skin was a greenish-yellow. It moved with unnatural speed and agility, its powerful limbs propelling it through the air as it descended upon an unsuspecting villager.

Kenji watched in terror as the creature's talons sank into the man's flesh, pinning him to the ground. The villager's scream was cut short as the creature's jaws clamped down on his throat, blood splattering across the cobblestones. The creature turned its head and locked its red eyes on Kenji. But then the ring on his finger pulsed, a firm reminder to keep moving.

"Kenji-sama, this way!" Yasuko shouted over the roar of the flames and the clamor of the villagers. They sprinted across the courtyard, staying low to avoid being seen. As they approached the outer wall, Yasuko pointed to a small, hidden gate. "Through here!" she urged. Kenji pushed the gate open, and they slipped through just as a section of the castle collapsed behind them with a deafening crash. They ran into the forest to escape the heat from the flames. Finally, Yasuko and Kenji stopped to catch their breath. Kenji turned to her, his face filled with gratitude. "Thank you, Yasuko."

She nodded, tears filling her eyes. She pointed to a large oak tree a short distance away. "I've hidden your horse, Tsuki, tied to that tree. She's ready for you. I also secured your katana to her saddle." Kenji glanced toward the tree and saw Tsuki, his loyal friend, tied securely and waiting for him. Her coat glistened in the moonlight, and she nickered softly in recognition. His weapon, the Tora Katana, was safely secured with its handle poking out of a long leather case attached to his horse. Kenji felt a burst of relief.

Yasuko approached, her eyes filling with tears of sorrow. "Kenji-sama," she said softly, her voice trembling slightly. Before she could continue, Kenji grabbed her hand and held it tightly. "Come with me," he urged, "I have strong feelings for you." Yasuko looked down at the ground. "I share those same feelings, but I must tend to my father who lives in the village and help get him to safety. Come back in two days, and I'll meet you at this oak tree." She pointed to the tree where Tsuki was tied. Kenji pleaded, "Let me go with you!" Before he could continue Yasuko held her finger to his mouth to silence him, "The guards will be looking for you, you must stay here and wait for me."

Kenji bent down on one knee, meeting her gaze. "I will come for you, Yasuko. But what if I cannot find you or something happens to one of us?" Yasuko looked directly into Kenji's eyes, then leaned in and whispered in his ear, "Nothing will happen, but if I am not here, find me in your dreams." She gently kissed his cheek and pulled back. "Kenji, you must go now and stay in hiding until we meet!" Yasuko pulled away from Kenji and began walking into the dark woods. Before she disappeared, Kenji shouted one last time, "Two days!" Then, in a rare moment of impulsiveness, he called out, "Yasuko, my heart belongs to you!"

She stopped and turned back, holding up two fingers before placing them gently over her heart. Without another word, she vanished into the shadows. Kenji's chest tightened as he wondered: were the two fingers a reminder of their meeting in two days, or was she telling him she felt the same?

Kenji rubbed Tsuki's neck. "We will wait for Yasuko." He then strapped the Jade Sword to the side of the saddle and climbed onto Tsuki to find a safe place to camp. Kenji waited in the nearby woods for two days, his thoughts consumed by the promise he had made to Yasuko. The days passed slowly, each hour filled with hope and anxiety. He spent his time in quiet reflection, the silence of the forest a relief to the chaos that had engulfed the Akurosai estate.

On the second day, at the first light of dawn, Kenji rode back to the oak tree. He scanned the area hoping to catch a glimpse of her figure emerging from the shadows. The memory of their last encounter played over and over in his mind, her final words echoing in his heart. He could still feel the warmth of her kiss and the gentle touch of her hand. But as Kenji drew closer, the only sound that greeted him was the soft rustle of the wind through the leaves.

Kenji's heart sank as he realized she was not there. The thought that something might have happened to her gripped him with fear, and his mind raced with possibilities. He wondered, had she been delayed by the dangers surrounding the village, or worse, had she fallen victim to the chaos that had consumed the estate? He felt intense guilt as he replayed their final meeting, knowing he should have followed her. *Why did he let her go*, he asked himself over and over. He stood beneath the oak tree, the very spot where they had promised to reunite, but the solitude was overwhelming. The tree, which had once symbolized hope and reunion, now seemed to feed his growing despair. Kenji sat leaning against the tree until the evening sun began to fade.

As the darkness fell upon the land Kenji decided to ride through the village to search for Yasuko. Kenji was shocked as he rode toward the once-bustling town. Every building was burnt to the ground, reduced to nothing but charred ruins. The overpowering smell of smoke still lingered in the air, clinging to everything like a shroud. The sight was almost too much to bear—what had once been a thriving community was now gone.

Kenji's heart ached as he took in the scene, his mind struggling to comprehend the enormity of what had happened. He decided there was nothing left to see so he rode to the Akurosai estate. The gates, adorned with the family crest, were twisted and broken, barely standing. Inside, the courtyard was a wasteland of debris and ash, with the outlines of what were once buildings now reduced to skeletal frames.

Kenji scanned his way through the ruins, his heart heavy with the memories of what had transpired here. He moved silently, his senses on high alert, scanning for any signs of movement or life among the rubble. The stillness was broken only by the occasional sound of shifting debris. But there was no sign of life. Realizing there was nothing left to see or do at the estate, Kenji decided it was time to move on. He rode back to the oak tree and waited. Two more days passed before Kenji mounted Tsuki to leave.

With a final glance at the smoldering village, he nudged Tsuki forward, leaving his past behind and heading toward an uncertain future... alone.

Kenji sat up and paused. Haruto ran both his hands through his hair and said, "Kenji, I am so sorry you had to experience such betrayal and loss." Kenji nodded. "I want to thank you for everything you have given me. I see now the lessons shared did not come easy. Thank you, Kenji!"

Kenji quickly diverted the conversation and said,

"Shall we continue?"

Haruto tentatively smiled and said,

"May I ask a personal question?"

Kenji nodded yes.

"What is your real name?" Kenji smiled. "I was called Langa."

Haruto smiled. "Thank you!"

He took a deep breath, steadying himself before delving back into his story. The firelight sparked and made a popping sound. Haruto leaned in closer, eager to hear more, his expression filled with anticipation. "After witnessing the devastation of the Akurosai estate and the sudden disappearance of Ryuji and the Shadow Blade, I decided I needed to disappear for a while. I was a dark skinned man living among ivory skinned people."

Chapter Six

THE DARKNESS CALLS

Kenji rode for days in search of a quiet, protected piece of land where he could find silence. Tsuki, his trusted friend, trotted steadily beneath him, her rhythmic gait providing comforting relief from his inner turmoil. The journey took him through dark forests, over rolling green hills, and across flowing streams. Each night, Kenji would find a secluded spot to rest, the distant calls of nighttime animals his only company.

Kenji exhausted but unable to to sleep stared at the night sky. His eyes traced the patterns of the constellations, each star a dot of light in the vast blackness. Kenji's mind wandered back through the tangled web of memories that had led him to this very moment. He remembered the terror and betrayal he felt when he first discovered Ryuji's dark secret, the pain of being accused and imprisoned, and the desperate escape from the burning estate with Yasuko's help. He missed her kind smile and soothing voice. He wondered if he would ever see her again.

His thoughts drifted further back to his childhood, to the days spent learning the ways of his people and the nights listening to his father's tales by the fire. His mother calling his name as he played with his friends, "Lan-GA!" She would yell from the family hut. He could almost hear the rhythmic beat of drums and the laughter of his siblings as they played under the watchful eyes of the elders. He thought of his journey across the ocean, the harsh life on the ship, and being found on a beach after the shipwreck.

The constellations seemed to blur as his mind moved through time, recalling the days of his training with Ryuji. He remembered the intense sparring sessions, the sweat and exhaustion, and the satisfaction of mastering new skills. He could still hear Ryuji's laughter and see his father's stern look as they trained in the courtyard. The memories of their friendship, once so strong and pure, now stained with sorrow and betrayal.

Kenji's heart ached as he thought of the children who had gone missing, their innocent faces haunting his dreams. He felt a deep sense of responsibility to stop the darkness that had taken hold of Ryuji and to protect the village and its people. This burden weighed heavily on him, more so with every passing day.

Kenji had always been a protector, a guardian of the people. The village had relied on his strength and wisdom, and he had never once let them down. But now, with Ryuji's betrayal and Yasuko gone, he felt the sting of his own failure. There was an intense guilt for not following his gut and sharing his secrets with Ryuji. He had trusted in his friend, shared his knowledge, his hopes, and his fears. That trust was broken, shattered like glass, and the fragments cut deep into Kenji's soul.

The constellations above seemed to form a map, guiding him on his path, reminding him of his purpose and the strength he had gained from his journey. But for now he must rest and wait. Kenji continued his travels across the vast landscape, the scenery changing from moment to moment. The days were long, but the beauty of the natural world around him provided a sense of peace he had not felt in a long time. As he rode through a particularly expansive field of tall brush, something unusual caught his eye.

Amidst the gently swaying grass, he noticed a strange flapping on the ground. It seemed out of place, a frantic movement that disturbed the otherwise calm landscape. Kenji's curiosity was stirred, so he guided Tsuki closer to the source of the commotion. As they approached, he saw that it was an animal, struggling and clearly in distress. Dismounting swiftly, Kenji moved through the tall brush with mindful steps, his eyes fixed on the flapping creature. His heart quickened as he drew nearer and recognized that the injured animal was a beautiful, large hawk. Its wings were spread awkwardly on the ground, one of them clearly damaged. The hawk's sharp, intelligent eyes were filled with pain and fear as it tried to rise, only to collapse back into the grass.

Kenji knelt beside the hawk, speaking softly to calm it. "It's alright, I'm here to help you," he whispered, reaching out slowly to avoid startling the bird further. The hawk's feathers were a rich, dark brown, with striking patterns that shimmered even in its weakened state. He could see that it was a magnificent creature, proud and powerful despite its current plight. Kenji carefully examined the hawk's injuries. One wing appeared to be hurt, likely from an attack by another predator. He knew he needed to act quickly to save the bird. Gently, he lifted the hawk into his arms, feeling its rapid heartbeat against his chest. Tsuki stood nearby, calm and patient, as if sensing the seriousness of the situation.

Kenji walked the injured hawk to his leather pouch where he kept his herbs and salves. Kenji selected a few key items from the pouch: some dried comfrey leaves and a small vial of oil to reduce inflammation and prevent infection, and a piece of soft cloth to serve as a bandage. He ground the comfrey leaves into a fine powder, mixing it with a bit of water to form a paste.

He noticed the hawk was a female. "There you go girl. Do you have a name?" Kenji murmured softly. "I'm going to call you Hikari, it means light. You are my first sign of light after such darkness." He smiled at the bird. "I'm Langa, but they now call me Kenji. This will help you to heal. You just need to rest and let the herbs do their work."

The hawk watched him with a hint of caution and trust, her sharp eyes never leaving his face. Kenji's calm demeanor and gentle words seemed to reassure her, and she allowed him to work without resistance. Once the comfrey paste was in place, he carefully wrapped the wing with the soft cloth, securing it but leaving enough room for the hawk to move.

He stroked the hawk's head gently, feeling the smooth feathers under his fingertips. Hikari let out a soft, grateful cry, her eyes closing momentarily as if in relief. Kenji smiled, feeling a deep sense of connection with the majestic bird. Kenji decided he would stay for a few days and build a camp before releasing his new friend Hikari back to her home. He wanted to ensure that the hawk was fully healed and strong enough to fend for herself. He guided Tsuki toward a quiet area near a gently flowing stream. The spot he chose was perfect, nestled near a grove of trees that provided ample shade.

The stream was clear and cool, its waters rushing over smooth stones. Kenji could see small fish darting about, and he knew this would be an excellent place for both him and Tsuki to rest and rejuvenate. He unsaddled Tsuki, allowing her to roam freely and graze on the green grass that lined the stream's banks. Tsuki lowered her head to drink from the stream, her muscles visibly relaxing as she settled into her temporary home.

Kenji set about establishing a comfortable camp. He gathered large stones to form a fire pit. Using fallen branches and dry leaves, he built a small fire. He then arranged his belongings around the campsite, and rolled out his tatami mat which was partially curled up on the ends. Next, Kenji turned his attention to building a more secure shelter for Hikari. Using his dagger, he cut branches to construct a sturdy frame, binding them together with strips of bark. He then wove smaller twigs and leaves through the frame to create a protective covering. The shelter was large enough to give Hikari space to move around comfortably while keeping her safe from predators.

Once the shelter was complete, Kenji gently placed Hikari inside, ensuring she had enough food and water. He sat beside her, speaking softly and offering reassuring words. "We'll stay here for a few days, Hikari. You need to rest and regain your strength. When you're ready, you'll fly free again." Over the next few days, Kenji and Hikari settled into a routine. Each morning, Kenji would check on Hikari's wing, carefully applying healing salves and adjusting the bandages as needed. He would then spend time foraging for food, gathering berries, nuts, and edible plants from the forest. The stream provided fresh fish, which he caught using a handmade fishing line. These meals sustained both him and Hikari, helping them grow stronger each day.

In the afternoons, Kenji would practice his martial arts and meditation by the stream, finding solace in the peaceful surroundings. Hikari, now more comfortable with Kenji's presence, would watch him intently, her observant eyes following his every movement. Occasionally, Tsuki would wander over, nuzzling Kenji affectionately before returning to her grazing. As the sun set each evening, Kenji would light the fire and sit quietly, reflecting on his journey and the events that had led him to this moment. He would often stare at the night sky, tracing the constellations and drawing strength from the stars and his ancestors. Hikari, perched nearby, seemed to share in these moments of contemplation, her presence a comforting reminder of the bond they were forming. On the seventh morning, Kenji woke to find Hikari stretching her wings, testing their strength. He could see the determination in her eyes, a clear sign that she was ready to take flight once more. With a sense of sadness and joy, Kenji carefully removed the final bandage from her wing, giving her one last check to ensure everything was in order.

Standing back, Kenji watched as Hikari spread her wings wide. The morning sun reflected off her feathers, highlighting their rich, brown hues.

With a powerful leap, Hikari launched herself into the air, her wings beating strongly as she ascended. Kenji's heart swelled with joy as he watched her soar higher and higher, her silhouette a beautiful sight against the clear blue sky. For a moment, Hikari circled above the camp, her dark eyes meeting Kenji's. She seemed to communicate a silent message of gratitude, an unspoken promise of friendship and loyalty.

Then, to Kenji's surprise, Hikari descended gracefully from the sky and landed at his feet. Her eyes looked up at him with determination. Kenji stared awkwardly, a surprised look on his face. He knelt down beside her, gently stroking her feathers. "Come on, girl. Go home!" he urged softly, pointing to the vast expanse of sky beyond.

But Hikari refused to leave. She let out a soft, insistent cry, flapping her wings as if to solidify her decision. Even when Kenji began breaking down the camp, gathering his supplies and preparing to leave, Hikari remained steadfast. As Kenji mounted Tsuki and prepared to continue his journey, he looked back at Hikari one last time. "I guess you're coming with us then," he said with a chuckle, shaking his head in disbelief. Tsuki started to move, and to Kenji's amazement, Hikari took to the sky, following them from above.

Throughout their journey, Hikari remained a constant presence, soaring above them with grace and agility. She would scout ahead, alerting Kenji to any potential dangers or obstacles. Her bright eyes missed nothing, and her cries served as both a guide and a warning. During the nights, Hikari would perch close by, her watchful eyes never straying far from Kenji and Tsuki. She became an integral part of their small, wandering family, her bond with Kenji growing stronger with each passing day. As they traveled together, Kenji felt a deep sense of companionship and trust with Hikari, knowing that she had chosen to stay by his side out of loyalty and mutual respect. She was a true friend.

Kenji looked at Haruto and let out a big breath followed by a short smile. Haruto felt an even deeper sense of connection to Hikari and her sons after hearing Kenji's story. Kenji's eyes softened as he reflected on the memories he had recounted. The bond between Kenji and Haruto had deepened with time, weaving a tapestry of trust and understanding. Kenji broke the silence with his voice, "There is more I must share." Haruto stretched his legs and prepared himself for Kenji's words.

After escaping the Akurosai estate and evading the dangers that pursued them, Kenji traveled for many days with Hikari soaring above and Tsuki carrying him along. Kenji knew he needed a place where he could find peace and rebuild his life, far from the chaos and darkness of the past. They traversed tall mountains and crossed wide rivers. Each night, Kenji would set up a temporary camp, and they would rest under the stars. He would stare and whisper to the constellations, hoping they would guide him to the sanctuary he sought.

One evening, after many weeks of travel, Kenji felt a sense of exhaustion creeping over him. They had been following a winding river through a particularly thick forest. The sun was setting, and it would be dark soon. Kenji decided to stop and rest for the night. He dismounted Tsuki and set up a small campfire. The fire crackled to life, its warm glow providing comfort to the growing darkness. He prepared a simple meal, using the last of their provisions.

As they settled in for the night, Kenji spoke softly to his companions, "We need to find a place we can call home. Somewhere safe, where we can build a new life. Tonight, I will perform a ritual ceremony to guide us to our new home." Kenji rummaged through his bag draped over the saddle and pulled out a small, leather pouch. From it, he took out several objects: a clear crystal, some dried herbs, and a moonstone etched with symbols. He arranged them carefully around the campfire, creating a sacred circle.

Kenji then pulled out a small drum he had made from the remains of a fallen tree. He began to beat it rhythmically, the deep, resonant sound echoing through the landscape. The steady beat seemed to blend with the sounds of the night, creating a haunting melody. Hikari watched intently, her head cocked to one side, while Tsuki paused in her grazing to listen. As the drumbeat filled the air, Kenji closed his eyes and began to chant softly, invoking the spirits of the land and sky. His voice was a low hum, blending seamlessly with the rhythm of the drum. He called upon the spirits to guide them to a place of safety and peace, a place where they could build a new life free from fear and darkness. The forest seemed to respond to his call. The wind picked up and stirred the leaves that had been resting on the ground. The river's gentle flow turned into a soothing melody, harmonizing with Kenji's chant. The air grew thick with a sense of anticipation, as if something significant were about to happen.

Kenji took a bundle of dried sage from his pouch and lit it with a branch from the fire. He waved the smoking sage around the circle, purifying the space and strengthening the connection to the spirits. The fragrant smoke filled the air. As the ritual continued, Kenji felt a deep sense of calm wash over him. His exhaustion seemed to melt away, replaced by a renewed sense of purpose. He could feel the spirits guiding him, their presence a comforting warmth that surrounded him and his companions.

When the ritual was complete, Kenji sat back, feeling a profound sense of peace. He looked at Hikari and Tsuki, who seemed to share in his newfound tranquility. "We will find our home," he said softly to his companions. "The spirits will guide us." That night, Kenji slept soundly, his dreams filled with visions of a beautiful, vibrant valley. In his dream, he saw a sparkling river winding through lush fields, surrounded by protective mountains. He saw himself and his companions thriving in this paradise, building a new life filled with peace and harmony. In his dream, he saw a woman standing near a meadow with her back turned. She had long, flowing black hair and wore a simple black kimono. There was an aura of familiarity around her, and he felt a deep sense of connection and tranquility. He kept trying to look at her face, but it escaped him. No matter where he turned, he could only see her back.

Kenji awoke with the image of the woman still vivid in his mind. He pondered the significance of the dream as he prepared for the day. There was something about her presence that felt like a beacon, guiding him to their future home. *Was this a sign from Yasuko?* he wondered. The next morning he packed their belongings and continued their journey, following the river deeper into the forest. As they traveled, the terrain gradually began to change. The crowded forest started to thin out, giving way to rolling hills and open meadows.

By midday, they reached a high ridge that overlooked a vast, hidden valley below. Kenji stopped in awe, taking in the breathtaking view. The valley was a massive expanse, surrounded by protective mountains on all sides. A radiant river wound its way through the center, flanked by fertile fields and groves of fruit trees. Wildflowers dotted the landscape, adding splashes of color to the lush greenery. It was as if he had been brought to the very doorsteps of his dream manifested.

Kenji's heart burst with hope. "This is it," he whispered to himself. "This is where we will build our new home." They made their way down the ridge and into the valley, exploring the land as they went. Kenji found a perfect spot near the river to set up a more permanent camp. The soil was rich and fertile, ideal for farming. The river provided a constant source of fresh water, and the surrounding mountains offered protection from harsh weather and potential threats.

Kenji went to work immediately, constructing a simple shelter for himself and a stable for Tsuki. He gathered materials from the surrounding forest, using his knowledge of building and crafting that he had learned on the Akurosai estate. Hikari continued to watch over them, often disappearing into the sky to hunt and returning with food. Over the next few weeks, Kenji worked tirelessly to cultivate the land. He planted seeds, tended to the growing crops, and built irrigation channels from the river to ensure a steady supply of water. Tsuki helped by carrying supplies and plowing the fields, while Hikari kept the area free from small pests and predators. Kenji carefully carved a hidden compartment into the rocky landscape behind the cabin, blending it seamlessly with the natural surroundings. This secret chamber, concealed by layers of stone, moss, and vines, was designed to protect the Jade Sword. The compartment was small but secure, with a cleverly crafted mechanism that only Kenji could unlock. It wasn't just a hiding place; it was a sanctuary for the sword, a secret place known only to him. Kenji understood the importance of keeping it safe, not only from thieves but from those who sought its legendary power. Here, nestled in the heart of the mountain, the Jade Sword would remain untouched and undisturbed, awaiting the moment it might be called upon by the One.

As the weeks turned into months, their hard work began to pay off. The crops flourished, providing a bountiful harvest. Kenji expanded their home, adding more storage and enclosures for his growing family of animals. He built fences to protect the fields from wild animals and created a comfortable stable for Tsuki. Kenji built a large enclosure in the back of the cabin for Hikari and her new family. She laid eggs, and soon, two small hawks, Yume and Kaze, hatched. Kenji felt a deep sense of fulfillment as he watched the hawks grow, knowing that their family was beginning to feel complete.

As much as Kenji loved his animals, he did miss human companionship. He longed for a family that he could share his life with, people to laugh with, to share stories and meals, and to find solace in during tough times. The solitude, while peaceful, often felt like a heavy cloak that he could not shed. Kenji's thoughts frequently drifted to Yasuko. He remembered the way her eyes sparkled with life, how her small dimples appeared when she smiled, and the quiet strength she carried within her. Though Kenji enjoyed his quiet life in the valley with his family of animals on his small farm, the memory of Yasuko left him with a deep, aching emptiness.

Each night he would create mental images of her in his head before he fell asleep. Yasuko's final words played out in his head, *Look for me in your dreams.* Driven by those parting words, Kenji would focus intently on drawing her into his dreams, as if by sheer will he could bridge the distance between them. His intention was to create a space where they could meet, even if only in the realm of dreams. But each night she was absent. Then one night, as Kenji fell into a deep sleep, she appeared. It was the girl in the simple black kimono with long, flowing black hair, standing near a rushing river. As Kenji approached her, she turned around, and it was Yasuko. She looked distressed and was speaking frantically, but her voice was drowned out by the roar of the river.

Kenji ran towards her yelling, "What is it, Yasuko!" Her voice was faint, but he could still make out the words, "Go to Master Takeda, he is at the old temple in the mountains." Before she could finish, her voice was swallowed by the noise, and the vision began to blur. Kenji reached out, trying to hold onto the image of Yasuko, but she began to fade, her figure dissolving like mist in the morning light.

When he awoke the message was clear: Master Takeda needed his help, and there was no time to waste. Kenji's mind raced as he recalled Ryuji's stories of the old temple in the mountains, a place steeped in mysticism. It was a secluded and ancient sanctuary, hidden deep within the forested peaks, where only the most dedicated monks had once ventured. The temple was rumored to be a place of great power, where the veil between the physical and spiritual worlds was thin.

Kenji packed his supplies and prepared Tsuki for the rigorous journey ahead. He checked his weapon, the Tora Katana, the Tiger Sword, which had served him well over the years. It was the very sword that Master Takeda had presented to him at the Akurosai estate so long ago. The blade was as sharp and lethal as the day it was forged. Unsheathing the katana, Kenji inspected the glowing metal closely, satisfied with its condition.

His gaze then shifted to the jade ring on his left hand. The memory of the day Master Takeda entrusted him with the guardianship of both the Jade Sword and the ring surfaced in his mind. To others, the ring appeared as a simple metal band, but when Kenji looked at it, the metal glowed softly with a light green hue, a constant reminder of his commitment. He recalled the vow he had made to Master Takeda, to protect the ancient artifacts, even with his life if necessary.

Kenji had hidden the Jade Sword in a secure place, knowing its location had to be kept secret at all costs. The hiding spot was known only to him, but even that wasn't enough. To ensure the sword remained concealed, Kenji had cast a protective spell—a complex incantation he had mastered through his practice. This spell created a barrier around the sword's location, making it far more difficult for anyone to find it.

Before Kenji left, he carefully opened the enclosure, releasing Hikari and her young sons into the open sky. "I need you to watch over the valley while I'm gone, Hikari," he said, his voice filled with trust. "I will be back in a few days." Hikari, the mother hawk, spread her wings wide, stretching them against the morning light. She tilted her head to the side, her intense eyes locking onto Kenji's as if to show her understanding and acknowledgment of his request.

The journey would require a full day of traversing difficult, snowy terrain. Kenji wore a black bear fur over his shoulders and a fur covering for his head. He took special care to ensure Tsuki was well-prepared for the journey as well. Kenji draped a heavy blanket over the horse's back, securing it tightly to keep the cold at bay. He also gave her a special concoction of herbs to protect her from the harsh cold.

It was a difficult journey, but Kenji knew he needed to get there as quickly as possible. He rode swiftly up the steep, rugged mountains, his heart pounding with urgency. The narrow passageways twisted and turned, leading them higher and higher up the unforgiving slopes. The air grew colder and thinner with each passing moment, biting at Kenji's skin and causing his breath to come in sharp, icy bursts.

Tsuki pressed on, her hooves striking against the stony ground with relentless rhythm. Finally, as they crested a steep ledge, the landscape opened up before them. In the distance, silhouetted against the darkening sky, stood the huge monastery, its ancient stone walls towering above the surrounding terrain. As Kenji approached the gate, two guards in armor appeared. Kenji nodded to the men and said, "I am here to see Master Takeda."

One of the guards eyed Kenji suspiciously before turning and leaving. A few minutes later, he returned with an older, tall monk draped in a large bear fur that wrapped around his shoulders. A small fur hat sat atop his head, its flaps hanging down over his ears, protecting him from the mountain's chill. Kenji dismounted his horse and bowed respectfully to the monk.

"I am Kenji, and I am here to see Master Takeda."

The monk hesitated, a hint of sorrow in his eyes as he met Kenji's gaze.

"I am sorry. Master Takeda is gone," he replied softly.

Kenji immediately responded, "When will he return?"

The monk cleared his throat before answering, "He will not be back. He's dead."

Kenji stared at the monk in disbelief, his breath catching in his throat.

"What happened to him? Can I see him?"

The monk bowed once more, his expression grave and respectful. "I am sorry," he began, his voice steady yet heavy with grief. "Master Takeda died during an attack by outsiders. His body has already undergone kaso." Kenji's heart sank as he processed the monk's words. He understood that kaso meant cremation—there would be no final viewing, no chance to look upon his master's face one last time. The rituals had already been completed.

Kenji returned the bow, his voice calm but filled with grief. "May I pay my last respects?" The monk nodded solemnly and walked over to one of the guards, whispering something in his ear before returning to Kenji. With another bow, he said, "You may come in and pay your respects." Kenji nodded in gratitude, then climbed back onto Tsuki and followed the monk through the gates and into the monastery.

When Kenji entered the monastery, he was in awe of the massive size of the grounds. The vast, open courtyard stretched out before him, blanketed in a pristine layer of glistening white snow that sparkled under the moonlight. The snow-covered ground was untouched, its surface smooth and undisturbed. Surrounding the courtyard were a series of stone buildings, their ancient walls built directly into the rugged mountain landscape. The buildings were connected by covered walkways, the roofs heavy with snow.

Kenji followed the guard and monk to a nearby stable, where Tsuki could eat and rest after the long journey. The monk then guided Kenji to a building reserved for sacred ceremonies. The building was a tall wooden structure with intricate carvings that were painted in a bright red with gold accents. Inside the building there was a strong scent of incense. The walls were adorned with tapestries depicting scenes of celestial beings. It was a place, the monks believed bridged the world of the mortal and the divine. Kenji removed his fur and placed his katana next to it. The monk paused to allow Kenji to prepare, he then nodded in silent acknowledgment and pointed towards a raised platform at the center of the room.

On the platform rested an ornate urn, its surface adorned with delicate engravings of warriors engaged in battle—a tribute to the warrior life of Master Takeda. The urn was surrounded by an array of offerings. There were carefully arranged bowls of rice, fruits, and incense sticks, each item placed with deep reverence. Kenji approached the platform and bowed deeply in honor of his teacher and master. Turning to the monk, he asked, "May I have a moment of privacy?" The monk smiled, bowed, and quietly stepped outside. Once alone, Kenji reached into a small leather satchel slung across his shoulder and removed a small container of herbs.

Holding the herbs over the flame, he watched as they ignited, releasing a thin stream of fragrant brown smoke that began to curl and swirl into the air. He walked to the urn and allowed the smoke to engulf the container. The smoke circled the urn several times, almost as if performing a ritual of its own, before gently rising toward Kenji. The tendrils of smoke reached his nostrils, filling them before slowly exiting through his mouth and rising into the air.

Kenji knelt and closed his eyes, sinking into a deep state of meditation. Almost immediately, a tunnel appeared before him in the darkness of his mind. He felt himself being pulled into it, rapidly accelerating through the tunnel's endless expanse. The walls of the tunnel were alive with ever-changing fractals, shifting and morphing into various colors. As he moved through the tunnel, the fractals seemed to dissolve and fall away, like fragments of a dream fading into the void.

Suddenly he felt as though he was in a dark room. A space devoid of light, structure, or any sense of boundaries. The blackness was absolute, disorienting, with no indication of where he was or even if he was standing or floating. Then, piercing the silence, he heard the voice of Master Takeda, soft yet commanding. "Kenji... You must save the girl." Kenji, feeling confusion replied, "What girl?" The voice urged him, "She is here, you must find her." Suddenly he felt as if Master Takeda had left. Kenji felt a sense of coldness overcoming his body as a female voice spoke, "You must go back now Kenji." In an instant, his eyes sprang open, the vision vanishing as quickly as it had come. He found himself alone back in the sacred ceremony room.

Kenji bowed deeply to Master Takeda's urn, a gesture of respect and acknowledgment, before turning to gather his belongings. The experience left him confused, but he knew he had to find answers. He quickly walked to the door, determined to find the monk who had brought him there and hopefully uncover the meaning behind this cryptic message.

Kenji approached the monk and bowed. "Did Master Takeda have a girl with him?" The monk looked away, avoiding Kenji's look as he replied, "There is no girl. It is late and the weather has turned, may we lay out a tatami for you tonight?" The cool air of the monastery pressed down on him as he lay on his tatami mat. His body rested on the familiar texture of the rice straw, yet his mind was far from at ease. He pictured Yasuko's face, her white skin and dark, piercing eyes. He hoped that she might reach out to him as she had before, guiding him through the tangled web of secrets surrounding Master Takeda's death. "Yasuko," he whispered into the stillness of the night, his heart heavy with the weight of unanswered questions. "Help me unravel what happened to Master Takeda and the mystery of the girl."

As Kenji drifted into a light sleep, his mind still buzzing with unanswered questions, he was suddenly startled by a gentle rapping on his door. The sound was soft yet insistent, cutting through the quiet of the night and pulling him back from the edge of sleep. Kenji walked to the door and was greeted by a thin, young monk. The monk held his index finger to his lips, signaling for Kenji to remain silent. With two quick taps to Kenji's chest, he motioned for him to step back into his room. The man held a single flickering candle, its light dancing across his face. He quietly slid the door closed behind him, ensuring they wouldn't be disturbed. He then bowed deeply as he whispered, "I am Tomo, a novice monk, I am sorry to disturb you Master Kenji." Kenji returned the bow, his curiosity aroused. "Why did you awaken me, Tomo?"

Tomo straightened up, his movements awkward and hesitant.

"I need to warn you," he began, his voice trembling slightly.

"The senior monks have taken the girl, and I fear they intend to harm her."

Kenji, still confused, asked, "Who is the girl? What happened to Master Takeda?"

Tomo's voice grew more serious as he continued, "Master Takeda came here some time ago to train our warrior monks. The girl was sent to live with him, and he took her in, caring for her in his private residence. Then, one day, a man arrived at the monastery, claiming to be her father and demanding to take her away."

Kenji's eyes sharpened as he focused on Tomo. "What happened to them?" Tomo swallowed hard, his voice faltering slightly as he recalled the events. "Master Takeda refused to hand the girl over. He told the man that she was not here and hid her. But that night, the man returned. He attacked Master Takeda and killed him. The man... he was no ordinary person—he was a demon."

Kenji's heart pounded as the weight of Tomo's words sank in. "The demon slaughtered several of our warrior monks before fleeing into the night," Tomo continued, his voice laced with fear and sorrow. "He caused great devastation. The senior monks believe the girl is somehow connected to this evil, that she is cursed, and that she must be dealt with..."

Kenji straightened up as he reached for his katana, "Can you help me find the girl?" Tomo nodded, "I know the way." Kenji followed Tomo through a long, dark corridor. Tomo walked ahead, his small frame barely illuminated by the low light. The air grew colder as they ventured further, and Kenji could feel the chill seeping through his fur cloak. After continuing for some time, they reached a door that opened onto an outdoor walkway connecting to another building. A blast of frigid air greeted them as the door creaked open. Snow was gently falling from the sky, and the white-covered ground sparkled in the moonlight.

Tomo glanced at Kenji and pointed to a tall building across the way. Without a word, they stepped onto the walkway, a suspended bridge covered in snow. The bridge swayed slightly with each step, the ropes creaking under their weight as they carefully traversed the narrow path. The snow crunched softly beneath their feet, and the wind picked up, causing the bridge to rock from side to side.

Kenji gripped the side ropes tightly, his breath visible in the cold night air, as he focused on the building ahead. As they neared the entrance, Tomo suddenly paused, his eyes scanning the surroundings for onlookers. He turned to Kenji, motioning for him to come closer. Leaning in, Tomo whispered, his voice barely audible over the wind, "You need to quietly go in and climb to the top of the tower. They have the girl in there."

Kenji's heart pounded as the weight of Tomo's words settled over him. "I'll gather your horse and meet you back here, and I can get you out of the monastery," Tomo continued. "Be careful, Master Kenji. They will be watching. Move quickly, but stay silent—we don't have much time." Kenji bowed to Tomo in silent thanks, then turned his attention to the towering building.

Tomo glanced around suspiciously before inserting a large key into the wooden door. With a quick turn of his hand, the bolt clicked, and the door unlatched with a soft creak. Kenji slowly drew his sword from its sheath. He held it upright in front of him in a defensive position, ready for whatever might await him on the other side.

As he entered the building he could hear the distant sound of chanting echoing off the walls. Kenji scanned the dark room, the only light coming from a torch mounted on a wall leading up a tall stairway. The chanting grew louder as Kenji moved closer to the stairs. The very walls seemed to vibrate with the energy of the chant, amplifying the sound as it traveled up the stairwell.

Kenji's pulse quickened, the hairs on the back of his neck standing on end as he moved forward. The narrow, wooden spiraling steps were worn smooth by countless years of use. He followed the stairs upward. Finally, after what felt like an eternity, Kenji reached the top. The stairs opened onto a small landing. The chanting was louder here, its source just beyond a heavy wooden door that stood slightly ajar, the faint glow of torchlight spilling out into the darkness. Kenji took a deep breath before peeking into the open door.

Inside, a series of stairs led down to an open room where a group of men in red robes stood in a circle. In the center of the circle was a large stone slab, and lying silently in the middle was a young girl, about ten years old. A tall man stood over her, holding a large dagger in his hand. The men in the circle began to chant even louder as he approached the girl. Kenji knew he had to act quickly if he was going to save her.

He stealthily descended the stairs toward the men in the circle. The men knelt around the stone slab, their bodies swaying slightly with the rhythm of the chant. The tall man standing over the girl raised the dagger higher, the chanting reaching a frenzied pitch as the moment of sacrifice drew near. With a burst of speed, Kenji dove over the girl and, in one fluid movement, cut her restraints. As he landed on his feet, he found himself face-to-face with the man holding the dagger.

The man's eyes widened in shock just as Kenji struck him in the mouth with the hilt of Tora Katana. His head whipped to the side, and a blood-covered tooth launched into the air. The men in the circle quickly stood up and began moving toward Kenji. A large, bald man with a thick beard walked toward the men surrounding Kenji and shoved several of the monks aside, launching their bodies into the air. Then he pointed at Kenji and flexed his muscular arms, which bulged from the cut-off sleeves of his robe. With a roar, he threw his arms into the air and charged.

Kenji drove Tora Katana deep into the wooden floorboards. As the man approached, Kenji braced himself by gripping the hilt of the weapon, then launched a side kick straight into the man's midsection, sending him flying backward. As the man stumbled and regained his footing, Kenji burst forward and dove for his legs, tackling him to the ground with a resounding crash. Kenji quickly slithered on top of the man's chest. Once in position, he reached behind the man's head with one arm and shoved the other arm across the man's own face. Locking his hands together, Kenji drove his shoulder into the bearded neck, choking the man until he gagged and fell unconscious.

Some of the monks turned and ran, while the remaining few charged toward Kenji, who was now gathering the Tora Katana and placing it into its home at his side. Before they could get close, he scooped up the girl and hoisted her over his shoulder, swiftly moving toward the stairs and the door. Kenji carried the girl down the stairs, his movements quick and focused. As he descended, he periodically checked to see if she was conscious. Her eyelids fluttered, a faint sign of life, but they never fully opened. Her breathing was shallow, and her body limp against his shoulder. As he reached the bottom of the stairs he looked back as he heard footsteps. Outside the door was Tomo.

Tomo quickly approached, his eyes scanning the area nervously. He pointed to another monk who was standing near a wall and motioning for Kenji. "There," Tomo whispered urgently, "a secret exit used for emergencies. It leads out of the monastery and into the forest. You can escape that way without being seen. Go now, Master Kenji!"

Kenji gently placed the girl on the front of his horse before mounting Tsuki. He draped his bear fur over her back, completely covering her. He rode through the snow, creating a fresh path that led to the monk standing near the main wall. Tomo gestured frantically for Kenji to hurry. As they neared the wall, Kenji spotted the hidden entrance. It was a narrow, concealed door built seamlessly into the stone. Tomo quickly unlatched it, revealing a dark tunnel beyond. Kenji glanced back at Tomo, who nodded, a silent farewell in his eyes.

The air inside was damp and cold, with the sound of Tsuki's hooves splashing through the muddy water that pooled along the uneven floor. The tunnel walls, slick with moisture and green moss, seemed to close in around them as they advanced. As they emerged from the long, dark tunnel that led into the woods, Kenji immediately looked down at the girl to check her breathing. In the faint moonlight, he could see a wisp of cold vapor escaping from her mouth, a small but reassuring sign of life.

The rhythmic motion of the horse seemed to soothe her, and she remained still as they moved through the forest. Kenji's eyes darted around, constantly alert for any signs of pursuit from the monks. After ensuring they were safe and far enough from the monastery, he decided it was time to stop and check on the girl. The girl's clothes were tattered, dirt-streaked, and torn. Her skin was unnaturally pale, and her face bore the marks of recent tears. Streaks of dirt trailed down her face, cutting paths through the grime on her cheeks. As Kenji's eyes traveled down her arms, he noticed her wrists had newly healed scars. Her skin was ice cold, and the cuts looked deep and fresh. He removed herbs from his saddle, treated her wrists, and covered them with fresh cloth.

He looked the girl in the eyes and softly asked,

"What is your name?"

Her eyes fluttered open, and she quietly whispered,

"Ayama," before closing them again.

Kenji carefully lifted her onto Tsuki, positioning her securely in front of him so he could keep her steady during the ride. He wrapped her in his fur cloak, covering her entire body and head to protect her from the elements. As they traveled through the forest and down the mountain, Kenji maintained a steady pace, mindful of Ayama's need for peace. The journey back to the cabin took half the night, with the forest gradually giving way to the familiar landscape of Kenji's valley. The rolling hills and lush meadows were a welcome sight after the previous day's daunting events. As they approached the valley, Kenji noticed Hikari, his loyal hawk, and her offspring circling the sky overhead.

As Kenji rode up to the cabin, Hikari swooped down and landed gracefully in front of Tsuki. She tilted her head back and forth several times, as if sensing the seriousness of the moment. "We have a new friend, and she needs our help," Kenji said softly, acknowledging Hikari's presence. Kenji quickly dismounted and gently lowered Ayama from Tsuki's back. The girl remained silent, her body limp with exhaustion. He carried her into the cabin, where he laid her down on a tatami mat.

Kenji set about making Ayama comfortable. He carefully removed her tattered sandals and covered her with a thick covering, tucking it around her to keep her warm. As he touched her skin, he noticed she was unusually cold. He then turned his attention to building a fire. The hearth soon crackled with a welcoming warmth. As the fire built up, Kenji took a moment to prepare a herbal remedy from the plants he kept stored in his cabin. He applied the soothing mixture to Ayama's wrists, where the newly healed scars were still tender and swollen.

Kenji stood vigil as she rested, his eyes never straying far from her. He moved quietly around the cabin, preparing a simple yet nourishing meal that would be ready for her when she awoke. He brewed a pot of herbal tea, its fragrant steam filling the room, and set out a bowl of rice and vegetables. As the hours turned into days, the food was replaced with fresh servings, and Kenji's watchful care remained constant.

Each morning, Kenji continued his daily routines, tending to the animals and maintaining the farm, always keeping one ear tuned to any sign of her stirring. At night, he would sit by her side. She would often stir about and whimper as she kicked her legs and thrashed with her arms. Kenji would gently hold her arms and ensure she was safe. When Ayama finally awoke, it was as if she had emerged from a deep, healing sleep. Kenji looked into her eyes and smiled. "Welcome back, Ayama," he said tenderly. "You're safe here. You must eat and regain your energy."

Kenji prepared a simple meal of rice for the girl, hoping it would help restore her strength. However, Ayama refused to eat it, her eyes filled with a lingering fear. Kenji sat beside her, speaking in a calm and soothing voice. "I know you've been through a lot," he said, "but you need to regain your strength. The food will help you feel better." Ayama glanced at the bowl of rice, then back at Kenji. She appreciated his kindness but knew that the food he offered wouldn't help her. Her true need was something she couldn't explain to him.

Over the course of the following days, Kenji continued to offer Ayama food, but she always refused. Each time, her refusal was gentle but firm, leaving Kenji increasingly puzzled and concerned. He couldn't understand why she wouldn't eat, and his worry for her grew with each passing day. It was early one morning when Kenji was startled by a sound coming from the back of the cabin. He awoke and noticed that Ayama was not on her mat. Alarmed, he grabbed his katana and cautiously approached the rear of the cabin.

As he rounded the corner, he was shocked by the sight that greeted him. Ayama was in a dark corner crouching over one of the farm's chickens. The animal lay completely still, its eyes wide open and lifeless. Ayama's mouth was covered with blood as she held the animal's limp neck in her small hands. Kenji froze, unable to comprehend what he was seeing.

Ayama looked up at him, her eyes begging for understanding.

"Kenji," she began, her voice just a whisper.

His hand held his katana tightly.

"What are you?" he asked, his voice filled with confusion.

"I'm sorry," Ayama said, tears welling up in her eyes. "I'm... different. I need warm blood to

survive. I didn't know how to tell you."

Kenji's mind raced, trying to process the revelation. He had saved her, protected her, and now he was faced with a truth he could hardly fathom. "You could have told me," he said finally, lowering his katana slightly. "We could have found another way."

Ayama looked down at the lifeless chicken, her face filled with guilt. "I didn't want to burden you. You've already done so much for me." Kenji took a deep breath, steadying himself. "We'll figure this out together," he said. "But no more sneaking around. We need to trust each other." Ayama nodded, grateful for his understanding. Kenji sheathed his sword and approached her. "Let's get you cleaned up," he said gently. "And then we'll talk about how to move forward."

Over the coming months, Kenji attempted to help Ayama understand who she was and unravel the mysteries of her unique nature. They spent countless hours together, learning and growing, as Kenji called upon the spirit world to better understand her condition. They would often read and write together. Kenji was in awe of Ayama's reading and writing ability for such a young girl. In addition to herbal medicine, Kenji introduced

Ayama to meditation techniques designed to help her control her cravings. They would sit together in the tranquility of the forest, Kenji guiding her through breathing exercises and visualization practices. Ayama learned to center herself, finding a calm within that helped her manage the constant hunger.

Kenji would take Ayama on hunts deep in the forest. When Ayama felt the urge, she would gently tap Kenji on the shoulder, a silent signal for him to stop the horse. Understanding her unspoken request, Kenji would halt Tsuki and watch as Ayama swiftly dismounted. She would gracefully disappear into the woods, her figure quickly blending into the shadows of the trees.

Ayama was adamant that Kenji not follow her or witness her feasts. She wanted to spare him the sight of her true nature in its rawest form, fearing it might change how he saw her. In the solitude of the forest, Ayama would track her prey with uncanny precision, her heightened senses guiding her to the source of warm blood she craved. She moved silently, her eyes glowing a faint red as she honed in on an unsuspecting deer or other small creature. The hunt was quick, her instincts taking over as she fed on the animal.

When Ayama returned, her demeanor was calm and stoic. Kenji never questioned her about what transpired in the forest; he simply offered her a reassuring smile and helped her back onto the horse. Ayama's small frame was filling out with healthy muscle from the farm work. Her eyes, which had once been clouded with fear, now sparkled with curiosity and confidence. She began to develop a routine of her own, taking initiative in the daily chores and even adding small touches to the cabin to make it more homely.

As time went on, Kenji became increasingly frustrated by his lack of understanding of Ayama's abilities. One day, as the evening chores were winding down, Kenji approached Ayama as she swept the floor of the cabin. "Ayama, I need to tell you something," he said with an air of seriousness.

Sensing the importance of his tone, Ayama placed the broom against the wall and turned to face him. "I am stumped by your abilities and who you are... You seem to share traits with a vampire, yet you do not feed on humans," Kenji admitted. "Your skin is only mildly effected the sunlight... and you grow like a normal girl?" He shook his head. "And you say you cannot remember anything other than your name?"

Ayama looked up at Kenji, feeling somewhat ashamed of her lack of memory.

"I'm sorry, but I can't remember anything before you found me."

"Master Takeda, the man who was taking care of you, was once my teacher. When I last

saw him many years ago, he shared a prophecy with me. That the One would come

forward who would bring light to the darkness."

Ayama looked at Kenji shyly. "Am I the One?"

Kenji responded, "I don't know. There is a tale of an ancient seer who lives in the

mountains, and I think we should seek her counsel. But before we do that, there's

something I must show you."

Ayama looked at Kenji with a sense of guilt. "I am sorry to bring this upon you, Kenji, I am open to anything that will help me understand my past." Before she could continue, Kenji held out his hand and said, "We are in this together!" Kenji turned to Ayama and said, "I must go and retrieve something of importance. Stay here. I don't want you to follow." With a serious look, he walked away, heading toward a small stone building nestled among the trees, its entrance partially obscured by overgrown vines. As he made his way past a group of tall trees, he glanced down at the jade ring on his finger, noticing how it seemed to vibrate more intensely with each step he took.

Reaching the building, Kenji slipped behind it to where a hidden compartment, cleverly camouflaged among the vines, was built into the rocky hillside. He crouched down, running his hand carefully along the uneven stone, searching for the exact spot that would trigger the opening. As he traced his fingers over the stones, he began counting aloud, "One, two, three, four." Kenji paused and moved his hand to the right. "One, two." At that moment, the mechanism engaged, and a nearby stone shifted slightly, revealing the concealed compartment embedded in the wall.

Kenji leaned forward and reached into the narrow tunnel that extended beyond the wall's surface. His fingers brushed against something solid, and with great care, he pulled out a long leather sheath. He then made his way back to Ayama, who was patiently waiting at the front of the cabin, her eyes filled with curiosity. Standing before her, Kenji slowly unfastened the sheath's clasp and opened it, revealing a sword encased in a beautifully crafted scabbard.

Kenji held the sword reverently in both hands. He looked at Ayama, his expression serious. "This is the Jade Sword," he said softly. "It has been hidden away for many years, waiting for the right time and the right person." Kenji then pointed to the hilt of the weapon, where a large jade stone was embedded, its once vibrant color now faded. "I want you to place your hands on this weapon," he said, his tone gentle but firm.

Ayama hesitated, her hands trembling slightly as she reached out toward the hilt. She sensed that this moment was more than just a test; it was a step toward discovering her true identity, her destiny. As her fingers wrapped around the weapon, Kenji's stare remained fixed on the jade stone, as if willing it to respond to her touch. Ayama looked up at Kenji, searching his eyes for reassurance, but nothing happened.

The stone remained dull and lifeless. Disappointment spread across her face as she released the handle, her shoulders sagging slightly. Kenji met her eyes, his expression calm but encouraging. "Try again," he urged gently. "This time, close your eyes and focus on your breath. Let go of any doubts and fears. Just breathe, and let the sword feel your energy." Ayama extended her arms, wrapping her fingers around the sword's handle. She closed her eyes tightly and took a deep breath. In her mind, a vision began to form—an older man standing before her. "Ayama, it is me, Master Takeda," the figure said softly before vanishing into mist. Kenji looked at Ayama, then at the sword's handle. The jade stone flickered briefly before quickly fading.

Ayama opened her eyes and looked at Kenji, confusion written across her face. "What happened?" she asked, her voice filled with uncertainty. Kenji, equally perplexed, responded quickly, "I'm not sure. The stone reacted, but only for a moment." He studied the sword and then Ayama, wondering what this brief glimmer could mean. "Try to recall what you saw in your mind. Did you see or feel anything unusual?" Kenji asked, hoping for a clue to understand what had just occurred. Ayama hesitated before responding, "I saw a man, and he said he was Master Takeda, but that was all that happened."

Kenji carefully placed the sword back into its scabbard. "I think we should take the Jade Sword to the seer in the mountains and seek her counsel on this mystery." Ayama gave a nervous smile and nodded in agreement. The next day, they gathered their supplies to journey deep into the mountains in search of Akiyama no Sora, known as "the sky of autumn mountains." They packed carefully, ensuring they had enough food, water, and warm clothing for the journey ahead. Kenji securely strapped the leather case holding the Jade Sword to Tsuki.

He also strapped Tora Katana to his back, while Ayama carried a small bundle of herbs and healing supplies. Before setting off, Kenji fed Tsuki a handful of specially prepared herbs for the difficult journey. She quickly ate the mixture, then responded by shaking her head and stomping her front hoof. They rode Tsuki for an entire day to reach the spot the elders spoke of, the place where the leaves change color. The journey was arduous, with narrow paths winding through snow-covered, rocky terrain. As they ascended higher, the air grew crisp and thin, making it more challenging to breathe. The vibrant colors of the leaves painted the landscape in hues of red, orange, and gold. The further they traveled, the brighter the landscape became, as if signaling their arrival.

However, as they ascended the mountain, a large, dark cloud gathered over the landscape, casting a shadow over the vibrant colors below. The once clear sky darkened, and the temperature dropped noticeably. Kenji glanced up at the cloud, his brow furrowing in concern. "We need to find shelter soon," he said, his voice tense. "That storm is coming fast." As he turned his head forward, lightning struck the ground in the near distance, illuminating the landscape with a blinding flash. The thunder that followed was deafening, reverberating through the mountains and shaking the very ground beneath them. The loud boom startled Tsuki, causing her to rear slightly before Kenji calmed her with a gentle pat and a few soothing words.

Ayama grabbed onto Kenji, holding his waist tightly. In the spot where the lightning struck the ground, a white light began to appear. It started as a faint glow, but quickly grew in intensity. Kenji reached over his shoulder and placed his hand on his katana, his instincts on high alert as the light expanded and became brighter. He squinted against the glare, trying to make sense of what he was seeing. The light took on a strange, orange glow.

As the light continued to brighten, it began to take shape, slowly forming the outline of a woman's figure. The form was delicate and graceful, almost angelic. Kenji's heart raced as his mind struggled to comprehend the apparition before him. "Ayama, we should dismount Tsuki slowly," he whispered. They both carefully climbed off the horse. Kenji secured the case holding the Jade Sword before Tsuki trotted away to a nearby clearing. The woman's form became more defined, her features gradually coming into focus. She appeared to be floating just above the ground, her long hair flowing as if moved by an invisible force. Her eyes were closed, and her lips were curved in a gentle smile.

As she opened her eyes, she looked directly at Kenji and Ayama, her presence comforting. Kenji felt a strange mix of emotions—awe, fear, and an inexplicable sense of familiarity. "Who are you?" Kenji called out, his voice strong and clear despite the howling wind and sprinkling rain. The woman smiled gently, her eyes filled with wisdom and compassion. "Do not be afraid," she said, her voice resonating like a melody that seemed to calm the storm around them. The howling wind began to subside, and the rain softened to a light drizzle. "I am here to guide you."

Kenji and Ayama exchanged glances, both of them feeling a strange sense of peace in her presence. The woman's aura was serene, and it felt as though she had brought a protective shield around them. Turning her gaze to Ayama, the woman continued, "Ayama, I have been waiting for you. I have seen you in my visions. You are a dhampir." Ayama's eyes widened. "A dhampir?" she repeated, her voice trembling. She had never heard the term before and now looked back with confusion. The woman nodded, her expression gentle and understanding. "A dhampir is a being born of both human and vampire blood. Your existence bridges two worlds, and you possess unique abilities because of it. You have felt the hunger, the strength, and the confusion of your dual nature, but you have also felt the compassion and empathy that makes you who you are." Kenji's grip on his katana loosened as he listened. "Why have you been waiting for her?" he asked, his voice filled with curiosity. "There is a prophecy," the woman explained, her eyes fixed intently on Ayama. "A dhampir will rise to bring balance between the light and dark worlds." Kenji stepped forward, holding out the Jade Sword with both hands. "I was given guardianship of this sword, waiting for the return of the One." The woman nodded, her expression serene but commanding. "Ayama, place your hands on the handle of the sword."

Kenji, his impatience getting the better of him, interjected, "We've already tried this..." The woman's eyes shifted to Kenji. "Do it again," she instructed firmly, leaving no room for argument. Ayama closed her eyes and placed both hands firmly on the handle of the weapon. The woman spoke softly to Ayama, "Relax and allow the sword to connect with your heart." As Ayama began to breathe slowly, an image formed in her mind. She saw a man lying on top of a woman, his sharp fangs glowing yellow in the dim light. A large ring on his finger shifted from black to crimson. Suddenly, two guards burst into the room, causing the man to lunge toward the window and vanish into the night.

The vision shifted, and Ayama saw the same woman giving birth. The newborn child wailed incessantly, refusing to feed on her mother's milk at first. As she lay in her mother's arms nursing, she suddenly clamped down and bit her, drawing blood. The mother tried to push her away, but the child kept feeding relentlessly. The image shifted to the mother sitting and crying while cutting her own wrists to retrieve blood to quell her babies thirst.

The image then faded, and another one appeared. She saw the child, now a toddler, feeding on a baby rabbit, her small mouth smeared with blood. Her mother stormed into the barn and yelled, "No, Ayama, no!" The image changed once more. Ayama now saw the girl, a little older being rushed to a man with a horse. The mother handed the man a bag of gold pieces and a map, pointing to the snowy mountains. The scene then shifted back to her mother, who was now alone. The man with fangs appeared, searching for someone. His anger flared as he began to attack and kill the woman.

Finally, Ayama saw herself at Master Takeda's home in the monastery. The same man appeared and attacked Master Takeda and the others. She then saw herself being dragged away by monks and locked in a small room. She sat alone for many days, until she began cutting her wrists with her nails, feeding on her own blood for sustenance. Suddenly a monk walked into the room and was shocked to see her mouth covered in blood. The image shifted once more as the monks took her to a large room and tied her up, preparing to sacrifice her.

Ayama then opened her eyes, feeling something shift in her hands as the tip of the handle turned and opened with a soft whoosh of air. The woman spoke softly, "Reach inside the handle and pull out the scroll." Ayama placed two fingers inside and felt a thick, paper-like material. She slowly pulled the paper from the handle. As her fingers brushed against the parchment, she felt a surge of energy pass through her, a connection to the powerful knowledge contained within. She looked up at the woman, her eyes filled with questions.

Ayama carefully unrolled the scroll, her fingers trembling with anticipation. As the parchment unfurled, she found it covered in strange markings she could not comprehend—lines threaded together with circular shapes, repeating across the page like a hidden pattern:

—O—O—O—O—O—O—O—O—O—O—O—O—

"What does it say?" Ayama asked, her voice trembling with anticipation. She clutched the scroll tightly, sensing the weight of its significance. As she stared at the mysterious symbols, something extraordinary began to happen—the shapes and lines on the scroll started to glow with a golden hue. The glow intensified, and the symbols seemed to lift off the parchment, floating in the air between Ayama and Kenji. The characters shifted and rearranged themselves, the once incomprehensible patterns transforming into words they could understand. Ayama and Kenji exchanged a glance, their eyes wide with awe and disbelief as the message revealed itself before them.

The child born of light and shadow, shall walk the path that few dare to follow.

A heart of courage, a spirit bright, shall banish the darkness, bringing the light.

When the endless loop is torn apart, the gate shall open, and destiny's course will start.

Balance restored, yet the light cannot stay,

For what ends at dusk is reborn with the day.

In that moment, the glowing symbols gradually returned to the surface of the paper, their golden light fading as they settled back into place. The characters, now fully formed and readable, glowed one last time before solidifying, becoming permanently etched into the scroll. The once-foreign symbols were now clear and understandable. Ayama and Kenji realized that the message was now a permanent part of the scroll.

They looked up from the paper and woman's image began to dissolve, her form becoming blurry and indistinct. Small flecks of color detached from her figure, swirling and dancing in the air like fireflies before merging into a shimmering cloud of mist. The spirit spoke, "Ayama, you are not the One, it will be your child who will restore balance."

As the last remnants of the woman disappeared into the mist, her voice echoed softly around them, carrying a final message. "Ayama you must fall in love and bring forth a child." Ayama handed the scroll to Kenji, who was now standing next to her. His eyes met hers, and they shared a silent understanding of the importance of this moment. Together, they walked to a large tree at the edge of the clearing, its branches providing a natural canopy from the drizzling rain. They sat on the ground, leaning against the sturdy trunk for support.

Kenji and Ayama stared at the verses, their minds racing to comprehend the prophecy's meaning. Kenji turned to Ayama with a serious look, "What happened when you closed your eyes?" Ayama paused, her eyes fixed on the scroll in her hands. The weight of what she was about to say hung in the air. Finally, she spoke, her voice filled with fear. "There was a vampire who attacked a woman. She had a child who was half-vampire, half-human. I think... I am that child."

Kenji's eyes widened as the realization washed over him. Memories of Sakura, the concubine who was attacked at Hirokazu's castle, flooded his mind. He had heard whispers of a child being born, but never could he have imagined that Ayama was the dhampir daughter of Sakura. Gently,

Kenji grasped Ayama's hand. "I knew your mother," he said softly. "I was aware of the attack. I believe you are the dhampir."

Ayama looked up at Kenji, "Am I to birth the One?"

Kenji paused before responding, "I do believe so."

He continued, "I believe that you will have a child one day who will fulfill this prophecy.

Your child will be the One."

With a renewed sense of purpose, they carefully rolled the scroll back up and secured it inside the handle of the Jade Sword.

Kenji stopped talking and looked at Haruto with a serious face. Haruto could sense the gravity in Kenji's voice, the weight of untold stories and the passage of time. Haruto, feeling the tension in the air, asked, "Where is Ayama now?" Kenji leaned forward, his eyes locking onto Haruto's with a profound intensity. "When she was old enough, I asked her to leave the valley," he began, his voice calm but laced with emotion. "I taught her all I could about herbal medicines and spirit work."

Haruto interrupted, "So, she left the valley?"

Kenji looked up, "I told her that she needed to create a family, fall in love, and do all the

things that I cannot. I wanted her to have a life beyond the confines of this isolated world.

By doing so she could start a family and perhaps fulfill the prophecy once and for all."

"But how could she live as a dhampir?" Haruto said with concern.

Haruto listened intently, his curiosity growing. Kenji continued, "I helped her find her way to a village where she could start a new life as a farmer. She had learned to control her blood thirst and protect herself from the elements. She took on a new name to signify her new beginning." Haruto, intrigued and puzzled, asked, "What is her name?"

"She changed her name to Hana," Kenji revealed, a hint of sorrow in his voice.

Haruto's eyes widened as the realization struck him.

"You mean my mother?" Haruto paused, his voice a low whisper, the revelation hitting him

with a massive wave of emotion.

Kenji nodded slowly, his expression softening. "Yes, Haruto. Your mother, Hana, was once Ayama, the girl I saved and raised. She is the reason I know you and why you are here today." Haruto sat back, absorbing the magnitude of Kenji's words. "My mother is a dhampir?" Kenji nodded. "Yes, your mother carries vampiric blood, but she does not feed on humans and is able to control her thirst."

Haruto, in disbelief, responded, "What does that make me?"

Kenji immediately answered, "Her son!"

The stories his mother had told him about her past suddenly made sense—the lessons in herbal remedies, the rituals of protection, the tales of vampires and dhampirs, the skills and knowledge she possessed... they all traced back to Kenji. "She never spoke of you directly,." Haruto said, his voice filled with awe and sadness. "But she always said that a great man taught her everything she knew."

Kenji smiled faintly, memories of Ayama... Hana—flooding back to him. "She wanted to protect you, to let you forge your own path without the shadows of the past. But know this, Haruto: everything I did for her, she has passed on to you. You do not seem to carry her vampiric blood, but you do carry her legacy." Haruto felt a deep sense of connection, not just to his mother, but to Kenji as well. The old man before him was not just a mentor to his mother he was the father she never had.

Haruto asked, his voice filled with concern,

"Where is my mother? Is she safe?"

Kenji responded with a reassuring nod.

"Yes, she is safe. Hikari and her sons check in with her often and bring her messages. They

ensure that she is well and protected."

Haruto breathed a sigh of relief, the worry in his heart easing.

"Thank you, Kenji. It means a lot to know that she is safe and looked after."

Kenji placed both hands on Haruto's shoulders and looked him directly in the eyes. "It is an honor to see her legacy live on in you, Haruto. She was like a daughter to me, and you are like a grandson. Remember, you carry within you the strength and spirit of those who came before you."

Haruto smiled. "I have one more question."

Kenji replied, "Yes, what is it?"

"If I am her son, then I am the One?"

With a serious look, Kenji responded, "Yes. That seems to be true."

Chapter Seven

RISE FROM THE ASHES

As the days passed, the full impact of Kenji's news settled deeply within Haruto. Needing time to reflect, he decided to go to the woods and hunt in silence with his handmade fukiya. He had spent hours selecting the perfect piece of bamboo, ensuring its balance and length were just right. Kenji had helped him craft the fukibari, the slender metal projectiles.

Now, as Haruto held one in his hand, he admired the craftsmanship. He stared at the long, sharp tip and sharp blade which were perfect for the hunt. He had only brought one projectile. Kenji would boldly state, "You only need one fukibari... it's one shot, one kill. The predator strikes once, and that's all that's needed to complete the hunt."

As he walked, the revelation that Kenji was not only his mentor but also the man who had raised his mother lingered constantly in his thoughts. Haruto felt a profound, unshakable connection to his family's past, along with an urgent need to reconnect with his mother and share this new-found understanding. Suddenly, many of her strange habits made sense. He remembered how she would always cover herself when exposed to the sun, how she rarely ate the food she prepared, and how she would often disappear for hours, only to return recharged and full of energy. Haruto felt a surge of empathy as he considered the constant burden she must have carried, concealing the truth of her existence. He realized how much she had sacrificed to protect him from a world he was only just beginning to understand. The weight of her silence, the quiet strength it must have taken to live in secrecy, overwhelmed him.

Haruto spent hours replaying Kenji's words in his mind. Images of his mother, Hana, and her life before she became the woman he knew swirled in his thoughts. He couldn't shake the feeling that he needed to see her, to understand her journey from Ayama the dhampir to Hana the mother, and how that journey had shaped her into the person she had become.

Thoughts of Rumiko could not escape his heart; she had been the light of Haruto's life, her presence a beacon of hope and joy in his darkest moments. Her laughter had a way of brightening even the bleakest days, and her kindness had left an indelible mark on his soul. They had made promises to each other, dreams of a future filled with love and happiness. But as the years passed, Haruto, unable to bear the pain of her possible absence, built walls around his heart to protect himself.

Yet, the thought of Rumiko remained a constant, haunting presence in his mind. He often found himself wondering about her, picturing her face, and hearing her voice in his dreams. Recently, he realized he could no longer remember what her voice sounded like, and this upset him deeply. He would try to relive memories, hoping to hear her voice one last time, but it always eluded him. Despite his efforts to move on, the love he felt for her refused to fade. The possibility that she might still be alive, somewhere out there, tugged at his heartstrings with an intensity that was impossible to ignore.

Haruto couldn't shake the overwhelming sense of urgency. His heart was heavy with the need to reconnect not only with his mother but also to uncover the fate of Rumiko, his true love. He had spent countless nights lying awake, haunted by thoughts of what might have happened to her.

As Haruto approached the edge of the forest, he knelt down and slowly removed his waraji, feeling the cool earth beneath his bare feet. The sensation grounded him, a quiet reminder of his connection to nature. Before stepping deeper into the woods, Haruto took a deep bow—not only to honor the hunt but also to symbolically release the mental burdens he carried. Kenji would often remind him, "To succeed, the mind has to be as clear as the path ahead."

His long bamboo blowpipe was securely tucked into the gray sash wrapped around his black kimono. In his left hand, he carried one slender projectile, its sharp tip pointed toward the ground. As he stepped into the forest, a transformation took place. His body crouched low, and his movements became more fluid and primal. He stretched his arms forward as if they had become the forelegs of a predator stalking its prey. With each step, he placed his hands lightly on the forest floor, followed by his legs, mimicking the stealth and grace of a hunting animal.

Haruto moved silently through the thick foliage, his body blending with the shadows cast by the towering trees. The forest seemed to breathe around him, and in his mind, he could hear Kenji's voice: "To truly hunt, you must become both the hunter and the hunted. The predator and the prey." As Haruto crept deeper into the woods, he observed the animals around him—deer grazing on fresh leaves, birds pecking at the forest floor. None of them noticed his presence; in fact, it was as if they accepted him as part of their world. His movements were so fluid, so in tune with the rhythm of the forest, that he didn't just become invisible... he became one with them.

Haruto felt a deep respect for the creatures he shared the forest with, but he knew what must be done. In the past, he had felt guilt for the animals and feared the hunt. But now he understood that he was part of nature's balance as both a custodian and a participant. Kenji often reminded him, "You must respect all that you take from the forest, but you must also leave no trace of your presence."

He came upon a large buck feeding in an open area near a stream. Its golden-brown coat sparkled in the sunlight, each movement catching the light as it grazed peacefully. The majestic creature stood tall, its antlers spreading wide like the limbs of a great tree. Haruto crouched low and studied the creature's movements, trying to connect to its pulse.

He closed his eyes, took a deep breath, and thanked the animal for its life. In the distance, he could hear the faint heartbeat of the buck, steady and rhythmic. When he opened his eyes, the animal stood frozen in its tracks, unaware of Haruto's presence. He slid the fukibari into the blowpipe and raised it to his mouth. With a deep inhalation, he released a powerful breath, sending the projectile flying from the bamboo shoot toward the unsuspecting buck.

The projectile struck the buck in the neck, and the animal dropped instantly to the ground in a cloud of dust. The impact was swift, sending a billow of dirt into the air as the creature collapsed. The forest fell into a temporary silence. As Haruto started to stand and move toward the fallen buck, the sound of hooves caught his attention. Two men on horseback rode into the clearing, the metal of their gear rattling with each movement. They were clad in black samurai garb, their helmets adorned with the crest of a dragon with a crimson red eye. The riders moved with authority, scanning the area as if they were searching for something... or someone.

One of the riders dismounted and knelt beside the buck. He pulled the projectile from its neck, lifting it to his face and inspecting the blood-covered tip before touching it lightly to his mouth, as if tasting the kill to determine its freshness. Standing up, he turned the fukibari between his fingers, his gaze shifting toward the trees, eyes shifting as though sensing someone watching. The man slid the fukibari into his pouch and mounted his horse once more. Without a word, he pointed in Haruto's direction, signaling to the other rider.

Haruto's heart raced as he began to crawl backward, trying to distance himself from the approaching men. Before they could spot him, he slipped behind the embankment near the river, keeping his body low against the ground. As the riders drew closer, Haruto grabbed a nearby stone and tossed it in the opposite direction, the rock echoing across the forest floor.

The men immediately turned their heads toward the sound, eyes scanning the thick brush for any sign of movement. Taking advantage of their distraction, Haruto slid silently into the river, the cold water wrapping around his body. As he entered the water, he held the bamboo blowpipe just above the surface, moving carefully to avoid making any ripples. Before fully submerging, he placed the blowpipe in his mouth, allowing him to breathe freely while remaining hidden beneath the water's surface.

The men rode to the edge of the river, scanning the area carefully before turning their horses and riding off. Once Haruto was sure the men were gone, he climbed out of the river, gathered the fallen deer, and dragged it back to the valley. When he arrived at Kenji's cabin, the old man was tending to the small garden outside. Kenji looked up as Haruto approached, sensing the determination in his stride.

Kenji stood up, his expression tense. "Haruto, are you okay? You are wet and look troubled." Haruto took a deep breath, gathering his thoughts before recounting what had happened by the river. Kenji listened calmly, then said, "Haruto, these men... they are with Ryuji, and they may be looking for us."

Before Kenji could continue, Haruto interrupted, "I need to travel to see my mother. I need to speak with her about everything you've told me, an d... I need to find Rumiko. I can't rest until I know what happened to her. I need to see if she's still alive." Kenji's eyes softened with understanding. "I will send Hikari's sons, Yume and Kaze, to check on your mother. Then we can decide if we must go right away."

Later that night, while Haruto and Kenji were asleep, they were abruptly awakened by a loud flapping sound coming from outside. Startled, they quickly got up and rushed to check the source of the noise. As they stepped outside, they saw Hikari's sons, Yume and Kaze, moving about in distress, their wings beating the air frantically. Kenji immediately recognized the urgency in the hawks' behavior. He bent down and began to soothe them with his words, his voice calm and reassuring. "Easy now, Yume, Kaze. What troubles you?"

The hawks gradually began to settle, their agitated movements slowing as they responded to Kenji's familiar presence. Kenji continued to speak softly, reaching out to gently stroke their feathers. "What has happened? Why are you so distressed?" Kenji looked at Haruto and spoke, his voice filled with concern, "I sent Yume and Kaze to your mother's village to check on her. I'm worried now for her safety."

Haruto's eyes widened, his face filled with fear. "What do we do?" he asked urgently, his heart pounding in his chest. Kenji's expression hardened with resolve. "We leave tonight!" he declared. They quickly returned to the cabin. Haruto gathered supplies, making sure they had enough food, water, and essential tools for the journey. Kenji, meanwhile, prepared his satchel with medicinal herbs and remedies, knowing they might need them along the way.

As they worked, Kenji spoke, his tone serious yet reassuring. "Haruto, Yume and Kaze are exceptional scouts. If they sensed something was wrong, we must take it seriously. Your mother is strong, but we need to be there for her." Haruto nodded, his worry noticeable but lessoned by Kenji's calm demeanor. "I understand, Kenji. I just hope we're not too late."

With their preparations complete, Kenji and Haruto readied their horses for the journey. Kenji would ride Tsuki, while Haruto would take the reins of Kumo, a name that means "cloud." Kumo was a beautiful mare with a coat of gray and white, her colors blending seamlessly like clouds against the sky. Kenji took a moment to speak to Haruto, looking him directly in the eyes. "We will get to your mother, Haruto. Stay focused and keep your wits about you. We'll travel as swiftly as Tsuki and Kumo can carry us."

Haruto took a deep breath, drawing strength from Kenji's confidence. "Let's go," he said, his voice filled with conviction. Kenji mounted Tsuki, his katana securely fastened to the horse. Haruto strapped his weapon to his back and mounted Kumo. They planned to ride straight through the night, stopping only briefly to let Tsuki and Kumo drink water and graze momentarily. The windy night air served as a constant reminder of the urgency of their mission, pushing them onward with relentless determination.

Kenji led the way, his experience with nocturnal travel proving invaluable. His eyes constantly scanned the terrain, ever alert for any signs of danger or obstacles. Just as the sun began to rise, they crested a hill and caught their first glimpse of the village in the distance. Haruto's heart lifted momentarily at the sight of the familiar surroundings. A thick plume of dark smoke was rising into the sky from the far end of the village, sending a knot of dread into Haruto's gut. "Kenji, look!" Haruto pointed towards the smoke, his voice tight with fear. "Something's wrong." Kenji's expression grew grim as he followed Haruto's gaze. "We need to hurry," he said, his voice calm but urgent.

As they approached the village outskirts, Haruto and Kenji were met with a scene of utter devastation. The once lively village was now a landscape of ruin and despair. Only three houses still stood, their walls blackened by soot and their roofs partially caved in. Everything else was charred and burned to the ground, reduced to smoldering heaps of ash and rubble. The air was thick with the stench of smoke and the smell of death.

Haruto's heart sank at the sight. The destruction was overwhelming, and the dark energy that lingered in the air was suffocating. It seemed to cling to everything, a reminder of the violence and hatred that had torn through his village. Haruto began to panic as he jumped off Kumo and sprinted toward Rumiko's home. Each step felt like a race against time, but as he approached the familiar path, his worst fears were confirmed. The house was completely burned to the ground, with nothing remaining. The roof had caved in, and the walls were reduced to piles of ash and debris. The fire had spared nothing, leaving the ground scorched, barren, and empty. The only remains were a set of bones on the ground. Smoke was still slowly trickling from the darkened remains. Haruto fell to his knees, the overwhelming sight stealing the breath from his lungs. "Rumiko," he whispered, his voice breaking with sorrow. He reached out to touch the charred remains, but the heat of the ashes burned his finger tips.

As Haruto knelt there, lost in his grief, an old woman walked by, her pace slow and steady. She carried a small bundle of salvaged belongings, her face marked with soot and fatigue. Haruto, desperate for any information, turned to her with a pleading look in his eyes. "Do you know Rumiko?" he asked, his voice filled with emotion. The woman stopped and looked at him, her eyes hollow and empty. She remained silent as tears filled her eyes, then turned and continued her labored walk through the chaos.

Haruto rose and hurried toward Kenji, who was approaching Hana's home.

"Rumiko is gone," Haruto blurted out as he reached him.

Kenji stopped and turned to face Haruto.

"Are you saying she has left?"

Haruto's voice trembled with emotion.

"She's either gone or dead."

Kenji placed an arm around Haruto's shoulders. "I am sorry." As Haruto approached the familiar path leading to his childhood home, his heart sank even further at the sight of the devastation that awaited him. The house, once a sanctuary filled with love and memories, was now reduced to a smoldering ruin. Haruto's breath came in deep gasps as he tried to process the scene before him.

One of the villagers, an elderly man named Masaru, called out, his voice hoarse from smoke and sorrow. "It was terrible. Hundreds of samurai came in the night, like shadows. They set everything ablaze and took all of the children with them." Haruto, his eyes wide with panic and tears streaming down his face, turned to Masaru. "My mother is Hana. Is she alive?" he asked, his voice trembling. Masaru looked at the ground, his face filled with pain. He then glanced at Kenji and Haruto. "She went in there." He pointed to what was left of Haruto's childhood home. Haruto felt as though the ground had been ripped from under him. He ran through his mother's doorway. The once-familiar opening was now just a blackened framework.

He stumbled inside, the smell of smoke filling his lungs. Inside, the devastation was complete. The interior of the house was unrecognizable, charred, and crumbling. As Haruto's eyes adjusted to the dim light filtering through the smoke, he saw a figure in the corner, leaning against a large supporting beam. His heart wrenched at the sight. There, slouched against the beam, was his mother. Her face was blackened from the smoke and soot, her beautiful black hair flowing behind her, now matted and singed. There was a trail of blood traveling down her kimono from a silver dagger sticking out of her chest. Her hand was still clutching the handle of the weapon.

Haruto rushed to her side, his body trembling, as he lifted up her head. "Mother! Mother, it's me, Haruto," he cried, his voice choked with emotion. "Please, wake up. I'm here now. You're safe." Kenji entered the remains of the house, his expression grim as he took in the scene. He knelt beside Haruto, his eyes filled with sorrow as he looked at Hana's still form. He gently placed a hand on Haruto's shoulder. "Haruto, she is gone," he said softly, his voice heavy with regret. "But I must act now to save her soul."

Haruto's breath caught in his throat, the weight of Kenji's words pressing down on him like a fallen tree. His mother, the woman who had been the center of his world, was gone. Kenji rose quickly and went to Tsuki, who stood just outside the ruined house. From his bag, he carefully gathered a selection of herbs and a talisman. The herbs were a mixture he had ground together for their cleansing and protective properties. The talisman was an intricately carved piece of wood, inscribed with ancient symbols of protection and peace.

Returning to Hana's side, Kenji set the herbs and talisman down and began to prepare for the ritual. "Haruto, we need to create a sacred space," Kenji instructed. "Gather stones from around the house to form a circle. This will help contain the energy and guide her spirit." Nodding, Haruto moved quickly, his movements fueled by a desperate need to help his mother one last time. He found stones scattered among the debris, the surfaces still warm from the fire. He carefully placed them in a circle around Kenji and Hana, ensuring that the space was enclosed. Kenji lit the herbs with a nearby dying flame, allowing the fragrant smoke to rise and swirl around them. The scent filled the air, creating a calming, purifying atmosphere. Kenji then placed the talisman gently on Hana's chest, his hands calm and focused. "This talisman will guide her spirit to the afterlife, allowing her to choose her new form," Kenji explained.

As the smoke continued to rise, Kenji began to chant softly. The sound was melodic and soothing. Haruto watched, his heart heavy but his mind focused on the importance of the ritual. He knew that this was the final act of love and respect he could offer his mother. The chant grew louder, resonating through the ruins of the house and out into the village. Villagers who had been tending to the wounded and clearing debris paused, drawn to the haunting beauty of Kenji's voice. They gathered quietly around the perimeter of the sacred space, their presence a silent testament to their shared grief and respect for Hana.

As the ritual reached its climax, Kenji raised his hands, directing the energy of the circle towards Hana. The smoke thickened, forming a protective veil around her body. The talisman began to glow faintly, the symbols pulsing with a golden light. Haruto felt a warmth spread through the circle, a comforting presence that seemed to wrap around him like a loving embrace.

Kenji spoke, his voice strong and clear, "Spirit of Ayama, Hana, mother, daughter, and protector, we release you from this earthly bond. You are free to choose your form in the afterlife." Kenji paused to wipe a single tear forming in his eye. "Your legacy lives on in your son and in the hearts of all who knew you." As Kenji finished the chant, the glow from the talisman intensified for a moment before slowly fading away. The smoke began to dissipate, and the air around them felt lighter, as if a great burden had been lifted. Haruto knelt beside his mother, tears streaming down his face.

He knew that Kenji's ritual had succeeded, he could feel that his mother's spirit was now at peace. But he could not help but wonder, *where was Rumiko?* Haruto and Kenji carried Ayama's body to the large fire in the middle of the village, their steps slow and reverent. She had been gently wrapped in a cloth that was tied with vines and twigs. Kenji placed sacred herbs within the folds to honor her spirit and cleanse her passage to the afterlife. The few surviving villagers had gathered around the fire, their faces solemn and respectful. They had come to to pay their respect. The air was thick with the scent of burning wood and the faint, fragrant aroma of the herbs.

As Haruto approached the fire, Kenji stepped forward to assist him. Together, they carefully lifted Ayama's body, their movements synchronized and gentle. Haruto's eyes were filled with tears, his heart aching with the loss of his mother. With a final, shared glance, they placed Ayama's body onto the flames. As the fire embraced her, a burst of sparks shot into the air, mingling with the rising smoke. The sound of the fire consuming the cloth and wood was a farewell symphony of crackles and pops. The villagers bowed their heads, whispering prayers and farewells. Kenji stood beside Haruto, his hand resting on the younger man's shoulder, offering silent support. Together, they watched as the flames danced around Ayama's body, slowly consuming it.

Tsuki and Kumo grazed in the tall grass, enjoying a rare moment of calm before the journey back to the valley. The air was quiet and still, a sharp contrast to the chaos and destruction that had recently swept through. Kenji stood nearby, his face reflecting the gravity of the moment. He took a deep breath and approached Haruto, who sat quietly on a fallen log near the fire, lost in thought. The weight of the past days pressed heavily on him, and the uncertainty of the journey back to the valley lingered in his mind. Haruto looked up at Kenji with an intense expression. "How could my mother kill herself if she was a dhampir?"

Kenji paused before speaking. "A dhampir can die from natural causes after many, many years, or be killed by a silver-tipped blade through the heart. I cannot say for certain why she chose to take her own life. Maybe she feared that Ryuji would trap her soul in the Shadow Blade. Maybe she was protecting you. I don't know if we will ever truly know." Haruto sat quietly letting the weight of Kenji's words settle. "Haruto," Kenji said, "I believe it is Ryuji who has brought this darkness upon us." He paused, allowing the weight of his words to settle. "With the recent disappearance of children, I believe he has reemerged and is looking for you." Haruto's heart skipped a beat, and he felt a chill run down his spine despite the warmth of the fire. "Ryuji?" Haruto echoed, his voice barely above a whisper. "But why? Why would he be looking for me?" Kenji took a deep breath, his eyes reflecting the firelight. "Ryuji is not just a man. He is a dark sorcerer, once a guardian like me, who turned to forbidden arts seeking power. When he disappeared years ago, it was predicted that he would rise again."

Haruto looked up, the weight of Kenji's words pressing heavily on him. Kenji's expression was grave as he continued, "Haruto, Ryuji is very powerful. He may have control of the Shadow Blade. This weapon is not just a mere sword; it is a dark relic of immense power. If he strikes you down with this blade, your soul will be trapped inside it, forever fueling its dark magic. This is how it is powered. Each soul it captures adds to Ryuji's strength."

Haruto's eyes widened in horror. "Trapped? Forever?" Kenji nodded solemnly. "Yes, Haruto. If Ryuji gains control of your soul, it will grant him immense power." Haruto quickly responded, "Then why not just destroy the sword?" Kenji sighed and replied, "I wish it were that simple. If we destroy the sword, every soul trapped within it will be lost for eternity." The full weight of the situation became painfully clear to him. Haruto stood up and asked Kenji, "There is one other thing."

Kenji smiled, "What is it Haruto?"

"Do you think that was Rumiko's body?"

Kenji took a deep breath.

"Haruto, I know Rumiko has meant a great deal to you for a long time. But I believe she's

gone, and it's time to let her go. Like with a newborn, if the cord no longer serves you, then

perhaps it's time to cut it."

Haruto nodded, "Maybe you are right."

Since it was getting late in the day and the sun would soon set, Kenji thought it best that they ride for a short bit then stop for the night and begin again by the light of day. They were both tired from the day's events, their bodies and minds weary from the emotional and physical toll of the recent devastation. As they rode, the remnants of the village gradually gave way to the quiet, undisturbed beauty of the surrounding wilderness.

After riding for about an hour, Kenji spotted a suitable clearing by a small creek. "Here," Kenji said, signaling Tsuki to halt. "This is a good place to make camp. The brook will provide us with fresh water." Haruto dismounted, his legs feeling the strain of the day's efforts. He led Tsuki and Kumo to the brook, allowing the horses to drink while he filled their water skins. Kenji busied himself with gathering dry wood for a fire, moving quickly despite his own fatigue.

Haruto lay on his tatami mat, his heart heavy with sorrow and uncertainty. The thin mat offered little comfort against the emotional weight bearing down on him. His thoughts were a fierce whirlpool, dragging him deeper into sadness with each passing moment. His mother, Ayama, was gone, her spirit now in the hereafter. The pain of her loss was a raw, open wound, and the reality that she was no longer there to guide him was almost unbearable.

Haruto missed his one true love, Rumiko. She had been his anchor, her presence a beacon of hope in his life. The thought that she might be dead filled him with a profound emptiness. But perhaps Kenji was right—it was time, once and for all, to let go of Rumiko. Haruto turned his head slightly, glancing at Kenji, who was meditating near the fire with eyes closed in deep concentration. Kenji had been a rock of strength and wisdom, guiding and teaching him. Haruto knew that Kenji's belief in him was deeply rooted, but he couldn't help the doubts that crept into his mind. If he's truly the Prophesied One, how would he ever stop Ryuji?

Haruto drifted off to sleep, the intensity of his thoughts slowly giving way to exhaustion. The dreams that came were restless and filled with images of his mother and Rumiko. Suddenly, in the late hours of the night, he was jolted awake by Kenji's urgent voice. "Quick, Haruto, wake up! There is danger in the valley!" Haruto sat up on his mat, his vision blurred and his heart racing. As he tried to shake off the remnants of sleep, he noticed Kaze, one of Hikari's sons, fluttering about on the ground. He was agitated, flapping his wings in a frantic manner as if he was trying to communicate something important to Kenji.

Kenji's face was intensely focused and serious. He knelt beside Kaze, listening intently to his distressed cries. "We must leave now, Haruto. Hikari needs us!" Haruto quickly rose to his feet, his mind snapping into focus. The urgency in Kenji's voice dispelled any lingering drowsiness. "What's happening, Kenji? What did Kaze say?" Kenji swiftly gathered their belongings. "Kaze brought news that Hikari and Zume are in trouble, and there are many men in the valley!"

Haruto's heart pounded in his chest as he grabbed his weapons and supplies. The thought of Ryuji's men being so close filled him with fear. "Do you think they're looking for me?" he asked, his voice tense. Kenji responded, "Yes!"

They rode Tsuki and Kumo through the night, with Kaze following overhead, the hawk's sharp eyes scanning the terrain for any signs of danger. As they approached the top of the mountains that protected the valley, a sense of danger grew within Haruto. When they reached the crest of the mountains, the sight that greeted them was one of complete devastation. Haruto's heart sank, and he felt as though the ground had been pulled out from under him again. The fields that once stretched out in a lush green expanse were now charred and blackened, smoldering in the aftermath of a recent fire. Smoke still rose from several spots, twisting and curling into the night sky.

Haruto's gaze shifted from the devastated fields to the small cabin that Kenji had built with his own hands. The cabin was now nothing more than a heap of ashes and burnt timbers. The roof had collapsed, and the walls were reduced to rubble. The sight of it filled Haruto with a deep sense of loss and anger. Kenji's face was a mask of controlled fury, his jaw clenched tightly as he surveyed the destruction. "Ryuji's men have been here," he said, his voice low and filled with cold rage. "They've left nothing but ruin in their wake."

Haruto dismounted Kumo, his legs feeling weak and unsteady. He walked slowly toward the remains of the cabin, his mind struggling to process the extent of the damage. Memories of happier times flooded his mind—working alongside Kenji on the farm, sharing meals by the fire, and training in the nearby fields. All of it was gone, reduced to ash and smoke. Haruto was relieved when he saw Ushi-ko hiding behind a small tree near the edge of the woods.

When Kenji walked to the back of the burnt-down cabin, he was heartbroken by the scene that greeted him there. The once lively and protective Hikari lay on her side, her eyes frozen in a lifeless stare, her body still and motionless. The great hawk, who had been a loyal guardian and true friend, was now gone. Next to her, her son Yume was pressed against her side, his feathers ruffled and stained with a trickle of blood, an arrow piercing though him and into Hikari. His body was still, the vibrant energy he once possessed now extinguished. The sight of the two hawks, who had stood by their side, reduced to such a state, was a blow Kenji had not been prepared for.

Kaze circled back and forth above them, his cries piercing the air and filled with grief and desperation. His movements were frantic and erratic. Every now and then, he would swoop down, attempting to nudge his fallen family members back to life with his beak, only to be met with the cold reality of their stillness. Kenji fell to his knees beside Hikari and Yume, his heart heavy with sorrow. He gently placed a hand on Hikari's lifeless body, feeling the chill of death that had settled upon her. "Hikari," he whispered, his voice breaking. "I'm so sorry. I should have been here."

He turned to Yume, brushing a hand lightly over the hawk's feathers, smoothing them down as if it could somehow erase the violence that had befallen him. In the distance, Kenji could hear the faint but unmistakable sound of horses approaching. The rhythmic pounding of hooves grew louder with each passing moment, signaling the imminent return of Ryuji's men. He looked at Haruto, with urgency in his eyes. "Ryuji's men are coming. Follow me."

Without waiting for a response, Kenji took off towards the edge of the woods. Haruto followed closely, his heart racing as he tried to keep up. Kenji led them to a dense thicket of shrubbery. He pulled back the thick branches to reveal a hidden alcove. Concealed within the foliage was an intricately carved wooden panel, nearly indistinguishable from the surrounding trees. Kenji pressed a lever with his foot, and with a soft click, the panel swung open, revealing a hidden compartment. Inside the boxed-out area was a large cache of weapons—swords, bows, arrows, daggers, and various other implements of war. Each weapon was meticulously maintained, their surfaces glistening even in the dim light of the trees.

Haruto's eyes widened in surprise and admiration. "I didn't know this was here," he said, his voice filled with awe. Kenji nodded, his expression serious. "I built this cache as a precaution, knowing we might one day need it. Take what you need." Haruto selected the ōdachi, a long bladed weapon. The ōdachi was a formidable weapon, with a blade much longer than a typical katana, designed for dealing significant damage from a distance. In addition to his loyal weapon, Tora Katana which was already strapped to his side, Kenji selected a wakizashi. This small sword was perfect for close quarter combat or as a back up weapon.

Kenji looked at Haruto with focused intensity. "There is something else I must show you," he said, his voice heavy with significance. Kenji quickly moved toward a small stone building nestled against the mountainside. The rough exterior was carefully camouflaged by long, trailing vines that seemed to embrace the structure. The building, almost hidden from sight, had clearly been constructed with secrecy in mind. Over the years Kenji had made sure the building was well hidden.

He walked to the side and pulled back a small tree that covered the stone wall. "Haruto, I have hidden the Jade Sword in this wall. I am the only person who knows where it is hidden. We cannot let Ryuji get control of the weapon." Haruto nodded, "I understand."

"I'm showing you this, Haruto, in case anything happens to me," Kenji said, his voice laced with urgency. As he spoke, he began counting the stones on the wall. "You must remember this... four stones down and two to the right." Kenji placed his hand on a small stone embedded in a larger one and carefully turned it. A soft clicking sound echoed through the air as the hidden mechanism sprang to life, causing a nearby section of the stone wall to shift and reveal a concealed compartment.

Kenji turned to Haruto, his eyes intense. "Did you see how I did that? It's vital that you know this!" His tone made it clear that the knowledge he was imparting was of the utmost importance. Kenji then removed the jade ring from his finger—the very one passed down to him by Lord Akurosai and Master Takeda. He carefully placed the ring alongside the Jade Sword inside the tunnel-like compartment. Looking directly at Haruto, Kenji spoke with grave seriousness, "You are the only other person who knows the whereabouts of the Jade Sword and ring. If something happens to me, you must take guardianship of them!"

Haruto nodded and looked towards the river, his eyes widening in shock. Hundreds of men on horses, clad in full samurai gear had filled the valley. They moved with precision and discipline, their horses snorting and pawing at the ground, eager to make war. The valley, which had once been a place of peace and tranquility, was now a scene of impending chaos. He could see the banners fluttering in the wind, each one bearing the unmistakable emblem of a dragon with red eyes.

Kenji's face was unmoving as he took in the sight. "We're heavily outnumbered," he whispered more to himself than to Haruto. His mind raced, assessing their options. "We need to move quickly," Kenji said, his voice cutting through Haruto's shock. "Position yourself behind those rocks. Use the cover to your advantage. I will advance first. You stay here and jump when I signal you." Haruto's heart pounded in his chest as he tried to process Kenji's words. "You want me to jump?" he asked, still grappling with the enormity of the situation.

Kenji turned to him, his eyes intense and serious. "If ever there was a time to use your gift, it's now. You have the ability to teleport instantly, right?" Haruto nodded. "I will distract Ryuji, and you jump in close enough to take him out. Your weapon is long, so you should be able to get closer. You have to get past the Shadow Blade and strike him in the heart with your sword."

Haruto nodded again, feeling a mixture of fear and determination. He had trained with Kenji for years, honing his skills and learning to control his unique abilities, but he had never faced anything on this scale. Kenji paused and looked Haruto directly in the eyes. "Our only chance is to get past the Shadow Blade and reach Ryuji at close range. Haruto, you have to believe in yourself and jump close to him when it's time." Haruto looked at

Kenji, confused. "How will I know it's time?" Kenji replied, "I will signal you!"

Haruto moved quickly to the cover of the rocks. From his vantage point, he could see the samurai spreading out, forming a tight and disciplined line as they advanced toward the river. Kenji put his katana in his scabbard and began to walk forward, his hands raised in the air as if he were surrendering. Haruto watched in stunned silence, his heart racing. *What was Kenji doing?* The older man's face was a mask of calm, his eyes fixed on the lead samurai on a horse, who had paused mid-charge.

The valley fell into a tense silence. The samurai leader, a large man wearing a helmet adorned with a dragon crest, raised a hand, signaling his men to halt. The warriors pulled up their horses, the beasts agitated by the abrupt stop. Kenji continued his slow and measured walk, his hands held high in a gesture of peace. Haruto's hand instinctively reached to his rear to grip his weapon, ready to spring into action at a moment's notice. He didn't understand Kenji's plan, but he trusted his mentor.

The lead samurai, rode to Kenji's feet and stopped a few paces away.

"Why do you approach us unarmed?" the samurai leader demanded, his voice a low growl.

"Do you wish to surrender?"

"Bring your leader, Ryuji, to me. This is between us!" Kenji's voice rang out with a commanding authority that echoed through the valley, cutting through the silence. As he spoke, a raven scattered from a nearby tree. He stood tall and firm, his hands still raised in a gesture of surrender. The lead samurai, who was about to turn away, paused and wheeled his horse around to face Kenji once more. The samurai warriors around him exchanged glances and shook their heads in confusion. "What makes you think you are in any position to make demands?" The samurai asked, his voice filled with anger.

Kenji took a step forward, lowering his hands slowly but keeping them visible to show he meant no harm. "Because this conflict will only end with Ryuji's defeat or mine," he said, his voice clear and unwavering. "Spare your men and your resources. Let us settle this honorably, warrior to warrior." Just then, the horses moved aside as if the seas were parting. The tension in the air was palpable, with every eye fixed on the approaching figure. From the rear, a man appeared, wearing an oni mask adorned with horns and sharp curved teeth protruding from the top gums. He rode a midnight-black horse, its coat glowing in the sunlight like polished obsidian.

The horse moved with a fluid grace, its powerful muscles rippling with each step. As he advanced, the samurai around him bowed their heads in respect, creating a clear path for him to meet Kenji. When he reached Kenji, the rider halted his horse and slowly removed his mask. It was Ryuji. His face was strikingly youthful, unmarred by time. His body was bold and strong, showing no signs of age.

Kenji stood his ground, his eyes locked on Ryuji. He was fully aware of the threat Ryuji posed and was prepared to face it head-on. Haruto, hidden behind two large boulders, watched nervously. His heart pounded in his chest, each beat echoing like a drum in his ears. Ryuji dismounted his horse, his dark armor reflecting the overhead sun. The black plates gleamed menacingly. His movements were smooth and controlled, exuding a confidence that bordered on arrogance. As he approached, his eyes locked onto Kenji's, a mocking smile playing on his lips.

"So, how have you been, old friend?" Ryuji's voice was smooth and taunting, carrying across the stillness of the valley like a serpent's hiss. "I see you have aged terribly!" His words were filled with sarcasm, a mocking grin spreading across his face as he took in Kenji's weathered appearance. Kenji remained steadfast. "Why do you bring war to my home?" he demanded, his voice filled with anger. He had known Ryuji once, long ago, but the man before him now was a twisted shadow of the person he remembered.

Ryuji laughed, the sound cold and devoid of any warmth. "This isn't war, Kenji," he replied. "You were always so righteous, so convinced of your own moral superiority. I don't want you... I'm here for Haruto, and I've waited long enough!" As Ryuji's words hung in the air, two men suddenly emerged from the ranks of the samurai, carrying a long black wooden box. The box was ornately carved with the image of a dragon, its eyes inlaid with glowing stones that seemed to shift from crimson to black. The men moved with precision, their faces stern and focused, as they brought the box to Ryuji and bowed their heads in respect.

Kenji glanced towards the boulders where Haruto was hidden, hoping that his student remained unseen. Ryuji approached the box with a sense of reverence, his demeanor shifting from mocking to serious. He placed his hands on the lid, tracing the intricate carvings with his fingers before slowly opening it. Inside, nestled on a bed of black fur, lay the Shadow Blade. The sword was as black as night, absorbing the light around it, and the hilt was adorned with a large crimson garnet stone that matched the dragon's eyes.

"This," Ryuji said, his voice filled with pride, "is the Shadow Blade. Forged in the darkest depths, it has the power to trap the souls of those it strikes down. And with it, I will claim both your soul and Haruto's, finally achieving the power I've sought for so long. But before Haruto, I will take you, old friend!" Ryuji then lifted the sword from its cradle. As he did, a dark energy seemed to pulse from the blade, spreading through his body. His form began to twist and contort unnaturally, as if the dark power within the sword was warping his very essence. His muscles bulged, and his eyes glowed with a crimson radiance.

A man in samurai armor approached Ryuji and carefully placed the oni mask back on his face, securing it tightly at the back. The mask, adorned with horns and sharp teeth that formed a mocking smile, bore a smear of dried blood on its forehead. Ryuji's eyes glowed a bright crimson red from behind the mask. Kenji stood his ground. "Why only one sword, Ryuji? Where are your twin blades?" Ryuji laughed. "I now have the Shadow

Blade, and that is all that's needed." Kenji watched in horror as Ryuji quickly raised the Shadow Blade over his head.

In an instant, Ryuji brought the weapon crashing down with terrifying force. The blade cut through the air with a chilling, almost otherworldly scream. Kenji's instincts kicked in. Without a moment to lose, he dove to the side, narrowly avoiding the deadly strike. The ground where he had stood exploded in a shower of dirt and debris as the blade struck with devastating impact.

Kenji rolled to his feet in one fluid motion, his heart pounding in his chest. He drew his sword in a flash, the familiar weight of Tora Katana grounding him amidst the chaos. His eyes locked onto Ryuji, who stood with a twisted grin, the Shadow Blade pulsing with dark energy in his hands. "You're quick, Kenji for an old man," Ryuji sneered, his voice echoing. "But you cannot escape me forever." Kenji steadied his breathing, focusing his mind.

Ryuji continued his onslaught, his attacks moving faster and faster, each strike fueled by the dark power of the Shadow Blade. Kenji's movements were quick and agile, but Haruto could see the toll the battle was taking on him. The once-fluid motions of his mentor were beginning to show signs of fatigue. Kenji's breath came in shorter gasps, and his movements became more labored, each one costing him more effort. Haruto's anxiety grew with every passing second. The battle between Kenji and Ryuji was reaching a fever pitch, and he could see his mentor struggling to keep up with the relentless onslaught. Kenji's movements, were becoming slower, his defenses weakening under the sheer ferocity of Ryuji's attacks. The clang of steel against steel rang out through the valley, accompanied by Kenji's harsh grunts and heavy breaths.

Haruto reached inside his kimono and touched the black opal necklace his mother had given him. As he watched Kenji, his anxiety grew, and he began tugging on the cord that held the opal stone. Suddenly, the cord unraveled, and the stone fell to the ground. Panic washed through Haruto at the sight of the fallen stone. He quickly glanced at Kenji, who was fading fast, then snatched the stone from the ground, gripping it tightly in his palm. Haruto whispered aloud, "Don't let go of the stone, no matter what you do."

Just then, Kenji looked in Haruto's direction. As Ryuji thrust the Shadow Blade toward Kenji's midsection, he shouted to Haruto, "Jump now..." Panic surged through Haruto. "Jump!" he yelled to himself, his voice breaking with desperation as he sprinted toward Kenji. The word seemed to hang in the air, both a plea and a command. Haruto screamed it again, his legs pumping furiously as he closed the distance. He yelled again, "Jump!" But his feet remained firmly on the ground; his teleportation, the gift that could have saved Kenji, eluded him in his moment of greatest need. The world seemed to slow, every second stretching into an eternity as he watched in horror. Kenji turned too late. Ryuji's blade was already descending, the dark energy surrounding it pulsating. Haruto could only watch, his voice hoarse and raw from screaming, as the Shadow Blade plunged into Kenji's chest. The impact was sickening, a thunderous boom that was followed by a burst of dark energy that sent shockwaves through the ground. "No!" Haruto's scream was a raw, guttural sound, filled with fury that echoed through the valley.

Haruto stood completely still just within reach of Kenji, his body rigid and unresponsive. A single tear rolled down his cheek. Ryuji turned his attention to Haruto, his eyes narrowing with predatory anticipation. The sight of the tear seemed to amuse him. "Well, boy," he snickered, "it seems it's your turn to fall." In a swift, merciless motion, Ryuji swung the Shadow Blade toward Haruto's midsection. The air around the blade crackled with dark energy. Haruto's mind screamed at him to move, to teleport, to do anything to evade the lethal strike. As the blade closed in, Haruto dropped his weapon to his side and whispered desperately, "Jump..." He willed his feet to move, to activate his gift and escape the impending blow. But his body betrayed him.

Time seemed to slow as the Shadow Blade made contact with Haruto's body. Dark energy surged through him, and he felt a searing pain like no other. The blade penetrated straight through him, the dark power attempting to claim his soul just as it had with Kenji. As he fell to his knees, Haruto held the black opal tightly in his hand as if it were his final moment of resistance against the encroaching darkness. Haruto could feel a presence trying to overtake him. Summoning the last of his strength, Haruto reached out with a trembling hand. His fingers brushed against the cold, lifeless hand of Kenji. This is how they would die, side by side, just as they had lived and fought.

A large raven landed near Kenji's head, its iridescent feathers shifting from deep black to subtle green with each movement. It hopped toward his hand, still clutching the Tora Katana, and began pecking at his fingers. Ryuji knelt down on one knee, removed his oni mask, and gently stroked the raven's feathers. The raven stopped pecking and turned its head toward Ryuji, as if to acknowledge his presence. Ryuji's eyes glowed a bright crimson as he stared at the remains of Haruto and Kenji, a smile spreading across his face. He bent over Haruto and yanked the talisman from his neck, the red thread snapping easily in his grip. Then, he knelt beside Kenji's lifeless body and pried his sword from his hand. The raven climbed up his knee and rested on his shoulder. Ryuji gazed into the polished blade of the Tora Katana—his reflection grinning back with a menacing smile.

CHAPTER EIGHT

TO CONQUER FATE

Thump, thump, thump... At first, it was subtle, then it grew louder and louder. *Where is it coming from?* he wondered. Then, he realized for the first time that it was his own heartbeat. He was alive. "Yurei, welcome home." The voice was soft like a whisper, gentle and soothing, yet familiar. The Loa Spirit spoke, "Yurei, you're back now. Don't open your eyes, just listen to my voice. You've been through a lot. It will take some time for everything to assimilate."

Yurei felt a deep, unfamiliar heaviness in his limbs, as if he were trying to move through water. His mind was foggy, filled with fragments of memories and sensations. He tried to focus on the voice, grounding himself in its calm presence. The Spirit spoke, "Yurei, there is something I must tell you. I promised you that I would always be by your side to protect you and watch over you, and I have. Yurei, it's me, Ayama, your mother. I am the Loa Spirit."

Yurei spoke in his thoughts, "Mother, why didn't you tell me before? All you said was that you were the Loa Spirit. Why did you keep this from me?" Ayama spoke in a soothing, gentle tone, "My son, before you experienced all that is Haruto, you would not have recognized me. That is why you hear me now as I truly am, your mother."

Yurei's voice trembled as he asked, "Mother, who am I now?" Ayama's presence seemed to surround him with warmth and comfort. "You are Yurei, but you also carry everything that Haruto has ever been—every experience, every emotion, every lesson. The soul of Haruto now resides in your physical form. You and Haruto are One. But it will take time for this to be completed."

"Mother, where is Kenji?" Yurei asked, his voice filled with a mix of hope and dread. The bond he shared with Kenji was profound, and the thought of his mentor being lost was almost too much to bear. Ayama's voice shifted slightly, as if the weight of her next words was too heavy even for her to bear. "I am sorry, my son," she began, her voice filled with sorrow. "But I could only save one of you. Kenji's soul is trapped inside the Shadow Blade, and only you can save him."

Yurei paused and then whispered, "How can I save him?" Ayama responded, "It will take a few days before you fully become one with Haruto. You will even look more like him as time passes. When the transformation is complete, you can help Kenji. But for now, you must gather your strength. When you are ready, I want you to take five deep breaths and then slowly open your eyes."

Yurei took a deep breath, counting silently to five before slowly opening his eyes. The view above him was a blur, and a familiar voice said, "Welcome back, Yurei!" He lay still for a moment before noticing something in his hand. As he slowly opened his palm, he saw a glistening black opal stone that suddenly shifted to a dark green and back to black again. He closed his hand firmly, feeling the warmth of the stone pulsing against his skin.

Aiko gently helped Yurei to his feet, her hands steadying him as he swayed, still overwhelmed by the weight of his new reality. She placed an arm around his waist, guiding him with a firm but gentle grip. The journey back to the cabin was slow, each step requiring a conscious effort from

Yurei as he adjusted to the new sensations coursing through his body. As they walked, the landscape around them seemed to blur and shift with each movement. Every now and then, Aiko would glance at him, her eyes filled with concern.

Upon reaching the cabin, Aiko opened the door and led Yurei inside. The air was filled with the comforting scent of herbs and incense, a familiar aroma that helped to ground Yurei in the moment. She guided him to a tatami mat she had set up ahead of time. She helped him sit down, and then gently eased him back until he was lying down. "Rest now," she said softly, adjusting the blankets around him. "You've been through a lot, and it's important to give your body and mind time to heal and absorb everything."

Yurei nodded weakly, his eyes closing as he sank into the comfort of the mat. The events of the past days, his merging with Haruto, the revelation from his mother, and the loss of Kenji. They all swirled in his mind like a chaotic storm. But here, in the safety of the cabin, he felt a small measure of peace begin to take root. He closed his eyes and rested his mind. As he lay there, he found himself drifting into a vision. He was standing in a vast, otherworldly landscape, the air vibrating with a golden light that seemed to pulse with a life of its own. The sky above was a shifting mosaic of swirling colors and broken fractals, hues of gold and crimson intermingling in a celestial dance. As he looked around, he saw a figure emerging from the radiant light. His heart skipped a beat as he recognized his mother, Ayama. She was surrounded by a warm, golden aura that seemed to flow from her very being. Her eyes sparkled with the same love and wisdom he remembered, and her presence brought a deep sense of peace to his heart.

She floated towards him, her movements gentle and graceful. When she spoke, her voice was a whispering echo, reverberating gently through the golden light. "My son," she began, her tone filled with tenderness, "when I crossed over, I chose to become a Loa Spirit so that I could remain by your side and protect you and save you from the darkness." Yurei listened intently, his emotions filled with longing and gratitude. The golden light around her seemed to intensify. "Mother, why did you kill yourself?" he whispered, his voice catching in his throat.

Ayama continued, her tone soothing and melodic. "It was the only way for me to avoid being trapped in the Shadow Blade. I realized that you and Kenji alone could not stop Ryuji. His power, fueled by the darkness of the Shadow Blade, was too great. You needed to be stronger, more resilient. I had a vision that you would pass, so I waited for you. I had to change your form. Ryuji, although a man, has become very powerful. But you, my son, with the combination of Haruto and Yurei, are more than a man."

Yurei's eyes widened with realization, the memory of his transformation flooding back. "You made me a vampire," he whispered, understanding growing in his heart. Ayama nodded, her expression sorrowful. "Yes, my son. It was the only way to save your soul from being trapped inside the Shadow Blade. The prophecy speaks of a 'child born of shadow and light.' I, your mother, carried the vampiric bloodline as a dhampir. Now that you carry the human soul of Haruto within you, you are also a dhampir, half human and half vampire. This means that you can live a very long time in the human world, but you cannot change others into vampires. You do, however, have the ability to travel between realms, which may be your greatest gift."

Ayama paused before continuing, allowing Yurei to absorb her words. "With your gifts as a vampire, Yurei, combined with the lessons of Haruto's life, you have the strength and abilities necessary to face Ryuji and fulfill the prophecy. It was a difficult decision, but one that had to be made to protect you and ensure you could achieve your destiny." Yurei felt a deep sense of gratitude, understanding the immense sacrifice his mother had made to protect him. "Thank you, Mother," he said, his voice filled with emotion. "I understand now. I will use this gift to honor your sacrifice and to defeat Ryuji."

Ayama's eyes softened, a mixture of pride and sadness in her gaze. "I know you will, my son. You have always had a strong heart, and now you have the power to match it. Remember, your journey is not just about defeating Ryuji, but also about understanding yourself and the balance you bring to the world." Yurei paused before speaking, his brow furrowing with a question that had haunted him. "Mother, when I faced Ryuji with Kenji, why couldn't I jump? It was the cause of his death!"

Ayama's expression grew serious, and she took a deep breath before answering. "Yurei, your inability to jump wasn't your fault. When you jump, you create a field of energy, forming a connection between time and space. But Ryuji, with his connection to the Shadow Blade, he may have disrupted that field. His dark power doesn't just affect the physical world—it interferes with the very fabric of energy that allows you to manipulate space."

She paused, her eyes locking onto Yurei's. "The Shadow Blade is more than a weapon; it's a bridge for a deeper force that distorts the natural flow of energy around it. In that moment, Ryuji may have used it to sever your link to the energy field, preventing you from jumping."

Ayama continued, "Regardless, you could not have defeated Ryuji as Haruto alone. It was your destiny to merge with him, combining his wisdom with your strength. Only together could you become powerful enough to face Ryuji. This transformation was necessary. Now, with your newfound abilities and the knowledge you possess, you are prepared to fulfill the prophecy and bring balance to our world... even if you cannot jump."

Yurei looked down, the weight of guilt still pressing on him. "But Kenji trusted me, and I failed him. How can I be sure I won't fail again?" Ayama spoke gently, "You won't fail, Yurei. You have grown stronger, and you have learned from your experiences. Trust in yourself and the training you have received. Kenji believed in you, and so do I. Let that belief guide you." She continued, "Remember the lessons Haruto imparted to you. You are not alone in this fight. You have the wisdom of those who came before you... and the strength of Aiko at your side."

"Mother, I have one last question."

Ayama nodded. "What is it, my son?"

"What happened to my brother Daichi?"

Ayama's form began to emit a soft glow.

"He volunteered as a samurai after you left the village. He said he wanted to defend his

home and find you one day. He is well and alive."

Before Yurei could reply, her voice echoed softly as it faded away. Over the next few days, Aiko tended to Yurei with unrelenting dedication. She encouraged him to take the time to meditate and connect with his new identity. The cabin became a sanctuary, a place where he could find solace and strength. When Yurei was feeling stronger, he began to practice martial arts and weapons training each day. The woods and its surrounding area provided the perfect sanctuary for his intense regimen.

Every morning at dawn, Yurei would rise with the first light to train his body and mind. He would start his day with a series of stretching exercises to limber up his muscles, ensuring that his body was ready for the rigorous challenges ahead. Each stretch was a ritual that connected him to his mentor. Standing barefoot on the cool grass, Yurei would begin with deep, controlled breaths, aligning his mind and body. He extended his arms upward, reaching for the sky, feeling the gentle pull in his muscles. His movements were slow and purposeful, each one designed to awaken different parts of his body.

He could feel the lessons from Kenji and Haruto flowing through his body, guiding and directing him. Kenji's teachings emphasized balance and precision, while Haruto's experiences added a layer of resilience and adaptability. As he moved through his stretches, Yurei's mind often drifted to memories of Kenji's patient instruction. He could hear his teacher's voice, calm and focused, correcting his form and encouraging him to push his limits. "Feel the earth beneath your feet, Haruto," Kenji would say. "Draw strength from it. Let it ground you."

Throughout his training, Aiko was a constant presence. Initially, she observed from a distance, her eyes filled with quiet curiosity. But soon, Yurei began to involve her more directly in his training sessions. He would call her over, demonstrating the finer points of combat techniques, explaining the philosophy behind each move and the importance of leverage, timing and technique. It was as if Kenji was speaking through him.

"Aiko," he would say, his voice calm and patient, "it's not just about strength. It's about understanding your opponent, anticipating their moves, and using their energy against them." He would have Aiko grab the collar of his kimono, guiding her through the motions with great care. "Okay, now reach your other hand around my waist. Good. Now, load me onto your hips." As she followed his instructions, Aiko lifted Yurei off the ground with surprising ease. "Now throw me!" he instructed.

Aiko executed the move, turning her hips in a circular motion and dropping Yurei into the dirt. The throw was quick and effective. Aiko proved to be an eager and attentive student. She mimicked Yurei's movements with precision, her natural grace and ability improving as she absorbed his teachings. Yurei took great care in correcting her stances, adjusting her grips, and refining her techniques. He was impressed by her quick learning and dedication.

During their training sessions, Yurei would often pause to offer detailed explanations that felt like Kenji's wisdom speaking directly through him. "Aiko, remember, it's ultimately about leverage. When you throw, it's not just about the strength in your arms. It's about how you use your entire body to create leverage and momentum." Aiko nodded, her eyes focused and determined. She repeated the move, this time with more confidence, her body flowing smoothly through the steps. Yurei observed her closely, making minor adjustments and offering encouragement. "Good, that's much better. You're getting the hang of it."

As the training wound down, they sat together in the grass, their bodies glistening with sweat from the intense session. The sun, just below the horizon, cast long shadows on the ground before them. Yurei looked at Aiko, his expression filled with pride. "I'm feeling more confident than ever in my ability to face Ryuji and the Shadow Blade." Aiko turned to him, "You have grown so much, Yurei. Your strength and skill are undeniable. Together, we can overcome this darkness."

Yurei smiled, "Something came to me when I woke up this morning."

Aiko, her curiosity aroused, asked, "What is it, Yurei?"

Yurei quickly responded, "I remember where the Jade Sword is located."

Yurei and Aiko began packing supplies for their journey to secure the Jade Sword and find Ryuji and the Shadow Blade, their movements filled with a sense of urgency. The cabin, usually a place of tranquility and rest, buzzed with newfound energy as they prepared for the journey ahead. Aiko went about collecting specific herbs and magic items from her shelves in the cabin. The cabin was a reflection of her gathered knowledge; each shelf was lined with carefully labeled jars filled with dried herbs and enchanted talismans.

Yurei packed his weapon, a sword that Kenji had given him. The katana held deep significance, not just as a weapon but as a symbol of their shared journey and the sacrifices made along the way. Yurei handled it with reverence, feeling the power it represented. The blade was sharp, its edge glowing golden-yellow in the light—a testament to Kenji's meticulous care. Yurei then carefully slid the katana into its scabbard, positioning it across his back.

As Yurei finished packing the katana, he turned to see Aiko preparing her own weapons with equal care. She selected a small katana called a wakizashi, its blade shorter but just as deadly. The hilt was intricately wrapped in dark leather, providing a secure grip. Aiko tested its balance, swinging it gracefully through the air before sheathing it with a satisfied nod.

In addition to her katana, Aiko carried two daggers, each hidden within the wide sleeves of her kimono. In her hand, she held her trusted walking stick, a gift from a dear friend. The stick was crafted from resilient hardwood, polished smooth and reinforced with metal bands for strength. At its top, a talisman dangled—a collection of feathers, beads, and a small animal's skull that swayed with each step she took. Aiko finished packing her horse, tightening the last strap and making sure all the supplies were secure. She turned to Yurei, a mischievous look in her eyes. "Yurei, I have a surprise for you," she said, her voice carrying a hint of excitement.

Yurei looked up, curious about what Aiko had in store. He watched as she walked behind the cabin, disappearing from view for a moment. The suspense built as he waited, wondering what she could possibly be hiding. Then, he heard the unmistakable sound of hooves on the ground, and his heart skipped a beat. Aiko emerged from behind the cabin, leading a magnificent horse. The horse's coat gleamed in the sunlight. Yurei's breath caught in his throat as he recognized the animal immediately.

"Tsuki, it's you!" Yurei exclaimed, his voice filled with a mixture of surprise and joy. Tsuki, neighed softly in response, her ears flicking forward as she recognized her old friend. Yurei stepped forward, his hand reaching out to stroke Tsuki's neck. The horse nuzzled against him, her warm breath a comforting reminder of the bond they shared. He felt a surge of emotion and memories flooding back.

"Thank you, Aiko. This means a lot to me!"

Yurei smiled as he stroked Kenji's old friend.

"Do you know what happened to my horse, Kumo?"

Aiko looked down. "I'm sorry, but I think she's gone."

Yurei nodded, then smiled and patted Tsuki.

"I'm grateful to have this old friend here. How did you find Tsuki?"

Aiko smiled. "I didn't; she found you. Tsuki has always had a strong connection with you. When your heart awakened, I believe she felt it and followed your pulse back to you." Yurei placed his hand on Tsuki and gently rubbed her neck. "I'm glad you found me, old friend." Tsuki shook her head and nudged him. Yurei looked at Aiko and asked, "Which way do we travel?"

Then his mother, Ayama, the Loa Spirit spoke in his mind. "I have another surprise for you. Look up." Yurei looked up at the vast blue sky, his eyes following the graceful sweeping circles of a hawk. The bird's powerful wings cut through the air with ease. As the hawk soared higher, his sharp eyes scanned the landscape below, ever vigilant. His feathers glistened in the sunlight. "Kaze," Yurei whispered, his voice filled with awe and reverence. Kaze circled above them, his sharp, piercing call—half squawk, half cry—echoing through the air. Yurei's mother spoke reassuringly, "Kaze will be your trusted guide."

Aiko looked at Yurei and enthusiastically asked, "Where are we headed?" Yurei looked up at Kaze and declared, "We're going to Kenji's valley!" They set out with Yurei riding Tsuki and Aiko on her black horse, Kuroguma, whose name meant "black bear." Tsuki moved with a graceful, steady pace, her ears flicking forward attentively. Yurei sat tall in the saddle, his eyes scanning the surroundings, always on alert.

Beside him, Aiko rode on Kuroguma, with his glossy black coat and powerful build he moved with a quiet strength and confidence. The horse's name, "black bear," was a testament to his formidable size and the fierce loyalty he had towards Aiko. As they rode, Kaze circled above them, his keen eyes ever watchful. The hawk's presence was a constant reminder of the guidance and protection that Ayama had promised. Every now and then, Kaze would swoop lower, his vision scanning the path ahead and the forest surrounding them.

They rode through lush forests and across vast landscapes, the journey a mix of breathtaking beauty and arduous travel. Aiko rode in the warmth of the sun, while Yurei carefully stayed within the shadows of the tree canopy. As the day wore on, and the sun began its descent behind the distant mountains. The air grew cooler, and the light took on a softer, warmer hue. Yurei and Aiko knew they needed to find a place to camp for the night before darkness fell completely.

As they rode over the crest of a hill, they spotted a lustrous stream below, its waters clear and sparkling in the fading light. "This looks like a good spot," Yurei said, pointing towards the stream. "We'll have fresh water for the horses." Aiko nodded in agreement. "Let's set up camp here," she said, guiding Kuroguma down the gentle slope towards the stream.

They dismounted and led their horses to the water's edge, allowing them to drink their fill. Afterward, they set up a temporary camp and built a small fire. Yurei and Aiko sat cross-legged on their tatami mats, their eyes lifted to the heavens, captivated by the sheer beauty of the night sky. It was a rare moment of tranquility amidst the storm they were facing, a chance to connect with the universe and reflect on their journey.

"The stars are so bright tonight," Aiko whispered, her voice filled with awe. "It's like they're guiding us, showing us the way." Yurei nodded, feeling a deep sense of connection to the cosmos. "They remind us that we're part of something much larger," he said softly. "That our journey, our struggles, are all part of something greater." Aiko smiled warmly, her eyes reflecting the light of the fire. "Everything happens for a reason, Yurei." He nervously smiled. "I know." Yurei felt a wave of energy surging through his body, a sensation that had become more frequent recently whenever he was near Aiko. It was as if her presence awakened something deep within him, stirring emotions and memories that had long been dormant.

He turned to Aiko, his expression serious yet filled with an intensity he couldn't quite explain. "Look at me," he said, his voice soft but insistent. She looked at him, her expression calm and comforting. "I am," she replied. "No, look me in the eye," Yurei urged, his voice carrying a deeper, almost pleading tone. Aiko turned to meet his gaze, her eyes surrendering to his.

There was a moment of silence between them, the air thick with unspoken emotions. "Aiko, I am having these powerful feelings," his voice trembling slightly.

Before he could say more, Aiko placed a gentle finger on his lips, silencing him with a tender gesture. "Shh," she whispered, her touch soft. She leaned forward and gently kissed him on the cheek, her lips warm and comforting against his cold skin. In that moment, Yurei felt a powerful wave of love and memories pass through his body. The sensation was overwhelming, a flood of emotions that brought tears to his eyes. He closed them for a moment, letting the feelings wash over him. When he opened his eyes, the words slipped out before he could stop them. "Rumiko?"

"Yes, Haruto, it's me, Rumiko," she said softly, her voice carrying the weight of years of longing and separation. Yurei felt a rush of confusion and emotion. "I don't understand, how?" he asked, his voice trembling with disbelief. Rumiko leaned in closer, her eyes reflecting the firelight with a tenderness that spoke volumes. "Before you became one with Haruto, you looked very different." She explained gently.

Yurei, struggling to process the revelation. Rumiko responded, "But I must confess, I was having feelings even then. But over the past few days you began to look like Haruto." She smiled, a warm, knowing smile that seemed to bridge the gap of time and space between them. "The truth of our love had bled through," she said. "Our souls were always entangled, even when we didn't fully understand it."

"Did you know it was me the whole time?" Yurei asked, his voice filled with wonder. Rumiko nodded, her eyes filled with unshed tears. "No, Haruto, but I have always been looking for you. When you left the village, your mother, Ayama, saved me. She became my tutor and taught me her secrets. After a short while I left the village, cutting my hair and assuming a new identity, all in search of you, my one true love."

She paused, taking a deep breath before continuing. "I studied the stars, mastering the ancient arts Ayama had imparted to me. Every night, I held a ceremony in the woods, hoping to attract you, to call you back to me. Your mother, as a Loa Spirit, guided you to me. That is how you found me that first night, Yurei. Our love had seeped through, transcending time and space."

Yurei felt a surge of memories and emotions, a flood of images and sensations that clarified the deep connection he had always felt but could never fully explain. He remembered the nights spent wandering, feeling an inexplicable pull towards a destiny he couldn't yet name. He now understood that it was Rumiko and his mother, guiding him, calling him back.

"When I first saw you," he began, his voice thick with emotion, "I felt something I couldn't explain. A familiarity, a sense of belonging. It all makes sense now." Rumiko reached out, the back of her hand gently caressing his cheek. "I felt it too," she whispered. "The moment I saw you, I knew. Our souls recognized each other, even if our minds didn't. The bond we share is ancient and unbreakable."

Tears welled in Yurei's eyes as he realized the depth of their connection, the profound love that had endured through so much hardship and change. "I can't believe it's really you," he said, his voice just a whisper. Rumiko nodded, her own eyes glistening with tears. "It's me, and I'm here with you now. We've found each other again, and nothing can separate us this time."

Rumiko smiled. "I have to ask you, do you want to be called Yurei or Haruto?" He smiled and laughed. "For now, Yurei, but I guess we can decide when this is all over. How about you, Aiko or Rumiko?" She laughed. "Rumiko sounds refreshing!"

They embraced, holding each other tightly, their hearts beating in unison. The world around them seemed to fade away, leaving only the two of them and the love that bound their souls together. For a long moment, they stayed like that, basking in the warmth of their reunion. When they finally pulled apart, Yurei looked into Rumiko's eyes, seeing the depth of her love.

"What do we do now?" he asked.

Rumiko smiled, a fierce light in her eyes.

"We face whatever comes next, together, forever."

Yurei nodded, feeling a renewed sense of purpose and strength.

"Together, forever." Yurei leaned over, placing his hand gently behind Rumiko's head, his fingers brushing against her short silken strands of hair, and kissed her. He could feel the coldness of his skin fading as he connected with her, the warmth of her lips igniting a spark that chased away the lingering chill within him. He then climbed on top of her and slowly pressed his lips to her neck, feeling her heartbeat resonate with his own.

The warmth of his breath lingered at her collar as his lips brushed against the delicate vessels tracing down her neck toward her chest. Deep, satisfying love now replaced the temptation of hunger. There was no desire to take anything more from Rumiko, but only to remain in this shared moment of connection. Rumiko whispered into his ear, "Be one with me, Haruto... Yurei. I am yours." Rumiko wrapped her arms around Yurei's waist, sliding her hands under his kimono and pulling him in closer, her nails digging firmly into his back. With a deep exhale he let his hips fall forward, his body pressing deeply into Rumiko. It was an unbreakable connection, their hearts beating in perfect unison.

For the first time, they became one... a bond that transcended time and space. Their souls were now entwined, bound together for eternity. They lay unclothed on a single tatami mat, the fire casting a warm, faint glow over their entwined forms. Yurei gently wiped away the beads of sweat trickling down Rumiko's back. He cradled her in his arms, her body fitting seamlessly against his, as though they were two halves of a whole.

Yurei could feel the gentle rise and fall of Rumiko's chest as she breathed, each breath a soothing rhythm that calmed his own racing heart. They lay together for many hours, their bodies nestled under the blanket of the night sky, the fire gradually dying down to glowing embers. Yurei held

Rumiko close, savoring the warmth and closeness they had found again. His breathing matched hers, slow and rhythmic.

As the night deepened and the forest grew quiet Rumiko began to stir. At first, it was a slight movement, her body tensing and then relaxing again. But soon, her stirring became more pronounced, and she began to whimper softly in her sleep. "No, Haruto, no," her voice filled with distress. The sound pierced through the quiet of the night, making Yurei's heart clench with worry. He held her tighter, hoping to soothe her with his presence, but her crying continued.

"Please, no, Haruto stop, get off me" she repeated, her voice growing more urgent, more desperate. Yurei's own heart pounded in his chest as he watched her struggle against the invisible torment of her dreams. He gently brushed her hair back from her face, whispering her name softly, trying to bring her back to the present. "Rumiko, it's okay. I'm here. Wake up, my love."

Her eyes finally opened, wide and filled with tears. She looked around, disoriented, before focusing on Yurei's concerned face. Tears filled her eyes as she lay trembling in Yurei's arms. "Rumiko, what's wrong?" Yurei asked urgently, his voice filled with concern and love. He tightened his embrace, trying to offer her comfort and security. Through her tears, Rumiko struggled to speak. "Something terrible is going to happen," she sobbed, her voice breaking with fear. "I saw it in my dream. Someone will die, Yurei."

A cold dread settled in Yurei's chest at her words. Gently, he cupped her face, wiping away her tears with his thumbs. "Rumiko, I heard you say, 'Get off me, Haruto, stop.' Was I hurting you?" he asked, his voice heavy with turmoil. Rumiko took a long, deep breath, trying to compose herself enough to explain. "In my dream, I saw a great darkness falling over us. There was a battle, and I could sense the presence of something evil, something powerful. I saw you, bravely trying to stop the darkness, but... but someone was struck down. I couldn't see who it was."

Yurei reached into his kimono lying nearby and retrieved the black opal stone his mother had given him. It was tied to a new cord he had added so he could wear it securely around his neck. The opal stone caught the moonlight, radiating with an inner glow that seemed almost alive. Yurei cradled the stone, his fingers tracing its contours, feeling the power it held. He turned to Rumiko, who lay beside him, her eyes wide with curiosity and a lingering hint of fear from her dream. Leaning closer, his voice gentle, Yurei said, "This stone means a lot to me. My mother, Ayama, gave it to me, and it has protected me through many trials."

Rumiko's eyes followed his movements, her expression filled with awe. Yurei carefully placed the necklace over her head, letting the black opal rest against her heart. The coolness of the stone seemed to soothe her, and she closed her eyes briefly, feeling its calming energy. "I want you to wear this," Yurei continued, his voice soothing. "It will protect you, just as it has protected me. It carries my mother's blessing. With this talisman, you will be safe."

Rumiko opened her eyes, tears settling at the corners. She reached up, touching the stone gently, feeling the smooth surface. "Yurei," she whispered, her voice filled with emotion. "Thank you. I will cherish this and keep it close to my heart." Yurei held Rumiko as she fell back to sleep, her breathing evening out as she found comfort in his embrace. He listened to the steady rhythm of her heartbeat, feeling a profound sense of peace and protectiveness wash over him. After some time, Yurei carefully slipped out of Rumiko's arms, ensuring she remained undisturbed. He tucked the covering around her, making sure she was warm and comfortable. Standing up, he stretched slightly, feeling the tension of the day's events and the emotional weight of their reunion.

He turned his attention to Kaze, who was perched on a nearby tree, the hawk's vigilant eyes watching over them. Yurei approached the tree, his movements silent. "Kaze," he whispered, looking up at the hawk. "Watch over her. I need to hunt." Kaze shook his beak from side to side, acknowledging Yurei's instructions. He let out a soft, affirming cry, his eyes flicking back to Rumiko. Yurei felt a surge of gratitude for the loyal bird's presence.

The hunger burning inside Yurei was becoming unbearable, a gnawing emptiness that he had been ignoring for days. He knew he needed to fulfill this hunger to maintain his strength and focus for the trials ahead. The transformation his mother had bestowed upon him required regular feeding, and he had pushed it to the brink. Moving quietly, Yurei slipped into the nearby forest, the shadows surrounding him as he ventured deeper into the trees. The forest was alive with the soft sounds of nightly creatures.

Yurei's senses sharpened as he moved through the trees, his eyes adjusting to the low light. His heightened senses, a gift of his vampiric nature, allowed him to see clearly even in the darkness. As he stalked through the forest, Yurei focused on the hunt. His hunger was not just a physical need; it was a primal urge that demanded satisfaction. He moved with the grace and precision of a predator, every step calculated and silent. His crimson eyes scanned the forest floor, looking for signs of potential prey.

It didn't take long for Yurei to catch the scent of a deer, a young buck grazing in a small clearing. He crouched low, his movements slow and silent as he approached. The deer, unaware of his presence, continued to nibble on the tall grass. Yurei could hear the steady beat of its heart, the rhythm syncing with his own. For a moment, he heard a second heartbeat, even more powerful than the deer's. Confused, he glanced around but saw no other animals nearby. He brushed off the sensation and focused on the hunt.

The buck barely had time to react before Yurei's hands closed around its neck, his strength overwhelming. He whispered a silent apology to the creature. The bite was quick and efficient, his fangs sinking into the deer's neck. Warm blood filled his mouth, the metallic taste both satisfying and energizing. Yurei drank deeply, feeling the hunger inside him abate as the blood filled him with renewed strength. He drank until the deer's heart stopped, then gently laid the lifeless body on the ground.

Yurei knelt beside the deer, placing a hand on its still-warm body as he took a moment to honor its life. He acknowledged the sacrifice it had made, offering silent gratitude for the nourishment it would provide. Wiping his mouth with the back of his hand, Yurei felt the warmth of the deer's blood surging through his veins, revitalizing him. The gnawing hunger that had consumed him moments before was gone, replaced by a deep sense of fullness and strength.

He rose to his feet, feeling more connected to the earth and his surroundings. The forest, once distant and quiet, now pulsed with life. Every rustle of leaves, every shift in the breeze, seemed charged with energy. His senses sharpened, attuning to a heartbeat that grew louder with each passing second.

Suddenly, a rustling sound nearby snapped his attention to the left. Yurei turned his head sharply, eyes narrowing and turning a crimson red. Emerging from the brush, a massive brown bear charged toward him, its powerful body crashing through the undergrowth with alarming speed. Instinctively, Yurei's body tensed, adrenaline flooding his system as he prepared to face the oncoming beast.

The bear let out a guttural roar as it leaped through the air, its powerful claws extended, aiming directly at Yurei. In an instant, the beast was upon him, its enormous weight crashing down with overwhelming force. Yurei was knocked onto his back, the impact driving the breath from his lungs. Instinctively, he raised his legs, bracing them against the bear's chest as it snarled and snapped, its massive jaws dangerously close. Every muscle in Yurei's body strained as he tried to keep the creature at bay, using the strength of his legs to push against the bear's crushing weight. He could feel his legs beginning to weaken under the bear's immense size, the strain becoming too much.

Just as despair began to creep in, Yurei heard a familiar voice—soft yet commanding, cutting through the chaos. It was Ayama, his mother, the Loa Spirit, her words echoing in his mind with clarity and urgency: "Yurei, jump!" In his mind, he saw Rumiko lying asleep by the campfire. A surge of her love coursed through him, and suddenly, he vanished from beneath the bear, reappearing beside Rumiko.

Yurei found Rumiko still peacefully asleep, the opal necklace resting against her chest. He took a deep breath of gratitude, relieved to have escaped the bear and to know that he could, in fact, jump. He glanced over at Kaze, who was perched on his branch, eyes surveying the surroundings. Yurei gave the hawk a grateful nod to be back once again. He wiped the bear's saliva from his face and let out a sigh of relief before nestling next to Rumiko. Wrapping his arms around her, he pulled her close. The warmth of her body and the steady rhythm of her heartbeat soothed his soul. He knew that together, they could face any challenge. With his hunger satisfied and his strength renewed, he felt ready to protect Rumiko and fulfill their mission. He was eager to share with her the return of his ability to jump.

Yurei wondered if this was his final assimilation with Haruto's soul. They awoke the next day with a renewed sense of purpose as they broke down their camp. Kaze took to the sky and they followed her lead. As Rumiko mounted her horse, Yurei placed a gentle hand on her back. "Hold on, Rumiko. There's something I need to tell you." Rumiko turned to him, concern building in her eyes. "What's wrong, Yurei?"

He smiled, his eyes bright with excitement. "Nothing's wrong. It's just... there's something I never told you. It's an ability that I had when I was Haruto, but I was always afraid to share it." Rumiko frowned, unsure. "I don't understand. What do you mean?" Yurei continued, "When I was Haruto, I had the ability to move my body from one spot to another almost instantly. I've always been able to do it, but with Kenji's training, I learned to do it in a flash. Then, something happened, and my ability stopped working."

Rumiko tilted her head to the side with a look of confusion. "For the first time, I think I understand," Yurei said, his expression intense. "It's you. You're the connection."

"Me?" Rumiko asked, looking bewildered. "What are you saying?" Yurei gently held Rumiko's hands, his stare unyielding. "Just stay right here," he instructed, his voice calm yet filled with anticipation. Slowly, he began stepping back, creating a growing distance between them. He counted under his breath, his eyes never leaving hers. At the count of ten, he paused, standing across the open space. Turning to face her fully, he called out, "Now, when I focus on you... watch what happens."

He stared at her eyes for a heartbeat, then gave a subtle nod and smile. In an instant, Yurei vanished from her line of sight, dissolving into thin air. Rumiko's eyes widened, searching in shock. Before she could catch her breath, she felt a familiar presence just behind her. Spinning around, she found Yurei standing only a step away, his smile warming her face. He leaned in and kissed her softly.

Rumiko wrapped her arms tightly around him, and as they slowly parted, their eyes met, filled with unspoken affection. Yurei softly murmured, "You are the light that guides my path." Rumiko smiled, her cheeks tinged with warmth, and replied, "And you are my light."

She then playfully pushed him back. "Hey, is this how you always beat me to our secret meeting spot?" They both burst into laughter, their voices echoing in the quiet space around them. Yurei smiled, his heart swelling with pride. "It feels like everything is falling back into place. I've missed the power to jump—it's a part of me, of who I am."

Rumiko gazed at him for a moment, then pulled him into a tight embrace. "I am so happy you found your strength again." Yurei smiled, "Your love fuels my strength."

"Let's go," Yurei said, his voice filled with conviction. He mounted Tsuki, adjusting his pack and ensuring that his katana was securely strapped to his back. Rumiko nodded, her eyes shining with determination. She mounted Kuroguma, feeling the powerful muscles of her horse beneath her. With a final check of their gear, they were ready to set off. Kaze led the way, his form a graceful silhouette against the brightening sky. Yurei and

Rumiko followed, their horses moving in unison. Though Yurei was in the shadows, the clear morning light illuminated the way. It was time to head to Kenji's valley and secure the Jade Sword once and for all.

CHAPTER NINE

AGAINST THE SHADOW

As they emerged from the forest, they were greeted by the sight of vast hills and meadows, bathed in the golden light of the rising sun. The sky was a brilliant blue, dotted with fluffy white clouds that drifted lazily overhead. It was a day filled with promise and hope. Kaze flew ahead, his vigilant eyes guiding them with unwavering precision. Yurei and Rumiko kept their focus on the hawk, trusting his instincts and the guidance of their ancestors. They rode at a steady pace, their minds fixed on the task ahead. Yurei remained careful to stay under cover, while Rumiko and Kuroguma basked in the morning light.

The journey took them across vast fields, the tall grasses swaying gently in the breeze, creating a sea of green that stretched out in every direction. Yurei and Rumiko rode in silence. As they reached the edge of the vast open field, the atmosphere began to shift. The bright, open sky above them seemed to dim, and a chill crept into the air. The vibrant green of the fields gave way to the shadowy outline of a dark forest ahead.

Yurei pulled Tsuki to a stop, his eyes focused on the tall, dark trees that loomed before him. The air around them felt heavier, charged with a strange energy that set his nerves on edge. Rumiko's horse, Kuroguma, suddenly reared up, sensing something unseen—a presence, like an invisible wall that seemed to repel them from entering the forest. Suddenly, Haruto's mother, the Loa Spirit, spoke to Yurei, her voice a soft whisper in his mind, "Kenji protected the valley with a shield of powerful spiritual energy. This forest is the first line of defense. It is imbued with the echoes of the past, a place where lost regrets and unfinished business linger."

Yurei listened intently, understanding the weight of her words. "To reach the valley, you must face what lies within these woods. Yurei, you may not be affected due to your dhampir blood, but Rumiko will be. The forest will test her resolve, conjuring visions of her deepest fears and regrets. Only by confronting them can you both pass through and reach the valley beyond." Yurei then asked, "Why can't I go alone and leave Rumiko here to wait for me?"

His mother's voice softened with a hint of warning. "The Forest of Lost Regrets is a place of profound magic, Yurei. It is not just a barrier but a trial by fire. If you go alone, the forest will not allow you to return the same way, and Rumiko would be left vulnerable and unprotected, prey to the forest's dark forces. The only way forward is together. Rumiko must face her past and her fears, or she will never be able to move forward. You must guide her, but she must take these steps on her own. This journey is as much hers as it is yours."

Yurei knew she was right; it was the only way to get the Jade Sword, end this madness with Ryuji, and save Kenji. He explained the situation to Rumiko, who understood and was ready to face the challenge together. As they stood at the edge of the forest, feeling the invisible force pushing them back, Yurei realized that physical strength alone wouldn't be enough. The forest's defenses were the result of Kenji's protective magic, designed to keep out intruders and safeguard the valley.

Determined, Yurei approached the forest's boundary once more, this time extending his hand slowly toward the invisible barrier. As his fingertips made contact, a ripple of energy surged through the air. The invisible wall gave way under the pressure of Yurei's hand, and he felt an opening forming in the barrier. The air shifted slightly, signaling that the forest was granting them passage.

"We can enter now," Yurei said, turning to Rumiko with a look of caution. "Stay close to me." Together, they stepped into the forest, the pathway closing behind them almost as soon as they passed through. The tall thick trees seemed to close in, and the shadows around them deepened. They guided Tsuki and Kurogumo through the narrow opening, the horses moving hesitantly at first. Yurei whispered soothing words to Tsuki, and Rumiko did the same for Kurogumo, urging them forward. Kaze, the hawk, soared overhead, gliding effortlessly above the tree canopy, untouched by the forest's dark magic.

As they ventured deeper into the woods, the air grew colder. The trees seemed to loom closer, their twisted branches reaching out like grasping hands. It was then that Yurei heard the voice of Ayama, the Loa Spirit in his head, "Mount your horses and stay close together." Yurei glanced at Rumiko and pointed to the horses. They quickly mounted Tsuki and Kurogumo, pulling their reins tight as they rode side by side.

As they moved through the forest, Kurogumo suddenly halted, his ears pointing forward as he stared intently at a dense wall of thorny vines that seemed to have sprung up out of nowhere, blocking their path. The vines were thick and dark, their sharp thorns glistening with what looked like drops of blood. Rumiko turned to look back at Yurei, but to her horror, he was nowhere in sight. Panic surged through her as she whipped her head from side to side, frantically searching for him, but he had vanished without a trace.

Just then, her attention was hypnotically drawn to the figure of a little girl running behind a nearby tree. The girl's movements were quick, as if she were more shadow than substance. Rumiko felt a strange pull toward the child and instinctively turned Kurogumo in the girl's direction. "Hey, you!" Rumiko called out, her voice trembling. The only response was a soft, mischievous giggle that echoed through the trees.

Rumiko dismounted her horse and tied him securely to a tree. She then turned toward the sound of the giggling and began to walk cautiously in its direction. "Please don't run, I just want to ask you a question," she called out. As she followed the girl deeper into the woods, Rumiko felt an inexplicable pull of invisible hands guiding her. She watched as the little girl climbed into a large open tree stump.

Suddenly a female voice echoed through the forest, "Ru-mi-ko!" There was something hauntingly familiar about it, a tone that tugged at the edges of her memory. Rumiko's heart pounded as she strained to listen, her breath catching in her throat. Then it hit her—the voice was unmistakably her mother's. A flood of emotions poured over her, a mixture of longing, sadness, and fear. *How could this be?* Her mother had been gone for years, lost in a violent encounter that still haunted Rumiko.

Without thinking, she sprinted toward them, her feet barely touching the ground as she ran. "Mother! Father!" she cried out, her voice choked with emotion. But as she reached them, something strange happened. They didn't react to her presence. They remained still, their eyes staring into the distance as if they didn't even see her. Rumiko's heart sank, confusion and fear pulling at her as she reached out to embrace her mother. But the moment she touched her, Rumiko's hands passed through her mother's body, as if she were made of mist. She stumbled forward, her arms grasping at nothing, and fell to her knees in the grass.

Rumiko's breath caught in her throat as she realized what was happening. The scene before her was not just an illusion but a replay of a memory she had long buried—a memory from her childhood, from a day she had tried so hard to forget. She had been walking back from the fields with her mother when they saw two men on horses approaching their home in the distance. Rumiko's mother paused, then pushed Rumiko behind her to hide. Crouching down nervously, she whispered, "Let's play a game. I want you to go back into the woods and hide until I find you." She gave Rumiko a gentle shove. "Go now! Hurry and hide, but promise me you won't come out until I find you." Rumiko nodded enthusiastically.

She ran deep into the woods, clutching her doll tightly, and hid inside a large tree stump. She sat there for hours until, finally, she heard her father's voice calling her name in a low whisper, "Rumiko, where are you?" She was shocked when she saw his face—swollen and red, his mouth still bleeding. "Where is Mother?" she pleaded, but her father only bowed his head in shame. The scene shifted, and she had a vision of two men dragging her mother away as she screamed. Her father remained outside, hiding, covering his face, and weeping.

The images around her suddenly dissolved like mist, fading away as if they had never existed. Rumiko blinked, disoriented, and found herself standing in the familiar warmth of her grandmother's home. She was no longer an adult, but a little girl once more, her heart heavy with the fresh grief of losing her mother. The room smelled of cedar wood and the faint aroma of her grandmother's herbal tea, a scent that always brought her comfort.

She looked up to see her grandmother, a figure of strength and kindness, bending down to meet her at eye level. Rumiko felt her small hand being gently cradled in the warm, comforting grasp of her grandmother's weathered fingers. "Rumiko," her grandmother said, her voice tender, "your grandfather and I will be taking care of you now." She handed Rumiko her doll and said, "Now go outside and make some friends!"

In an instant, Rumiko found herself no longer a small child but a teenager, standing alone with Haruto at their secret meeting place. The memory was so vivid, it was as though she had been transported back to that very night. She watched in horror as the black sludge of the Kurokawa consumed her body. Rumiko could feel the fear and panic of that night as if she were reliving it all over again. Her chest tightened, and her vision dimmed. She remembered the helplessness, the terror of feeling her life slip away. She saw Haruto bravely climbing on top of her to save her life, only to be carried away by the guards and thrown into a jail cell. She could feel the weight of Haruto's absence.

The vision shifted, and Rumiko found herself in a time after Haruto had left. She saw herself in a vision, with Hana, Ayama by her side. Ayama was kneeling close, carefully administering a handful of herbs that brought her back from the Kurokawa's dark sleep. Her voice was a soft, urgent whisper as she leaned closer, eyes filled with worry. Ayama spoke softly, "You are not safe here," her words heavy with fear. "You must leave the village before it's too late." Rumiko watched as she lay there, vulnerable and confused, struggling to process the urgency in Ayama's voice. She saw herself nodding faintly, the weight of Ayama's warning sinking in like a spear in her chest.

Her presence was a beacon of light in a dark time, her guidance both a comfort and a lifeline. With every instruction, Ayama imparted not just knowledge but also the courage Rumiko would need to survive beyond the safety of her home. Rumiko watched, both as an observer and a participant, reliving the moment when her world had changed forever.

She saw herself meeting Ayama in secret. Her mentors voice was firm as she shared with Rumiko what she knew—how to move unseen, where to find refuge, and the ways to protect herself from those who would do her harm. She watched as Ayama came upon her with her familiar "crooked walk" and long gnarled stick in hand to support herself. Each leg was an effort as she slowly advanced forward.

But as Ayama drew nearer, her gait transformed. The heavy steps became light, each stride fluid and effortless, as if she were shedding her years with each step. Rumiko watched as Ayama handed her the walking stick. Ayama smiled, "I want you to take this with you on your journey's." Rumiko interrupted, "Don't you need your stick to walk?" Ayama laughed, "Some things are not as they seem."

Rumiko's heart swelled with emotion as she relived these moments, but before she could speak, a soft rustling to her side caught her attention.

She turned to see Yurei standing next to her, a gentle smile on his face, his presence grounding her in the moment. He nodded reassuringly, as if to encourage her to listen to the vision before them.

Rumiko turned her attention back to Ayama, the vision of her mentor glowing softly in the dim light of the forest. "Rumiko," Ayama's voice was gentle, yet it carried a weight of wisdom and love, "you have come so far, and you've faced so much. Remember the lessons I taught you, and trust in your strength. The path ahead is difficult, but you are not alone. I will always be here for you. You have the power to overcome your fears and fulfill your destiny. The death of your mother was a tragedy, but it does not define you. Her love, her sacrifices, have shaped you into the strong and resilient woman you are today. Let her memory guide you, but do not let it hold you back. You are destined for greatness, Yurei and Kenji need you to be strong."

As Ayama's words resonated within her, Rumiko felt a flood of warmth and courage. The heaviness in her heart began to lift, replaced by a renewed sense of purpose. The image of Ayama slowly dissolved into mist, her reassuring smile the last to fade away. Suddenly, the thick forest canopy overhead parted, allowing a stream of sunlight to pierce through the gloom and bathe the forest floor in a golden glow. Ahead of them, the forest opened, revealing the entrance to Kenji's valley.

Yurei looked out over the valley, his heart heavy with sadness. The once lush and vibrant landscape was now a scorched, barren expanse of land. The trees that had once stood tall and proud were reduced to blackened stumps. The fields, once filled with wildflowers and green grass, were now a desolate wasteland, the soil charred and lifeless. Everything that Kenji had created was gone, reduced to ashes.

Yurei rode next to Rumiko across the blackened soil, their horses' hooves stirring up small clouds of soot with each step. The silence was heavy, broken only by the distant, mournful cry of Kaze as he circled above. Yurei turned to Rumiko and pointed ahead as they rode. "It's back here, behind where the cabin once stood," he said. Rumiko followed closely on Kuroguma as they approached a stony hillside. Yurei pulled the reins on Tsuki, bringing her to a stop, and then dismounted. He scanned the hillside, his eyes searching for a series of stones that marked the spot where the Jade Sword was hidden.

Yurei began counting the stones, tracing their edges with his fingers as he carefully moved in different directions. He began counting under his breath, "One... two... three... four." Finally, he paused, his hand hovering over a particular stone. "Right here, this is it," he said, his voice filled with relief. Yurei removed a small rock from the hillside, revealing a flat stone beneath it. He pressed down on the flat stone, feeling it give way slightly under the pressure. The stone shifted, and with a faint click, the mechanism engaged, causing a nearby rock to slide open. Yurei reached into the hidden compartment and carefully pulled out the leather scabbard. He slowly removed the Jade Sword, the stone embedded in the handle was covered in a layer of dust. He then reached in again and retrieved a jade ring that had been tucked inside.

Yurei wiped the ring on his kimono, clearing away the cloud of dust that had settled on it. Slowly, he placed the ring onto his left hand, watching as the metal adjusted and adapted to slide over his thick finger. Rumiko stood silently, watching him. As Yurei held the sword in his hand, the jade stone on his left ring finger began to vibrate and flicker, resonating with the energy of the sword. The gentle vibration traveled through his hand, filling him with a sense of connection to his memories of Kenji. He remembered standing here with Kenji just hours before they both would die at the hands of Ryuji. The anger built inside him, simmering like a storm ready to break.

Sensing his turmoil, Rumiko placed her hand on Yurei's shoulder and said softly, "It will be okay, Yurei. We will stop Ryuji and save Kenji's soul. I promise you, we will make things right." Yurei nodded as he stared at the Jade Sword, "Let's find Ryuji!" Yurei strapped the Jade Sword to Tsuki and rode toward the edge of the forest. As they reached the dense tree line, he paused and looked around one last time before heading into the thick woods. Kaze circled overhead, his persistent cries echoing through the air as if calling out to the spirits of his brother Yume and his mother Hikari. They moved quickly through the Forest of Lost Regrets, finding the journey much easier this time. As they exited the forest, Rumiko remarked with a grin, "That was a lot easier!" Yurei chuckled, sharing in her relief.

CHAPTER TEN

FATE

The sun climbed higher in the sky, its warmth a constant companion as they pressed forward. The morning passed quickly, but as the day wore on, the heat intensified, making the journey increasingly challenging. Yurei stayed in the shadows as much as possible to avoid the harsh sunlight. Despite his efforts, the relentless sun seemed to pursue him, and frustration began to build within.

They had been traveling for hours, and despite the beauty of the landscape, Yurei felt a growing sense of impatience. He was eager to make progress, to get closer to their goal, but the endless fields and meadows seemed to stretch on forever. The realization that they were not progressing gnawed at him further. Rumiko noticed his agitation and tried to offer words of encouragement, but Yurei's frustration was growing. Finally, unable to contain it any longer, he brought Tsuki to a halt and signaled for Rumiko to stop as well.

"Rumiko, we need to stop," Yurei said, his voice tight with irritation. Rumiko reined in Kuroguma and turned to face Yurei. "What's wrong Yurei?" she asked gently. Yurei dismounted, running a hand through his hair in exasperation. "We're not making enough progress," he replied, pacing back and forth. "We've been riding for hours, and it feels like we're getting nowhere."

Rumiko slowly dismounted her horse. She approached Yurei with a calm demeanor, her presence radiating a soothing energy. She reached out and placed a gentle hand on his arm, feeling the tension coiled beneath his skin. "I understand your frustration," she said softly. "But we need to be patient. This journey is going to take time. We can't rush it." Yurei responded with irritation, his eyes flashing with a mix of fear and anger. "I don't know where we are going, Rumiko, and it will be dark soon!" he snapped, his voice rising. The uncertainty of their path and the encroaching night were fraying his nerves.

Before Rumiko could respond, a familiar and comforting presence filled Yurei's mind. It was his mother's voice, clear and resonant, speaking to him from beyond the physical world. "My son," Ayama's voice echoed in his thoughts, "it is time to close your eyes and listen to the heartbeat of the forest. Feel the darkness that is Ryuji; he is waiting for you. Listen to the pulse of darkness." Yurei's eyes widened at the sound of his mother's voice. It was as if a wave of calm washed over him, momentarily silencing his fears and frustrations. He closed his eyes, taking a deep breath to center himself.

Rumiko watched him, her expression shifting from concern to understanding. She knew that Yurei had a deep connection with his mother's spirit and that he needed this moment to regain his composure. She stepped back slightly, giving him space while remaining close enough to offer support. Yurei focused on the rhythm of the forest, trying to tune out his own anxieties. He could hear the rustle of the wind through the trees, the gentle flow of a nearby stream, and the faint calls of creatures in the forest. He slowed his breathing, matching it to the natural cadence of the world around him.

The sounds of the forest blended into a symphony of life, and within that symphony, Yurei began to sense something else. It was a faint, almost imperceptible pulse, a dark rhythm that grew beneath the surface. It was the presence of Ryuji, the man who killed Kenji and ultimately brought so much pain and suffering. The darkness felt cold and oppressive. Yurei opened his eyes, his look sharper and more focused. "I can feel him," he said quietly, looking at Rumiko. "Ryuji's presence is out there, waiting for us. We're on the right path, but we need to proceed carefully."

Rumiko nodded. "Then we'll listen to the forest and follow its guidance," she said. Yurei climbed back onto Tsuki, feeling the familiar strength and warmth of his loyal friend beneath him. The bond they shared was deep, forged through countless journeys. He knew that Tsuki understood him in ways that words could not fully convey. Closing his eyes, Yurei placed his hand gently on Tsuki's neck, feeling the steady rhythm of her heartbeat. He began to take deep, slow breaths, focusing on syncing his own heartbeat with hers. The sensation was calming, a silent conversation between man and horse that spoke of trust and mutual respect. The world around them faded into the background as Yurei concentrated on the connection. In this moment, there was only the steady thump of Tsuki's heart and the deep, rhythmic breaths of her rider.

Yurei could feel the tension in his body easing, his mind becoming clearer and more focused. He let go of his frustration and impatience, replacing it with a sense of calm determination. He trusted Tsuki to understand his silent instructions, to follow the path that he could not see with his eyes but could sense with his heart. Suddenly, Tsuki sprang to life. Her muscles tensed and then relaxed as she moved forward with a smooth, purposeful gait. Yurei kept his eyes closed, trusting completely in Tsuki's instincts and their shared connection. He could feel her hooves striking the ground with precision, avoiding obstacles and navigating the uneven terrain with ease.

Tsuki's movements were fluid and confident, her strides long and steady. Yurei sensed her responding to the subtle shifts in his posture and the gentle pressure of his legs, guiding her without the need for reins or vocal commands. It was a dance they had perfected over years of riding together under Kenji's tutelage—a seamless blend of human and animal instinct.

As they moved through the forest, Yurei could feel the subtle energy of the land guiding them. The presence of Ryuji's darkness was still there, a cold, heavy weight that seemed to hang in the air. But now, it was as if they were following an invisible thread, a path laid out by the heartbeat of the forest itself.

Rumiko followed closely on Kuroguma, her eyes alert and watchful. She marveled at the sight of Yurei and Tsuki moving as one, their connection powerful. Kaze circled overhead, his cries providing reassurance and guidance as they continued their journey. The forest grew thicker, the trees towering above them like ancient guardians. Despite the growing darkness, Yurei felt no fear. With Tsuki beneath him and the forest guiding them, he knew they were on the right path.

They rode for what felt like hours as the day turned to dusk, the rhythm of Tsuki's hooves and the steady thump of her heartbeat grounding Yurei in the present moment. Each step brought them closer to their goal, each breath filled him with renewed focus. The crushing weight of Ryuji's darkness grew stronger. Finally, they emerged from the thick forest into another clearing. The area was dominated by a massive, ancient tree that stood in the center. Its gnarled branches stretched out like twisted arms, and its roots formed a complex network that spread across the clearing. The air was thick with a dark, tangible energy.

Yurei opened his eyes, feeling the presence of the ancient tree and the power it held. He gently patted Tsuki's neck, a silent thank you for her guidance. "We're here," he said softly, his voice filled with hope. They immediately dismounted their horses. Yurei and Rumiko knew they had little time to prepare for the confrontation that awaited them. Yurei instructed Kaze to fly overhead and watch out for Ryuji.

Rumiko moved quickly and efficiently, gathering her magic potions and herbs from her pouch. She laid them out in a neat array on a flat stone, their colors vivid and striking against grey stone. Alongside her potions, she placed her katana and her trusted walking stick. Yurei, meanwhile, checked the straps of the Jade Sword on his back, making sure it was secure and ready for quick access. He could feel the weight of the weapon pressing against him—a reminder of the legacy he carried and the battle he was about to face.

"We don't have a lot of time," Yurei said, his voice tense but controlled. He glanced around the clearing, his eyes scanning every detail, every shadow. He could feel the presence of Ryuji's darkness growing stronger, like a storm gathering on the horizon. Rumiko nodded. "I have an idea, Yurei, something that might work." Yurei turned to her, giving her his full attention. "I've been trying to figure out how we can destroy Ryuji without trapping Kenji's soul forever. I think I can build a bridge between the Shadow Blade and the Jade Sword."

Yurei nodded. "Yes, tell me more." Rumiko continued, "The Jade Sword is deeply connected to Kenji as he was once the guardian of the sword. I can place an ancient spell on it that will allow his essence to be channeled into the Jade Sword. Once the spell is activated, you'll need to connect the Jade Sword to the Shadow Blade. This will create a bridge for Kenji's soul to travel through. I can't guarantee it will work, but it's worth a try."

Yurei nodded, his expression focused. He reached behind and pulled the weapon from his its home. He could feel the weight and the powerful legacy it carried. He looked at it intensely, contemplating the significance of what they were about to do. After a moment of silent reflection, he handed the weapon to Rumiko, his eyes meeting hers with a silent vow of trust. Rumiko took the Jade Sword and laid it on the ground. She prepared a protective barrier around the katana. She began to mix her potions, her hands moving quickly, combining various herbs and magical ingredients with precision. The air around them seemed to fill with energy as she chanted incantations.

Yurei watched her for a moment, his admiration for her skills deepening. He then closed his eyes, centering himself. Amid the gathering darkness, he could hear his mother's voice loud and clear in his head, a beacon of guidance and strength. "Remember, my son, you must connect the Jade Sword to the Shadow Blade when the spell is complete. This is the only way to create the bridge for Kenji's soul to travel."

As Rumiko's chanting grew louder and more intense, the protective barrier around the Jade Sword began to glow with a radiant green light. Yurei opened his eyes and stepped forward, ready to fulfill his part of the plan. The final confrontation was approaching, and with Kenji's spirit and Rumiko's magic, he felt prepared to face the darkness of Ryuji.

"We're almost ready," Rumiko said, her voice calm despite the intensity of the situation. She finished her preparations, standing up and gripping her walking stick with complete focus and determination. "This barrier will hold, but we need to act quickly. Ryuji won't wait long before he strikes. Remember, if you need to jump, do it—but stay out of the range of the Shadow Blade, as it may disrupt your ability!"

Yurei nodded as he lifted the Jade Sword and held it firmly at his side. The ring on his hand began to vibrate and glow. Rumiko nodded and gave him a look of approval. "Just be careful, Yurei. We still have a lot of catching up to do!" With that, Yurei smiled and stepped toward the edge of the barrier that Rumiko created, his weapon drawn and ready. He focused his mind, pushing away any lingering doubts and fears.

Rumiko looked down at the opal necklace that Yurei gave her and pressed it against her heart and smiled. The forest around them grew unnaturally silent, the usual sounds of forest creatures fading into nothingness. It was as if the entire world was holding its breath, waiting for the inevitable clash of light and darkness. Yurei's senses were on high alert and ready for the confrontation.

Overhead, a piercing cry broke the silence and echoed through the forest walls. Yurei and Rumiko both looked up simultaneously to see Kaze circling in the sky as a mass of shadows approached. Kaze swooped down to Yurei, flapping his wings urgently as if to warn him of the impending danger. Yurei watched intently as a cloud of ravens drew closer, their black feathers shifting in unison like the waves of an ocean. The sky had become a sea of darkness. Their wings beat like a drum, a warning of something far greater.

Suddenly, a low, menacing laugh echoed through the clearing. Yurei instinctively brought his katana to the ready, eyes scanning the edge of the woods. From the thick shadows, a figure emerged. Ryuji appeared, wearing the familiar oni demon mask smeared with blood. The ravens descended from the sky, circling above him. One by one, they began to merge, their forms dissolving into black smoke that enveloped Ryuji. The smoke covered his body and began to shape itself into a billowing black cape.

He moved with an unsettling grace, the fabric fluttering around him like a living entity. The cape itself seemed to pulsate with a life of its own, its edges moving and curling up in unison. The Kurokawa's black sludge had permanently encased Ryuji's form. It clung to him, ascending the fabric of his cape and intertwining with his very essence. The dark mass reflected the moonlight, its movements synchronized with Ryuji's breaths. For the first time, the Kurokawa and Ryuji had become a single entity, bound to darkness.

His eyes glowed with a deep crimson light that radiated through his oni mask. Ryuji carried his twin blades, but today, Kenji's sword, the Tora Katana, was at his side. In his hand, he held the Shadow Blade, the weapon pulsing with energy, as if breathing in the air around it. Ryuji snarled, his voice filled with contempt as he took a step forward, the dark shroud of the Kurokawa swirling around him. "I thought I already killed you, Haruto," he taunted, his eyes filled with disdain. "Or is it Yurei now?" Yurei held the Jade Sword in a defensive posture. He stood tall, his stance strong and steadfast as bared his fangs at Ryuji. The air between them burned with tension. "My name is Yurei," he replied. "But I carry Haruto's spirit within me. You may have thought you defeated us, but we are stronger together."

Ryuji laughed, a harsh, grating sound that echoed through the clearing. "How touching," he mocked. "Two souls in one body, clinging to each other for strength. How pathetic. I see you've gotten your hands on the Jade Sword. I'm guessing this was Kenji's doing before I trapped his soul forever!"

As Ryuji advanced, his hand tightened around the handle of the Shadow Blade. Yurei could feel the dark power radiating from it, a constant reminder of the deadly threat it posed. "How fitting that it will be Kenji's soul, powering the Shadow Blade, that will be your undoing!" Rumiko stepped forward, her eyes blazing with anger. "You underestimate us, Ryuji," she said, her voice filled with conviction. "We have the strength of our ancestors and the power of our bond."

Ryuji's crimson eyes shifted to Rumiko, his lips curling under his mask. "Ah, the little witch," he laughed. "Do you really think your feeble magic can stop me?" Rumiko's grip tightened on her walking stick, her knuckles white with the force of her grip. She felt the protective barrier she had created pulsating around them, its energy flowing through her. "It's not just my magic," she said. "It's the strength of our hearts, the power of our love, and the spirits who guide us. You cannot defeat that." Ryuji's eyes blazed with fury as he laughed aloud, the Shadow Blade glowing with dark energy. "Enough talk!" he roared, lunging forward with ferocious speed.

Yurei's instincts kicked in, his body reacting to Ryuji's incoming assault. He quickly evaded the attack, feeling the rush of air as the Shadow Blade narrowly missed him. The blade struck the ground with a deafening impact, sending shockwaves rippling through the earth. The force of the blow was immense, and the ground trembled as if in fear of the weapon's dark power. The shockwaves radiated outward, toppling small trees and sending loose debris flying through the air. Yurei felt the ground beneath his feet shudder, but he kept his balance, his eyes never leaving Ryuji.

Ryuji pulled the blade from the earth with a snarl. As he turned to face Yurei, the dark force of the Kurokawa traveled up his body like a living shadow. The cape seemed to twist and surge with life, its edges flickering and twisting as he moved. Yurei took a deep breath, centering himself. He could feel the presence of Haruto within him, their combined strength filling him with power.

Ryuji's face twisted with anger and frustration. "You can't escape me forever, Yurei!" he yelled, his voice echoing with a dark resonance. He lunged again, the Shadow Blade cutting through the air like the hiss of a snake. Rumiko watched from within the protective barrier, her heart pounding with anxiety and hope. She continued to chant softly, her voice a steady rhythm as she finalized the spell to connect with Kenji. As she chanted, she felt the barrier weakening.

Sweat beaded on Rumiko's forehead as she watched Yurei struggle to get close enough to Ryuji's body. Her heart pounded in her chest, each beat echoing her mounting anxiety. Every time Yurei got close, the Kurokawa would lunge at him like the tentacles of a sea creature, snapping with violent intent. The shadowy coils struck with terrifying speed, forcing Yurei to dodge and weave, his movements growing more desperate with each failed attempt. The Kurokawa was alive, anticipating his every move, blocking his path and pushing him back with relentless aggression. The swirling vortex of blackness repelled Yurei's every attempt to make contact with the Shadow Blade, leaving him increasingly frustrated and desperate.

The sight of Yurei's struggle worried Rumiko. She knew that time was running out, both for her spell and for Yurei's strength. She chanted louder, willing her magic to hold just a bit longer, her eyes never leaving Yurei as he fought valiantly against the oppressive force surrounding Ryuji. Suddenly, amidst the chaos, Yurei could feel time slow. The sounds of the battlefield faded into the background as a familiar, comforting voice spoke to him. It was his mother, her voice clear and calm in his mind. "My son, you must now trust in Haruto. Close your eyes and listen to your inner spirit. Let go of your fear and doubt. Feel the energy of Haruto within you."

Yurei took a deep breath, closing his eyes as his mother instructed. He blocked out the sounds of Ryuji's mocking laughter and the whisper of the Kurokawa. Instead, he focused inward, sensing the presence of Haruto's spirit intertwined with his own. The connection was profound, a merging of past and present. As Ryuji intensified his attacks, Yurei kept his eyes closed and focused on the sensations within. He felt the energy flowing through him, the shared wisdom and strength of Haruto guiding his movements. It was as if his body was moving on its own, driven by a force greater than himself. Each step was executed with flawless precision, as though choreographed by an unseen hand.

Ryuji's attacks became more frenzied and desperate. He swung the Shadow Blade with brutal force, aiming to overwhelm Yurei with sheer power. But Yurei, with his eyes still closed, moved with an almost supernatural grace, anticipating and evading each blow. With a final deep breath, Yurei opened his eyes, now glowing with a bright crimson hue. He saw Ryuji's next move before it happened, his katana already in motion to meet it. The blades clashed with a resounding impact, the force of the collision sending shockwaves through the clearing.

As the weapons connected, Yurei could feel time slow to a pause. The world around them seemed to freeze, their bodies locked mid-action. A bright golden light emanated from the swords, illuminating the darkened clearing with a brilliant glow. The light pulsed and expanded, creating a sphere of radiance that pushed back the encroaching shadows. In that suspended moment, Yurei could feel the presence of Kenji. The jade stone embedded in the base of the swords blade began to glow. Within the light now emanating from the jade stone, a spectral image of Kenji appeared. The familiar voice of his mentor echoed through his head, "Yurei, it's me, Kenji." He could see Kenji advancing forward, reaching towards him. Yurei extended his hand towards Kenji's image.

In that instant, Yurei felt the dark hold of the Kurokawa making its way up his legs. It was a cold, insidious sensation. The icy strands were creeping over his skin, tightening their grip with every passing second. He could hear Rumiko's voice like a distant echo, "Yurei, break the connection now before it consumes you!" In that instant, Yurei felt a surge of energy pulling him out of the vision. Time began to speed up as he glanced at Rumiko, who was pleading with him to come back.

Ryuji suddenly sprang to life as the two swords broke their connection. With a deafening explosion, the swords separated, launching Yurei and Ryuji in opposite directions. Ryuji landed on the ground near Rumiko's barrier, while Yurei was thrown onto an embankment on the other side, much farther away from her. The Shadow Blade and the Jade Sword landed near each other, sticking straight into the ground. Rumiko held her ground, her walking stick firmly anchored into the earth. A glowing blue energy pulsed down the length of the gnarled wood, spreading outward to encircle her body and form a protective barrier.

Her body began to shake and throb as she gripped the stick tightly with both hands. Then, like a distant echo, a familiar voice rang through her head. "Rumiko, it's me, Ayama. You can let go, everything will be okay." Ryuji suddenly turned his attention toward Rumiko, lifted his leg into the air, and delivered a powerful side kick straight through her walking stick. Splinters flew as his leg smashed through the wood, shattering it into pieces. The blue energy flickered and vanished, just like the voice in her head.

Yurei looked on in terror as the Kurokawa snaked around Rumiko's legs, its black coils tightening with every second. The dark, strands pulsed with life, anchoring Ryuji to her body like chains. Rumiko's eyes widened in fear as she struggled against the unnatural force pulling her down, but the Kurokawa's grip was relentless, its power feeding off her helplessness.

Ryuji's eyes grew brighter as if he was drawing strength from the Kurokawa's connection. Yurei glanced frantically between the Jade Sword and the Shadow Blade, both weapons still lodged in the ground. He hesitated, torn between securing the weapons—keys to stopping Ryuji—and saving Rumiko. In his desperation, his mother's voice echoed in his mind, clear and commanding. "Jump, Yurei! Jump now!"

Without hesitation, Yurei sprang into action, propelling himself forward with supernatural speed. In an instant, he was on top of the Kurokawa that was swallowing up Rumiko. As Yurei shielded her with his body, he could hear Rumiko's muffled cries beneath him, her voice strained and panicked, "Haruto, stop! Get off me! Let me go!" Ignoring her plea, Yurei extended his arms, wrapping them tightly around the pulsating, mass that was consuming Rumiko. Ryuji was anchored to the Kurokawa and bound to Rumiko through its chain-like strands. This connection kept him tethered, unable to move freely. The Shadow Blade lay far out of reach, lodged in the ground and glowing faintly.

Hissing with fury, he reached down to his leg and pulled a sword from its scabbard. It was the Tora Katana, the weapon he had seized from Kenji's lifeless hand after striking him down. Ryuji raised the sword above Yurei's body and, with a powerful downward strike, drove it into Yurei's back. Yurei felt the cold metal pierce his flesh, sharp, searing pain radiating through him. Beneath him, the Kurokawa convulsed violently, its dark form acting as a shield and preventing the Tora Katana from reaching Rumiko's body.

Yurei resisted with all his strength, desperately trying to stop the sword from reaching Rumiko. But as thoughts of his love for her filled his mind, the Kurokawa suddenly turned to water, causing the Tora Katana to slide effortlessly through Yurei and into Rumiko. The pink-tinted liquid cascaded down Rumiko's sides like a waterfall, soaking into the dirt-covered ground below.

They lay motionless. Ryuji drew his dagger and turned toward Yurei, who was face down on top of Rumiko's body. Seizing Yurei's hand, he sliced through the finger that bore the jade ring. The severed finger fell, and the ring slipped free, rolling across the ground.

Ryuji left the katana embedded in their bodies as he turned to secure the jade ring. He bent down to the ground to pick up the ring as a smile spread across his face.

But as he reached for the ring it suddenly vanished. Ryuji's eyes shot upward, just in time to see the jade ring fly straight into the hand of a tall man wearing a garnet ring on one hand. His nails were long, sharp, and curled down at the tips. Beside him stood a wolf-like creature, its brown fur marked by a contrasting white stripe running down its back. It rose onto its hind legs, its long claws raking the ground. Saliva clung to its jaws, stretching in thin strands toward the earth. The creature glanced up at the tall man, then back at Ryuji, snapping at the air with its jagged, blood-stained teeth in a menacing display.

The man was long and lean, with shoulder-length black hair neatly slicked back. His unusually pale skin contrasted starkly with his blood-red eyes. His jaw was square, and his face was defined by sharp, angular features. He wore a long, flowing black coat made of fine silk, which seemed to dance around him as he moved.

Ryuji locked eyes with him. "Nikolai, it's you!"

The man's lips twisted into a mocking smile. "Ryuji!"

He slipped the jade ring onto his finger and pointed toward the Jade Sword. The weapon tore itself free from the earth and leapt into his hand. Ryuji reached for the Shadow Blade that was planted in the ground. As he pulled the sword from the ground, Nikolai rapidly turned his body. With a swift, commanding gesture, he raised the Jade Sword high and cut into the fabric of the veil, slicing through the threads to create an opening.

The air in front of Nikolai began to ripple, distorting and twisting violently into an invisible vortex. The swirling winds whipped around, pulling in loose debris and darkening the space around them. Without a moment's hesitation, Nikolai stepped into the opening, disappearing into the swirling void. The wolf-like creature stood in front of the vortex, snarling and barking at Ryuji. It then turned and leapt into the opening, vanishing into the darkness.

Ryuji, clutching the Shadow Blade tightly, sprinted toward the vortex and, with a burst of speed, dove through just as it began to close behind him. In an instant, they were gone, leaving Yurei and Rumiko lying like a lifeless mound. Yurei lay on top of Rumiko for days, with the Tora Katana still embedded in his back. They remained there, unmoving, like a monument to a failed destiny and a broken fate.

Yurei carefully removed the Tora Katana from their bodies and performed the rites to cremate Rumiko, honoring her spirit before he moved on. The weight of his grief and guilt was almost too much to bear as he wandered the countryside, his steps heavy and aimless. Each day bled into the next, the world around him a blur of muted colors and indistinct sounds. The vibrant energy that had once driven him seemed to have drained away, leaving behind a hollow shell of the warrior he had once been. He had vowed to never wield Kenji's sword again. He had failed his mother, Kenji, and even Rumiko. It was time for him to put his weapons to rest. Yurei walked to a sandy meadow by the river. Dropping to his knees, he wept as he dug into the sand with both hands—one of them missing a finger.

The weight of his failures pressed heavily on his shoulders, each tear a reminder of his regret and sorrow. Yurei's hands moved erratically, creating a shallow grave in the soft earth, his mind flooded with memories of those he had let down. He remembered his mother's kind eyes, always full of hope and pride, now shadowed by disappointment. He saw Kenji's stern but loving face, the mentor who had believed in him and trusted him with his teachings. And Rumiko, whose faith and support had been his anchor, now seemed like a distant dream. They were all erased from his life.

With a heavy heart, Yurei placed Kenji's sword into the hole he had dug. The blade, once a symbol of honor and strength, now felt like a relic of a past he could no longer uphold. In his hand he held the opal stone his mother had given him. He had removed it from Rumiko's body and was ready to bury it with the Tora Katana. He then heard his mother's familiar voice in his head, a gentle, soothing presence that brought a flicker of warmth to his cold, weary heart. "Yurei, it's me, mother. I have something to share with you."

Yurei froze, his breath catching in his throat. He had not heard his mother's voice in so long, and the sound of it was like gentle touch to his aching soul. He closed his eyes, as sand drifted between his fingers. "Mother?" he whispered, his voice trembling with emotion. "Is it really you?"

"Yes, my son," the voice replied, filled with a tenderness that only a mother could convey. "I
am here, always watching over you. There is something important you must know."

"Tell me, Mother," he said softly, his voice barely audible.

"Yurei, I want you to take the katana and stone from the ground. You must do as I say."

With a deep breath, Yurei reached for the weapon and stone, pulling them from the ground as sand and dirt poured off them. His hands trembled as he stared at the weapon. His mother spoke softly, her voice gentle yet firm, "Yurei, you must close your eyes and hold the stone tightly in your hand." Yurei hesitated for a moment, before closing his eyes and letting the warmth surround him completely. With his vision darkened, his other senses heightened. The warmth from the stone seemed to pulse in time with his heartbeat, creating a connection that transcended the physical.

"Yurei, I want you to slowly open your eyes," his mother urged, her voice gentle and reassuring. In that instant, he heard the familiar cry of Kaze, the hawk, circling overhead. Yurei let out a deep breath, his heart pounding in his chest. He felt a strange, powerful energy in the air around him. Slowly, he opened his eyes. Standing before him was a familiar looking woman. She had a radiant glow about her, a soft light that seemed to emanate from within. She was wearing a black kimono that matched her dark hair. Her long, black hair flowed down her back, glistening like a river of midnight silk. Her head was bowed, her eyes were closed.

Kaze, the hawk, landed at his feet and looked at the girl with his head tilted. Yurei's breath caught in his throat, his mind racing. He whispered, "Rumiko, is it you?" She lifted her head and slowly opened her eyes revealing a crimson glow. With a confused look she said, "Who is Rumiko?"

PART TWO

CHAPTER ELEVEN

WHO IS NIKOLAI?

"We will call him Nikolai!" Ambrose announced proudly as he stared deeply at his newborn son, the only child to survive after so many attempts to bring life into their dark world. Nikolai had a full head of jet-black hair and stared at his father with piercing, dark eyes. It was late into the night, and the moon cast its amber light through a square opening in the wall, illuminating the room with a soft, gentle glow. Shadows danced along the walls, as if they, too, bore witness to this rare and precious moment.

After countless tries, Seraphina had finally carried a child to full term. Her long black hair rested on her shoulders as sweat trickled down her neck past her freckles and onto Nikolai. Exhausted but overjoyed, she cradled her first living child, whispering, "Our Nikolai will be our miracle." The Dragomir family lived high in the secluded reaches of the Carpathian Mountains in Eastern Europe. Isolated from the outside world, it was just the three of them—Ambrose, Seraphina, and their son, Nikolai. They lived a quiet life in a timber-and-stone house, built long ago by Ambrose's own hands and weathered by the passing of time.

Tall grasses and thick, lush greenery bordered the property's edges, forming a natural barrier against the outside world. The house itself was cloaked in moss and vines that crept along the wood and stone, with the occasional rough rock surface peeking through. It seemed almost as if the house had grown organically from the earth, blending seamlessly into the wild landscape.

Nikolai had never seen another person aside from his parents. His entire world was confined to their remote farm, hidden far from the nearest village. Days often passed in silence as he tended to the animals they raised for sustenance. Alongside his daily chores, he helped grow vegetables to feed the livestock they relied upon, carefully tending to each plant that helped sustain the animals.

But most of their food came from hunting, a skill his parents had taught him since he was old enough to walk through the forest. In addition to the pigs and chickens they kept on the farm, they relied on two loyal hunting dogs, always at Nikolai's side. The dogs were his constant companions, quick to pick up a scent and unyielding in their devotion. He called them Bela and Sable. Bela, a female, had a light tan coat marked by a dark line down her back, while Sable's darker fur was distinguished by a pale stripe along his spine.

When Nikolai was just three years old, he went on his first hunt. His parents had taken him deep into the woods to search for small game like rabbits and squirrels. They dressed in warm furs for the occasion, as the air was growing colder, and a light mist coated the leaves and forest floor. Each breath left a faint trail of vapor that quickly disappeared into the morning air. Nikolai, barely taller than his father's knees, walked between his parents, his small steps matching their careful, silent strides. His father, Ambrose whispered as they walked under the forest canopy, "Okay my boy, we must stay in the shadows and out of the light."

Nikolai looked up, his thick black hair falling over his forehead, and nodded to his father. As they walked through the forest, his mother gently grabbed the back of his shirt to stop him. His father, who was a few steps ahead, paused and looked back with a silent smile. His mother understood that this meant he had spotted an animal. Ambrose motioned for Nikolai to come closer, then pointed to a group of rabbits grazing on tall shoots of grass. Without saying a word, he bowed his head to the animals in a silent show of respect. Nikolai closed his eyes and mirrored his father's gesture perfectly.

His father then removed the sling from his belt. It was a simple yet sturdy weapon, crafted from braided leather with a small pouch in the center. Wrapping one end securely around his hand, he placed a smooth, round stone into the pouch. He then shifted into a low crouch and began spinning the sling, building momentum. With a quick flick of his wrist, the stone launched through the air and struck the largest rabbit with a soft thump.

The animal fell to the ground, a small trickle of blood expanding in its fur. Ambrose looked at Nikolai to see his reaction. He stared at the fallen animal as if hypnotized by the stillness that seemed to fill the air. His father nudged him to go forward and retrieve the rabbit. As Nikolai stood up and carefully made his way over, his mother joined Ambrose, wrapping her arm securely around his shoulder. Together, they watched their son take his first steps into the solemn ritual of the hunt. Nikolai crouched beside the rabbit, hesitating for a moment before looking back at his parents for approval. They both nodded, smiling warmly. It was silent gesture encouraging him to go ahead.

Nikolai lifted the animal off the ground and brought the wound to his mouth. He looked at his parents one last time before feeding on the animals warm blood. For Nikolai, this was all he had ever known. Days were spent learning how to use the land and its creatures for survival. His father had established a perimeter around their living area, marked by specific trees that Nikolai was strictly instructed never to cross. These boundaries defined his world yet also sparked his curiosity. His father would often caution him, saying, "There is great danger beyond our home, and we must never tempt it."

Both his parents would warn him of dangerous creatures lurking beyond, that would pose a great threat. But as Nikolai grew, so did his curiosity. The forest beyond the marked trees called to him with a quiet, irresistible pull. He would often find himself staring at the boundary, wondering what mysteries lay hidden in the shadows beyond his home.

They would all feast on the warm blood of animals. It was their only means of survival; without this sustenance, they would perish. But this was something they had not yet revealed to Nikolai.

His mother would insist, "We cannot keep the truth from him. We must tell him what we

are; it's the only way for him to be safe."

Ambrose ran his fingers through his short dark hair, his expression troubled. "And what

exactly do we tell him? That we're vampires?"

Seraphina stepped closer, a look of empathy softening her features. "Yes, vampires. We have chosen to follow the true path..." Before she could continue, Ambrose interrupted, "Just because we've chosen to survive on animals alone doesn't mean Nikolai will... or can make the same choice. He is our only son, and we must protect him from himself."

"But we must..." Seraphina began, but Ambrose cut her off sternly. "For now, we say nothing. This is the only life he knows, and it will stay that way." Nikolai would often ask to walk the boundaries in solitude. His mother would warn him to stay in the shadows, avoid the sunlight and take the dogs. He would begrudgingly nod and then disappear into the woods with Bela and Sable at his side. His father didn't like him wandering alone, wary of the hidden dangers beyond their farm. But Seraphina would gently remind him, "If we don't let him move freely, he will become restless. He needs to feel that he has his own place in this world, even if it's just within the boundary."

Nikolai walked slowly along the perimeter, his two dogs following close behind. As they approached a large oak tree marked with two carved lines and a circle between them, signaling the boundary, Nikolai stopped and gazed intently at the ground beyond. Sable and Bela hesitated, sensing his intent, and slowly backed away as Nikolai placed his foot just beyond the border. He waited a moment to see what would happen before slowly placing his other foot over the boundary. He laughed out loud and announced, "Nothing!" as he turned to his dogs, both of whom were crouching on the ground. He called them to come to him, but they refused. Motioning with his hand, he urged, "Come on!" But they stood firm, unmoving, their eyes fixed on him with an uneasy stillness. Nikolai walked back to the dogs and motioned them, "All right, but next time I'm coming alone!"

Ambrose and Seraphina had vowed to follow the true path, a commitment to sustain themselves without ever feeding on a human. They took this vow very seriously, fully aware of the price it demanded. Both were born of the Nocturni, a lineage of purebred vampires who possessed the rare ability to procreate like humans. As Nocturni, they had the potential for immortality, but only if they feasted on human souls. Without this ritual, they were bound to survive on the warm blood of animals alone.

However, the blood of animals provided only temporary strength, not true longevity. Feeding solely on animals meant that, over time, they would age and ultimately perish. Unlike those vampires who embraced eternal youth by consuming human souls, Nocturni like Ambrose and Seraphina knew that their choice would lead them down a finite path.

Many years before, a great divide fractured the Nocturni, splitting them into two factions. One group, the Virescent, took a vow to safeguard life's mysteries without bending them to their will. They followed the natural order of birth, life, and death, believing it was not their right to feed on humans. They held that those who did so severed their connection with the sacred and were bound to an eternal sleep. The name Virescent, meaning "becoming green," symbolized their return to nature and the cycle of renewal.

The Virescent believed they should only take what the earth itself provided, using its gifts with respect and reverence. The other group, known as the Immortalis, or "undying," was seduced by the allure of eternal youth. They fed on human souls, adding years to their lives with each soul consumed. Yet every soul they devoured was torn from the cycle of existence itself.

However, because they consumed the souls of the living, the Immortalis could no longer return to the great cycle. The system rejected them, leaving their essence fragmented and incomplete. Severed from the resonance that bound all things, they became hollow—forever removed from all realms, unable to integrate back into the weave of existence.

For the Nocturni following the path of the Virescent, attempting to bring a child into the world without consuming human blood was fraught with difficulty. As a couple, they had tried unsuccessfully for over one hundred human years. Time and again, Ambrose returned to the fields to bury another lost child, each burial deepening the sorrow that bound them.

As he looked across the barren field, filled with row upon row of burial mounds, a rare tear formed in his eye. Their vow to follow the true path was tested with each loss, yet they clung to it, hoping that one day their commitment would yield the miracle they yearned for. With the birth of Nikolai, their long-awaited miracle was finally fulfilled. Yet Ambrose carried a secret—a silent, dark burden he kept hidden from Seraphina. Although they shared a deep bond, he had never told her the truth about his past. Ambrose was far older than his beloved wife; when they first met, he had assured her they were of the same age and that he had been a lifelong follower of the Virescent path.

In reality, Ambrose had already lived for more than a century before meeting Seraphina. His youthful appearance was a remnant of a darker past, for he had once feasted on human blood as an Immortalis. Those who become Immortalis bear a tell-tale mark: faint "bite mars" scarred into the neck. No matter how carefully they try to hide them, the scars show themselves. Only with time—and abstinence from feeding on human souls—do the marks begin to fade.

He had turned away from that path long before meeting Seraphina, seeking redemption through the ways of the Virescent. Yet he chose to keep his past hidden, hoping that if Seraphina ever uncovered the truth, she would find it in her heart to forgive him.

For a vampire born of the Nocturni, aging stops upon reaching adulthood, provided they continue to feed on humans. However, by consuming only animal blood, they age slowly and, eventually, will perish. Ambrose had chosen this path long ago, but he now felt the weight of his years pressing upon him. After failure upon failure in creating a child, he decided to take matters into his own hands.

Late one night, he quietly slipped out of the cabin while Seraphina sat alone, absorbed in her reading. A weathered manuscript lay open in her lap, its pages filled with fading symbols. She traced the lines slowly, as if searching for meaning beyond the words themselves.

Moving silently through the forest, Ambrose tried not to dwell on the act he was about to commit. With each step, he felt the weight of his decision pressing upon him. He glanced back as he quickly crossed the boundaries he himself had set, feeling a wave of dread fill him. Once he was far from their home, his steps became focused and silent. His entire demeanor shifted as he crouched low, moving like a predator in search of prey. He lifted his head occasionally, sniffing the air as he moved his nose from side to side, sharpening his senses in search of any trace of life.

With unnatural speed, he descended from the high mountain where their home lay hidden among the clouds. The forest blurred around him as he moved, covering in moments what would have taken hours for a mortal. He reached the outskirts of the village, where the scent of humans filled the air, rich and tempting. The familiar yet forbidden smell stirred something deep within him, igniting a primal urge he had suppressed for centuries.

He waited in the shadows, watching as a family hurried down a dirt pathway. The mother pulled her child along, prodding him to keep up. Ambrose crouched low, his eyes shifting to a lone man staggering along the edge of the woods. The man was clearly intoxicated, swaying as he struggled to keep his balance, oblivious to the presence lurking nearby.

Ambrose crept closer to the man his fangs beginning to form, drawing in a long breath before lunging forward and sinking his teeth into his neck. The bite was quick and deep, cutting off any cry. He drove his fangs in further, locking his grip as he dragged the man into the cover of the woods. Warmth flooded his body as he felt the man's life melting away.

The power of taking not only the mans life, but his very soul poured through Ambrose's very being. Yet tangled with his guilt was the intoxicating rush of pure ecstasy, a sensation that satisfied him to his very core. When it was over, Ambrose buried the body beneath the earth. He stared at his blood-stained hands, a prickling sensation rising along his neck where the hidden markings began to stir. Reaching up, he rubbed the spot, smearing blood into the rough edge of his newly grown beard. He reassured himself, if this brings us a child, perhaps even Seraphina could forgive it. But the full truth remained buried, even within himself.

"We must tell our son the truth of his existence!" Seraphina's voice was filled with concern. Ambrose rose from his chair and glanced outside to see what Nikolai was doing. "And what exactly do you want to tell him?" he asked. Seraphina spoke in a low, urgent whisper, "It's time he knows what he's capable of." Ambrose knew she was right, they would all be safer if Nikolai understood his gifts. "Alright, I'll take him into the woods today." Before he could continue, Seraphina interrupted firmly, "We will take him into the woods."

Together, Ambrose and Seraphina led Nikolai deep into the forest, walking in silence until they reached an area filled with shadows. Ambrose turned to face Nikolai, who now stood taller than his mother but still a few inches shorter than his father. Nikolai looked up, meeting his father's eyes with an expressionless stare. Ambrose cleared his throat and began, "My son, you have abilities that are very special...abilities that set you apart." He glanced at Seraphina, who nodded encouragingly. "Your mother and I share these same skills, though ours have faded with time." Ambrose took a few steps back and then he closed his eyes.

Without warning, his form began to flicker, pulsing in and out of view, until he finally vanished completely. Nikolai's eyes widened in shock, and he jumped back. "Father... where are you?" he called, his voice filled with confusion. A moment later, Ambrose began to flicker back into view, his form glowing faintly as he reappeared fully before Nikolai.

He looked at his mother, who smiled. "Can I do this as well?" he asked. Seraphina laughed and replied, "Yes, we all can!" She then flickered and moments later reappeared beside Ambrose. "We call it cloaking," she explained, "because it lets you become invisible and move unnoticed." Nikolai, his curiosity aroused, asked, "How do I do this?" Ambrose stepped in front of him and said, "Close your eyes and take a deep breath." Nikolai closed his eyes. "Now, picture yourself in complete darkness... now release the breath." Instantly, Nikolai vanished from view.

"Father, can you see me?" Nikolai's voice called from the emptiness. Ambrose looked around, but his son was nowhere to be seen. "No, Nikolai, we cannot see you." Just then, Ambrose felt a hand on his shoulder, and Nikolai's voice whispered in his ear, "Father, this is amazing." A moment later, Nikolai flickered back into view, fully visible once more.

Ambrose and Seraphina gave Nikolai a stern warning not to trifle with this gift. "My son, your mother and I have shared this with you because we trust you. But you must be more careful than ever, as you have not yet mastered this skill. True mastery takes time," Ambrose cautioned.

Seraphina then interrupted, "Stay out of the elements until you've mastered your cloaking. If you suddenly reappear in the sun you could be in grave danger." Nikolai looked at his father, then his mother, and nodded solemnly. She continued, "Even the rain can reveal your form, you must be careful."

Nikolai was more excited than ever to hunt. He would sit, invisible among the creatures of the forest, lingering in the shadows, unseen as he observed in silence. Every now and then, he would suddenly begin to flicker back into view, startling the animals and sending them running. He asked himself, *How do I control this gift?* He wondered if it required more concentration or perhaps less? No matter what he tried, he would unexpectedly reappear.

As time went on, Nikolai gained more control over his cloaking ability. He often walked with Bela and Sable to the edge of the boundary, instructing the dogs to stay until he returned. They would heed his command, sitting patiently and waiting. Nikolai ventured into the shadows of the forest, careful to remember his path back. He tried to walk in a straight line, keeping mindful of the sun's position in the sky. As he pressed farther through the lush greenery, he suddenly heard footsteps. Closing his eyes, he drew in a long breath and exhaled, causing his form to vanish from sight.

He sat silently in the shadows as a man and a dog walked through the forest. The man wore black and brown furs draped over his shoulders and a small fur cap, carrying a bow with an arrow at the ready. Suddenly, the man stopped and crouched down, signaling his dog to halt with a hand gesture. He then pointed up at the sky as a flock of pheasants flew overhead. The dog froze as the man aimed his bow skyward and released an arrow.

Nikolai watched as a pheasant fell from the sky, an arrow piercing its breast. The bird tumbled down, landing softly among the leaves. The hunter signaled to his dog; however, the animal turned toward Nikolai, who sat several feet away, still invisible, and began to growl. Nikolai began to panic, glancing frantically to each side, unsure of what to do. He slowly stood up and started to move away, but the dog charged toward him as though it could see him. The hunter rose to his feet, whistling for the dog.

As the dog closed in, Nikolai realized he was cornered and made a dash toward an open clearing where the sunlight poured down. Thinking he would remain invisible, he stepped into the light. But as he entered the clearing, his form began to flicker, and he reappeared fully, exposed under the bright sun.

Panicked, he immediately covered his face with his hands and sprinted back toward the shadows. But as he reached the trees, a sharp, stinging pain erupted on the backs of his hands. He turned them over and saw fresh burns on both, their skin sizzling and a thin wisp of smoke rising. The smell reached his nostrils, a stark reminder of what he had done. Fear hit him like a wave. *How would he explain this to his parents?* Nikolai ran as fast as he could back to the dogs and then toward home. He couldn't hide the burns from his parents, as they needed immediate attention. He decided he would tell them he had fallen off a ledge into a sunny clearing, where he burned his hands.

Nikolai waited almost two years before he started venturing away from the boundaries. As he approached the trees marking the boundary, Nikolai glanced down at the backs of his hands, now etched with the permanent scars from last time. They served as a vivid reminder of the consequences he faced when he ventured too close to sunlight. He clenched his fists and watched as the scars protruded upwards like coiled snakes. Today he had left the dogs behind and told his parents he was hunting for small game.

He carried a sling wrapped in his belt, along with a small leather pouch filled with smooth, round stones. Nikolai walked slowly past the boundary and into the shadows of the forest. He kept an eye out for small creatures, knowing he needed to return with something from his hunt to satisfy his parents' curiosity. The forest was quiet as Nikolai walked, careful to stay within the shadows. He passed the spot where he had once seen the hunter, but this time only the gentle sound of a nearby stream filled the air. Deciding to venture farther, he continued deeper into the woods, going farther than he had ever gone before. After a long walk, he noticed it was getting late and realized he should turn back. Just as he turned, he heard a sound behind him.

He crouched down, closed his eyes, and cloaked himself into invisibility. As he sat quietly, a girl with a woven basket approached, stopping by a bush to pick berries. She looked to be about Nikolai's age, with shoulder-length brown curly hair that caught the last bit of sunlight. She wore a woolen overdress, its earthy tones blending seamlessly with the forest, covering the tattered sleeves of her coarse linen tunic. Her feet were clad in worn leather boots, and a brown scarf draped loosely around her neck, dancing gently in the breeze. She smiled as she plucked a berry and slipped it into her mouth.

Suddenly, a man's voice called from beyond the bushes, "Come on, Mira, we must go now." Nikolai shifted his leg, causing some leaves to rustle. The girl paused, looking in Nikolai's direction, then turned and walked toward the man's voice.

Each day, Nikolai returned to the woods in search of the mysterious girl. She was the first female, other than his mother, that he had ever seen. Before encountering the hunter, he had imagined that the world consisted only of his family and the creatures of the woods. Seeing this new girl brought Nikolai a sense of hope for the first time. After many weeks without a single glimpse of her, she suddenly reappeared—alone. She walked into the same clearing and began picking berries. This time, she seemed to dance as she moved, singing softly to herself. Nikolai sat cloaked in the shadows, watching her. He decided that he would try to follow her home.

The girl, Mira, wore the same woolen dress. Nikolai followed her, staying in the shadows. He figured he would trail her for as long as possible, knowing he could always cloak himself if needed. She followed a winding path that snaked down the mountainside, a river rushing ran beside it, tumbling over rocks. As she skipped along the dirt trail, she began to hum. It was a soft melody like a child's lullaby.

Nikolai hid near the edge of the woods, ducking behind a fallen tree. The wood was soft and moist, having collapsed in sections, creating large openings. He positioned himself within one of the openings, careful to keep his head out of view. The earthy scent of decomposing bark surrounded him as he watched and listened in silence. He continued following her down the winding path, he noticed the sky had suddenly darkened with thick clouds rolling in overhead. A sudden flash of lightning split the sky, illuminating the landscape for a brief moment. Nikolai was torn between seeking shelter and continuing to follow the girl.

Realizing the risk of being exposed by the rain, he decided it was best to hide inside a nearby cave. Taking a deep breath, he closed his eyes and, with a sudden flicker, vanished completely from view. Nikolai sprinted across the open area to the edge of the cliff and slipped into the cave. He crouched in the corner, remaining completely invisible. Closing his eyes tightly, he focused his energy on maintaining his cloak.

The silence was interrupted by an unexpected sound. His eyes snapped open—only to find a pair of striking sky-blue eyes staring directly at him. It was the girl. She tilted her head slightly and asked, "Who are you?" Nikolai realized he was no longer cloaked and the girl could see him.

"I am Nikolai. What is your name?" he asked, even though he already knew.

He didn't want to confuse or scare her.

She glanced down at the ground and smiled. "I am Mira."

They sat in the darkness of the cave as the rain poured down outside, the steady rhythm

echoing through the hollow space.

Nikolai found himself staring at her golden brown hair, its radiance catching the faint light.

He had never seen another female before—certainly not one with hair so luminous. She smiled, then playfully pushed his shoulder, snapping him out of the trance he had suddenly

fallen into.

"Are you even listening?" she asked. "Where are you from?"

Nikolai hesitated for a moment, then silently pointed toward the mountains.

Her energy captivated him as she spoke endlessly, finishing one sentence only to begin another without pause. Nikolai listened, entranced, his eyes fixed on her as she filled the silence with words. Suddenly, the sun broke through the clouds, casting light into the cave's opening. Mira glanced at the sky, then back at Nikolai. "I have to go. Can you meet me here tomorrow?"

Before he could answer, she had already crawled out of the cave in a flash, disappearing into the daylight. Nikolai sat there, nodding to himself, still absorbing her presence long after she was gone. When the rain cleared, Nikolai quietly exited the cave and made his way home. He couldn't stop thinking about his encounter with Mira. He also wondered why his parents had kept the village and its people a secret. *What else were they hiding from him?*

When Nikolai returned home, he hurried through his chores, eager for morning to arrive so he could return to the cave. He told his parents he was going hunting for small game with his sling. Gathering several round stones, he prepared for his journey. As he walked toward the woods, his mother stepped outside and called after him, "Take Bela and Sable!" Nikolai paused mid-step, his shoulders slumping in disapproval. "But Mother, I hunt better alone. Please, I want to practice my cloaking!"

Seraphina shook her head before replying begrudgingly, "Okay, but stay in the shadows and don't be gone all day." She watched as he walked to the edge of the woods, then disappeared from sight as he cloaked himself. Nikolai went to meet Mira nearly every day he could. To avoid suspicion, he always brought home animals they could use for clothing and insulation for the cabin.

He loved sitting with Mira, listening as she told story after story. She spoke of her life on her father's small farm and how her mother had died long ago from an accident. The word "death" confused Nikolai. His parents had never spoken of such a thing. But he understood that she meant she was now gone.

Mira also told him that her father was very strict and gets very angry if she is late. She looked outside the cave and pointed to the position of the sun in the sky, "I must go!" Nikolai was beginning to feel something inexplicable when he was with her. It felt like a wave of energy that pulsed through his very being. "Please don't leave just yet!" Nikolai then reached into his leather pouch and pulled out a delicate white flower—its petals shaped like tiny bells, trembling in the breeze. "This is for you," he said, his voice quieter than before.

Mira cupped the flower in her hands, her eyes softening.

"A snowdrop? But they only grow in the deep woods."

"Then it suits you," Nikolai replied, "because there is no other like you."

She blushed, but before she could respond, she glanced at the sun and gasped.

"I really must go!"

She leaned forward, took Nikolai's hand, and pressed a gentle kiss against it. Her warm lips brushed the scars on the back of his cold hand as her soft blue eyes lingered on him. Nikolai smiled, a rush of energy surging through his body. And then, in an instant, she was gone.

Nikolai fell under her spell of innocence. He spent every minute he could with her, often lying to his parents about where he was to quell any suspicions. At first, they only sat inside the cave, but soon, they began walking the paths in the woods. Nikolai insisted they stay hidden beneath the trees, out of sight. He didn't want to arouse her suspicions about why he always avoided the sunlight. Nikolai had never seen a female human before, so he assumed Mira might be just like him. The first time she stepped directly into the sun, he reacted instinctively.

They were walking along a dirt path when Mira suddenly jumped into the sunlight to pick a flower. Nikolai lurched forward, grabbing her and pushing her back into the shadows. "You must be careful! You'll get burned!" he warned. Mira laughed as she stood up, brushing dirt from her clothing. "How can the sun burn me?" To prove her point, she extended her hand into the sunlight. Nothing happened. Before Nikolai could stop her, she grabbed his wrist and pulled his hand into the light. The moment the sunlight touched his skin, a sharp sizzling sound filled the air, followed by a thin wisp of smoke curling from his arm. Nikolai jerked his arm back violently and yelled, "No!" Mira took a step forward, raising both hands in alarm. "I'm so sorry! But what ails you?"

Nikolai held his injured arm close to his chest. "I do not know. My mother and father have this condition as well. But Mira, I have to tell you... you are the first girl I have ever seen." Mira tilted her head, her brown curls falling into her view. "What do you mean, I am the first?" Nikolai frowned. "I have never left our home until I saw you. My parents think I am hunting, but they have forbidden me from leaving the marked area around our cabin."

Mira interrupted, "But why would they hide you from others?" Nikolai sighed. "I don't know. I feel there is much they have hidden from me, and it's time I uncover the truth." Nikolai hid the burn on his arm and headed home.

When Nikolai returned to his family's cabin, he waited until he was alone with his mother to ask her some questions. The sun had begun to set, and this was the time the family tended to the gardens to avoid exposure to the sun. Seraphina was tending to the plants, her head completely covered by a scarf. Her long hair fell in front of her face, hidden beneath a black veil. "Mother, why are there no others like us?" She was crouching in the dirt, scraping the soil with her tool. "Because it is only us who live here; there are no others."

Seraphina brushed the dirt from her hands onto her pant legs and stood up. "My curious son, why do you ask such questions?" She began walking toward the cabin, and Nikolai hurried behind her to keep up. "Mother, why are there no others? We cannot be the only ones!" Seraphina stopped in her tracks causing Nikolai to slam into her. She abruptly turned and faced him, "My son, there are others far from here, but we are not like them. We are different and can only survive on warm blood."

Nikolai demanded, "Who are the others?"

"They are humans," she whispered, "and they fear what they do not understand. We must

stay away from them; it is not safe for us or for them."

Seraphina began to walk away, and Nikolai followed.

"But Mother, why?"

As she walked ahead, she pleaded, "No more talk!"

As Nikolai lay in the darkness of his straw mat, he decided it was best not to persist with his questions, as Mother might become apprehensive about his hunting ventures.

Nikolai got an early start and finished his chores before heading to the woods to hunt. He spent the better part of the morning searching for small game to appease Mother. By midday, he had killed two hares, their warm bodies limp in his hands. Steam lifted from the animals, the scent of warm blood alluring, tempting his taste buds

He wrapped the animals in cloth and hid them on a low-hanging tree limb, making sure to take note of the spot so he could retrieve them later. Mother always reminded him to keep his stomach full and never travel without sustenance. "A starving body is a weak body," she would say, her crimson eyes piercing through him like a cold breeze. She would often warn him, "Hunger dulls the senses, slows reflexes, and leaves one vulnerable. And vulnerability can mean death." For now, he thought, *my hunger will have to wait.*

As he turned the corner near the edge of the woods, he saw Mira in the distance; she was wiping tears from her eyes. He became concerned and hurried his pace. When he got to their meeting spot at the cave, her blue eyes were surrounded by redness that could not hide her recent tears. Nikolai sat facing Mira and reached for her hands. "What is the matter?" he asked, holding her snow-white fingers gently in his own. Mira turned her head to the ground to avoid his look. Nikolai pressed, "Please, Mira, what is it?"

Slowly, Mira raised her head and met Nikolai's eyes. "My father has become suspicious and has forbidden me to leave. I had to sneak away to come here. I am fearful that he may have followed me." Nikolai tilted his head in concern. "Why do you fear your own father?" Without a word, Mira lifted the front of her shirt, revealing deep black bruises marring her pearl-colored skin. Wrapped around her wrist was a tightly wound gray cloth, stained with a blackened circle of dried blood.

Nikolai reached for her injured arm. "How can I help you?" Before she could respond, he demanded, "Did your father do this to you?" Mira whispered solemnly, "Yes." Nikolai began to slowly unravel the makeshift bandage covering her arm. As he slowly turned the last piece of cloth he saw the cut on he wrist covered in dried blood. Holding back his anger Nikolai asked,

"What happened to you?"

Mira spoke through her tears,

"My father demanded to know where I was going off too. He kicked me and I fell and

injured myself."

As Nikolai looked at her arm, her voice faded into the distance. He became entranced by the wound, the dark stain of dried blood drawing his focus like a beacon. Everything around them blurred as a deep, insatiable hunger began to stir within him. As he held her arm he slowly squeezed harder until a drip of fresh blood appeared. Mira tried to free her arm from his grasp and pleaded, "Nikolai, you're hurting me." Nikolai leaned toward her arm, his mouth parting as his teeth shifted, their tips sharpening into fine points. He lowered his head towards her arm when she suddenly pushed him away. Mira looked at him in disgust. "What are you?"

Before he could answer, she scrambled toward the cave's entrance and fled. Nikolai sat stunned, shaken by his own uncontrollable hunger—a primal urge that had consumed him. His hands trembled as he stared at them, as if they belonged to someone else. *What had I almost done?* he pleaded silently. "Who am I?" he cried aloud.

Nikolai crawled to the entrance of the cave, closed his eyes, and willed himself to cloak. His body flickered for a moment before vanishing from view. Once invisible, he left the cave and lingered in the shadows near the edge of the woods, listening for Mira. But it wasn't his ears that found her—it was his sense of smell. He lifted his nose, and Mira's familiar aroma drove him forward.

He followed the trail as he moved quickly along the edge of the forest, careful to stay out of the sun. He hurried along a well-worn path as her scent became more distinct. It was a mixture of wildflowers and earth, laced with the faintest trace of blood—a tantalizing blend that drove him forward. But to what end, he had not yet considered.

As he moved along the shadows, he kept asking himself: *What was it that took over? Why was I so entranced by her wound?* The more questions he asked, the faster he moved toward the unrelenting scent that called to him. Still cloaked, Nikolai reached the end of a path that opened into a vast field, where a small cabin stood. A trail of smoke lifted from a stone chimney that was awkwardly balanced on the rooftop. The smell of burnt timber mingled with the familiar essence of Mira, filling his senses. Nikolai was beginning to tire from the strain of Mira running off and his lack of sustenance.

His cloaking was growing weaker as he moved closer to the cabin. Stealthily, he made his way to the side of the structure and crouched in the tall grass near the stone foundation. He decided to hide, uncloaked, in the shadows and try to regain his strength. Nikolai sat on the ground, breathing heavily, as thoughts of what could be happening to Mira raced through his mind. *What was he going to do?* he wondered. *Would Mira even want to see him now? But what if she was in danger from her father?* He could not escape the gnawing fear growing inside. He closed his eyes to gather his thoughts when a loud bang, followed by a scream, came from inside the cabin. His eyes popped open. *Mira. She had to be inside,* he thought.

He closed his eyes tightly and willed himself to cloak. After a deep exhale, he opened his eyes and looked at his own arm that was now invisible. Nikolai quickly stood up and moved to the front of the cabin, the scent of Mira's blood stronger than ever. As he rounded the corner, Nikolai noticed that the front door was partially open just as a gust of wind slammed it against the doorframe.

Nikolai, still cloaked made his way to the door and slowly opened it. Inside he saw a large man with his back turned. Mira was on her knees in front of him, her brown hair streaked with red. He gripped her hair tightly, his fingers tangled in her bloodied locks. The man was wearing a gray woolen tunic that fell past his waist. He had an auburn colored beard and short hair. Small red bristles sprouted from the folds of his neck. He was very tall, with a broad, powerful frame—more like an ox than a man.

Mira was whimpering. As Nikolai entered the cabin, a deep anger surged within him.In the center of the room, the figure dropped Mira to the floor and turned just as Nikolai flickered into view. The intruder met his eyes and let out a deep, guttural growl, followed by, "You!" Without a word, Nikolai opened his mouth wide, revealing sharp, pointed teeth. Large, claw-like nails sprouted from his fingertips. He crouched low on all fours like a predator, digging his claws into the wooden planks before launching himself forward in a single leap, slamming into the man's chest and knocking him backward into a heavy wooden beam.

The impact sent the beam rocking from side to side before the weakened roof gave way, collapsing on them with a deafening crash. Clouds of dust, dirt, and debris filled the air. Nikolai crawled out from under the wreckage, lifting wooden beams off of his head. He was exhausted, hungry, and spent. With what little energy he had left, he dug through the remains in search of Mira. He called her name. "Mira!" But all he heard was the groaning voice of the man.

As he dug through the wood, he finally saw a sign of Mira. It was her curly, blood streaked hair draped across a large piece of wood. He pulled the beam from her head to reveal her lifeless body. There was a trickle of blood running down her forehead, her eyes closed like a child peacefully asleep.

Nikolai was angry and confused. This was his fault—he had caused this terrible tragedy. The man stood up, lifted a large wooden beam, and struck Nikolai in the back of the head, knocking him unconscious and sending him crashing into the rubble. He then bent down and hoisted Nikolai's limp body over his shoulder. Stepping carefully through the debris, he made his way outside the collapsed cabin and into the open field.

Without hesitation, he began walking toward the well. As he walked, his mind drifted back to the well. It was a place of deep regret for Ulrich. First, it was his wife, Danica, who perished, and now Mira was gone too.

He had met Danica when he was a younger man, and she was still little more than a girl. After her parents perished from disease, she survived alone, eventually wandering onto his farm. He found her one day asleep beneath a cluster of trees near his cabin. She was in rough shape, so he carried her into his cabin and slowly nursed her back to health. It took a long time before she finally spoke, but she never talked about her past—only that her parents had died from an illness and that she had gotten lost while searching for help.

As time went on, Ulrich and Danica developed a routine. She tended to the farm and prepared meals, while Ulrich did the hunting and preserved the food for storage. They rarely spoke, but their arrangement seemed to work. Ulrich found himself staring at her when she wasn't looking. Danica had red, curly hair that cascaded past her shoulders. Her pale skin was dusted with freckles on each cheek. She was unlike any woman he had ever seen.

Ulrich prepared her a sleeping area in the cabin while he slept in the barn. It wasn't the ideal sleeping arrangement but he felt like it was the proper thing to do. One night, while alone in the barn, he was startled by a sound. He jolted awake to see Danica standing before him. She extended her hand as if to reach for him, her bright blue eyes offering a silent invitation.

For a moment, neither of them spoke. Then, she took a step closer, her fingers trembling slightly as they brushed against his. Ulrich intertwined his fingers with hers and followed her into the cabin. She lay down on the straw mat, pulled him in behind her, and wrapped his arm around her body as she drifted off to sleep. For the first time he felt a comforting warmth.

This became part of their nightly routine. At bedtime, Ulrich would wait in the doorway, and Danica would take his hand, leading him to her mat. There, they would lie together, his arms wrapped tightly around her. She embraced the warmth of his beard as it pressed against her shoulder. As the days passed, their nights grew more intimate, and they came together as one.

In time, Danica became pregnant and gave birth to a daughter they named Mira. She was a spirited child, born with a full head of curly golden-brown hair that matched her lively nature. Ulrich had hoped for a son but was surprised by the depth of his affection for Mira. He would lift her onto his broad shoulders while he worked in the fields, her laughter ringing through the air with each bounce of his stride. The two became inseparable, often leaving Danica alone.

As Mira grew, Ulrich would take her into the woods, letting her pick berries while he hunted. Danica stayed behind at the cabin, drowning in her loneliness. One day, while Ulrich and Mira were away, a man came to the cabin. He was alone and searching for food. The man, was long and thin with a square jaw and kind face hidden under a layer of dirt. Danica felt a sense of duty to help him, just as Ulrich had once helped her. She wiped the dirt from his face with a dampened rag. She then prepared him a meal and sat in silence, watching as he ate. The two did not speak. When he finished his meal, he stood, smiled, and then left.

As time went on, the man returned on the same day each week to share a meal with Danica while Ulrich was away hunting with Mira. They would sit, talk, and eat together, Danica sharing pieces of her past and simply enjoying the company. The man sat quietly, smiling and listening, but he spoke nothing of his own life.

One day, as they sat and ate, Ulrich unexpectedly returned early from the hunt with Mira. When he opened the cabin door and saw Danica with the man, rage consumed him. He pointed to Mira, who stood behind him in the doorway. "Go to the edge of the woods and gather more berries!" Mira protested, "But Father..." Before she could continue, he demanded, "Go now!"

Ulrich turned to Danica, who now stood beside the man. He pointed at her. "Step aside. Now." The man raised his hands in the air, signaling Ulrich to stop. This only enraged him further. Beads of sweat rolled down Ulrich's forehead, soaking into his red beard, which burned as fiercely as his flushed skin. His fury boiled over as he pushed his way across the room and seized the man by the collar. He dragged him through the doorway and into the front of the cabin. He held the man in front of his face and lifted him off the ground and struck him in the stomach, launching him onto the ground with a thud.

Ulrich made his way to the man who was lying in a cloud of dust. As he slowly sat up, Ulrich kicked him squarely in the teeth, knocking him back to the ground. In the distance he could he hear the muffled cries of Danica. The man slowly crawled away and never returned. Ulrich did not say a word to Danica and this time he forced her to sleep in the barn. He couldn't bear the pain of thinking that Danica had been disloyal to him after everything he had provided for her. This angered him to no end.

Danica was at the well, drawing water early one morning while Mira slept. Ulrich quietly approached as she leaned over the stone well, her head tilted downward into the dark void. As he walked towards her he stared at her long curly red hair for one last time. Ulrich grabbed her by the legs and lifted her into the well. Her final words were, "No." As she fell into the blackness.

Ulrich had tried hard to forget that day, even convincing himself that she must have fallen in on her own. The truth was too much to bear. As he approached the well with Nikolai slumped over his shoulder, he thought, I will get rid of this demon, and then I will find his nest and destroy any others. Ulrich had grown suspicious and had been watching Mira and Nikolai for some time. Ulrich grabbed Nikolai's shirt, tore a piece from the bottom, wiped it across Nikolai's face, and then tucked it inside his tunic. Without hesitation, he dumped Nikolai into the well. Nikolai plummeted into the darkness, landing with a quiet splash in the depths below.

As Ulrich turned toward the fallen cabin, he thought, I will find those who caused this destruction, but for now, I must bury this secret along with Mira. Ulrich dug a small grave and gently placed Mira's body inside. He had wrapped her in a wool covering and laid a bed of rocks upon the earth for her eternal rest. With the last handful of dirt, he whispered a final goodbye to the one person he had loved more than anyone.

Determined for vengeance, Ulrich gathered men from the nearby farms and told them that a demon had taken his child. The locals were well aware of the stories—tales of creatures said to dwell deep within the mountains. It had been a very long time since someone was attacked. The men were eager to help, driven by the fear of losing their own families to such darkness.

Ulrich's fellow farmers trusted his word and would follow him to the ends of the earth. He was a man of few words, speaking only after listening carefully. They knew him as someone to be respected and, when necessary, feared. His strength was unquestionable. When his wife, Danica, died in an accident, he stepped up and cared for Mira as only a father could. If he said a demon had taken his child, then a demon would die by their hands.

Ulrich and four other men hiked into the darkness of the mountains, their breath visible in the cold night air. Each man was led by a hunting dog, the animals straining against their tethered ropes, noses low to the ground. Stories had been told of vampire demons whose scent was so potent that only animals could perceive it. It was said that humans could not detect it, for they were merely prey to these creatures. The dogs would be able to smell the pungent aroma that came from the vampire creatures. The men carried large spears strapped to their backs. They would use the dogs to track the demons, driving them out into the open where they could be trapped.

Ulrich purposely did not tell the other men that he had trapped Nikolai inside the well. For all he knew, Nikolai would die at the bottom the same way Danica had perished. Besides, he did not want to risk the men growing suspicious of Danica's death. They hiked up the mountain, following the trails in search of any sign of the creatures. Once they reached an open field bathed in moonlight, Ulrich pulled out the piece of cloth he had taken from Nikolai. Holding it high, he addressed the group. "Men, I was able to take this piece of clothing from the demon!"

He then bent down on one knee as the four dogs surrounded him, lunging forward to sniff the cloth. Ulrich stood and lifted the cloth into the air. The dogs leapt at him, whining and barking. He tucked the cloth inside the fur-lined cloak that draped over his body. Ulrich addressed the group once more. "We will find the nest, and then we will stand back." One of the men interrupted, "Why stand back? Why not attack?"

Ulrich looked at them sternly. "It was my daughter who was taken. I will decide what we do and I have a plan!" The men stood in silent agreement as they wrestled with the dogs, who were anxious to hunt. The men followed the dogs as they pulled them along an invisible trail only the animals could perceive. They hiked through the late night and into the early morning. Ulrich paused the group near the edge of a river as the sun rose over the horizon. "We will let the dogs regain their strength and drink while we rest in the sunlight."

The dogs were tied to a nearby tree after they had their fill of water. The men had all heard the stories of these creatures—beings that lurked in the shadows, fearing the sunlight. They knew they would be safest in the open, bathed in direct light. Cautiously, they moved to the center of a wide, open field. While the others rested, one man stood guard, his eyes scanning the tree line for any sign of movement.

Nikolai lay in the black murk at the bottom of the deep well. Only his mouth and nose remained above the thick, sludgy water that filled the pit. His eyes suddenly sprang open as he stared into the long tunnel that led into even deeper darkness. *Where am I?* he thought. *What happened?* He silently begged for an answer. He remembered Mira's face, her delicate curls drifting gently in front of her eyes as she spoke. His thoughts raced to the cabin—to her father, gripping her by the hair as she begged. Then he remembered her lifeless body resting silently in the wreckage. He was weak and exhausted, but he knew he had to escape. He willed himself to bend his legs and stand.

As he pulled himself up, he felt something beneath his feet. He tried to steady himself and gain traction, but his footing failed. He slipped backward and was swallowed by the dark water. When his head burst from the blackness, he spat out a flood of water, gasping for air. As he coughed, he glanced to his side and saw what had caused him to lose his balance—a large bone rising to the surface, followed by two smaller ones.

Nikolai finally found his footing, standing on something just below the surface. He looked up into the black void, searching for any possible way to escape. *The well is long and narrow,* he thought. *If I can stretch my legs to each side, I can use the claws on my hands and feet to gain traction as I climb.* But he knew this would be no easy feat as his strength was nearly gone. He had to escape this predicament and feed so he could hunt for the man who entombed him in the well. He looked down at his open hands—his claws were retracted. He needed anger to bring them to life.

Closing his eyes, he pictured Mira's lifeless body lying beneath the rubble of the cabin. A surge of energy coursed through him as he screamed her name through the tunnel above him, "Mira!" The sound traveled upward and disappeared into the open void. He felt something in his hands and looked down. Sharp, pointed claws emerged once more. Each nail was wide and curved toward his palms, its surface rough and jagged. They were yellowish-brown, darkened at the tips, and stained crimson.

He reached up and grasped the stones lining the well. With a burst of strength, he lifted himself from the water, which cascaded down his body and vanished into the blackness below. As he planted his feet against the stones, the sharp nails on his toes dug into the wall, securing his grip. He looked down and saw the remains of a torso rise to the surface. Bones protruded from the blackened, waterlogged carcass, which bobbed lifelessly in the water below. Nikolai looked up and summoned every ounce of energy to climb out of his temporary grave.

Ambrose had become worried by Nikolai's sudden disappearance. "Our son has never returned late, let alone been absent for an entire night," Seraphina said, looking back at Ambrose with worry. "I will stay here with Bela, and you take Sable and search for Nikolai." Ambrose gathered Sable, tied a rope around his neck, and headed into the woods and down the mountain. He was careful to stay in the shadows as the sun rose above the horizon.

Ulrich and his men were now well-rested and decided it was time to hunt, as the creatures would avoid the sun and remain in the shadows of the woods. They, however, would travel in the open sun. Ulrich gathered the dogs, pulled out Nikolai's cloth, and let them smell it. The dogs went wild, fighting over the fabric. They rolled around on the ground with excitement.

With their noses to the earth, the dogs led them toward the forest's edge, where the mountain began to rise. Reluctantly, the men followed as the hounds plunged into the darkened woods. The men hiked up the mountain for most of the day before finally resting along a riverbank as the sun began to show its last bit of light. In the distance, they spotted a thin trickle of smoke rising above the tree line. One of the men stood up and announced, "Look, Ulrich! There's smoke, someone or something has a fire." Ulrich slowly rose to his feet and said, "We will draw them out and then trap them!"

Nikolai slowly made his way up the darkened well, his claws scraping against the moss-covered stone walls. Each nail was caked with blackened grime, leaving faint streaks along the damp surface as he climbed. Each movement was driven by the thought of finding the man responsible for Mira's death and trapped him in this well. Despite his complete lack of strength, Nikolai forced himself through the dark tunnel.

As he pressed on, he finally saw a glimmer of light shining from the well's opening. With the last of his strength, he pulled himself over the wall and onto the dirt-covered ground. The moment his feet touched the earth, his knees gave out, and he collapsed under the shade of a tree and onto a pile of cold, wet leaves, their dampness seeping into his tattered clothing as he gasped for breath. Nikolai lay on the ground with his eyes closed, finally slowing his breathing enough to form a coherent thought. He pictured his mother staring at him, reminding him, *"You must always make sure you eat. A starving body is a weak body!"* She had repeated those words over and over again. Nikolai knew he needed to get to the hares he had hidden earlier. With a little luck, they would still be warm.

Ambrose hiked down the mountain all day, relying on Sable to track Nikolai's scent. But as the hours passed, Sable grew increasingly confused, distracted by other lingering scents that kept redirecting his path toward the cabin. Frustration mounting, Ambrose stopped in his tracks and looked at the position of the Sun in the sky as the day was winding down. "We have to find Nikolai. We cannot go up the mountain—we must go down." Ambrose looked down the mountain and wondered, *where could Nikolai be?* Sable whined and pulled against the lead, his instincts urging him in the opposite direction. But after a moment of hesitation, he lowered his head, sniffed the ground, and reluctantly followed Ambrose's lead.

Ulrich and the other men followed the smoke to a small cabin hidden among the trees. They tied the dogs to a nearby tree, far enough away to avoid arousing suspicion. Silently, they took cover among the trees, watching and waiting. Ulrich leaned in and whispered, "Let's stay here and see if anyone comes outside. If the fire is burning, someone must be inside." They sat quietly, observing for some time when, suddenly, a woman stepped out of the cabin. She paused in the doorway and called, "Bela, come now!"

A dog sprinted toward her, rising onto its hind legs to snatch a piece of meat from her hand. The woman then led the dog to a small barn in the back before returning and going inside. Ulrich signaled for the men to move farther back, away from the cabin, where they could speak freely. They followed as he walked toward the dogs. Gesturing toward an open field bathed in the last bits of daylight Ulrich said, "It seems the woman is alone. We'll dig a deep hole, conceal it beneath the leaves and timber, and then drive her into our trap. We will then use her as bait to get the rest of them."

One of the men interrupted, "She looks like a woman. How do we know she's a demon?"Ulrich replied, "Because they hide within men and women, and when provoked, they reveal their true form. We cannot trust that she is merely a woman." The man hesitated before speaking one last time. "But what if she doesn't change?" Ulrich stepped closer, locking eyes with him. "If she is just a woman, then when the sun rises tomorrow it will not harm her and she will just be stuck in a hole."

The men found a patch of soft earth and began digging with their spears. The soil was loose and easy to break apart. Sweat beaded on their foreheads as they worked in silence, the rhythmic thrusting of their spears into the ground the only sound breaking the stillness. As the hole deepened, they exchanged uneasy glances. "How deep should it be?" one of them finally asked, his voice just a whisper. Ulrich paused, surveying their progress. "Deep enough that she won't escape," he muttered. "Keep digging."

The men continued working until the hole was twice as deep as the tallest among them. One man climbed into the pit, stretching his arms over his head to demonstrate its depth. Satisfied, the group laid long branches across the opening in a woven pattern before finally covering it with loose leaves. Ulrich opened his leather pouch, retrieving his flint and steel. He then gathered some dry tinder to start a small fire. "Men, we will get close enough to set the house on fire and drive out the demon. One of you will have the dogs ready to chase her toward the hole. Two of us will wait nearby with our weapons to keep her trapped inside." The men nodded in approval as Ulrich assigned each of them a task. He would wait near the hole to guide her toward the trap.

Once the fire was burning, they lit broken tree branches to use as torches. The firelight danced across their faces as they slowly walked toward the cabin, torches in hand. As they neared the home, the dog began barking from within a small barn at the rear. The men quickened their pace, spreading out around the house before setting it ablaze. The fire spread quickly, engulfing the cabin. As the men waited nearby, the front door burst open, and the woman rushed out, frantically waving her hands in the air.

She started to run toward the barking dog when one of the men released the hounds. They sprinted toward her, closing the distance in seconds. As one of them leapt at her, she threw up her arm, deflecting the dog with her forearm. The animal whimpered before landing hard on its side. Another dog latched onto her leg biting down with a growl. It frantically shook its head from side to side trying to release its grip. The hounds began barking as the surge of the woman's scent agitated them. She turned toward the barn and yelled, "Bela!" just as the flames consumed the structure. The dogs had now surrounded her, and one of the men approached with his spear aimed at her. Without hesitation, she spun away from the cabin and sprinted toward the open field—where Ulrich was waiting.

When she reached the field, Ulrich stood on the far side of the hidden pit, his spear pointed directly at her. Seraphina was alone and frightened, she knew she had to cloak herself. As she ran towards Ulrich she closed her eyes and began to flicker and then disappeared. A moment later, the top of the hidden pit collapsed, sending debris tumbling into the hole. Ulrich took a few tentative steps forward and used his spear to push aside the remaining branches and leaves. When he peered into the pit, he saw the woman's body flicker in and out of sight before finally hitting the ground and collapsing. She now lay motionless, fully visible, like a discarded lump of waste.

Nikolai had crawled all the way to the path that led to the food he had hidden. He was exhausted and spent but forced himself to his feet. Leaning against a tall boulder, he looked up at the full moon hanging in the clear night sky. He wondered what his parents must be thinking. *Would they be angry at him, or would they come looking for him?* At this point, he didn't know what was worse—them finding him or not finding him. Either way, he knew he had to forge onward. Nikolai slowly made his way to the branch where he had hidden the hares. He was devastated to find the cloth he had wrapped them in torn apart on the ground. Both carcasses lay nearby, mostly shredded by a scavenger. He fell to his knees and tore at the last remains of the animals in search of a single drop of warm blood.

Nikolai rolled onto his back and stared at the night sky. He closed his eyes, searching for a sliver of hope. He lay there, breathing slowly, drifting in and out of his thoughts when, suddenly, he felt something wet on his face. He opened his eyes—it was Sable, his dog, licking his face. He then heard the familiar voice of his father, Ambrose. "My son, what has happened to you?" His father knelt down and placed his hand on Nikolai's cold, blackened face.

Ambrose helped Nikolai into a seated position and poured water into his mouth. He then rinsed off his own hands and wiped the dirt from Nikolai's face. They sat silently for a moment, with Ambrose holding him in his arms as he had when Nikolai was a child. Ambrose broke the silence with a whisper. "The sun will rise soon and you are weak and must feed. I will leave you here with Sable while I hunt for you." Nikolai nodded before closing his eyes. Ambrose turned to Sable, who seemed to understand the weight of the situation. "I want you to watch over Nikolai while I find him warm blood."

Ambrose quietly disappeared into the darkened forest. He would return a short time later with the warm carcass of a small deer. The animal was barely alive when Ambrose returned. He crouched down near Nikolai and bit into the animals neck to start the flow of blood. He then laid the wound near Nikolai's mouth as he slowly drank. In time, Nikolai recovered his energy, but he was still exhausted from the ordeal.

Ambrose waited until Nikolai was coherent and able to speak clearly before he asked what had happened. Nikolai left out much of the truth but confessed to his father that there was a dangerous man who might be looking for him. Ambrose looked at Nikolai sternly. "We must go back to the cabin. Your mother may be in danger." Nikolai felt a surge of guilt as he considered the danger he had invited into their quiet lives. Ambrose gave

Sable a drink of water and a handful of herbs before they headed back up the mountain while the sun slowly rose in the distance.

Seraphina lay in the cold, moist pit, facing the ground. She was partially covered in wet leaves and branches. Standing around the pit were three men and Ulrich, all pointing their spears at her, their expressions grim. She slowly turned her head, the leaves pasted to her face, and looked up at the men. Ulrich spoke. "You have brought this upon yourself. Where is the rest of your kind? Answer me, demon, or you will burn!" Seraphina lowered her head to the ground as the first light of the sun began to make its way across the landscape.

As Ambrose and Nikolai hiked the path up the mountain, Sable became agitated and began to pull at the lead, practically dragging them along. Ambrose tried to calm her with his words. "Easy, boy. What's wrong?" Sable looked at Ambrose for a moment before settling down. For the entire walk, Nikolai was silent, and Ambrose asked few questions. When Nikolai finally spoke, Ambrose was surprised. "Father, I fear Mother may be in serious danger. We must hurry!" As Nikolai and Ambrose neared the open field by their cabin, they saw a trickle of black smoke rising into the air. Nikolai tried to push past his father but was stopped. "Don't go any further. There are humans nearby—I can smell them."

Ambrose guided Nikolai and Sable behind a nearby group of trees to hide. They crouched low as Ambrose pointed to four men standing in a circle in the distance, holding spears. Ambrose looked up at the sun, which hung high in the heavens, nearing its zenith. He realized that Seraphina was either burned in the cabin fire or captured by these men. Regardless, they didn't have much time, as the sun would soon become their greatest enemy.

They silently made their way around the forest's edge, staying low and remaining camouflaged in the overgrowth. Ambrose kept Sable close, and he knew to remain still, as they had hunted together many times. Nikolai was still weak but pushed himself forward in spite of the guilt that consumed him. When they got close to the men, Ambrose decided he would cloak himself and slowly walk to the area where the men were standing. Nikolai and Sable would remain on the side in case Ambrose had any trouble.

Nikolai pointed to four dogs, all tied to a nearby tree in the distance. Ambrose acknowledged him with a nod. Ambrose slowly closed his eyes and began to flicker before fully disappearing. He stealthily made his way across the clearing, knowing that the sun was nearing its apex and that he could not uncloak and face its deadly rays.

Nikolai watched from the shadows holding Sable close to his chest nervous with anticipation. Ambrose quietly made his way within arm's reach of the men as the nearby dogs began to bark relentlessly at his scent. As he approached, he saw that the men were surrounding a large pit. As the sun shifted to its highest point in the sky, there was a familiar scream coming from within the hole. It was Seraphina, and the sun's rays were now reaching her body as she turned and tried to hide from its grip.

Ambrose reacted by pushing the men aside with one powerful swing of his arm. Ambrose stared into the hole in horror as smoke rose from Seraphina's body. He dove in, his arms and legs extended as he landed on top of her. His body began to flicker as he came into view. He pulled Seraphina to the side and over his shoulder as he clawed at the muddy walls of the hole. The wet mud gave way, causing him to fall forward. As he hit the ground, he tried to cover Seraphina as the sun's rays consumed them.

Nikolai watched as smoke rose from the hole. He could smell the scent of burnt flesh filling the air as Sable pulled away from him and ran toward the men. As Sable leaped into the air toward one of the men with his back turned, the man quickly spun around, his spear pointed directly at Sable. Nikolai watched as Sable landed, the spear piercing his body. He closed his eyes and forced himself to cloak. He flickered before disappearing and sprinting across the open field. As he approached the pit, his claws extended from his hands and feet.

He attacked the men, slicing his hands from side to side in a frantic motion, blood filling the air. Then men reacted by turning in confusion as they could not see their invisible attacker. He pushed the men into the pit where his parents were now burning. Nikolai looked up and saw a familiar face—Mira's father, Ulrich, the man who had left him to die in the well. Ulrich swung his spear back and forth as he declared, "Stop hiding! Make yourself seen, demon!"

Nikolai, still cloaked slowly walked up to Ulrich and stood just out of his reach. As he swung the spear one last time, Nikolai stepped in close to him, sliced his throat with the claw on his index finger before biting down on his neck and devouring his essence. The blood rushed into him, warm and flowing, carrying more than just life. Each drop was a stream of hidden code. Ulrich's soul signature—his very DNA unraveled like threads of light and data, pouring into Nikolai's veins.

In moments, every trace of Ulrich was gone—erased from existence. Nikolai pushed his empty shell into the fiery pit. He then walked over to Sable who was barely breathing. He gently stroked his fur before pulling the spear from his body. Nikolai leaned forward and bit into the wound and drank his blood. He could feel Sables heart fading and disappearing. He then instinctively sliced his own wrist with his nails and allowed his blood to fall into Sables wound. Nikolai looked down into the pit one last time as the nearby dogs, still tied to a tree, began to bark. He then turned to Sable, who was still lying on his side.

He let out a breath as his eyes snapped open—now a deep crimson red. In an instant, Sable sprang to his feet, shaking his head from side to side before rearing up on his hind legs. His body had doubled in size as he clawed at the ground, his sharp teeth snapping at the air. Nikolai remained cloaked to avoid the sun. He walked into the shade and came back into view, knelt down, and called Sable to him.

His once familiar dog was now an immense beast. He smiled at him and stroked the white stripe that ran down his back as he hissed and growled.

Leaning into his pointed ears, he whispered, "Are you hungry, boy?" He then pointed to the dogs tied to the trees. "Go get them, boy!" Sable ran across the field and leaped into the air at the barking hounds. Nikolai turned his back and walked away as he heard the dogs whimper and cry. He then paused, looking at his nail, where a single droplet of blood clung. He brought his hand to his face, stared at it for a moment, then licked it clean and said aloud, "I don't understand the fuss, I think I rather like the taste of humans!" His fingers brushed across the small marks that had suddenly appeared on his neck. Nikolai walked into the woods at its darkest point and disappeared.

Chapter Twelve

THE CITY OF BUDA

Nikolai and Sable wandered, studying the humans. He fed on animals, with the occasional human for good measure. However, he was careful not to attract attention when he fed. He would cloak himself, becoming invisible, and observe human behavior from the shadows. Eventually, he grew bored of merely watching and sought to blend in, learning to act as one of them. Nikolai traveled to a nearby village where people were always on the move—merchants, laborers, and travelers passing through without question. He found clothing to help him fit in. At first, Nikolai was nervous to speak to the humans for fear of being exposed. But over time, he realized something peculiar—if he locked eyes with them, even for a moment, he could subtly influence their thoughts.

Eventually, their path led them toward the Danube River, the great waterway that connected kingdoms and carried merchants, soldiers, and wanderers to distant lands. Nikolai had overheard whispers in the village taverns about the city of Buda. It was the heart of the Hungarian kingdom, filled with wealth, power, and opportunity. In order for him to travel to this far-off land, he would need to secure a riverboat and a captain without arousing suspicion. Nikolai had found it relatively easy to obtain gold as currency. With his ability to control the minds of lower-level beings, he could get his hands on nearly anything he desired, including a riverboat and its captain.

He approached the captain, an old man named Hans, and offered him one bag of gold before their departure, promising a second upon their safe arrival—no questions asked. However, there were some conditions: the captain could only bring one assistant, and Nikolai would bring a live sheep. He told them it was meat to feed his dog, Sable. But in truth, it was warm blood for both of them, a way to curb his hunger and remove the temptation of devouring the captain and his assistant.

The captain's assistant was a boy named Imre. He was rail-thin, with coffee-colored skin darkened by a mixture of sun and dirt. He was a likable lad with a constant smile, always eager to follow Hans's instructions. The journey would take approximately two weeks. Hans looked at Nikolai as he picked at his teeth with a small stick. "I can't guarantee anything," he said, pointing toward the sky. "It's all in the hands of the Almighty, and the mercy of the river herself. We will travel as fast as she will take us."

Nikolai looked the man directly in the eyes, as if casting a spell on him. The old mans eyes were like black orbs, surrounded by bloodshot, red threads. "We will get there quickly, and you will tell no one of this journey." Hans stared at Nikolai and nodded in agreement. He looked like he had lived well past his prime, and life on the river had carved deep lines into his weathered face. His skin was tanned and leathery from years spent beneath the sun, and his fingers were gnarled like tree branches. Nikolai continued to stare at Hans, telling himself he would not be tempted to feast on this old man, as there wasn't much to take. The boy however was a different story.

Life aboard the riverboat was cramped and uncomfortable. The vessel itself was around forty feet long by ten feet wide. It was built like a barge, with a flat bottom made from sturdy timber. Hans had traveled this route for a long time, while his assistant, Imre, was just learning the ways of the river. Hans had taken Imre in as his own son when he found the boy wandering along the riverbank as a small child. Imre had been starving and alone, so Hans brought him aboard and cared for him.

Hans would often joke, "I could feed Imre an entire horse, and he'd still be a tree branch."Nikolai wore a gray tunic with a black cloak and hood covering his head. He carried a small dagger hidden beneath his cloak, though it was more of a tool than a weapon. In his observations of humans, he noticed one clear sign of their weakness: they always carried weapons. He believed it was because their bodies were inherently frail. He, on the other hand, was a weapon himself and had no need for such trinkets.

Nikolai spent his days beneath a hemp-woven canopy to avoid the sun, while Sable sat obediently by his side, always alert and aware of everyone's next move. Nikolai kept the sheep tied to the side of the boat. She was white, with shades of gray running along her back. She mostly stood idle, occasionally letting out a low cry. At night, Nikolai would stand at the front of the boat, watching the stars in the sky. He would find himself thinking about his father and mother and the journey that brought him to this moment.

After a week traveling down the river, his hunger began to grow. He caught himself staring at young Imre wondering what he tasted like. His thoughts were interrupted by his own guilt. He would tell himself, "Control yourself. We need to get to our destination." He had brought the sheep for this very reason, knowing he and Sable would need to eat. Tonight, he thought, was an excellent night to feast. The captain and Imre slept on the boat while it remained tied to a tree along the shoreline, the gentle swaying of the river guiding their breathing.

Nikolai untied the sheep and quietly escorted it off the boat to the shore. He found an open area in the moonlight and secured the animal to a tree. Sable eagerly approached, circling the sheep before pawing at the ground in front of it. His claws suddenly extended from his paws as he reared up on her hind legs, arching his back. Nikolai ran the back of his nails down the light-colored stripe along Sable's spine.

Nikolai walked behind the sheep and wrapped his arms around her body. Then, he extended his pointer finger as a large nail grew from it. With a swift movement he sliced the animal throat. Before a single drop could fall to the ground he had pressed his mouth to the wound and drank. As the animals heartbeat quickly faded, he released his hold and let Sable finish off his leftovers. The blood gave him a brief surge of strength, but it was hollow, fleeting. What he truly craved… what his body demanded—was the taste of human life.

They finally arrived as the sun dipped below the skyline of Buda. The city's war-torn air was thick with the scent of smoke, spices, and secrets. Nikolai thanked Hans and Imre with an extra bag of gold pieces, a reminder of their shared secret. Nikolai led Sable to a wooded clearing to hunt. "Listen, Sable, I want you to eat while I find myself a meal. I will come back to this very spot to find you." Sable clawed at the ground before disappearing into the woods.

Nikolai decided he would not cloak himself, but rather walk among the locals and blend in. He pulled his black hood over his head and his scarf up over his face as he moved toward a crowded district, where the sounds of conversation and laughter filled the air. The cobblestone street wound down a long stretch before disappearing into the darkness. On each side stood wooden-framed buildings with stone facades and thatched roofs. Thin trails of soot and smoke poured from the chimneys into the night sky. The buildings rose two stories high, each with a balcony jutting out from the upper floor. Women leaned out of open, shuttered windows or looked down from the balconies—some wearing very little, strutting from side to side like bait on a fishing line.

On the streets below, small groups gathered around open fire pits, drinking and murmuring beneath the glow of the dancing flames. Nikolai stood in awe of the activity and bustle unfolding in every direction. The scent of warm blood hung thick in the air, tempting his hunger. As he walked he was drawn to a tent filled with herbs and medicines. Nikolai stepped inside and began to browse the selection of brightly colored herbs that lined the makeshift table where an old woman sat. Her head was tilted downward as she snored softly, hunched over on a low wooden stool. Just as Nikolai looked away, her head snapped up with unnatural speed, and she spoke. "What do you need, dear man?"

The woman had thinning white hair protruding from beneath a faded blue scarf that clung to her scalp. Her body lurched forward with a creak of bone, unable to fully straighten. She had one milky eye, and nothing but a hollow socket where the other should have been. Her lips were cracked, flaking with a chalky white crust that clung to the corners of her mouth. Nikolai stared at her as he stepped closer, his eyes deepening, pulling her into sharp focus. His voice dropped low, almost serpentine. "I am hungry, old woman, and it's not food I need." His words hung in the air like a spell, coiling around her like a snake. The old woman stood, her head barely reaching Nikolai's waist. "If it is blood you seek, go to The Red Rose," she said through a raspy cough. Then, without another word, she slouched back onto the stool and began to snore softly once more. Nikolai stepped out of the tent and continued down the damp, uneven streets. Activity pulsed in every direction, sights and sounds clawing for his attention. He had only ever known quiet villages, isolated and sparse. This was something entirely different, and his vampiric senses surged beneath the surface. He was alert to every heartbeat, every whisper, every drop of blood in the air. Its scent pulled him forward, subtle at first, then growing stronger as he approached a weathered stone building. A single red rose was painted, almost discreetly on a small stone near the door.

Nikolai stepped toward the entrance, where a large, round man stood silently on watch. His bright blue eyes were focused and unblinking as he stared straight ahead, not even acknowledging Nikolai. His head was bald, and a thin mustache drooped past his cheeks like twin blades. Before

Nikolai could speak, the man slid open the door and motioned for him to enter. Inside, the space was dimly lit, with low ceilings intricately carved with creatures bearing exposed breasts and pointed teeth protruding from their snapping mouths.

Beneath Nikolai's boots lay a masterpiece of woven artistry, its colors still vibrant despite years of wear. Deep crimson reds and icy blue trim formed a complex web of interlocking geometric shapes. A thin man with a long, pointed nose sat in the corner playing a lute. He sat cross-legged on a faded red cushion, gently plucking the strings with his eyes closed. The melody was soft and delicate, a whisper of something forbidden.

Nikolai paused and listened. It was the first time he had ever heard music. His parents had never introduced him to it, and in the small villages he had passed through, it simply did not exist. His focus was interrupted by a female voice coming from nearby, "Welcome to The Thorned Rose... How may we fill your appetite sir?"

As Nikolai turned, the woman moved closer. She had short black hair that stopped at her ears. Her eyes were narrow slits, like two dark stones, unblinking, and impossible to read. She wore a long flowing black robe that was opened in the front revealing her naked body. Gold bangles with elegant engravings hung from each wrist. She stepped in swiftly, pressing her nose to Nikolai's neck and taking a deep inhale and licking his throat where two small bumps lifted at her touch. Then, she sniffed a few more times before smiling at him with an audible purr. "I am the House Mother and I know exactly what you want."

She then locked her arm around Nikolai's and lead him towards a doorway with a painted red rose. They entered a small room, where the woman asked Nikolai to sit on a cushion before disappearing through a red velvet curtain. As Nikolai lowered himself onto the weathered cushion, the smell of warm blood began to gnaw at his nerves. His hunger was growing by the moment, and now his patience was too. Suddenly, the woman reappeared with two girls. One had flowing black hair that cascaded down her shoulders, past her waist. The taller girl had sand-colored hair and pale skin. Both wore crimson robes that clung to their bodies like wet paint on canvas.

"These are my Vermilion-Courtesans," the House Mother said, her voice rich with pride. "They do more than offer pleasure. They offer memory, vitality... ecstasy. But only to those who can endure it." Nikolai said nothing and stared at the girls, his thirst overwhelming. "They will tell you when to stop, do not take more than is allowed, or you will not leave." She bent down to Nikolai's level and extended her open palm. Her long black fingernails curled at the tips like the beak of a raven. Without a word, Nikolai handed her the remainder of his gold and stood. She then handed him a thorny rose and left him with the girls.

The dark haired girl extended her hand to Nikolai, he could see her breast poking out from her robe. A series of scars circled her nipple like a map. Nikolai quickly looked away as his excitement stirred. The girl led him through the velvet curtain into a small room. Once inside, she pushed Nikolai onto a red velvet divan, a low couch with a curved back that rested against the wall. She asked, "Which of us do you want?" Nikolai pointed to her, and with that, the pale girl slipped out of the room.

He was now alone, his thirst mounting like never before. The girl smiled as she extended her hand and pointed to the rose. Nikolai handed it to her, careful not to cut himself on the thick thorns sprouting from the stem. She then turned and walked to a small modest wooden table resting in the corner. She placed the rose on the table and gathered a small cup filled with a finely ground brown herb. She bent down and used the nearby candle to light the herb. A trail of smoke immediately filled the air, curling up into the girl's nostrils and drifting out the other side and back into her mouth.

The girl turned with the cup in hand and smiled at Nikolai. She glided across the room and climbed onto his lap and straddled him. The bumps on his neck swelled and lifted, his tongue begging for her streaming essence. She leaned into his face to kiss him. As their mouths connected she released a plume of smoke into his mouth. Nikolai pulled it deep into his lungs and exhaled it through his nose.

She had the cup in one hand and the rose in the other. She gently pressed a pointed thorn against her skin and closed her eyes. She let out a loud moan as the barb pierced her skin. She placed the silver cup beneath the dripping blood. Nikolai watched as the cup slowly filled. The girl then handed it to him, and without hesitation, he drank every drop. Her scarlet essence coated his tongue, flooding him with a torrent of energy.

He closed his eyes and leaned back, his hands falling to his sides. In his mind, a tunnel appeared before him. He felt his body accelerating through a rotating sphere of ever changing, colored fractals. Each color was more vibrant than the last. Suddenly, he had the sensation of arriving somewhere. He now stood in an empty space with no walls and no structure, only darkness, devoid of light. In the center of the void, he saw a black garnet stone pulsing like a heartbeat, drawing his full attention.

The heartbeat grew louder and louder until he could feel it thudding within his own chest. It was as if he had connected with something sentient... something alive. The rhythm was not just a sound, but a presence, syncing with his breath, his blood, his very thoughts. For a moment, there was no separation between himself and the stone. Then, a voice echoed in the dark. Not spoken aloud, but felt inside his mind, "Come to me." He suddenly opened his eyes as the girl leaned in and kissed Nikolai's neck, her tongue tracing the raised bumps that had now swelled beneath his skin.

Nikolai walked back to the wooded area where he had left Sable earlier that night. The sun was beginning to rise, and he decided he should feast one last time before retreating to the shadows. He found a large buck feeding as the first light broke through the trees. Silently, he tackled the animal and drank most of its blood. Then he dragged the remains into the tree line where he met up with Sable. "Come here. I brought you some leftovers," he said, dropping the deer to the ground. Sable began to feast.

Nikolai became obsessed with returning to his courtesan each night. As he sat on the red velvet divan, Nikolai spoke to the girl for the first time. "What is your name?" The girl looked away shyly, pulling her long hair around her shoulder to temporarily conceal her face. "We are not allowed to be called by names." Nikolai insisted, "Did you ever have a name?" She suddenly turned and pulled her long black robe closed. "When the other girls and I talk, they call me my birth name Velora. But our mother will not let us have names." Nikolai continued, "Is she your mother?" Velora looked down at the faded red rug beneath her bare feet. "She did not birth me. But she makes us call her Mother."

Nikolai returned to Velora nearly every night, feeding on her blood and slipping into visions. Each time, the image of the black garnet stone appeared. It pulled him toward it, all of his senses blending together. He could smell, taste, touch, and feel its essence, calling to him, beckoning him like an old lover.

After just a few days, Nikolai found lodging in a forgotten corner of a small stone room attached to a crumbling bathhouse that had long since fallen out of use. The entrance was hidden behind a walled garden overgrown with ivy, and the only light came through the cracks in the old wooden shutters, which Nikolai kept tightly closed. The owner, a merchant, had asked no questions and accepted gold without hesitation. Sable stayed in the open courtyard at the back, and Nikolai would often release him at night to hunt in the nearby woods while he visited Velora at The Throned Rose. Sometimes he would feed; other times, they would simply talk. He would always slip her extra gold pieces for her time.

One night, as Nikolai left The Thorned Rose, he was quietly followed by a woman dressed in a square-shaped black veil that hung delicately from her face, concealing her identity in the shadows of the narrow street. She moved carefully, keeping to the darkness and avoiding the breeze so Nikolai would not catch her scent. She would secretly follow Nikolai and other vampires from within the shadows of the city. Her name was Lady

Morovia, and she was an outsider who had only recently arrived in Buda. Her journey had begun much farther upstream along the Danube River. She had traveled not only to escape her past, but to uncover answers to a greater truth.

Until recently, she had lived with a powerful vampire named Soren. He kept her hidden away in a remote castle nestled deep in the mountains, far from the eyes of men and other Nocturni. Soren lived alone in a castle that had been left to him by his family long ago. As a young boy, he showed signs of deep unrest. He struggled to control his hunger and, on multiple occasions, killed and drained the entire human staff. If he wasn't given warm blood, he would scream, cry, and destroy everything in sight.

When he reached his teenage years, Soren grew large and powerful. During a violent outburst, he threw both of his parents from the top window of the castle. They fell into the open courtyard below and burned to ash beneath the searing rays of the afternoon sun.

Soren remained in the castle alone. But at night, he would venture into the surrounding woods to hunt large predators like wolves, boars, even bears. He was careful not to travel far from his home, for he had committed the ultimate sin of the Nocturni: killing another vampire. But even worse, his own parents. Though many years had passed since that grave transgression against his parents, Soren still hid deep within the mountains.

When he was a growing boy, he had been taught the two sacred rules of vampire existence: 1. They must remain hidden in the shadows and only feed in public during the blood moon. 2. They must never take the life of another vampire, should they do so, they must be destroyed.

Soren eventually fed on human hunters, and once he had tasted human blood, it became impossible to resist. Over time, the weight of isolation wore on him, and he grew increasingly restless. He began venturing to nearby villages under the cover of night, capturing humans to feed on in secret. One evening, while wandering into a village in search of warm blood, Soren met a man he believed he could trust. His name was Marek.

Marek was a local who had grown up in the mountains. He knew the forests, the secret paths, and the rhythms of life that most outsiders overlooked. He was no stranger to the things that lurked in the darkest corners of the world. Though he was human, he had ties to those who practiced and lived by the dark arts. Perhaps this was why he didn't flinch when he saw Soren's pale skin and crimson eyes. Rather than running or resisting, Marek offered Soren help.

"Please do not feed on me," he said calmly, careful not to beg, if he was to earn Soren's respect. Soren stared at him, fangs bared, saliva dripping from his upper lip. Marek continued, "You can kill me, yes. I am just one man. But let me live, and I can bring you a steady supply of fresh blood, more than you could ever take by force. I know the villagers... who is sick and dying, who is fresh and vibrant, who will be missed, and who will not. I can bring you vagrants, prisoners, and orphaned children. Let me keep you fed."

Soren and Marek formed a partnership that satisfied them both. Soren could feed in isolation, and Marek enjoyed a steady stream of gold and protection. Marek arrived with a woman for Soren to feed upon. She had a kind face and sad eyes. When the woman begged for her life, Soren listened... for the first time. She had shoulder-length brown hair and soft blue eyes. Her name was Morovia, and she had once served as a Vermilion-Courtesan. But she was older now, no longer considered worthy by those who fed on blood. She was like a cow that no longer produced the same quality of milk, forgotten, discarded, and marked for death. Among the Courtesans, when age stole their allure, this fate had a name: they called it *"culling the herd."*

Morovia was the first human, aside from Marek, that Soren trusted. Even with Marek, he knew it was gold that kept him loyal, nothing more. But Morovia listened. She spoke to him. She struck a chord in him that had never been touched before. To him, humans were a meal to be consumed. But with Morovia, he saw something more. As time passed, they grew close, and Soren began asking her questions about life as a human. In return, she asked about his past, though Soren mostly edited the truth, keeping the darker details to himself. He trusted her, but he didn't want to frighten her with his misgivings. Over time, she became less a captive and more of a mother to him.

One night, Soren brought something special to share with Morovia. He entered her chambers with an object resting in both hands, covered by a black veil. Morovia stood, surprised by Soren's unexpected appearance. "What is it that you have in your hands, Soren?" He slowly removed the veil to reveal a black garnet stone. It was about the size of a child's closed fist, black in color, yet it seemed to pull light from all directions. Soren explained that it had been entrusted to his father and then passed down to him.

"This stone is said to be the crystallized heart of a fallen Keeper, the one who dared to journey beyond the known realms and plant a seed of darkness." He paused before continuing, "This stone, when touched by a worthy soul, it will become more than stone. It will awaken." Morovia carefully looked at the garnet, "Has anyone made it to the furthest realms?" Soren looked up at her, "Not yet." Morovia stepped closer to Soren to inspect the stone. She quietly whispered, "May I?" as she reached for it. Soren pulled away slightly. "Open your hands. Let me place it there."

She slowly opened her palms wide, the creases in her skin stretching as she accepted the stone. A burst of coldness surged through her entire body as the weight of the stone pressed against her hands. Instinctively, she closed her eyes and let the chill pass through her entire being. Her face tightened, and for a moment, she couldn't breathe. It was as if her inhale had been frozen in time. Then, as the cold breeze released from her body, a sudden swoosh of air escaped her lips, and the stone seemed to exhale with her. Her eyes snapped open, and her pupils had temporarily darkened, like small garnet stones. Soren smiled and laughed, "There is great power waiting to be unleashed from this stone."

Morovia's eyes began to shift back to blue as her face relaxed. "What more do you know about this stone?" Soren and Morovia sat on her bed. It was a sturdy piece of furniture with an oak frame. The mattress was made of a woolen blanket layered over scattered hay. The relationship she had built with Soren was one of quiet trust. He seemed more interested in keeping her around as company than as a meal to be forgotten. Despite her awareness of his hunger, Morovia strangely felt safe in his presence. There was a stillness to him when they were alone, as if some part of the darkness had learned to rest.

Soren stared at the stone, still resting in her open palms. "My mother told me, when I was younger, that the pulse of this stone could only be awakened by a Nocturni of great significance, one touched by both darkness and light." His voice softened slightly, "She said it would respond only to the one destined to restore balance, or destroy it completely." They both sat in silence, eyes locked onto the garnet's surface.

Morovia was careful to watch where Soren kept the stone. She felt a pull to return to it later when she was alone. The challenge was that Soren rarely left the castle. Marek was the one who brought supplies, food for Morovia and humans for Soren. Gold was never a problem. Soren's family had long ago hidden away a fortune in ancient coins and precious metals, more than enough to keep Marek loyal, and the castle fed.

The Blood Moon was a sacred time for vampires. It was the only night each year when they could converge with others of their kind and feed publicly in select locations. The gatherings were more than rituals... they were celebrations, almost festival-like in nature. Vampires would travel from distant regions to meet in secluded areas, hidden from the human world, to feast and revel under the crimson moon. These locations were carefully chosen and planned well in advance, aligned with ancient ley lines.

Marek tentatively approached Soren during his weekly food drop, this time empty handed. He ran his fingers through his reddish brown hair and exhaled slowly. "Soren, sir, I'm having trouble finding suitable humans for you to feed upon this time. But fear not, I have a suggestion, and the timing couldn't be more aligned." He continued, "There have been whispers among certain types of a Blood Moon festival coming in two days." Soren tilted his head and thick neck to one side, letting it crack. "Tell me more." Marek went on to explain the details of the festival, intriguing Soren even further. Still, a thought lingered in the back of his mind. If he were to leave the castle for even a few days, Morovia would need protection. The roads would be restless during the Blood Moon, and rogue vampires were known to emerge from the cracks of the world. They were parasites who lived like rats and vultures, feeding only on the weak and timid. They had a keen sense for finding the fragile, the forgotten, and the unguarded.

He shared with her the deepest secrets of the vampire, including how to weaken them, how to slow their healing, and even how to destroy them if it ever became necessary. He showed her how to prepare a dust that could be used to disorient a vampire. It was made from ground flecks of silver mixed with specific herbs and crushed into a fine powder. Soren explained that he had built a tolerance to using silver over time by gradually exposing himself to it. But for most vampires, the mixture would be enough to slow them down and leave them disoriented.

Marek took Soren in a horse-drawn cart across the landscape to a secluded area far from the villages and bustle. Soren remained discreetly hidden in the hemp-covered back, staying out of sight and shielded from the sun. They traveled the entire day, crossing grassy fields, weaving through narrow forest paths, and avoiding well-trodden roads.

It was nightfall when they finally arrived at the festival. It was held in an open field, fenced in on all sides. Twisted tree limbs and large boulders encircled the grassy clearing, forming a natural enclosure that felt sacred and secret. As they pulled up in the cart, Soren slid open the hemp cover and looked out into the gathering. The enclosure was quickly filling with people from every direction. Some were dressed in fine clothing, escorting companions who walked with grace and quiet smiles. People of all kinds attended as guests: children, women, and the elderly. In a corner of the fenced area, men sat cross legged, their faces hidden behind masks, painted white with lines and circular shapes that formed geometric patterns. They tapped lightly on hand drums, creating a rhythm that gently pulsed through the air like a subtle heartbeat.

Soren exited the carriage, handed Marek a bag of gold pieces, and asked him to return before the first light of day. He then entered the enclosed area and made his way toward the others, who were talking in small groups. He listened as they spoke with excitement about the midnight ceremony, when the Blood Moon would appear in full view. Some mentioned a fierce hunger after days of fasting to sharpen their appetite.

In one area, fires burned beneath large boiling pots. Women stood at these stations, stirring the contents with thick wooden poles as steam curled upward into the night air. Nearby, small ceramic cups were laid out in neat rows on a large wooden table, while another woman poured the warm contents into them. Torches were lit at each corner of the fenced area as the music grew louder and more intense. Others began to chant and dance, their bodies swaying with the rhythm. Eyes closed, they moved in a trance-like ecstasy, shaking and writhing.

Soren could feel his own tension begin to melt away as he slipped into the group trance. There was a connection, a pulse driving his body to move with the others. He pulled his shirt from his body and threw it to the ground. Lifting his large, muscular arms into the air, he tore away his remaining clothes and surrendered to the rhythm. His legs moved instinctively, carried by the same primal energy that now possessed the entire gathering.

The enclosure was now filled with bodies moving in unison, packed together like a litter of kittens. As night neared the midnight hour, the clouds broke open across the sky, revealing the Blood Moon. Groups of women walked through the crowd and handed out cups filled with a liquid tea. The moon hung low and heavy on the horizon, a deep crimson disc that pulsed like a wound. Its light bled across the field, painting the dancers in hues of red and orange. The drums suddenly stopped. The dancers froze, their eyes locked on the large red disc that stared back from the heavens. Slowly, as if moving by some unseen command, they raised their cups into the air and drank. The warm concoction they swallowed was laced with ergot, a potent fungus that would soon blur the line between shadow and light. At that moment, the vampires slowly turned toward their mostly unaware guests who had just drunk the tea. Most had no idea of the Blood Moon's true purpose. Yes, some had come as willing sacrifices, but others believed they were honored guests attending a sacred ritual. The truth, however, was far more perverse. This was not a celebration. This was a Blood Bath.

Heavy rain began to fall from the night sky. The vampires lurched onto their victims and drank. A red river poured in every direction, covering the ground with pools of blackness that reflected the rich hues of the red moon. Rain drops splashed into the puddles of essence, mixing and diluting them creating a mirror of broken faces.

Soren could not control his hunger. He dove towards a nearby woman with yellow hair, dressed in all white. She pulled her dress open revealing her pale breasts and smiled, as if offering herself to his rage. His fangs tore into her chest as she let out a deep moan of acceptance. The ergot-tainted blood hit his tongue with a burst of unnatural warmth. Energy flooded his body, racing through every vein like wildfire. In an instant, his skin shifted from icy cold to burning hot.

The bumps on his neck swelled and rose, as they did for all of the vampires feeding. A resonance ignited, binding them together in a single current. The world around them began to shift, as if a veil had been torn away. The threads separating physical reality from the Astral Plane grew thin, almost transparent, like strands of light pulling apart to create an opening. Through this rift, beings could now pass freely, lingering just beyond the edges of perception. They stirred in the shadows of the in-between, drawn to the sudden opening in the veil. The red light from the moon split into ribbons, twisting and spiraling through the sky before pouring into the passage. The faces of the guests and vampires became distorted, melting and reforming into monstrous shapes as they welcomed these entities.

The Blood Moon was the one night when beings from both the physical and astral realms could cross paths. Some came seeking lost memories, others came to feast, and a few were drawn simply by the chaotic energy that bled through reality itself. It was a celebration of the collective darkness, where time unraveled and the laws of nature bent to the will of the unseen. The beings that crossed between the layers of consciousness had access for one night only, a night that served as both a feast and a festival.

The ground beneath Soren's feet seemed to breathe, shifting like an ocean wave. He could no longer tell if he was floating down a river or drowning in the scarlet-soaked earth below. Soren continued to drink until he fell into a stupor. His body felt as though it were melting away, sinking into the ground and disappearing into the earth itself. It was a half state of awareness that some vampires entered when they over consumed blood. He lay alone in the grass when the rain began to fall even harder. Opening his eyes, he felt the red wash from his face, pooling around his head to form a dark halo on the ground.

He closed his eyes and saw flickers of sparks appearing at the corners of his vision. Then, an image of Morovia formed and she was holding the garnet stone tightly in her palms. Soren knew he needed to get back to the castle, but for now, he couldn't physically move. He was temporarily stuck in this half plane of existence.

This was her chance to escape Soren once and for all. Morovia had been searching for a way out for some time. She had been quietly stashing gold pieces, packing away food, and gathering basic supplies for her departure.

Before heading to the barn to saddle her horse, she returned to Soren's chambers for the one thing that could help her most, the garnet stone.

Nikolai was spending more and more time with Velora. He found himself at The Thorned Rose nearly every night. He would release Sable to hunt while he sat by Velora's side—talking, sipping on her essence, and slipping into trances. In some ways, she reminded him of his lost love, Mira. It wasn't her appearance, but rather the sound of her voice. Despite her circumstances, she always carried a seed of hope. In those states, he saw the garnet stone pulsing like a heartbeat, calling to him. It would light up like molten gold, glowing and swirling from within. He would speak to it with his thoughts: *Find me, and I will find you. Call to me, and I will answer. Seek me in the physical realm, and I will seek you. I am here.* Nikolai knew in his core that the stone was trying to find him just as much as he was trying to find it. He did not yet understand its significance, but he could feel its call, pulling at something deep within him.

Morovia traveled along the Danube River toward her new home. In her dreams, she saw it calling to her, urging her to travel to the city of Buda. It was there that she hoped to unlock the secrets of the garnet stone. She took the gold she had stolen from Soren and found herself a temporary room for boarding. As a former Vermilion-Courtesan, she was adept at finding the places where vampires secretly gathered and fed.

She would concoct the mixture of Silver Breath that Soren had taught her to disorient vampires. At night, she waited outside the Red Parlors. They were establishments frequented by vampires. These places could be identified by a red emblem on the door or wall, often depicted as a red rose or another ruby-colored symbol.

Lady Morovia wore a long black woolen overcoat with a hood that concealed her hair, and a black veil that covered her face. The veil was secured to the side of her hood. Beneath the coat, she wore a long dress that brushed against the tops of her leather boots. She covered her neck with a mixture of blood and sweat to attract vampires. As they drew near, she would lift her veil and blow the Silver Breath from a hollowed wooden straw into their faces, causing them to stumble back, disoriented and gasping for air.

In that moment, she would place the garnet stone near their face to see if there was any reaction. After many days of failed attempts, she decided to give it one final try. She was following a tall, thin man with pale skin that seemed almost translucent. As he approached her, she blew the Silver Breath into his face. He stumbled back... and then it happened. The stone flickered gold for a brief moment before fading away. The man was now on the ground, lying back and rubbing his eyes. She crouched down and brought the stone near his face, and it began to glow a golden yellow. The light poured through his translucent skin.

Then she heard a voice behind her. She whipped her head around. "I'm Nikolai," the man said, his voice low and unwavering, "and I think that stone might belong to me." She responded quickly. "I am Lady Morovia, and I can help you uncover your true purpose." Nikolai knew that Lady Morovia was an important part of uncovering the true potential of the garnet stone.

They traveled together to Nikolai's home so he could inspect the stone more closely. When they arrived, she placed the stone on a small wooden table that sat near the wall. The moment she uncovered it in Nikolai's presence, the stone began to glow. Inside the garnet, a cloud of golden colors began to swirl and blend together. Nikolai approached and stared at it intently, drawn in by its pulsing light.

Lady Morovia stepped back as Nikolai leaned over the stone, placing his hands above it. Slowly, he lowered his open palms and gently pressed them against the stone's surface. His eyes locked shut. She watched as Nikolai's body began to shudder, the veins in his neck protruding like coiled serpents. With his eyes tightly closed, Nikolai could feel himself connecting to the stone. It was as if the stone had become his heart, beating like a drum.

As Morovia watched, the veins in his neck began to pulse and slither, shifting from side to side as if rearranging themselves. In his vision, Nikolai saw a large man with strong arms and short, dark hair. He didn't recognize the man, but it was Soren—restless, searching, and clearly looking for Morovia. When Nikolai opened his eyes, he turned to her and described what he had seen, then asked, "Who is he?" Lady Morovia turned away shyly before speaking. "I was once a Vermilion-Courtesan... but I was given to that man as a final offering, when I was no longer considered useful." Her voice trembled slightly, but she steadied it with a deep breath. "They said I had outlived my beauty and my use. But he didn't kill me. He kept me."

She then pulled her scarf aside to reveal a series of healed scars along her neck. There were four puncture marks, now closed, protruding from her skin like silent reminders of what she had once endured. Next, she rolled up her sleeve and showed Nikolai a thick scar across her wrist, healed into the shape of a jagged crescent. It was deep purple and red, raised above the surface like a permanent brand. "They could no longer take blood from my body," she said softly. "So please... don't think of taking me. I have far more to offer you alive."

Nikolai had no interest in feeding on Morovia. His mind was fixed on the man from his vision, Soren. He knew Soren was coming, and he wouldn't just be looking for Morovia; he would want the stone as well. But Nikolai wasn't willing to give it up. Too much had happened for the stone to arrive at his feet, and he sensed there was an important reason it had come to him. "I think we should take the stone to a Courtesan named Velora," he said. "She is my confidant, and when I feed on her blood, I see visions. Perhaps she can help us unlock this mystery."

Lady Morovia nodded in agreement. She knew a confrontation with Soren could end badly for them all. Vampires were strictly forbidden from killing their own kind—but what she didn't know was that Soren had already broken that law by murdering his own parents. Still, she understood one thing clearly: if he found them, she would be the first to die. And if pushed far enough, he was capable of killing Nikolai too.

They wrapped the stone in a small piece of fur that was soft, dark, and lined with the faint scent of smoke. Nikolai tucked it carefully into an inner pocket of his long black coat, made of heavy wool and reinforced at the seams with leather. The coat fell past his knees, its collar high and stiff to guard against wandering eyes.

Before they headed to The Thorned Rose, Nikolai released Sable to hunt. He knelt down on one knee as Sable lifted her forepaws and climbed onto him. "I have to be gone for a while. Go to the woods and hunt... I'll call for you later." With that, Nikolai let out a sharp whistle through his lips, and Sable sprang to his feet and disappeared into the night.

Nikolai and Lady Morovia arrived at The Thorned Rose and met with Velora just as she was finishing with another client. The Mother of the house allowed them in to see her after a quiet exchange of gold pieces and a simple nod. When they entered Velora's room, Nikolai quickly eased any suspicion with a brief introduction. "This is Lady Morovia," he said. She nodded to Velora in quiet acknowledgment. "She can be trusted, and she carries the stone I've seen in my visions with you." Nikolai reached beneath his coat and pulled out the wrapped stone. With a sense of urgency and excitement, he lifted it into the air. As he unwrapped it, the stone began to flicker with a golden light, pulsing brighter with each passing second.

"I think I should enter a trance while drinking your blood... with the stone present," he said. "I believe it has far more to show us." Velora faintly smiled to show Nikolai her trust, but she felt uneasy about Lady Morovia. There was something about her presence that didn't sit right. Sensing the suspicion, Lady Morovia broke the silence. "I was once a Vermilion-Courtesan you know...," she said, pulling back her sleeve to reveal her scars. "I can help you with your healing... I know ways to ease your pain."

Velora had endured terrible suffering during her Bloodwaking, the ritual of draining small amounts of blood from the body to be consumed by another. Among courtesans and mothers, it was said, *"Only through Bloodwaking can the visions come."*

She let out a soft breath and nodded.

"Yes, I'm often in great pain. Your help would be welcome."

"When you're finished with Master Nikolai, I'd be happy to treat you," Lady Morovia replied, pulling out a small vial of liquid and smiling.

Nikolai sat back on the black velvet divan, his posture relaxed but his gaze intense as it settled on Velora. There was a quiet sensuality in the way he looked at her, both sexual and almost reverent. Morovia immediately picked up on the connection between them. A flicker of jealousy rose within her as she watched their silent exchange. She wondered, *how deep this bond truly ran and whether Velora would get in the way of her plans.* Velora lit the small circle of brown herb that rested on a plate in the corner. Smoke swirled and danced through the air, curling into her nostrils. She moved gracefully across the room, her short black silk robe flowing around her.

Nikolai sat with the garnet stone resting in his open palms. Velora stepped in front of him, leaned forward, and locked her lips to his, releasing the plume of smoke into his mouth in a slow, deliberate breath. She lifted the rose from Nikolai's hand and pressed a thick barb into her flesh. It pierced with a wet pop, and the blood pooled into a ceramic cup below. She handed the cup to Nikolai. He closed his eyes and savored every drop as it touched his tongue, rich with warmth and a faint metallic taste. Morovia tried to hide her growing uneasiness as she watched it all unfold. She knew Nikolai needed this connection if she were to uncover the stone's true power. But she couldn't help but wonder... *did Velora really need to be part of this long term? And worse, would she become a dangerous distraction for Nikolai?*

As he lay back on the divan, Nikolai felt his body fall away as he slipped into a deep trance. In his mind, he could see fractals of colored light merging and shifting, reforming into endless geometric shapes. The shapes began to fall away into an endless expanse until he arrived in complete darkness. He felt no sense of space or depth, but only an infinite, silent void.

Then, a vision emerged from the stillness: the garnet stone, glowing from within, calling to him from a realm beyond the physical plane. Its light pulsed like a heartbeat, beckoning him forward. But the vision also carried a message, he could not cross into that higher realm yet. First, he would need to move through the physical world and sow the seeds of his presence. To break through, he had to awaken something ancient—through blood, through sacrifice, through creation. Only then could the path open fully to what lay beyond.

As he lay there with his eyes tightly closed, his pupils darted from side to side beneath his lids. Morovia and Velora watched as the stone grew brighter and brighter, casting a yellow glow that slowly filled the room. Moments later the stone began to dim as Nikolai reawakened into reality. When Nikolai finally opened his eyes, he remained silent. He did not share what he had seen. He finally stood and asked to go outside to be alone with his thoughts. Morovia offered to help Velora treat her wounds.

They remained in Velora's room as she slowly removed her robe, revealing scars that spread across her breasts and down her arms. Some were fresh, while others had hardened into permanent reminders. She hid her face behind her hair as Morovia quietly examined her body. "Do not feel ashamed," Morovia said gently. "I can help you." She turned away and retrieved two small vials from her leather satchel. Uncorking one filled with a clear liquid, she said, "This will help heal your wounds." She poured a few drops onto the back of her hand and gently rubbed it into Velora's scars. Velora stood still, flinching slightly as the cold medicine touched her skin. When she was done, Velora pulled her robe back over her body, covering herself completely.

Morovia then asked, "Do you feel any pain?"

"Yes," Velora replied. "All the time."

"I want you to drink this. It will help with your pain."

Velora lifted the small vial to her nose and sniffed it cautiously before pulling it away.

Morovia encouraged her gently, "I know it isn't pleasant, but it will help you."

Velora closed her eyes and drank the liquid.

Morovia smiled to herself as she watched Velora begin to gag and choke. Her eyes bulged, shifting into darkened orbs. As Velora collapsed to the floor, Morovia calmly knelt beside her. Just then, Nikolai entered the room. "What has happened?" he demanded. Morovia looked up from Velora, who now lay unconscious. "She took ill," she said with authority. "I think you may have taken too much blood from her."

A sudden knock came at the door just before the House Mother entered. She took one look at Velora lying on the floor with Nikolai at her side, trying to wake her. The House Mother's eyes tightened. "What has happened to the girl?" she demanded. Then, pointing at Nikolai, she added, "The vampire is responsible. The human can leave!" Morovia picked up the garnet stone and placed it inside her coat. The round, bald man who guarded the front door appeared behind her, grabbed Morovia firmly by the arm, and pushed her toward the exit.

He then nodded at Nikolai, signaling him to follow behind him. The rules of the house were clear: if a vampire took more than what was allowed from a courtesan, he could not leave. What happened to such vampires was never spoken of. Nikolai knew there was nothing he could do for Velora now and he had to escape this predicament. He closed his eyes, and his form began to flicker until he vanished from sight.

He placed his hand gently across Velora's face one last time, then turned and sprinted toward the exit and out the door. The bald man and the house mother looked at each other with perplexed expressions, unsure what to make of what they had just witnessed. Nikolai remained cloaked as he sprinted down the cobblestone street, catching sight of Morovia moving quickly away from The Thorned Rose. When he came within arm's reach, his form began to flicker, then fully returned to view.

He grabbed Morovia by the arm and spun her around sharply. "What happened back there? Where is the stone?" he demanded. She pulled her veil aside, revealing a smile. "I'm so glad you escaped—and that you're okay." Then she reached into her coat and pulled out the stone. "I have it right here. We are safe." Nikolai snatched the stone from her. "What really happened to Velora?" Morovia tilted her head slightly, feigning confusion. "Whatever do you mean? The girl was clearly ill. I could see it the moment we arrived."

Nikolai glanced around, making sure not to attract the attention of passersby. "She was fine. I've sipped her essence many times...always careful never to take too much." Morovia stepped closer to him, her tone softening as if to placate him. "You got what you needed from her. We don't need her anymore. It's probably better this way. We're stronger as two, not three." Nikolai looked down at the ground, memories of Velora's kind smile flickering through his mind. "I have something to share with you, Nikolai," Morovia said, "but it must wait until we return to your quarters."

They walked in silence to Nikolai's quarters, neither speaking the entire way. When they arrived, they stepped inside, and Morovia closed the door slowly, with purpose. Before Nikolai could speak, she turned to him. "I know you're distressed by Velora's death," she said softly, "but we are stronger together." Nikolai stood in stillness, absorbing her words. "You've tasted my loyalty," she continued. "Now taste eternity with me. Make me yours, not just for power, but forever. Change me, Nikolai."

Nikolai stood in silence. He was lonely and had been for so long, secretly aching for the presence of another. First Mira, then his mother, and now Velora—the only women he had ever known were all taken from him. This, he thought, might be his only chance at companionship. But he had never turned someone before. It was not a simple act. It was a covenant. A powerful step he had never dared consider. But here before was a willing participant, one who accepts the depth of this act.

He stepped toward Morovia and gently took hold of the back of her neck. His fingers brushed against the fabric of her scarf, slowly unraveling it until it slipped away. As her throat was exposed, he could feel a warmth begin to rise within him. It was a hunger, yes, but also something deeper. A connection... a calling. Without a word, he leaned in and sank his teeth into her neck. Morovia let out a sharp gasp, her body arching instinctively beneath his touch. Her hands gripped his arms, not in resistance, but in surrender. He held her carefully, lowering her to the floor with reverence as her breathing slowed.

With each draw of her blood, he felt her life and essence pour into him... all of her fears as a human, her longing, her desire to belong all vanishing into his body like smoke dissolving into air. He could feel her soul unweaving, not in death, but in transformation. He stood over her and pulled up the sleeve on his dark coat. With a flick of his finger, he slit his own wrist with his claw. A thin cut opened, and his essence dripped down onto Morovia's begging tongue.

Just then, the door burst open. Soren stood in the doorway, a small acorn-sized shard of the garnet stone glowing in his hand. Across the room, the larger garnet rested on a nearby table. It suddenly responded, pulsing with golden light that filled the room. Soren stepped forward, muscles flexing, his sharp teeth bared in warning. "Who are you?" he growled. "And what have you done to Morovia?"

Nikolai stood before Morovia who was now curled up on the floorboards. He wiped the blood from his mouth with the back of his hand, never breaking eye contact. "I am Nikolai," he said, his voice calm and focused. "And you must leave now... or I will destroy you."

Morovia lay on the floor, gasping for air, caught in a half state between human and vampire. Her limbs twitched as the transformation flowed through her, unfinished and unstable. Across the room, Soren's eyes locked onto Nikolai with burning fury. He dropped the small shard of garnet to the floor and in the next instant, he lunged toward Nikolai. With a roar, Soren charged across the room, his fangs bared and claws extended, every muscle rippling with rage.

But just as he closed the distance, Nikolai vanished. His body flickered and then disappeared entirely, cloaking himself in the shadows. Soren skidded to a halt, eyes wide with confusion. He whipped his head from side to side, scanning the room. "Where did you go?" he growled. "Show yourself, coward!" Soren flew into a rage, grabbing the table that held the garnet stone. As he lifted it over his head, the stone tumbled to the floor and rolled to a stop. He hurled the table across the room, narrowly missing Morovia, who lay convulsing on the ground. Nikolai stepped directly in front of Soren, still cloaked from sight. He stared at him and smiled.

But suddenly, he felt something grip his leg. It was Morovia. She had latched onto his ankle, her nails digging deep into his skin, eyes wild with confusion and desperation. Nikolai gasped and began to flicker. Within seconds, his invisibility faltered, and he appeared fully in Soren's view. Nikolai reached for Morovia's satchel lying nearby. He grabbed the blow-pipe protruding from the top and placed it into his mouth. As Soren straddled him, Nikolai blew the Silver Breath into his face. The cloud of silver filled the air, and Soren laughed and blew it back at him. Nikolai shook his head violently from side to side as he tried to stand.

Soren lunged forward and seized Nikolai by the throat, his grip tightening with monstrous strength. With a guttural growl, he drove Nikolai backward, forcing Morovia to release her grip. The two men crashed through the wall with an explosion of stone and splinters, tumbling into the courtyard outside.

Nikolai hit the ground hard, flat on his back, with Soren landing atop him. Debris and dust rained down around them, rising into a swirling cloud that caught the light of the full moon. Nikolai was still blinded and disoriented from the Silver Breath. As Soren tightened his grip around

Nikolai's throat, Nikolai summoned his remaining strength and managed to roll Soren off, reversing their positions. The chokehold broke, and Nikolai rolled free, coughing and gasping for air. Without hesitation, he let out a sharp whistle that echoed through the night.

Moments later, Sable leapt into the courtyard. He reared up on his hind legs before launching himself at Soren, his jaws sinking into his neck with savage force. While Soren struggled beneath Sable's weight, Nikolai stepped back through the opening in the wall and retrieved a small dagger that Morovia had in her bag. Its handle was wrapped in weathered leather, and its blade glowed, coated in silver.

Nikolai climbed on top of Soren, his breath ragged, his mind clear. With both hands gripping the dagger, he drove the silver-coated blade straight into the center of Soren's chest. Soren let out a deep roar, a sound filled with rage, pain, and disbelief. A final burst of air escaped his lungs in a harsh hiss. Then, silence. His body began to convulse violently. The flesh around the wound blackened, cracking like burned parchment. His limbs stiffened and his eyes rolled back as if trying to escape death itself.

Within moments, his once-powerful frame began to deflate, muscles collapsing inward as though drained of all life. His skin shriveled, tightening over bone, until he was nothing more than a withered husk that crumbled and disappeared into the night breeze. Soren was gone, erased from existence. All that remained was the small garnet stone Soren had carried. Nikolai picked it up and turned it in his hand, watching as it began to glow faintly at his touch.

Nikolai then walked over to Morovia, who lay on the floor pleading and thrashing. Without a word, he knelt beside her and plunged the blade into her heart. Then he stood and walked away. He also gathered the larger stone with the smaller piece, cradling them carefully in his arms. Stepping outside the front door, he let out a sharp whistle. Sable came running to him from the shadows, and together they walked down the cobblestone street, once again disappearing into the darkness.

Chapter Thirteen

JAPAN

Nikolai arrived in Japan in the year 1603. He and Sable had traveled nearly fifty years along the Silk Road—a long, winding journey filled with hard-won lessons. Nikolai was no longer the same man who had once stalked the streets of Buda. He had lived, fought, and endured more than any mortal could in a single lifetime. Along the way, he had left his mark—not just in legend, but in blood. He turned women into vampires, then impregnated them, spreading his lineage across continents like seeds scattered in the wind. He called them his *Matremorphs,* mothers who would raise young vampire orphans into adulthood.

Matremorphs are sacred vampire matriarchs, once human and now immortal, gifted with the rare power to bear and raise the next generation of Nocturni. They serve as living vessels of Nikolai's lineage. It was one of the rare gifts of the Nocturni: the ability to bear children. Through them, he cast his shadow far and wide across the physical realm.

Now, after many years of travel, he had crossed the world and arrived in Japan—a country that had finally found peace after many years of civil war and unrest. The turning point came on October 21, 1600, at the Battle of Sekigahara, where the army led by Tokugawa Ieyasu secured a decisive victory. In 1603, Ieyasu was officially appointed Shogun by the Emperor, marking the beginning of the Edo period—an era that would be remembered for its lasting peace... Or so it seemed.

During his travels he met other vampires, but none had made it this far across the world. He was the first to step onto the shores of this strange land. The people looked different and he looked different than them. They spoke with a strange tongue too. If he were to survive he would need to understand the language. One skill Nikolai had developed along the Silk Road was the ability to consume the blood-memory of others. He learned it from a man named Batu, whom he met in a small town on the outskirts of the Taklamakan Desert. Nicknamed "The Sea of Death," the region was a vast expanse of sand dunes—harsh, unforgiving, and filled with secrets lost to time. Nikolai had ventured there after hearing whispers of a man who could unlock memories through blood. He was a sorcerer, some claimed, who had lived beyond his natural years by devouring the minds of others. Batu was no myth.

He found him inside the narrow entrance of a cave that expanded as you walked deeper within. The sand-colored tunnels twisted and opened into a vast chamber that resembled a cathedral. The ceiling arched into a high dome, worn smooth by time. In the center of the room sat a man, cross-legged on a silk pillow. His long black hair swept past his shoulders like a dark cape. His face was covered in markings, geometric lines and shapes inked into his flesh with sharpened bone.

As Nikolai stepped forward, the man slowly opened his eyes and, without hesitation, spoke in Nikolai's language. "I am Batu." Nikolai bowed and asked, "How do you speak my tongue?" He had traveled the Silk Road for many years, and understanding foreign languages had always been a challenge. So he was genuinely surprised that Batu spoke his native language with such clarity. Batu spoke calmly. "I can consume the memories of others... including the languages they speak. I have mastered all tongues." Nikolai leaned forward, intrigued. "But how is that possible?"

Batu opened his mouth, revealing pointed, sharp teeth. "I am like you. But there is a way to absorb the blood-memory of others. Would you like to see?"

Batu stood up and walked toward the arched doorway. He was wearing a long robe of crimson and gold thread, its hem frayed with age as it dragged across the stone floor. As he passed through the entryway he spoke over his shoulder, "Come, this isn't something you see, you must experience it." Nikolai followed him down a narrow corridor, the walls rough with sandstone and lined with faint etchings worn by time. The hallway opened into a small, dimly lit chamber. A single candle flickered on a low stone shelf.

In the far corner, a bald man sat hunched on the floor, knees pulled to his chest. He wore a tattered brown robe, and his pale, dust-covered skin gave him a ghostlike appearance. He looked to be a monk. His eyes were distant, as if he had already surrendered his soul. Chains bound his wrists, and a blood-stained white cloth was tied around his mouth. Batu bent down to the mans level and smiled. As he reached towards the mans gag, he flinched and pulled back. Batu spoke in a low whisper in language Nikolai did not understand. He slowly untied the cloth and the man began to speak quickly in strange words.

Batu turned to Nikolai, his expression solemn. "You must drink from this man," he said, "but you cannot kill him. He must be brought to the very edge... to death's doorstep... and then you must let go." He stepped closer to the hunched figure and knelt beside him, gently tilting the man's head to expose the vein in his neck. "This is not about feeding," Batu continued. "This is about remembering. You are not just taking blood... you are taking memory, experience, knowledge. But if you take too much... it is lost forever, and so is he. When you drink go to his mind, not his heart. That is where the knowledge is hidden."

Nikolai knelt down and gently placed a hand on the shivering man's shoulder. The man flinched at his touch but did not resist. Leaning in,

Nikolai pressed his lips to the skin. His fangs slid effortlessly beneath the surface, piercing his flesh with ease. Warmth rushed to meet his tongue as a wave of blood, thick with life and memory filled his body. He normally drank to fill his hunger. But this time he imagined who this man was?

As he drank, a strange sensation began to rise within him. It was more than sustenance. Images flickered across his mind like distant lightning. Whispers of forgotten names, fragments of language, flashes of emotion... fear, joy, sorrow, all coalescing into a single memory. Nikolai pulled away from the man and sprang to his feet, a strange energy pulsing through him. His lips parted, and unfamiliar words poured from his mouth. Foreign syllables and words formed in his head. He stroked the emerging bumps on his neck as waves of memory poured through him... moments, faces, and voices that did not belong to him.

It was as if he were living fragments of another man's life, layered on top of his own. He turned to Batu, eyes wide with awe. "What is this? I feel... split. As if I am two men at once." Batu smiled knowingly. "Good. That means the memory has taken root. Now choose what you wish to keep, and the rest will fade." Nikolai looked down at the monk, now slumped against the wall, his head bowed. The man could no longer speak and could barely move... only faint, broken mumbles escaped his lips. His consciousness had been drained to a single drop of memory.

Nikolai used his new skill to travel the Silk Road, gaining knowledge and mastering the customs of countless cultures. He didn't read books, he read minds. When he arrived in Japan, Nikolai immediately cloaked himself to remain unseen. He had the smaller piece of the garnet stone forged into a ring worn on his finger, while the larger piece was securely mounted onto a leather collar he crafted for Sable. It was the perfect way for them to find each other if ever separated. When the stones were near each other, they would emit a faint vibration.

Sable stayed hidden in the nearby woods while he sought out his first victims, carefully selecting those whose blood-memory would offer the most value. It didn't take long for Nikolai to master the language and customs of Japan. Through blood-memory, he absorbed centuries of knowledge in mere days. Initially his presence was quiet and ghost-like, and soon, he began to gather followers. They were men who had lost their place in the new order but craved purpose.

After Tokugawa Ieyasu rose to power and unified Japan, many samurai found themselves without masters. These masterless warriors, known as Ronin, wandered the land with broken loyalties and blades still at their sides. Nikolai offered them what no daimyo could: power beyond life and a new code, forged in darkness.

Nikolai knew that to build real power, he needed to master the weapons of the land he now called home. The warriors here fought primarily with long blades that were elegant, precise, and deadly. He sought out a revered sword master, but instead of training for years to learn the weapon, Nikolai used his blood-memory ability to steal the master's knowledge in a single night.

He then sought out the legacy of the great Sengo Muramasa, the legendary sword smith. Though Muramasa had long since died, his work was said to live on through his former apprentice, *Tetsuo no Yoru*… known more simply as Tetsuo. The swords of Muramasa had been banned by Tokugawa Ieyasu himself. Many believed Muramasa to be a madman who imbued his weapons with a bloodthirsty lust. It was said that once one of his blades was drawn, it had to taste blood before returning to its scabbard, or it would turn on the one who wielded it. This is exactly what happened with Ieyasu's half-brother. He was found with his own weapon piercing his heart. Many called it suicide, but Ieyasu knew the truth: the blade had turned on him and taken his life. From that moment on, all Muramasa swords were outlawed, and possession of one was considered an act of defiance against the Tokugawa regime.

When Ieyasu rose to power, Tetsuo vanished into hiding. But Nikolai, using his blood-memory abilities, was able to track him down. Tetsuo, bitter and disillusioned, was more than willing to help Nikolai forge a weapon capable of unraveling everything Ieyasu had built... even the legendary shogun himself.

Together, they created the Shadow Blade—a weapon of immense, unnatural power, forged from the ashes of fallen warriors and burned monks. But this blade did more than kill: it trapped the souls of its victims, feeding on their essence and growing stronger with every soul. They kept its true nature a secret, ensuring that Ieyasu and his army would be unprepared for the horror Nikolai would unleash.

Nikolai sat alone in the main chamber of Kōfu Castle. He, his three Ronin, and Sable had easily taken the fortress from the local garrison. The castle was once ruled by Takeda Shingen who died in 1573. The clan's dominance crumbled after his son, Takeda Katsuyori, was defeated by Oda Nobunaga and Tokugawa Ieyasu at the Battle of Nagashino in 1575. Now, the stronghold was defended only by a scattered force loyal to Tokugawa, but unprepared for the kind of darkness Nikolai brought.

The once-proud banners of the Tokugawa now lay in tatters, replaced by a single black cloth bearing a new name: *Yami no Shujin,* "Ruler of Darkness." It was a message, sent not in words, but in conquest—directly to Tokugawa Ieyasu himself. Nikolai stared at the Shadow Blade, its obsidian-black surface drawing in light from every corner of the chamber. The sword rested on a wooden table. Beside him, Sable lay curled on the floor as he gently stroked his back. The sound of footsteps suddenly disrupted Nikolai's silence. It was Makage, one of the Ronin who had sworn loyalty to him.

He wore a tattered earth colored kimono, its edges frayed from countless battles, and his hand rested lightly on the hilt of his sword. A strip of dark cloth was tied around his face, concealing the lower half, but his eyes never left Nikolai. "My lord," Makage said, his voice low like a growl, "a rider has been spotted near the southern gate. He carries the seal of Tokugawa." Nikolai did not rise. He continued stroking Sable's fur, his gaze fixed on the

Shadow Blade resting on the table. "Then it begins," he whispered. Sable shifted slightly and let out a low whine.

Tokugawa Ieyasu was now in his sixties, a seasoned warrior shaped by decades of battle and politics. Though he still sought the essence of life, he knew his time was drawing near. What mattered now was legacy. He had outlived and outmaneuvered his rivals, and peace had finally settled across the land under his rule. But that peace was now threatened. A new, shadowy force had emerged. He was a figure calling himself *Yami no Shujin,* the "Ruler of Darkness." No one had seen his face. He was a mystery, cloaked in fear and forging a path laid in blood. He wielded a weapon said to defy nature itself... a blade capable of undoing everything Ieyasu had built.

He sat elevated on his tatami mat in Edo Castle, a symbol of quiet dominance. The chamber was spacious and serene, its walls lined with beautifully painted shoji screens depicting mountains, cranes, and flowing rivers. Ieyasu's hair was tied in a traditional topknot, with streaks of gray running through the sides. Age had thickened his frame, and he now carried the weight of both power and years. The extra folds of his ornate kimono helped conceal his broadening form, offering a dignified stature despite his growing discomfort.

His legs and back throbbed with pain, a constant reminder of battles fought long ago, but he endured them with unshakable discipline. His spine remained straight, his expression unreadable, as his closest advisors entered the chamber and knelt in silence before him. Ieyasu spoke with the authority of a seasoned warrior, "We must stop this force that threatens to overtake us with its darkness," he said, his eyes scanning the room to access the reaction. "But this is not a battle to be won through brute strength alone. No, this enemy feeds on fear and chaos. It is not war we must make, but something far sharper. Only cunning and strategy will bring this shadow to its knees."

A long silence followed his words, as if even the room itself understood the weight of what lay ahead. "We will devise a strategy to destroy this enemy once and for all," Ieyasu continued. "We will draft our plan and then send a messenger to Kōfu Castle." His advisors nodded and bowed in approval, eager to witness what the great leader would command next.

Nikolai unrolled the scroll bearing the seal of Tokugawa Ieyasu and read its contents aloud, his voice echoing softly against the stone walls:

"If you wish to claim power in this land, you must prove your mettle, your sword against

ours, warrior to warrior. I am an old man and cannot face you myself, but I will send my

bravest warrior and our strongest weapon."

He read the words again, slower this time, as if weighing in on each syllable. A slight smile curled at the corner of Nikolai's mouth. "So... the old lion wishes to send a cub with sharpened teeth," he whispered to himself. Makage, his loyal Ronin, stepped forward from the shadows. "You cannot trust him. It's a trap." Nikolai placed the scroll on the table beside the Shadow Blade. "It doesn't matter," he said calmly. "I possess a weapon beyond their comprehension. Nothing can stop me." Sable rose to his feet, stretched his limbs, and let out a low growl as he pawed at the floor. This was his silent way of telling Nikolai he was ready for whatever lay ahead.

Ieyasu doubted he would ever marry again. He sat alone in his chambers, a single candle flickering on a nearby table. His union with Lady Tsukiyama remained a chapter of his life he rarely spoke of, it was a time stained by betrayal, blood, and deep regret. Though their marriage had once been forged for political strength, it had brought more unrest than unity. He thought often of the choices he had made, and the lives those decisions had unraveled. So much was lost, he mused silently, and truly, so little was ever gained. Though her execution had silenced a potential conspiracy with the Takeda clan, it had also torn apart his family, leaving scars he bore not on his body, but deep within his legacy.

He had given the order himself, the execution of his own wife. Lady Tsukiyama, once a trusted partner, had been discovered conspiring to marry their son to a daughter of the Takeda house. The Takeda were not merely rivals; they were a threat to the fragile unity he had fought so long to build. Their bloodline, once powerful and defiant, had nearly toppled his plans for a unified Japan. But worse was him ordering his son to commit seppuko, and taking his own life. Now, with a new darkness rising, Ieyasu found himself recalling a secret buried deep in the folds of his past.

There was one Takeda son, just a child at the time, whom he had secretly spared. Rather than ordering the boy's death, Ieyasu had sent him in silence to a remote mountain monastery. There, away from politics and vengeance, the boy was raised in isolation under the strict discipline of warrior monks. *He would be a man now,* Ieyasu thought. *Hardened by silence and tempered by spirit. Perhaps this forgotten heir, cleansed of his clan's ambition, could serve a new purpose.*

He would send word for the return of Takeda Shin. Perhaps the young man's service to Ieyasu could redeem his family's past... and ease the deep guilt Ieyasu still carried. The last time he saw the boy was many years ago. Takeda Katsuyori, the last head of the Takeda clan, was defeated by Oda Nobunaga and Ieyasu at the Battle of Tenmokuzan in 1582. It was there, amidst the smoke and ruin, that Ieyasu found the child. He was just five years old, crying beneath a scorched ash tree. He was wrapped in a tattered, bloodstained cloth, his face streaked with ash and tears. Ieyasu did not see him as a threat, but a reckoning. The boy would be spared... not out of mercy, but as an offering of redemption.

But before any command left his lips, Ieyasu knew he must first seek the favor of the kami. Within the quietest wing of Edo Castle, far from the eyes of retainers and courtiers, stood his private shrine—a sanctum known only to a select few. It was here, in stillness and humility, that he addressed the heavens. He stepped barefoot onto the polished wood, the air scented with faint sandalwood and smoke. Before the modest altar, Ieyasu knelt.

He lowered himself onto a small cushion, worn by years of secret prayers. The silence was sacred. His hands came together. His head bowed. Before him sat a slender wooden tablet. Upon which were etched the names of his wife, his son, and Takeda Shin.

Then, in a soft whisper, he began: "Compassionate one who hears the cries of the world, I, Tokugawa Ieyasu, humble in spirit yet burdened by command, have taken life where I feared betrayal, have spilled blood not in war, but in peace. My wife, Tsukiyama. My son, Nobuyasu. I sent them to death with my own word. But today, I spare one life, Takeda Shin. Not for politics, but for peace. May this act ease the chains of karma. May the boy carry the light that I extinguished. Let the wind carry this prayer to your ears. Let my deeds find balance through this offering of mercy. May he be the one who brings true peace to the shadow that threatens us all." With these words, he placed a single stick of incense before the altar. The flame flickered, the smoke rose... and with it, Ieyasu's silent hope that his karma might shift, if only by a thread.

Days later, Nikolai received a second scroll bearing the seal of Tokugawa Ieyasu. The old warlord had responded to Nikolai's acceptance of his first challenge. The terms were now clear: they would meet beneath the cover of darkness, under the light of the full moon, to settle it once and for all. No more messages and no more maneuvers. Just one final confrontation, weapon against weapon.

Ieyasu was surprised by the strength and stature of Takeda Shin. The last time he had seen him, he was just a small, frail child. Now, before him stood a man—tall and composed. His head was cleanly shaved, and his muscles rippled beneath the torn folds of his gray kimono. He wore wide hakama pants and traditional waraji sandals, his posture was calm yet commanding. Shin bowed deeply before Ieyasu, his movements sharp yet reverent. Behind him stood two monks, their expressions unreadable. Each held a long shakujo—monastic staffs tipped with iron rings and capped with short spear blades that clinked faintly as they walked.

Now a man, Shin was well aware of his family's past. He had spent his entire life in a remote mountain monastery, trained in silence as a warrior-monk. Though the monks had sworn never to reveal his origins, one among them eventually broke that vow. The old monk Daji, believed Shin deserved to know the truth, that he was the last living son of the Takeda bloodline. In secret, Daji told him what he knew of Shin's ancestors. These stories of honor, downfall, and legacy became the fire that fueled Shin's will, pushing him to train harder, not just as a monk, but as a warrior destined for something greater. Daji would remind Shin, "You must train hard, you're destined for more than this mountain."

Though Shin often doubted his place in the world, his natural talent for combat was undeniable. He excelled in every form of training: bo staff, blade, endurance, and strategy. But there was one ability that frustrated his teachers more than any other. Shin had an uncanny gift for throwing his sword with pinpoint precision, striking targets from long distances. What he saw as instinct and skill, the monks saw as reckless deviation from the path.

"A blade is sacred... an extension of your arm," one would scold. "To release it is to sever yourself from your purpose. What you do is madness." They would strike his hands with a wooden training sword, the bokken, in an effort to correct what they saw as dishonorable behavior. Ieyasu looked the boy and up and down, "Come with me, let's walk in the garden." He gave a subtle wave to the guards, signaling them to remain behind, then turned and gestured for Shin to follow.

The warrior-monk bowed slightly, pressing his hands together in quiet respect before stepping forward. His head lowered, he moved with the silent grace of his training, his waraji sandals brushing softly over the polished floor as they passed through the open shoji screen and toward a row of manicured pines just beyond the veranda. Ieyasu explained the situation to Shin... that he would soon face a formidable warrior. But there was a plan, and if executed well, it could lead not only to Shin's freedom, but also to the redemption of his family's name. They walked in silence for a moment along a neatly manicured pathway, the stones beneath their feet polished smooth by generations of wear.

"I am told you possess a... unique skill with the sword," Ieyasu said at last. "Something your teachers have called *Kyōki no Michi*—the Path of Madness." Shin turned his head slightly, as if ashamed to hear the name spoken aloud. Ieyasu stopped walking and looked directly at him. "Please. Demonstrate." He nodded toward his own katana, resting at his side. Shin stepped behind the old master and, with swift precision, reached around his body and drew Ieyasu's weapon before he could even flinch. The blade whistled through the air as Shin spun in a full circle, his eyes scanning the entire garden. As his body reached 180 degrees, he released the sword from his hand, sending it flying in a perfect arc.

The weapon cut through the cool, crisp air, guided by Shin's precise intention—free from any grasp for the first time. It reflected the sunlight as it flew, silent and straight, like an arrow released from a divine bow. The katana sliced cleanly through a thick tree branch, severing it before embedding itself upright into the earth several paces ahead—its hilt still trembling from the force. A single leaf floated down behind it, landing gently atop the severed branch. Ieyasu broke his serious demeanor and laughed aloud. "Sometimes the greatest strategy," he said, "is breaking from tradition. Or in your case, severing it."

Nikolai would face Ieyasu's chosen warrior at a neutral location—near the foot of a sacred mountain under the light of the full moon. Ieyasu agreed to be present, and in a gesture of honor and consequence, he pledged to commit seppuku should his warrior fail. In preparation, the warrior monks forged a weapon unlike any other for Shin. Set into its hilt was a polished jade stone, luminous and pure. The blade itself was crafted with sacred rituals, folded steel, and prayers whispered into the metal as it cooled.

As the steam rose from the glowing metal, Shin sat nearby in silent meditation, surrounded by the monks who had raised him. They sat cross-legged around the fire, their heads bowed in reverence as the ritual continued. Each whisper, each breath, was a prayer woven into the very essence of the blade. It was more than a weapon; it was a vessel of balance, meant to counter the darkness of the Shadow Blade. Infused with the energy of clarity and protection, it was bound to Shin by purpose and spirit. Only he could wield it. And only he could unleash its true secret.

But the monks, wise in foresight, added a safeguard to the weapon. Hidden within the handle they placed a sacred scroll—etched with prayers and symbols from the gods. The monks meditated and the message was simple but absolute: should the blade fall from Shin's possession, it could not be handled by any ordinary hand. Only the One who had been chosen, by fate and circumstances, could hold it without consequence. But this message was hidden deep within the symbols the monks had received from the gods. Yet even this truth was concealed within the symbols, a hidden code the monks themselves could not decipher—meant to be revealed only to the One.

Nikolai and Sable traveled to the foot of the mountain where he would face Shin alone. His Ronin offered to accompany him, but Nikolai insisted they go alone and that help was not needed. "I will face him alone," he said calmly, his voice carrying the weight of finality. Whether it was arrogance, confidence, or something deeper. Perhaps a belief that destiny required no interference, only Nikolai knew. He walked ahead with Sable at his side. He was his loyal companion, always moving in perfect silence, his gaze alert and ever watchful. As he approached the clearing the full moon hung low in the sky. The surface was a bright orange hue that gazed onto the landscape.

Old memories stirred in Nikolai's mind with each step. He had traveled farther than most could imagine, lived more lives than any man could bear. He had worn the faces of different ages, tasted the blood of kings and commoners alike. His hands had delivered death, his name whispered across continents like a myth. But this moment, this confrontation… was unlike any he had ever known. It was not conquest he sought now, but closure. His seed had been planted in the soil, scattered like dark pollen across the landscape. And now, here he stood at the farthest edge of the known world, not just to conquer—but to complete his fate. As he stepped into the clearing, bathed in the moon's low orange glow, he drew the silver box from his robe. The night fell still around him… no wind, no sound. Even the trees seemed to hold onto the silence. With care, he slowly untied the thread and lifted the lid. Inside sat a small black stone. Its surface was impossibly smooth. But it wasn't the texture that drew the eye—it was the way it seemed to drink in the moonlight, bending it into itself. Beneath its dark exterior, faint crimson veins flickered and pulsed, like fire trapped in stone. Then, it shifted… *just slightly*. Nikolai's eyes opened wider. Without hesitation, he closed the lid with a soft snap and smiled. He had carried this black stone along his journey, across continents. He had only opened the box once before.

Nikolai knew that to add decades to his existence and become powerful he had to drink blood and learn as much as he could. This would be his path: to travel farther than any vampire had dared, to cross continents and past the realms not as a monster, but as a seeker of something greater. He glanced down at the garnet ring on his finger. The stone pulsed faintly, as if breathing. It was said to be a piece of the crystallized heart of the one who had traveled beyond the physical veil and past the Astral Plane. The fallen Keeper who had tried to bend the realms to his will. A heart turned to stone… *a curse turned into a compass*. And it was guiding him.

It was during his journey along the Silk Road that the name Ashkaran was first whispered during a blood memory. As Nikolai drank from a woman, a vision overtook him: the face of an old man cloaked in shadows… and a river of darkness winding endlessly through the void. They called it, "The Eye of the Goddess." Nikolai set off to find the man named Ashkaran and this mysterious river.

It was along a series of jagged mountains that he first saw it. A clear river cascading down rocky cliffs in ribbons of white and blue. The water glowed in the moonlight, pure and alive. But as it reached the base of the cliff, something unnatural occurred: the water darkened instantly, transforming into a thick, black stream as it spilled into a waiting lake of shadow.

There, along the base of the river, Nikolai spotted a fire pit formed by a half-circle of carefully stacked stones. An old man sat at its edge, warming his hands over the flickering flames. His long white hair cascaded past his shoulders, curling around his face and merging seamlessly with a thick, tangled beard. He wore a weathered, earth-colored robe, its fabric frayed and marked by years of wear. As Nikolai approached, the old man spoke without turning. "I have been waiting for you. Take a seat." Nikolai settled onto a dried-out log, worn smooth with age and turned on its side near the fire. The old man stared into the flames as they crackled and popped. "If you wish to drink," he said quietly, "you must first understand what it is you're drinking."

The old man, Ashkaran, told him the legend of Thal-Torren. Thal was neither goddess nor mortal, but a radiant energy... an eternal presence that existed between day and night, between knowing and dreaming. She was not female in the physical sense, but an embodiment of feminine essence. Thal held the energy of acceptance, of gentle mothering, of tender, boundless compassion.

She was a gentle watcher of endings, of reflections, and the final breath of the day. She walked the veil that separated two realms: the physical world and within the Astral Plane, along the Imagination Fields. She was one of many who had surrendered to this sacred role as a gatekeeper of twilight. She did not speak in words, but in sensations... like warmth on the skin just before nightfall, or the soft whisper of breath as a soul crossed into slumber. Thal was felt, not seen. Known, not named.

Her purpose was clear: to walk alongside the living during twilight, those still moments when the day gave way to night and consciousness drifted into dreams. She was there only to guide the sleepers into peace. She was not allowed to linger, not to attach, and never to interfere.

But one evening, she paused longer than permitted. That night she saw a man named Torren. He was a warrior-poet, caught between his longing for love and his thirst for war. As the words of his poems floated through his consciousness, she listened. Not with compassion, but with longing. This was the first sacred rule, and now she had broken it. Each night she returned, drawn to the ache in his voice and the beauty of his sorrow. She listened to his poems of love, letting them echo through her being.

For the first time, she imagined herself not as a watcher, but as a woman—a real girl, in love for the first time. And in doing so, she broke the second rule. Night after night, she returned to him. She watched, she listened. And as Torren whispered his verses into the dark, longing for the one he loved, Thal imagined she was that girl... the one his soul reached for through every word. One night, however the words changed. They no longer spoke of love—but of grief, sadness... and then, goodbye. When she returned again the following twilight, the energy was gone. And so was Torren.

Thal panicked. In her desperation, she crossed into the physical world—not as light, but as a mortal girl. In doing so, she had broken the final rule. She believed if she stayed only through twilight, she could return before the gate closed. Thal was unfamiliar with moving as a girl. Her new form felt strange and awkward, each step was unsteady. She bumbled through the world in quiet confusion, until at last, she began to recognize fragments from Torren's memories.

A large tree stood nearby, the very one where he had once sat, and read his poetry aloud beneath the rustling leaves. *Yes,* she thought. *This is it.* Nearby, she saw the old barn where Torren would sit and write. The structure leaned with age, draped in cobwebs and dirt. She cautiously moved toward it, her borrowed body trembling with unfamiliar weight.

Inside, the last bits of sunlight pierced the cracks in the wood, spilling across the floor. Night would be here soon. In the distance, she saw the table where he used to write. The light pooled across its surface, circling a lone piece of paper and a quill. They sat abandoned, as if it were his final message.

A long rope hung behind the table, suspended from a ceiling beam. It swayed gently from side to side, taut in the middle, held down by what it carried. Thal rushed toward it. There, slumped on the floor beneath, was Torren. His eyes were open, his gaze locked and distant, a look of sorrow frozen on his face. On the desk was not another poem, but a goodbye to the cruel, lonely world Torren had once known.

Unfamiliar emotions began to swirl within Thal as she realized what she was seeing. Outside, the sunlight was fading behind the trees, and night was creeping over the horizon. Thal ran to the doorway and looked into the distance—just as the opening to the Astral Plane sealed shut, permanently closed to her.

The realization struck like a falling star: she was trapped in the physical realm, alone, bound by sorrow, and no longer a divine being. She would walk the countryside confused and crying. For weeks she did nothing but weep, her sorrow unending. Her tears became thick and black, as if twilight was crying for her. With each tear came a primal scream, raw and haunting, echoing across the landscape. Her cries became so powerful that cracks split the cliff sides, and the earth opened into a vast valley. She stood at its edge, black tears streaming down her face, pouring into the emptiness below—filling the newly formed basin with her grief. Thal-Torren became the stuff of myth and legend... a name whispered across generations.

No longer a radiant keeper of twilight, she was now a being of sorrow and shadow, bound forever to a place just beyond the Astral Plane. To repeat her story over and over again. Not quite mortal, not quite divine, she was suspended in *The Eidon*—a world shaped by memory, belief, and story.

Nikolai closed his eyes while he listened to the story, taking in every word as if it were a drop of warm blood. The old man stopped talking and looked at Nikolai as he opened his eyes. Nikolai spoke, "I now understand and wish to drink." Ashkaran nodded, and together they walked toward an opening in the cliffside that led into a narrow cave. The air grew cooler as they stepped inside. At the far end of the cavern, a large eye had been carved into the stone wall. Its shape was elegant and feminine, the outer edges darkened and outlined like the curve of a woman's hips. In the center of the pupil, there was a small circular spout, plugged with a smooth, round piece of wood. A dried black trail streaked downward from it, like a tear that had bled through time.

Ashkaran stepped forward, holding a small clay cup in his weathered hand. He placed it beneath the spout and twisted the wooden plug with slow, measured care. A thick stream of black liquid oozed from the opening and poured into the cup. Once filled, he turned the plug again to seal the flow. He turned to Nikolai, cup in hand, his eyes solemn. "This is her sorrow," he said. "Drink... and be changed."

Nikolai closed his eyes as he brought the cup to his lips. The liquid was cold and sharp as it touched his tongue. It swirled through his mouth before sliding down his throat—smooth, deliberate, and sentient. He could feel it moving through his body, clinging to his essence like a living shadow. Tears began to build behind his eyes. He felt the growing pressure, the urge to open them. As his lids parted, thick black liquid spilled from his tear ducts and dripped into the clay cup below. The old man stepped forward and calmly placed a flat piece of wood over the vessel, sealing the contents inside. Ashkaran looked at Nikolai and spoke with quiet gravity. "This substance is pestilent. It preys on the weak and the fragile... and as it consumes, it will grow."

Nikolai carefully tucked the sealed vessel into the folds of his robe. As he crossed over an embankment, he saw Ieyasu and the monks awaiting his arrival. Two large fire pits blazed on either side of the clearing, flames dancing into the night sky. Three monks stood near Ieyasu, who was kneeling solemnly on the ground. From where he stood, Nikolai could smell the warm blood of the soldiers and horses hidden just beyond the hill, their presence inviting. But he wasn't concerned as he had a plan.

He would defeat their chosen warrior, then strike down Ieyasu himself. And if he could trap them both within the Shadow Blade, he would become unstoppable. Nikolai looked at the blade and smiled, imagining the power it would hold with their souls sealed inside. This, he believed, was how his legend would grow, how he would surpass every seeker before him. He imagined that if he could master the physical realm, he could break through it... and reach whatever lay beyond.

During his long journey along the Silk Road, Nikolai had used blood-memory to peer into the minds of mystics, monks, and seers. The very ones who had glimpsed realities that few dared speak of. Through their visions, he assembled a map in his mind, not of lands and borders, but of worlds layered upon each other. At the base was the physical realm... the world of flesh, stone, and time-bound mortality. The place where hunger ruled and blood had meaning. This was the domain he walked in now, where swords clashed and legends were born.

But beyond that was the Astral Plane—a world of thought, emotion, and energy. A place where dreams took form and souls could travel without bodies. He had visited it before in trances and rituals, sensing its tides and shadows. It was vast and filled with beings that had no names... wandering aimlessly, echoes of the past, and fragments of futures yet to be. Yet even that was not the end.

There was another place—*The Eidon.* Some called it the Cultural Realm, though such a name barely captured its weight. It was the farthest any seeker had ever gone. The word Eidon is ancient and means, *"the place of all that has been, or the I Am."* The Eidon is the realm of the seen... not as it is, but as it is remembered. It is the world stitched together by story. A plane not of flesh or thought, but of meaning itself. It was where archetypes live, where myths are born, and where every story ever told whispers from the walls. It was a realm where belief becomes form, where legends echo long after truth is lost. And Nikolai... intended to rule it. To take hold of The Eidon would mean more than power, it would mean dominion over story itself. Every legend, every belief, every fear carved into human memory flowed through that realm. If he could conquer it, he could bend meaning to his will.

And beyond it? He believed there was something greater still... a final veil, a place where time unraveled and space folded like parchment. A realm beyond myth, beyond memory. To master The Eidon was not just to become a god among men. It was to challenge the gods themselves. To go beyond was to defy creation itself.

Nikolai stepped forward into the clearing, while Sable lingered at the edge of the woods. He walked to the center, drew the Shadow Blade, and lifted it high into the air. The moonlight seemed to be drawn into its black surface before he drove the blade into the earth. The ground vibrated, and the hilt trembled with a life of its own. Nikolai then stepped back a few paces and raised his hands into the air.

In the distance, Ieyasu sat motionless. His short sword, the wakizashi, lay before him. Three monks stood around him, quietly chanting. Without a word, Ieyasu gave a small nod in Nikolai's direction. Just as Nikolai turned his eyes from the shogun, a figure emerged from the shadows. It was Takeda Shin. In his hand he carried the Jade Sword, its tip pointed toward the ground as he calmly walked forward. He wore a tattered gray kimono, the sleeves torn off to reveal his muscular arms.

Takeda stepped into the moonlight. "I am Takeda Shin," he declared. "I come to earn my freedom and to defend my legacy and homeland." Nikolai laughed, brushing his hair back with one hand. "First, I'll take your weapon. Then I'll take your home," he said with a smirk. "You cannot stop me. This is more than will... it is fate." Shin stepped back, gripping the Jade

Sword with both hands. His knees bent, posture grounded, eyes locked on Nikolai as he moved forward with complete focus.

Nikolai clasped his hands mockingly behind his back, standing before the Shadow Blade still embedded in the earth. Takeda began to circle him, and Nikolai mirrored his movements, his hands still resting calmly behind him. Then, without warning, Nikolai smiled and reached over his head, seizing the hilt of the Shadow Blade with both hands. In one fluid motion, he tore it from the ground in a sweeping arc and brought it down toward Shin's head with devastating force.

Shin reacted quickly and stepped aside. As the Shadow Blade hit the ground, the earth shook causing a ripple that knocked Shin backwards. As he hit the ground he held the Jade Sword tightly, careful to not drop it. Nikolai wrenched the Shadow Blade free from the trembling earth and began to advance, his steps slow and focused.

"You have no chance," he said, his voice cold and certain.

"I'm going to kill you... and trap your soul inside this blade."

He raised the weapon slightly, then pointed it toward Ieyasu.

"And then...together, we'll take your leader."

Shin rolled backward onto his shoulders and sprang to his feet, landing squarely to face Nikolai. Without hesitation, he charged forward, meeting his opponent's blade in midair. The clash rang out like thunder... metal against metal, sending a spray of sparks into the night. Nikolai swung the Shadow Blade with relentless force, but Shin countered each strike with disciplined precision. Blow after blow, Shin matched him, and slowly, Nikolai began to sense... he was losing. In a moment of calculated desperation, Nikolai broke from the rhythm of battle and lunged toward Ieyasu, who remained kneeling among the monks.

Ieyasu, sensing the sudden shift, reached for his wakizashi. But before he could act, Nikolai leapt into the air and landed before him. Ieyasu began to turn the blade inward for his final act of seppuku, but it was too late.

In one swift motion, Nikolai drove the Shadow Blade straight through the old leader's chest.

Ieyasu dropped the weapon to the ground and reached for the Shadow Blade which was now through his body and deep into the earth behind him. Shin watched in horror as Ieyasu's very soul was torn from his body by the Shadow Blade. Like a stream of black smoke, it rose from his chest and spiraled into the blade, vanishing within its dark core.

Before he could react, he felt something powerful slam into his back, it was Sable. He had leapt from the shadows to aid Nikolai, his fangs sinking into Shin's shoulder as he yanked him backward. The monks, now rising from their positions beside Ieyasu, turned toward Shin and shouted, "Now!" This was his signal to act.

Despite the pain, Shin fought against Sable's grip. With a burst of strength, he raised the Jade Sword overhead and hurled it toward Nikolai. The blade cut cleanly through the air, not aiming for Nikolai directly... but beyond him. The sword struck the very fabric of reality, embedding itself midair with a strange, vibrating hum. A soft ripple formed where it landed, like light warping on the surface of water. Then, with a flash, the blade sliced downward, tearing open a glowing vertical wound in the world itself. A sudden rush of wind followed—a vacuum pulling inward with tremendous force. Nikolai, startled, tried to wrench the Shadow Blade from the ground. But it was too late. The pull was relentless. He released the weapon and turned just as his body was lifted, sucked into the breach... his scream lost to the void.

As he crossed the threshold, his form began to flicker and distort, warping like smoke caught in a storm. He turned his head, eyes wide, staring back as the portal began to close. The last sliver of moonlight pierced the darkness... and in that final moment, Nikolai dropped the black stone though the opening.

When the stone struck the earth, it came to life. It pulsed, aware and sentient. It could feel everything around it: the monks kneeling in stunned silence before Ieyasu's empty body, the Jade Sword resting beside Shin, Sable retreating into the shadows of the forest. The horses coming over the hillside. And it could hear the faint, pulsating resonance of the Shadow Blade still lodged in the ground. The small black form slithered forward, inching toward the weapon like a parasite finding its host. It climbed the blade, coiling around the hilt, and began to merge... melding with the metal until the sword and the black stone became one.

Ieyasu could still sense his own consciousness, but he could no longer feel his body. He existed in thought, but not in form. His mind drifted, drawn deeper into a vast, insatiable void of darkness. He could not see, smell, taste, or touch... but he could intend. And in those intentions, he felt anger, fear, and confusion. There was no light... only a relentless, unforgiving blackness. He remembered his life, his physical self... but now he was driven by thoughts that were no longer entirely his own. Dark impulses crept in like vines wrapping around his mind. He tried to resist, calming his thoughts through meditation, attempting to neutralize the pull. But the darkness seeped in every time, breaking through even the stillness of his breathless form.

Ieyasu's physical death was kept an absolute secret and was never to be spoken of. His council quietly found a man who resembled him closely. The double was kept hidden from the public eye, used only when necessary. Behind the scenes, a council of three was formed with trusted advisors who would secretly govern the country until a plan could be made to stage Ieyasu's "natural" death. If the truth were ever revealed, it could shatter the legacy he had built and plunge the nation back into chaos.

Nikolai was trapped in an in-between world... a threshold between the physical realm and the Astral Plane. It was a place beyond time and structure, often whispered about in half-remembered visions. Some called it The Liminal Space—a fractured bubble suspended between worlds, neither here nor there. It was a realm without clear shape or form, where gravity flickered and direction dissolved. Thought repeated and echoed endlessly. Sound had no source and light appeared but cast neither shadow nor warmth. There were no walls... no sky and no death. Only awareness trapped in a slow, unraveling mind.

He had consumed souls, and reached the very edge of creation. But here, in the stillness between worlds, none of that mattered. In this suspended void, Nikolai drifted—stripped of dominance, devoid of flesh, left with nothing but looped consciousness... forever circling the same thoughts. As he drifted, he could see the wound in the threads of reality that had sealed him into this existence. It was a long, straight cut. It was now closed, its edges fused like scar tissue across the fabric of space. Faint drizzles of light slipped through the seams, offering Nikolai the smallest flicker of hope.

Ieyasu's soul was also trapped... but within the Shadow Blade. His plan had been to offer himself as bait for Nikolai. This would allow Shin to throw the Jade Sword at the precise spot they had determined in advance, an area where the threads of the veil were already thin. As the monks sat in meditation near Ieyasu, they chanted incantations meant to further weaken the boundary between realms.

But Ieyasu had not anticipated becoming imprisoned within the blade. He believed he would either take his own life through seppuku or find a way to escape before Nikolai killed him. Nikolai's plan had failed as well. Blinded by his own arrogance, he had underestimated the old warrior. Though the black stone was now fused with the Shadow Blade, feeding on its dark energy, powered by the soul of Ieyasu. Nikolai too was trapped, a prisoner of his own making.

Makage, Nikolai's loyal Ronin, was nearby when his master was imprisoned. He and Sable attacked the waiting samurai, drinking their blood until the fields ran red. Days before Nikolai faced Shin, he had bestowed the vampiric gift upon Makage... binding him to Nikolai. His final command had been clear: if anything were to happen to him, Makage was to build an army.

The monks and Shin secured both the Shadow Blade and the Jade Sword, fleeing under the protection of two warrior-monks. The Council of Three granted Shin his freedom, honoring the role he played in the battle. Together, they transported the weapons to the powerful Akurosai estate. There, Shin would serve as the guardian of the weapons, sworn to protect them from ever falling into the wrong hands. At the estate, he was also entrusted with the role of teacher and mentor... guiding the next generation of warrior-monks. After years of service, he would come to be known with honor and reverence as Master Takeda.

Unbeknownst to anyone, the black stone was quietly gathering power. Master Takeda kept the Shadow Blade and the Jade Sword in close proximity, allowing them to maintain a subtle resonance. Together, but separate, they were opposing energies locked in silent tension. But he was careful to keep them far enough apart to prevent catastrophe. He knew the Shadow Blade was not merely a weapon, it was a vessel of torment. If drawn by the wrong hands, it would likely drive the wielder to madness... or worse, compel them to take their own life.

When the monks first studied the blade, their thoughts grew dark and distorted. Even holding it for only moments outside its scabbard brought a suffocating wave of despair. Whispers filled their minds. Thoughts that were foreign, unrelenting... as if the blade itself hungered for death. They attempted countless rituals and incantations in hopes of releasing Ieyasu's soul, but all efforts failed. In the end, it was decided that the sword would be sealed and locked away for safekeeping.

What they did not realize, however, was that the small piece of black stone that had housed itself in the weapon, had learned to leave. It moved in silence, slipping in and out of the Shadow Blade unnoticed. It fed on the essence of the most vulnerable... young children, whose spirits were still close to the veil. After each feeding, it would return to the Shadow Blade, merging with it once more and strengthening the weapon from within. Whispers began to spread among the people. They spoke of a darkness that flowed like a river, devouring innocence wherever it touched. In time, they gave it a name: Kurokawa... *the Black River*

Nikolai remained trapped for many years. During that time, the virus of vampiric blood quietly spread and strengthened, thanks to Makage and his seed. The infection grew in secret, its reach expanding beneath the surface of society. It became increasingly difficult for Japan's leaders to silence the growing myth. Whispers of shadow-born creatures and blood-drinking demons circulated among villagers and soldiers alike. In response, a new force was formed named the Oni-gari, or demon hunters. These were elite warriors, specially trained to track and destroy vampires before their influence could spread any further.

There was a quiet war brewing between the ruling samurai of Japan and the vampires that had begun to invade the land. The conflict was rarely spoken of in public, but it simmered beneath the surface. There were hidden battles fought in the shadows of forests, far from the eyes of the common people. Even Master Takeda had joined in the hunts. Though his primary role was as guardian of the sacred weapons, he saw value in understanding the enemy. He studied the vampires by testing their strengths, identifying their weaknesses, and documenting their tactics. His goal was not merely survival, but preparation. He sought to train a new generation of warriors who would be ready when the darkness rose again.

At the Akurosai estate, beneath layers of stone and secrecy, Takeda had even gone so far as to capture and interrogate the creatures. He created the kakebako, the bamboo enclosures that housed captured vampires. Deep in the cold, narrow corridors of the estate's hidden dungeon, he subjected them to tests and trials. Some of them were cruel, some methodical—his goal was seeking to understand the essence of their unnatural resilience. It was here that he began to understand their strengths and their weaknesses.

After many human years trapped inside the Liminal space, something happened. The Shadow Blade had begun to awaken—its pulse growing stronger with the rise of the Kurokawa. Sable was drawn back to the very place where Nikolai had been trapped. The garnet stone on his collar began to glow faintly, its light intensifying as he approached the wound in the veil.

Inside the void, Nikolai began to flicker. His form was transforming between shadow and substance. A small tear shimmered in the threads before him. As his body began to solidify, he looked down at his hands. His claws were growing long and jagged, driven by his desire to escape. He reached toward the opening and began to claw at it, scraping violently against the fragile seam between worlds.

As he clawed, a faint seam in the veil gave way, splitting wider with every strike of his growing talons. His body flickered between form and formlessness, caught in a violent tug-of-war between realms. The opening widened further, and the beam of light from Sable's garnet collar poured through like a lifeline. Nikolai grasped the outer edges of the tear. With a silent scream, he pulled himself forward, ripping through the boundary as the light burned across his skin. Inch by inch, he dragged himself through until, with one final push, he emerged into the physical world... reborn in the glow of the moonlight. He lay on the ground, staring up at the tear as it slowly closed, then vanished into the night. Nikolai lay still beneath the golden light—free at last. Sable ran to his side, circling him anxiously.

The hunt for the Shadow Blade had begun, along with his vengeance against Takeda Shin. Nikolai scoured the countryside in pursuit of the blade, going so far as to kill Hirokazu, the brother of Lord Akurosai. He ravaged Hirokazu's estate, leaving a trail of bloodshed—and impregnating Sakura, the lord's concubine. A child would then be born from Sakura. Later, in his obsessive search for their daughter, he would kill Sakura. The hunt would eventually lead him to the mountain monastery where Takeda had taken refuge with the now older child, Ayama.

Takeda knew Nikolai would come. He hid Ayama in a small, sound-proof cell designed to mask scent and odor. There, he hoped to keep her safe from the darkness that now crept ever closer to their doorstep. He also knew that Nikolai was searching for the Jade Sword in addition to the Shadow Blade. The Jade Sword had been securely hidden by Shin's protégé, Kenji—but the Shadow Blade had vanished along with Lord Akurosai's son, Ryuji.

When Nikolai arrived, he slaughtered several monks before finding Master Takeda alone... with a single monk standing guard before him. Shin knelt calmly, his weapon laid out before him. Nikolai sneered. "Do you think you'll stop me by taking your own life?" The monk stepped forward, placing himself between Nikolai and Takeda. Nikolai laughed and advanced.

Then, without warning, the monk turned to face Takeda Shin. With a single, clean stroke, severed his head. As the head fell to the floor, Nikolai opened his hand, revealing his long talons. He slashed the monk's throat in one swift motion, spilling his blood across the stone. Suddenly, Nikolai could smell and taste silver in the air. It was sharp and metallic, burning his senses as its essence filled the room. He turned to find several warrior-monks surrounding him, their spears glowing with silver-tipped blades.

Takeda had studied the nature of vampires for years. He knew their strengths, but more importantly, he understood their weaknesses. These monks were trained by Master Takeda for this very moment. Nikolai knew he was vulnerable against so many wielding silver. Rather than risk defeat, he fled and went into hiding.

The pulse of the Shadow Blade had weakened, and so Nikolai vanished into the shadows... waiting for the perfect moment, the moment when the Shadow Blade would fully awaken and call to him. He and Sable remained hidden, watching and waiting. Then there was a stirring in the ether... the Kurokawa was gaining strength, and Ryuji was building an army. Nikolai could feel it—an unmistakable vibrational shift that echoed through his core. Using the garnet stone, Nikolai and Sable began to track the current of energy, drawn toward the storm that was rising once again.

When Ryuji confronted Yurei and Rumiko, Nikolai had been there from the very beginning. He lingered in the shadows, cloaked invisible and patiently waiting for the perfect moment to strike. It was when Ryuji became tethered to Rumiko by the Kurokawa that Nikolai emerged, seizing the Jade Sword. It was the only artifact capable of tearing through the veil. He wanted to get control of both weapons, but he knew that Ryuji would follow him though the opening.

Nikolai had long hungered for control of both sacred weapons, the Jade Sword and the Shadow Blade. Possessing both would grant him power beyond comprehension. But he also knew something else: Ryuji would not let him escape. The bond he forged by the Kurokawa would compel him to follow... *and he did.*

When Rumiko awoke she was alone, a voice in her head speaking. *Rumiko, it is me Ayama the Loa Spirit. I saved you.* Rumiko opened her eyes and stared up at the night sky, where countless stars glittered like scattered embers across the vast, dark canvas above. The air was still, and for a moment, everything felt suspended in time. Then she heard the voice... soft, familiar, echoing not in her ears, but within her mind. "It's me Ayama, right now you may not remember me, but in time you will."

"What happened?" Rumiko asked, her thoughts forming words in the silence between worlds. The Loa Spirit spoke gently, "Do not be frightened. Your name is Rumiko, and I saved you from death. You are now in the physical realm. Everything may feel foreign and unfamiliar... but do not worry. We will help you remember who you are." Rumiko slowly began to sit up, her body feeling strange... heavy, yet distant, as though she were moving through water. Her limbs responded sluggishly, and every sensation was filled with an odd detachment, like she was wearing a body that wasn't quite her own.

She looked down at her hands, turning them over slowly, as if seeing them for the first time. Her skin was pale, almost translucent beneath the moonlight, the veins beneath faintly glowing. Rumiko cleared her throat and whispered, "What am I?" She was standing in an open field, surrounded by towering trees whose branches swayed in the night wind. A cool breeze swept across her face, carrying unfamiliar scents of earth, pine, and something else... *something warm and alive.*

The Loa Spirit responded in a voice that drifted like smoke, "I will tell you everything. But first, you must regain your strength. You must feed." Rumiko blinked, confused, but the hunger was already stirring inside her. It wasn't the sharp pang of starvation she felt. No... it was colder, deeper, a hollow ache nestled in her core that begged to be filled. She didn't fully understand the urge, but she could smell it. The scent of blood was strong and nearby.

Her nostrils flared as she twitched her nose, instinct guiding her. Her senses sharpened, vision locking, the world around her fading into shadow and scent. Her eyes shifted to a glowing crimson hue as she dropped into a low crouch... animalistic and alert. She sprinted across the field like a predator, running on all fours. Each of her limbs struck the earth in perfect rhythm, her movements fluid and impossibly fast. As she neared the tree line, a large buck stepped into the clearing, its antlers catching just a hint of moonlight.

Before the creature could react, Rumiko lurched forward with an eruption of motion and hunger. She crashed into the buck, toppling it to the ground in a blur of effortless force. The animal let out a single, startled snort, its eyes wide with fear. Then her teeth sank into its neck. Warm blood gushed into her mouth, and poured down her chest. Slowly, the ache within her began to ease. It was now replaced by a rush of power and memory.

The Loa Spirit spent days trying to convince Rumiko of who she was... and that this name, *Rumiko*, truly belonged to her. Just as Yurei had once forgotten he was Haruto, this was Rumiko's turn to realign with her true self. But before Ayama could reunite her with Yurei, there was still work to be done. Rumiko remained unstable, her hunger barely controlled.

Ayama, the Loa Spirit could not risk a reunion... not yet. Not while there was still a chance she might attack the one she was destined to remember.

Then, just a few days later, Ayama felt it... a sharp disturbance rippling through the Astral Plane. Something had torn into the Liminal Realm, like a claw dragging across the veil between worlds. It was not subtle. It was violent, deliberate... and growing stronger. Something was trying to breach the Astral Plane itself. Ayama stood still, listening... not with ears or body, but with spirit. Whatever was coming, it wasn't just a threat. It was a reckoning.

The Liminal Realm was a ghostly veil stretched between the physical and astral planes. It was a realm of in-betweens and unfinished echoes. It was a shifting landscape of pale grey light, where matter drifted between form and formlessness. Gravity here was unreliable. Time flowed like liquid and existence itself felt unanchored and untethered. The air vibrated with a low, fading resonance. Then, a sudden rupture sliced through the fabric of the realm. A rift opened, and Nikolai stepped through, his long coat trailing behind him like smoke.

Sable stood watch in the physical realm, the garnet stone attached to his collar glowing steadily, as Nikolai disappeared into the Liminal space. The Jade Sword was clutched firmly in his grip, its edge glowing faintly with a pale green light. It pulsed, sensing the shift in energies. Nikolai turned slightly, his eyes resting on the still-rippling opening behind him. The tear widened and then Ryuji emerged. He moved silently, the Shadow Blade in his hand quivering with power, as if the weapon itself recognized where it had arrived.

The two men locked eyes across the shifting terrain. Nikolai's voice cut through the heavy stillness, echoing with sharp clarity. I see you followed me, Ryuji. I'm not surprised." Ryuji chuckled dryly, his tone cold still. "Don't act like you don't need me." Both were still in physical form, but their bodies had begun to flicker. Nikolai looked down at his hands as they faded in and out of view. "And you need me, unless you've figured out how to cut into the Astral Plane without the Jade Sword," he said. Ryuji remained silent as the air around them suddenly cooled and began to swirl. The realm shifted, unstable, their forms phasing in and out.

Nikolai's voice sharpened. "The realm is waking. We cut now, or we are consumed." Ryuji stepped closer, his body stabilizing slightly in Nikolai's proximity. The Jade Sword began to vibrate in Nikolai's hand as he raised it overhead. The Shadow Blade in Ryuji's grip throbbed like a living heart. With a powerful swing, Nikolai drove the Jade Sword deep into the Liminal membrane. The fabric of the realm tore open, and a blinding light poured through the gash. A massive ripple surged outward, forming a swirling vortex. The pull was immediate and unstoppable. Both men were sucked into the breach, swallowed by the roar of energy—as the Liminal Realm collapsed into silence once more.

CHAPTER FOURTEEN

INTO THE REALMS

The Loa Spirit struggled to convince Rumiko that she was, in fact, *Rumiko*. Though she existed now in a body, she felt like a shadow of something lost. There was a gnawing emptiness inside her, and the name Rumiko felt hollow... like an echo from a dream she couldn't remember. Whenever Ayama gently called her by that name, she would always respond the same way: "Rumiko? Who is Rumiko?" The Loa Spirit spoke, her voice laced with warmth and patience. "She is powerful, vibrant and she has a beautiful heart."

At that, Rumiko would press her hand to her chest, fingers splayed as if trying to feel something that wasn't there. Then, with two fingers tapping lightly against her sternum, she'd say quietly, "I have no heart." The Loa Spirit spoke softly. "There is one who will open your heart..."

Rumiko interrupted before she could finish. "I can't remember any part of who I once was." She knelt down and plucked a single blade of grass, holding it up between her fingers. "How is it I know this is a blade of grass... but I don't know who I am? Let alone who you're talking about?" The Loa Spirit could feel a deep disturbance in the Astral Realm. She knew she had to help Rumiko rediscover her true self, before it was too late. It was time to introduce her to her son, Yurei.

Yurei had been wandering for some time, mourning the loss of Kenji, his mother, and his beloved Rumiko. When Ayama spoke to him for the first time in what felt like ages, Yurei was overwhelmed with relief just to hear her voice again. But when she introduced him to Rumiko, his heart nearly stopped. Even though she didn't quite look the same, he knew. Despite that, her first words were: "*Who is Rumiko?*" He knew it was her.

Ayama was able to speak to them both, individually, within their thoughts. She had saved them each in her own way, and for now, she could still reach them—if only for a little while. She spoke to Yurei softly: "Listen, my son. I can only speak to you both for a short time longer. There has been a disturbance in the Astral Plane. We must help Rumiko reconnect to her true self. And the only way to do that... is with your help." Yurei asked, "How can I help?"

The Loa Spirit whispered... though only Yurei could hear her: "I will guide Rumiko to lie down and close her eyes. When I do, you must quietly introduce the scent of the herbs I had you gather. They will place her into the same sleep you once fell into. It is the only way to make her whole again... and stop the Shadow Blade."

Rumiko was growing increasingly frustrated with her existence. Even though she couldn't feel the connection to her true self, Rumiko... she knew she needed answers. Ayama gently instructed her to lie down and close her eyes. Rumiko heard the voice in her mind, "Close your eyes. Breathe in deeply... and exhale slowly." Yurei had been gathering a series of herbs that the Loa Spirit had guided him to find. He had ground them into a fine mixture. The brown blend now sat in a small mound on a flat stone.

Yurei took a branch from the nearby fire and brought it toward the plate. He knelt quietly beside Rumiko and lit the herbs. A small trail of smoke lifted from the mound, curling through the air before finding its way to Rumiko's nose. Ayama whispered, "Breathe in deeply... but do not exhale." Rumiko inhaled and held her breath. "Now breathe out," the spirit said. She repeated the cycle five times, while Yurei continued to tend the flame... adding a fresh pinch of herbs with each round, the smoke growing denser with every breath.

Rumiko could feel her body begin to slip away. Her hands and legs grew heavy, almost distant, as if they were falling from her. A small tunnel began to form between her eyes. She stared into it, feeling her inner self being drawn toward the opening. In front of her, she saw colored fractals emerge, like shifting panels of stained glass they began morphing, rotating, and expanding in an array of colors and patterns. She felt herself being pulled forward, deeper into the spiraling light, until suddenly... everything stopped. A pause, a stillness, as if she had arrived somewhere.

She was no longer a body, no longer Rumiko as she knew herself. She had returned to the very beginning... before flesh, before thought, before memory. She was now a conscious thread of DNA—thin, spiraling, and luminous. She twisted slowly in a space without gravity, an ancient strand of identity, encoded with ancestral truth. Then came the voices... not from around her, but within her. Whispers echoing from countless lives and lineages, layered like songs sung over each other:

"I am weak..."

"I am strong."

"Obey."

"Resist."

"You belong to us."

"You are free."

The voices clashed and merged, rising into a chorus of emotion and contradiction. Each word pulled at her coil, bending and stretching her very code, testing the foundation of who she was... *and who she could become.* She hovered, waiting for the promise of form. She could hear the distant voices as she floated in her mothers womb... *"You will be beautiful...*

You will be strong... You will be perfect." It was darkness first... then there was light. She saw herself as an infant... emerging into the world, cradled in her mother's trembling hands. She felt the warmth, the overwhelming love, the deep connection to the two souls who had created her.

In a single breath, she relived her entire childhood. Every emotion... joy, pain, sorrow, love all returned in vivid clarity. She watched herself grow. Saw the moment her eyes first lingered on Haruto with affection. Then, piece by piece, her life unfolded before her. She saw Yurei complete as Haruto, and the love they shared... sacred and eternal. She witnessed their union, their connection, the merging of two souls into one as they made love.

She watched Yurei stand bravely before Ryuji, fighting to save her. And she heard Ayama's voice again, softly telling her to let go. And she did. She saw herself perish, be saved, and be reborn... as she is now.

Rumiko felt herself being pulled toward a tear in the Liminal membrane, the same breach that had consumed both Nikolai and Ryuji. With a sudden pull of energy, she was swept through, carried into the second rift created by the Jade Sword. The pull was swift and unrelenting, her essence unraveling as it poured into the Astral Plane.

The Astral Realm was the first level of existence beyond the physical world. It is where restless spirits wander and ghosts linger. It is the realm of guardian angels and shadow creatures, where dream weavers shape visions and nightmares take form. It is the place humans enter when they dream. But no living human has ever passed beyond the Astral Plane. This is where Rumiko began to unfold, drawn into one of the lives she had lived before her most recent incarnation.

She had arrived where all beings arrive when they enter the Astral Plane, the Hall of Mirrors. She looked at her hands now translucent, and saw the ground beneath them. But it was not earth. It was a swirling vortex of galaxies and distant constellations. With each twinkling star, she felt unseen eyes gazing back at her. Above her, shattered pieces of mirror floated in slow orbit, forming multidimensional shapes. Within each shard, she glimpsed flickering images of memories, faces, and moments from lives being lived across time and space.

As she gazed out toward a horizon that bent and warped like heat waves, she saw a reflection of herself in a small broken mirror. Suddenly, her form flickered and her essence was pulled into the mirror. The entire existence she had experienced as Rumiko was now deeply buried as a new voice emerged. She was in her body, but not as who she once was but in a new form.

From a distance, a voice called out, "Ren, your food is ready!" She looked around, the final traces of Rumiko fading from her form. She was now ten years old, living on a small farm nestled in the mountains. Following the voice, she made her way to a small wooden table behind the barn. A light-haired boy sat waiting, smiling warmly at her. His name was Daito and he was her best friend.

When Nikolai and Ryuji entered the Astral Plane, they looked at one another and smiled. Their bodies had become translucent, drifting like clouds across the cosmic landscape. Below them, the ground radiated with stars and galaxies that flickered and watched as they passed. Multidimensional shards of broken mirrors floated across the skies, reflecting realities both foreign and strange. Spirits and ghosts that roamed the realm stirred at their arrival. The energy shifted—everything moved away from them, sending vibrations rippling through the realm to announce their presence.

Nothing had ever torn into the Astral Realm so violently. Though it was a place filled with creatures and chaos in every direction, it was also a realm of rules and order. Everything had its place and purpose within this swirling pool of madness. But now, Ryuji and Nikolai had entered. Their goal was clear: to unify the realm under complete darkness. To annihilate the dreams and the dreamers. To spread a corruption so deep it would twist the very nature of the Astral Realm itself.

They would do it by trapping its inhabitants within the Shadow Blade. Each soul, each nightmare, each stolen fragment of consciousness would become fuel. By powering the weapon, they could bend the laws of the realm to their will...and forge a new order out of the chaos. From there, they would possess the power to advance into the Cultural Realm—called *The Eidon,* the place of all that has been. Though they never spoke of it explicitly, they both knew: they needed each other. And if they were to control all things, they would have to go all the way—to the Creator itself.

They stood in the Hall of Mirrors, gazing at the floating shards of glass. Their plan would begin with the Jade Sword: cutting into dreams and intentions, enslaving the souls within, and feeding them to the Shadow Blade to build its power. Nikolai's form glided across the landscape toward the horizon, then leapt into the air and drove the Jade Sword into a mirror. The glass shattered into countless fragments—each one carrying the reflection of a life.

Ryuji followed close behind as the black mass of the Kurokawa broke away from his body and transformed into a flock of ravens. Each bird darted into the shattered fragments of glass before circling back and plunging into the Shadow Blade, carrying the trapped souls with them. Nikolai erupted into wild laughter. "It's working!" he cried, eyes filled with madness.

Together, they moved like shadows across the Astral Plane—shattering mirrors, slicing through dreams, cutting deep into the fabric of intention. They left ruin in their wake, a harvest of souls fueling the weapon that would soon bend reality to their will. They knew time held no meaning in this realm, so there was no need to rush. They would take all they could, for only then would they have the power to break through to The Eidon and beyond.

The Astral Plane was vast and infinite... but not in the way space is infinite. It stretched beyond the stars, an ever-shifting ocean of consciousness. Its size wasn't measured in miles or years, but in the intensity of emotion and thought. It was every dream, every memory, every fleeting desire that had ever existed. This realm was a dimensional ecosystem, structured like a giant webbed mandala. Within its chaos existed systems and order. Each sector was divided into region-like zones, each with its own function and energy signature.

There was the Imagination Field, where dreams and nightmares unfolded. This is where humans often drift when they sleep... where the subconscious takes shape, and thought becomes form. There was the Seed Garden, where intentions either wither or manifest. It's covered with translucent soil, and within it, intentions appeared as seeds. This was the place where reality often took root—long before it bloomed in the physical world.

There were the Ghost Fields, where those who refused death still wandered. These earthbound spirits, tethered by echoes of unfinished business, drifted between the physical and the Astral realms like slow moving fog. There was the Realm of the Ancestral Guides—the domain of the Loa Spirits and guardian angels. It was home to those who walk beside us through life... the hidden hands that guide us, the whisper of intuition we hear in moments we can't explain. It was here that Haruto and Rumiko were saved by Ayama, the *Loa Spirit*, when they died.

And deep within the Astral Plane lay the Hall of Mirrors... the endless loop that twists and folds on itself like a Möbius strip. Here, souls walked the same path over and over, trapped in repeating cycles until they finally gained awareness. The Astral Plane defied all known geometry. It bended and twisted endlessly, reflecting infinite possibilities within its mirrored depths.

Rumiko was now Ren, a mountain girl in another life where she had once existed. She had returned to a moment, a dream that had always felt like a whisper in the back of her mind. Here, time rippled sideways. Past and future collapsed into a single breath, and Ren remembered everything... *and nothing.*

Ren and Daito had been best friends for as long as they could remember. They had lived near each other since infancy, and now, just ten years old, they spent nearly every day together. Their families lived on neighboring farms tucked into a lush, green mountainside. They shared a field between them, and everyone... adults and children alike... took part in tending the crops and caring for the animals.

Their days were a blend of work and play—though for them, it mostly felt like play. Each afternoon, as the sun reached its peak in the sky, they would meet for lunch. It was always just the two of them. They'd eat quickly, laughing between bites, trying to leave enough time to explore the forest trails or climb the rocks by the stream before returning to their chores.

Today was the day they would walk the rope bridge. It was a tradition among the mountain kids—a rite of passage whispered about in secret. The bridge stretched across a deep ravine, made of worn wooden planks and suspended by two thick ropes, each tied securely to a towering tree on each side. Hidden deep within the woods, the bridge had always been forbidden. Ren and Daito had been warned by their parents never to cross it. But the temptation was too great.

On the far side, where the rope met the base of a gnarled oak, a handful of names had been carved into the bark—memorials of those who had crossed before. Ren had stared at them for years, wondering what it felt like to add her name. But the bridge was old and weathered now. It was still passable... but dangerous if one wasn't careful.

Daito was a good two inches shorter than Ren. He admired her—not just as a friend, but because she could do everything he could do. She was a fast runner, climbed like a cat, and could even jump higher than him. He often forgot that Ren was a girl, which wasn't hard to do considering she wore her hair short. While every other mountain girl had long, flowing hair, Ren flat-out refused. Her mother didn't mind much—even with short hair Ren came home with her hair tangled into knots. On more than one occasion, her mother would grab her by the head, pluck out a pinecone, and exclaim, "Your hair is a bird's nest!"

She'd then drag Ren to the nearest comb and yank it through the mess as Ren's body recoiled in pain. Daito approached the bridge and cautiously extended a leg to test its strength. The structure wobbled slightly, releasing a low screech as the ropes rubbed together. Specks of dust drifted from the wooden planks at the center, forming a cloud that caught the sunlight as it passed through. Daito watched the dust swirl and fall into the deep ravine below. At the bottom lay a dried riverbed, littered with jagged rocks.

A knot formed in his stomach as Ren stepped up beside him. She stood silently at the edge of the bridge, eyes locked on the tree on the far side. Without a word, she stepped forward. Suddenly, a loud boom cracked overhead. Daito flinched and lurched forward. Ren grabbed his arm and pulled him back just before he stumbled onto the bridge. It was thunder, rolling in from the gathering clouds.

They looked up as large raindrops began to fall. Neither moved. Eyes closed, they stood still as the droplets bounced off their faces, the forest around them darkening with the approaching storm. A sudden crack of thunder jolted them into motion. Without a word, they turned and sprinted toward the nearby path. Ren took the lead, weaving through the woods with Daito close behind as they raced back to the farm.

The next day, Ren and Daito returned to the bridge right after lunch. When they arrived, the bridge was soaking wet and swaying slightly under the weight of the water. Daito stepped toward the edge, but Ren quickly warned him to stop. "It's really wet. We need to give it another day," she said, glancing up at the sunlight pouring through the tree canopy. "One more day should do it." Ren turned toward the path and shouted as she took off running, "Chase me to the farm!"

When they arrived at the bridge the next day, Ren was ready. She had been planning this for quite some time. Daito was surveying the bridge, gently shaking it to test its stability, while Ren secured her knife in its sheath. She tightened the leather strap and pushed the handle all the way in. The sheath hung just past her hip. Her plan was simple: she would go first, and Daito would follow ten steps behind. She believed this was the safest approach, as it would distribute their weight instead of concentrating it in one spot. Once they were both safely on the other side, they would celebrate by carving their names into the tree.

Ren walked up beside Daito as they both stared at the tree on the other side. Daito looked up at Ren, "Are you ready?" She smiled, "I'm ready." Ren stepped onto the bridge first, gripping the rope handles as it swayed from side to side. The structure wrenched and screeched as the ropes rubbed against each other. She looked down and saw dirt crumbling and falling below. A knot formed in her stomach, but she forced a smile and turned to Daito.

Letting out a breath, Ren straightened her posture and steadied herself. "Come on, get ready," she said. She began to move forward slowly as Daito counted her steps. As she neared ten, he felt the weight of the moment pressing down on him. He hesitated, reluctant to step onto the bridge—but he knew how important this was to Ren. So, in spite of his fear, he forced himself to take the first step.

When Ren reached the middle of the ravine, the bridge began to sag slightly. She paused, realizing the structure was arching under her weight. She looked back at Daito, who was getting closer. "Stop there... We need to spread our weight out or it'll break in the middle. Let me get to the other side, then you can come. Just stay there for now." Daito hesitantly nodded as he grabbed the ropes on both sides and stood firm.

Ren slowly made her way out of the sloping center and began the upward climb as the bridge arched. Her final few steps were within reach. She exhaled and smiled with relief. When her foot touched the grassy edge, she let out an audible laugh and turned to Daito—who stood frozen, unmoving. Her smile quickly faded when she realized Daito wasn't going to move on his own—and she couldn't go back across now; the bridge wouldn't hold both their weights.

"Daito, you can't stay there. You have to come across." Ren noticed his arms trembling as he stared down into the ravine. "Look at me. Don't look down. Just listen to my voice." Daito slowly lifted his head and met her eyes. "I want you to move forward very slowly." But Daito turned his head away and begged. "I want to go back." Ren knew there was no way he could as he was too far across. He had to keep going.

She tried to remain calm, guiding him one step at a time. Slowly, Daito crept his way to the center of the bridge. When he looked up, Ren was kneeling at the far edge, her hands outstretched, a strained smile on her face as she pleaded, "You have to keep going!" Gripping the side ropes tightly, Daito continued forward, scaling the bridge step by step. But as he neared the final ten feet, one of the ropes gave out under the strain—and with a sharp, echoing crack, it snapped.

He froze, his fingers locked onto the rope. Daito looked back in horror as the bridge behind him began to collapse into the ravine, boards tumbling one by one like falling roof tiles in a storm. Wind rushed upward as the structure gave way. Panicked, Daito clung to the remaining rope and began climbing upward toward Ren, using the bridge like a ladder. His legs scrambled for footing while his hands gripped the fraying rope with everything he had, his heart pounding as he tried to escape the void below.

Ren lay on the edge of the ravine, her torso hanging down and arms fully extended as she frantically reached for Daito. What remained of the bridge now dangled beneath him as he climbed, every movement shaking the unstable ropes. He was within arm's reach. He looked into Ren's eyes—and she smiled back, trying to hide her fear. As his hand touched her warm palm, the last rope began to unravel. He slipped. Ren grabbed for the sleeve of his shirt as his hand slid from hers, fingers vanishing inside the fabric until she was left holding a single loose thread. Daito fell. Ren watched in horror as his body hit the riverbed below. The sound echoed through the valley and into her very soul. Gone... gone... gone. She was left alone, holding the blue thread.

Ren felt an immense guilt over Daito's death. But no one blamed her—except herself. Many weeks passed, and Ren refused to speak to anyone. She had always been close to her father, and he was beginning to worry. Her father found her sitting alone in a quiet corner of the barn. Father was a lean man with a speckle of grey hair on his mostly bald head. He was much older than mother and had his daughter Ren much later in life. She was their only child after many failed attempts.

Ren looked up at him as he approached, squinting into the light. His voice was gentle and compassionate. "Ren, you cannot carry this weight alone." She buried her face in her hands and began to weep. He knelt down slowly, bringing himself to her level. "Ren, I have something I'd like to show you." In his hand, he held something delicate—an iridescent feather danced in the sunlight, shifting from deep violet to emerald green, then to a brilliant sapphire blue. Ren wiped her tears with the back of her hand, trying to focus on what he was holding.

She slowly extended her hand. "May I touch it?" Her father nodded and smiled. Turning her index finger, Ren gently stroked the feather. The moment she made contact, she felt it—a subtle warmth and a gentle hum that resonated through her fingertip and into her chest. It was as if the feather recognized her.

Her father spoke softly, as if addressing a fragile creature: "It is called the bird of a thousand wings. My father's father told him that this bird flies so fast, it can pass beyond the veil where spirits walk. I want you to hold onto the feather as you mourn Daito." Ren nodded, her eyes fixed on the delicate plume in her hands. In the distance a voice echoed across the field, "Ren! Come Now!" Father quickly stood up and tapped Ren on her back, "Hurry along, Mother is calling."

That night, Ren couldn't get the feather out of her mind. She tucked it beneath her hand, resting it under her ear as she turned onto her side and adjusted the edges of the straw mat beneath her. The hum was still there like a lullaby—soft and steady as it followed her into sleep. In her dreams, she found herself back at the bridge. This time, she was alone, and it was the day before the crossing... when it had rained. She stood watching as the bridge absorbed the weight of the storm. She could feel it as if she were the bridge itself—heavy and weakened, the ropes sagging and straining beneath the water.

Then, the rain stopped. Sunlight pierced through the clouds, drying the ropes. But instead of growing stronger, they became brittle and weak—withered, fragile threads stretched to their limit. She felt the realization settle in: it hadn't been her fault after all. But somehow, that didn't change the ache in her chest—because Daito was still gone. Standing at the edge of the empty bridge, she called out into the silence, her voice trembling. "Daito... where are you?"

Then, halfway across the bridge, she saw him. He was walking slowly toward the other side. His skin shimmered with a soft, inner light, as if illuminated from within. He paused, turned back, and smiled gently at Ren. "It's not your fault, Ren," he said, his voice calm and clear. "It's time to move forward." When he reached the other side, he looked back one last time and smiled—then vanished like mist into the light.

When Ren awoke in the morning, the feather was gone. She searched everywhere, but it was nowhere to be found. She spent the morning hiking down into the ravine and up the other side, where the lone tree stood bearing the names of those who had crossed. At the edge of the cliff sat a small bundle of dried flowers left by Daito's family. Ren gently brushed off the dust and debris, then set the flowers upright with care. She stood and turned to face the large oak tree. At its base lay the last remaining rope, its ends frayed, lonely and weathered by time.

The bridge itself had been completely dismantled by then by nearby villagers. Ren removed her knife from its sheath. As she stared at the blade, she caught the reflection of her almond brown eyes and held the gaze for a moment. Then, Ren turned and pointed the knife at the tree, carving Daito's name deep into the bark. Pale yellow wood emerged beneath the surface as the bark gave way, each character etched with care and depth. When she came to the final line, she slid the knife back into its sheath and slipped her hand into the leather satchel strapped across her chest. Inside was the blue thread from Daito's shirt. She held it for a long moment, staring at it as tears welled in her eyes. Then she carefully tucked the thread securely into the edge of a loose piece of bark on the tree.

As she turned and walked away, she felt a hum in her core... a subtle vibration that pulsed through her chest like a small, fluttering heartbeat. She turned back to look at the tree—and saw it. A small, iridescent bird was dancing around Daito's name. Its feathers glowed softly as it hovered in front of the bark and gently pulled the blue thread free with its beak. Then, it tilted its head toward Ren in a gesture of acknowledgment before ascending into the sky, carrying the thread with it.

As it spiraled upward, the thread unfurled and twisted beneath it, forming a vortex above Ren. The hum grew stronger, resonating through her body, until she felt a sudden pull—followed by a release... as her soul was swept upward into the opening. This was Rumiko's karmic loop—an echo of lifetimes repeating, open at last. But she was more than just Rumiko. She was the sum of all who came before her, the seed of all she is yet to become. She is a universal being—woven from stardust, and destined to live across many lifetimes, across many forms. In each incarnation, she carries forward the wisdom of the past and the ache of unfinished stories. Her soul is ancient, her essence is cyclical. She is not bound by a single name or timeline. She is a weaver of worlds, a bridge between what was and what will be. With each life, she ascends to a new realm.... growing, evolving, and expanding through the ever-changing tapestry of existence. In every incarnation, she experiences a different expression of love, each one a sacred thread in the soul's long weaving.

Just as she knew with Daito, there was *philia*—the deep, loyal bond of friendship and shared truth. In that life, their connection was not born of passion, but of mutual respect, unwavering support, and soul-level recognition. The thread created by this experience will not only shape Ren and Rumiko, but all who have ever felt unseen yet deeply known... all who have loved without conditions or timelines... all who have stood by someone, even as the world unraveled. For in the vast weaving of the soul, no thread of love is ever lost—it becomes part of the pattern that guides others home.

The Loa Spirit knew this when she saved Rumiko and Haruto. She understood that together, they were the only ones who could mend the fracture forming in the veil. Rumiko, a Universal Soul—ancient and multidimensional. Haruto, always in the shadows, was her guardian and compass, helping her remember when she forgets. The battle ahead would not begin in the physical realm. It would start in the Astral Plane... a place of dreams and distortions. It was in this space that the true war would be waged. A war not only for balance, but for the control of all beings. Rumiko would need to remember all that she was not just as Ren and not just Rumiko. But the soul behind all names... one that had crossed lifetimes to stand at this very moment.

Yurei sat beside Rumiko, watching her lie completely still. Her hands rested over her stomach, her chest rising and falling in slow, measured breaths. Her face was calm, but her eyes moved rapidly beneath closed lids—caught in the grip of some unseen vision. He had been waiting for hours, trying to stay grounded. But something didn't feel right. *Too long*, he thought. Her stillness no longer comforted him, it gnawed at him. The longer she remained under, the more restless he became.

"I need to go in after her," he muttered aloud. "Something's wrong." A voice echoed in his

mind. "Wait." It was Ayama, the Loa Spirit. She didn't speak with breath, but with vibration.

"You feel it too," he said. "Don't you?"

"Yes. There's a disturbance. The veil is open, and Ryuji and Nikolai have entered. Now is

the time for you to follow."

Yurei asked, "Where is Rumiko?"

The Loa Spirit whispered, "She is there too."

He looked up at the sky as crimson and black clouds rolled across the landscape, swirling like ink in water. The Loa Spirit spoke again, "The ripples from the damage they are causing will only grow more severe. You must go now." Yurei took a deep breath and replied, "Yes, now."

As Yurei prepared the herbs, the Loa Spirit reminded him, "I will stay at your side throughout your journey and show the way to Rumiko. But I can only go with you into the Astral Realm. Beyond that is forbidden." Yurei sat beside Rumiko and held the black opal stone his mother, Ayama the Loa Spirit, had given him. He rolled it in his palm several times, letting it pass the gap where his finger had once been, before lifting it to his lips, kissing its surface, and whispering, "Rumiko."

Carefully, he tucked the stone into the bottom hem of her kimono. From his sleeve, he drew a length of silk string and a bone needle. With the skill his mother had endowed him with in his youth, he began to slowly stitch, until the round stone was secured within the fabric's base.

Yurei took a stick from the nearby fire and touched it to the bundle of dried brown herbs resting on a smooth piece of bark. The herbs caught fire quickly, releasing a thin ribbon of smoke that rose and curled into the air like a living thread. He leaned forward, inhaling deeply as the smoke spiraled toward his face. It entered his nostrils in a slow, steady stream. He held the smoke in his lungs before releasing it from his mouth with a burn and familiar aftertaste. He repeated the process again and again before finally closing his eyes as the world around him began to shift.

Ryuji and Nikolai caused immediate devastation to the Astral Plane as they cut and tore through the Hall of Mirrors. Reflections shattered, time-lines splintered, and memories bled across realms. But it wasn't enough.

The Astral Plane is a realm of consciousness... woven from thought, emotion, and belief. It reshapes itself in response to will. It does not die easily. For every mirror they broke, another shifted its angle. For every path they severed, new ones began to form. If they were to truly dismantle the Astral Realm, they would need to corrupt its foundations... the Imagination Fields, Seed Gardens, Ancestral Fields, and the karmic loops. With this kind of devastation, they would weaken the veil itself and make the boundary between realms thin and unstable.

As they tore into the fabric of dreams within the Imagination Field, their first act was to trap the dream weavers within the Shadow Blade. These were the guides who walked beside those who slept—guardians of the dream paths and protectors of subconscious realms. With their removal, the balance was broken. Dreamers began to spiral, caught in endless nightmare loops—trapped in an infinite cycle with no escape. Their physical bodies fell into a coma-like state, lying perfectly still as if in deep sleep. But for those who awoke, the nightmare had followed them back. They were trapped between dream and waking, unable to tell what was real.

Men turned on their spouses. Children lashed out at their parents. The boundaries of the mind had fractured. The attack on the Imagination Fields continued to weaken the veil, allowing even more darkness to pour into the physical realm. Shadows crept through forgotten doorways. Whispers threaded themselves into the thoughts of the vulnerable. The world began to shift under the weight of Ryuji and Nikolai's destruction. They both knew: the weaker the veil became, the easier it would be to cut into the Cultural Realm—*The Eidon,* the place where all collective memory, story, language, and identity reside.

If they could infect that realm, they wouldn't just dismantle individuals—they would erase entire civilizations from the inside out and reshape it to their will. The Imagination Fields stretched out in every direction... a vast, surreal landscape of rolling green meadows and whispering hills. The grass glistened with iridescent tones, changing slightly with each breath of wind, responding to silent thoughts.

Above, the sky pulsed with color and motion. Small storms would gather, born from the fragmented remnants of dreams. Wisps of ideas drifted upward, coalescing into vibrant, swirling clouds. They formed miniature vortexes that appeared suddenly, sparkled briefly, then vanished like forgotten thoughts. Some clouds crackled softly with distant laughter or echoes of whispered stories. Others wept silent tears of raindrops that fell from the sky.

Scattered across the meadows stood towering, ancient looms—woven not from wood or metal, but from light and memory. These were the sacred stations of the dream weavers. It was here they spun golden thread from inspiration and dreams manifested. The delicate strands were used to mend broken dream paths, repair torn symbols, and reweave the frayed edges of sleeping minds. Each loom sang softly as it worked, a chorus of lullabies for the dreamers.

But now, a dark shadow hung over the Imagination Fields, cast by the actions of Ryuji and Nikolai. That darkness had broken free from the Astral Plane and begun to seep into the physical realm—starting with the youngest and most vulnerable... the children. A small boy stood before his mother, clutching a picture he had carefully scratched into the back of a dried toadstool using the point of a stick. His bare feet were dusty, and his cheeks smudged from play, but his eyes grew with excitement.

He stepped beside her and gently nudged her leg to get her attention. His mother, who wore her long black hair pulled over one shoulder, paused in her work. She turned to him, her expression softening. Kneeling down to his level, she tucked a strand of hair behind her ear and smiled. The boy held out the toadstool, pointing proudly to the rudimentary image he had etched into its surface.

"What is it?" she asked, her voice warm and curious as she examined the strange figure. It was round and spider-like, with rows of jagged lines underneath that resembled legs. Its eyes were large and circular, darkened with heavy rings for pupils. Its mouth stretched wide, filled with sharp, triangular teeth that bared like a warning. The boy suddenly raised both hands and clawed at the air, letting out a dramatic growl.

"It's a demon!" he shouted. "And it's going to eat you!"

His mother gasped in mock fear, placing a hand over her mouth, eyes wide with playful

alarm. "Oh no! What should I do?"

The little boy smiled and whispered, "Run!"

Laughing, she turned around to play along—but the smile fell from her face.

Standing in front of her was the very creature he had drawn. Somehow, impossibly, the crude lines carved into the toadstool had taken shape and manifested into form. It stood there, alive, breathing, its eyes just as wide and empty, its teeth jagged and glowing in the light. The boy looked up at it, still grinning. "I told you," he said.

This was the darkness that had bled into the physical realm. Husbands and wives turned on each other, their bonds fraying under the weight of Ryuji and Nikolai's disruption. One man found himself trapped in a nightmare loop. He was caught in a dream where he was both the attacker and the victim. Each time he struck, he felt the blow land on his own flesh. He could feel the warm blood stain his hand and simultaneously pour from his body. The violence was raw, savage, and painful. Each time he cried out in pain, he heard his own voice echoing back in rage. His wife, sleeping beside him, was ensnared in the same dream. In her vision she saw her own look of terror staring back as she violently attacked herself. She watched herself pinned to the ground and, at the same time, doing the pinning. The sensations mirrored back and forth in a desperate spiral.

They shifted between helplessness and aggression to terror and guilt. Both were locked in a cycle they couldn't escape. What began in the dream soon spilled into waking life. Still mentally trapped in their sleep, they began to lash out, attacking each other's physical bodies. Both were deeply driven by the parasitic influence of a violence they couldn't control. Their bodies bore the marks of blood and bruises, violence and regret. They stared into each other's eyes, searching for a trace of hope.

But all they found was rage and fear, reflections of a love lost to the shadow of Ryuji and Nikolai—locked in a loop of pain as they lashed out again and again... trapped in a nightmare from which they could not awaken.

Chapter Fifteen

BEYOND THE EIDON

Ren awoke to the warm sun bursting across her face. She slowly opened one eye, blinking up at the pale blue sky. So much had happened to bring her to this very spot... she was alone, hidden in the tall grass. She shifted, stretching her sore limbs as she sat up. Her back was stiff, her muscles aching from three nights of sleeping on the ground. She was fifteen now. Her parents had both died from a strange illness that swept through the countryside. Ren had been spared—saved at the last moment when her mother's sister took her away just before the sickness reached their home.

She stayed on her aunt's farm, but life there was harsh. Ren was treated less like a niece and more like a servant. She spent her days doing grueling labor in the fields, and her nights cleaning the house and preparing meals. Her Oba was a bitter, lonely woman who never married and never truly loved. She was stern and short-tempered, and carried the weight of her regrets like stones in her heart. Her only outlet was taking it out on Ren.

She insisted Ren grow her hair long, claiming it was a woman's duty. Every night, she would sit Ren down and roughly drag a wooden comb through her tangled hair, tearing at the knots without mercy. This was why her real mother let her cut her hair short in the first place.

"Your mother is gone," she would repeat, "and you must grow your hair to attract a husband… otherwise, you'll be alone forever." Ren had heard those words so many times, they lost all meaning. But in her heart, she knew one thing: she couldn't stay. Late that night, she slipped out the door and disappeared into the darkness.

She was only a teenager, but she was tough and capable of handling herself. She had proven it time and time again, standing her ground against boys and even grown men who had tried to overpower her. There was something instinctual in the way she fought, a raw and natural skill rarely seen, especially in someone so young. After Daito died, the grief hardened into anger, and that anger lived in her body like fire. It drove her into conflict after conflict.

Ren carried an energy she didn't fully understand. While other girls her age dreamed of marriage, she was drawn to war. She was glad to be free from her Oba, but now she was alone—hungry and in need of shelter. She knew she couldn't survive long living like an animal in the wild. She had packed a small bag with only the essentials: a dagger, a fire-starting kit, and a worn water skin. It wasn't much, but it would have to be enough.

Ren walked to the edge of a nearby lake. The water was still and silent. As she bent down to scoop some water into her hands, she paused. The surface held her reflection—her long black hair falling over her shoulders like a blanket as she pulled her kanzashi from her head. This was the only gift her mother had given her. It was a long, slender metal hair hairpin that she had sharpened at the end so it could be used as a weapon.

Gripping her hair, she pulled it over one shoulder and pressed the sharpened end to it. Slowly, mindfully, she began to saw through the thick strands, her eyes locked on the girl in the water. The quiet was shattered as a large white crane descended into the lake, its wings stirring the surface.

Ripples spread outward, distorting Ren's reflection until it vanished completely.

She cut her hair to the length of a boy's and wrapped a gray cloth around her neck and face before heading toward a nearby village. Her hope was to find food and supplies, then move on. She figured that if she could pass as a boy, no one would give her trouble. And if they did, she was ready for that too.

She approached the edge of the village and crouched behind a cluster of trees to observe. It was a small farming village with just a handful of thatched-roof homes, a rice field, and a dusty road that slipped through the middle. A thin ribbon of smoke curled up from the village, carrying with it the mouthwatering scent of roasted meat. The smell drifted toward Ren, tempting her hunger.

After foraging some berries and refilling her water skin, she settled in for the night, planning to enter the village at first light. Sometime deep into the night, as she slept beneath a tree, a rustling in the nearby shrubs jolted her awake. She froze and laid completely still. Two men had tumbled through the brush, laughing loudly and tripping over their own feet. Ren quietly crawled behind a thick tree trunk and watched as they staggered in her direction.

They had been drinking and now they were looking for a place to sleep it off. One of the men swung a paper lantern lazily from a short bamboo stick. As he walked he tripped on a root sticking out of the ground and lurched forward. "Awwww..." he shouted, stumbling forward and flailing his arms. The paper lantern slipped from his grip and crashed into the dry grass with a loud thud. The bamboo frame cracked, and the candle inside flickered wildly. A small tongue of flame licked at the straw and twigs nearby. Within seconds, the brittle underbrush caught fire. The men cursed and stumbled back, drunken laughter giving way to panic.

Ren knew she had to act. If she didn't reveal herself, those two fools would set the entire forest ablaze. She sprinted toward the fire, which had already devoured the grass and was climbing the trunk of a nearby tree. She emptied her water skin over the flames. The blaze hissed, steam curling upward, but it wasn't enough. Dropping to the ground, she snatched up a freshly fallen branch still heavy with lush green leaves and began beating at the embers, fanning them down before pressing the leaves to smother the heat.

As she fought the flames, a sudden splash of water fell over the burning patch, dousing what remained. Ren's eyes shot toward the shadows, where a teenage boy stood holding an empty water skin. Instinctively, she pulled her scarf higher, covering her neck and face.

The two drunken men began shouting, "Hey there!" Their slurred voices caught the boy's attention, and without hesitation, he ran toward them. Ren slowly rose and watched as the boy closed the distance. The men dove forward to grab him, but he stepped aside, and they stumbled to the ground in a heap.

He planted a foot on one man's chest and pointed toward Ren. "Leave him be, or you'll answer to me." Ren started toward them, realizing the boy had mistaken her for a boy. He turned to her. "Are you all right?" Ren gave a short cough and lowered her tone from behind the scarf. "I'm fine. They would have burned the whole village." The boy smiled. He was long and lean, with black hair tied back in a messy topknot. "Then you may have saved my people," he said, nodding in thanks. He pointed down the path to where a faint light flickered in the distance. "We're staying there. This fire would surely have spread to us. Thank you. What is your name?" She paused, turning her head slightly to disguise her voice. "I am Ren." The boy nodded. "Come with me, Ren. You'll be safer with us."

His name was Souto. He had fallen in with a small band of Ronin who had slowly gathered companions along the road. What began as one wandering, masterless samurai had grown to three—plus the boy, who served as their errand runner. On this night, they had sent him to fill their water skins. Souto was fifteen and had joined the group after running away from home. His mother had died of illness, driving his father into a darkness that consumed him. The abuse became too much for Souto, so like Ren... he left.

Ren decided it was safer to keep her true identity hidden. Souto introduced her to the group, and they agreed to let "him" travel with them so long as "he" helped with errands. When they asked why he kept a scarf over his face, Ren claimed to have scars from a fire. She worked hard and kept quiet, so they did not press the matter further. Ren spent much of her time with Souto, gathering food and supplies for the group. When they traveled, the two would sometimes slip into villages under cover of night to steal what they needed.

One evening, Ren found a gold ring and gave it to Takahiro... known to all as the Old Crow. There was also Kenzo and Shinsuke. None of them used their given names anymore; each preferred the nicknames they had each chosen. Kenzo, short and sharp-eyed, was called the Fox. Shinsuke was known as Iron Head, for he always wore his battered jingasa... (war hat), no matter the weather or time of day.

Ren approached the old man with care. His hair, still black as a crow's despite his years, framed a face marked by a long, beak-like nose. He sat on a log, sharpening his dagger, when she stepped forward and held out the gold ring. He smiled faintly and gave a small nod as he grabbed the ring. "Good find." Ren nodded and walked away. She rarely spoke to the group, but she felt a quiet closeness to Souto, who filled nearly every moment with questions... he often answered himself. Ren listened, nodding along, holding onto every word. He was the first boy she had been around since Daito. It felt good to have a friend she often thought, but it was hard for her to communicate without arousing suspicion.

"Okay, Ren... you ready?" Souto asked with a grin. She gave a silent nod, adjusting the scarf over her face as they stepped into the bustling village. Travelers were setting up tents along the narrow road, their stalls overflowing with skewered meats, steaming rice cakes, and baskets of fresh produce. The air was thick with the scent woodsmoke, mingling with the distant sound of merchants shouting over one another to catch the attention of a passersby.

Ren and Souto split apart as they stepped into the bustle of the bazaar. Souto wandered beneath a canvas awning where an old man sold baskets of fresh produce. While Souto distracted him with questions about the ripeness of his melons, Ren slipped in silently and began filling a rough hemp bag with vegetables and dried roots.

Ren would slip away to their meeting spot, empty the bag, and then head back out. They repeated this over and over until their haul was full. Sometimes, Ren also crept along the shoreline, stealing any unattended fish left caught in nets. This was the system they followed as they traveled with the Old Crow, Fox and Iron Head. Ren was able to disappear and reappear with various trinkets she gathered and stole along the way. This kept the three at bay. They were just happy "he" went beyond what was expected.

Ren stayed with the group as they drifted from one place to another, never lingering long enough to be remembered. They had no horses, only a stubborn ox that pulled their single cart. Its wheels groaned with every rut in the road. The cart carried bundles of bedding, hemp covers for shelter and a few battered pots, and whatever food they hadn't yet eaten. As the weeks passed, Ren began to regret hiding her identity as a female... but she knew she was safer this way. At least, that's what she kept telling herself. Other than her father, every man she had ever been near had tried to touch her in ways that filled her with anger. She was safer as a boy, even if it meant keeping silent.

Ren enjoyed her time with Souto; they made a good team. He kept her entertained with his never-ending stories, and he never pressed her about her silence or the scarf she wore. Souto was grateful to finally have someone who would listen to his endless tales and commentary. An adventurous soul, he longed for freedom. His mother had been his closest ally and friend, but when she passed away, he was left alone with his father. His father wasn't a bad man, but tragedy has a way of changing people. Loneliness and age crept in, making him forgetful and impatient. He had little tolerance for the restless energy of a teenage boy. Sometimes he would even forget Souto's name, and when frustration boiled over, his anger would spill into violence.

It had been a long day, and Ren and Souto were sitting at their secret spot, a narrow alcove between two jagged rocks along the shoreline, where they stored the day's haul. They did this at every stop along the way... hiding everything they collected and then dividing it up amongst the group. The Crow and his men didn't seem to mind. They weren't much of warriors anymore, more interested in finding a jug of sake than in securing paying work as Ronin.

The Crow was old now, and his reflexes were not what they once were. In his time, he had been a tough man, but these days his body was failing him. Fox was the only one of the three who could still handle himself. Younger than the others, he was quick and agile. The Crow often wondered about Iron Head. He seemed more story than substance, talking endlessly in tales that rarely made sense and often contradicted themselves. The Old Crow sometimes suspected that Iron Head had simply found the helmet and invented the rest. He didn't care either way; he enjoyed the man's company regardless.

The Fox had grown suspicious of Ren and Souto, thinking they might be skimming off the top and keeping the best for themselves. So, he decided to follow them in secret. Ren and Souto sat side by side on an overturned log, gazing at their biggest haul yet. Ren smiled beneath her scarf. Souto clapped his hands together in delight. "Can you believe this? We have enough supplies for weeks!" Ren nodded and pointed to the neat rows of produce and rice. "What if we took the supplies and went out on our own? We don't need them—they do nothing for us." He leaned closer, his hand reaching for her scarf. Slowly, he began to unravel it. Ren instinctively pulled back, but he persisted. "It's okay, Ren. I know."

As the scarf fell away, her face emerged... there were no scars, just two almond-colored eyes that met his with a touch of fear. Souto stared for a moment, then leaned toward her. She pulled back just as a voice rang out: "You're a girl! And you're stealing our food!" It was the Fox, he had been hiding behind a tree. He jumped into the clearing with a knife clenched tightly in his hand. The Fox walked over to Ren and Souto, "Stand up now!" He directed.

They slowly rose to their feet, hands held in the air. As Souto straightened, the Fox lunged toward Ren with a knife. Souto shoved her aside, sending her sprawling to the ground, then stepped in behind the Fox as he stumbled forward. With a sharp kick to the back, Souto sent him crashing face-first into the dirt. Souto moved in to finish him, but the Fox suddenly whipped his hand around, flinging a fistful of dirt into Souto's eyes. Souto staggered back, clawing at his face.

The Fox followed with a vicious kick that dropped Souto to the ground. In an instant, he straddled him, knees pinning his arms, the knife raised high in both hands. Out of nowhere, Ren leapt onto the Fox's back, her scarf snapping tight around his throat. She locked her legs around his waist, riding him as he thrashed, pulling the scarf tighter... and tighter. She then felt someone from behind her grabbing at her shoulders. It was the crow he had heard the confrontation and came to investigate. He struck Ren multiple times until she released her hold on the Fox. She fell backwards as the Crow dragged her across the ground. As she struggled to get away she bit his leg. The Crow released his hold and screamed out in pain.

Ren lay there for a moment, breathing heavily. A sudden scream from Souto jolted her. She turned just in time to see the Fox drive the knife into his chest. Souto arched his back, his eyes finding hers one last time. Forcing herself to her feet, Ren leapt onto the Fox's back. Wrapping her arm tight around his neck, she began to strangle him. He coughed and gagged before collapsing forward onto Souto's lifeless body. Ren pushed herself to her knees, the taste of blood swirling in her mouth. Nearby, the Crow lay crumpled on the ground—his broken body failing him once more. She looked back at Souto, completely still, the Fox draped over him like a shroud. Gathering what little strength she had left, Ren snatched a few supplies before disappearing into the shadows once more.

Yurei felt his body slipping away, dissolving like mist. Colored fractals blazed past him at an unfathomable velocity, each flash carrying the echo of a memory. He saw himself moving through every moment he had lived—first as Haruto, then as Yurei. A force began to draw him forward, pulling him through an opening in the Veil, across the Liminal membrane, and into the Astral Realm. Here, there was only presence... no form, no horizon, no movement. Nothing to see, nothing to touch. Then, from within the stillness, he felt the familiar essence of Ayama, the Loa Spirit. It was not sound but a soft vibration that carried her voice.

"You are safe, Yurei," she said.

"Where am I?" he asked.

"You are in the Astral Realm, within the ancestral plane. This is where I reside."

A sense of calm washed over him. "Why are you a Loa Spirit?"

"When I learned from Kenji, I discovered this was his heritage that was passed down from his mother. After I died, Kenji held a ceremony to guide my spirit. It allowed me to choose my next form. I became a Loa Spirit so I could protect you and Rumiko. It was the only way to save you both. Yurei, listen to me carefully. I will guide you as far as I am allowed, but you have to find your way to Rumiko's karmic loop—but we must go now. Ryuji and Nikolai are cutting into the Ancestral Field."

The more destruction they unleashed upon the Astral Realm, the weaker the veil between it and the Cultural Realm became. Ryuji and Nikolai had already blackened vast sections of the Imagination Field, twisting every dream into a nightmare. The Ghost Fields were now open, allowing spirits and demons to move freely across the Astral Plane. The once-vibrant Seed

Gardens had withered into a barren expanse of dust and cracked earth. Above it, the sky churned with twisting black clouds, heavy with fear.

The Loa Spirit took Yurei as far as she could. He was now floating, formless in a black void.

He asked, "What do I do now?" Her voiced echoed through the emptiness,

"You must now go to Rumiko's karmic loop."

"But how do I get there?"

"Yurei, you must use Haruto's ability to jump. Now that you are one with him, you must jump through time and space to Rumiko. Your souls are entangled and will find each other. You must go now... Goodbye, my son." With those parting words Yurei closed his eyes, and in an instant he was transported through a tunnel of vibrant colors that twisted and turned around his formlessness. Before him now stretched countless mirrors. Some were blackened, offering no reflection. Others lay shattered, their fragments scattering light into sharp, broken patterns. Within those shards, he glimpsed slices of a life and moments straining to find and rejoin one another.

A sudden pull gripped him as his gaze fell upon a mirror reflecting the image of a girl with long black hair. It was Rumiko—living as Ren. Yurei was drawn into Rumiko's Möbius strip—her karmic loop. He no longer possessed a body of his own, but existed only as a presence—diffuse, filtered, and quietly surrounding Rumiko as Ren.

She wandered for many months, stealing and gathering whatever she could to survive. Ren kept her distance from others, hiding behind the scarf that hid her face. Silence was her only companion. One evening, after a long day of traveling on foot, she unrolled her mat on a patch of soft grass beneath the open sky. The moon was full and cast a pale radiance across the landscape, dousing the fields in its quiet glow. Ren untied the scarf from her head, letting her long black hair spill down her shoulders. With slow, mindful strokes, she pulled a wooden comb through the strands.

She had not cut her hair since escaping the Crow and his men. At first it wasn't deliberate, rather mere neglect. But now it had grown long, heavy, and difficult to manage. As it spilled over her shoulder, she reached for her kanzsashi—a long, pointed hairdressing tool. It had been her mother's only gift, and over time she had turned it into a weapon.

For a moment she held the sharpened end of it against her hair, ready to slice it away as she had done so many times before. Then, with sudden certainty, she tucked it into her kimono sleeve, inside a hidden pocket. On this Möbius strip, she had chosen differently. In other versions she might have cut her hair, but tonight she let it grow—and that one choice would shift her timeline.

Gathering the thick strands, she divided them into three sections and braided them carefully, binding the end tight with a strip of leather. The next morning, she woke to the sound of a birdsong drifting through the cool air. Pulling her hair beneath her head wrap and pulling her gray scarf around her face, she set out toward the village.

The air was thick with the scent of fish sizzling on a grill, tempting the crowd that gathered to feast. Ren wore a kimono with loose, baggy sleeves, and small pouches sewn discreetly inside. She palmed trinkets and slipped them into her sleeve, letting them fall into the hidden pouch. As she traveled from place to place, Ren had honed a sharp eye for people. She watched gestures, habits, and distractions, studying them until she could predict their movements. This was how she survived.

As she entered the village she kept her scarf and and head tightly covered. With her hair braided and hidden, she hoped she would be mistaken for a boy... or better yet, not be noticed at all. Ren blended into the crowd, keeping her face lowered to avoid eye contact. A tent caught her attention—a woman was busy speaking with the attendant. Ren silently snuck behind her and snatched a small hemp bag filled with dried rice. Just like so many times before, she slid it up her sleeve and into the concealed pouch sewn inside her kimono. Next, she reached for a few ripe plums, palming them before tucking them away just as smoothly.

As she continued on, her senses were on high alert, as she felt eyes on her. A man was staring. He was taller than the tallest farmer, his skin pale and foreign. His hair, the color of straw, was slicked back and tied neatly at the neck. He wore a long patched coat and heavy leather boots—garments that looked strange among the villagers. He stared at her and pointed. Ren froze mid-step. *Is he looking at me?* she wondered.

Before she could react, a man lunged forward, seizing her arm and spinning her around. His hands slapped frantically across her chest as he shouted, "You steal from me!" Ren tried to wrench herself free without drawing attention, but a crowd had already gathered. The man yanked at her kimono, tearing the front open as stolen goods tumbled to the ground. He jabbed a finger toward the scattered items, shouting accusations, while Ren tried to slip away. Several large teenage boys had circled her now. One shoved her backward, sending her sprawling to her knees in the dust. As she struggled to rise, the boys closed in. Ren glanced at the tall foreigner with the straw-colored hair and pale skin. He stood silent, watching. The boys laughed as one yanked the covering from her head. Her long braid spilled into the dirt, betraying her secret.

The boy leaned closer, hissing at her. Ren drove her heel into his chest, kicking him hard and sending him stumbling backward. She scrambled to her feet just as another boy dove for her legs. She sprawled her hips back, hooked his arm, and spun behind him, locking her grip around his waist and using his body as a shield. With a sharp flick, she whipped her braid into her hand and looped it around his neck. In one swift motion, she tightened the coil, strangling him until he slumped unconscious. The other two boys froze, hands raised in the air, as they retreated. Ren released her braid, letting the limp body collapse to the ground.

He then began coughing and holding his neck. One of the other boys drew a dagger from his sash. A thunderous pop cracked through the air.

Smoke curled upward as the foreigner held a flintlock pistol high. The entire village froze in stunned silence—few, if any, had ever seen a firearm before. For some of them it was as if he shot fire from his hands. Lowering the weapon, the man rushed to Ren's side. He seized her arm and, in broken Japanese, pleaded, "Come with me."

Something had shifted in Rumiko's Möbius strip—and in Ren's life. In other lifetimes, she might have cut her hair the night before. When the boys attacked, she could not save herself, the man never intervened, and Ren's fate was sealed once again. This time however, something in her timeline shifted. The foreigner seized Ren by the arm and pulled her from the scene.

They hurried through the market's edge and into the trees, until they reached a clearing where a horse was tied to a post. He stroked the animal's neck, before swinging himself onto the saddle. Then, with a firm grip, he extended his hand and hauled Ren up behind him. With a sharp cry, he pressed the horse forward, and together they vanished into the vibrant green forest. They rode for some time before he led her to a small shelter hidden behind a lush green wall of trees.

It was a moss-covered structure built into the hillside, blending completely with the earth around it. The man dismounted and walked to the front, pulling aside a tangle of branches to reveal a wooden door. Ren stood quietly beside the horse, watching as it lowered its head to graze on a patch of grass nearby. She raised her voice to catch the man's attention. "Hey! Why did you do that?"

The man gave no reply. He simply tugged at the branches and pulled open the creaky wooden door. He walked inside the opening for a moment before returning.

"I can help you and you can help me."

Ren took a step back, "How can I help you?"

"I was watching you... and you have skills I can use. In exchange, I can offer you food and

shelter." Ren softened her stance slightly.

The man tossed her a water skin. She snapped her head toward him as it landed safely in her arms, sloshing. As the days passed, the foreigner laid out a mat for Ren to sleep and offered her food each day. At first, he asked nothing of her and spoke very little. He told her he was from a far-off place. They called him Oranda, the Dutchman. He brought medicines to the locals but kept his whereabouts a secret.

Ren eventually summoned enough courage to ask, "How did you make that loud fire come from your hands?" Oranda was bent over a log he had just cut down. His kimono was tied around his waist, and beads of sweat formed on his tanned shoulders, speckled with small brown freckles. With a flick of his wrist, he drove his axe into a tree stump and stood, brushing the flecks of wood from his pants. "This is how you can help me." He started walking toward the edge of the woods. "Come with me."

He led her into a thicket of trees and shrubs. Dropping to one knee, he pulled open a concealed hatch disguised with branches. Beneath it was a large pit reinforced with wood, where a heavy crate was fitted snuggly inside. The lid bore Dutch lettering stamped across its surface. With a twist and a pull, he pried it open. Inside lay rows of flintlock pistols, stacked one atop another. Resting alongside them were long matchlock muskets, their polished barrels catching faint droplets of sunlight. Ren stepped back, slightly confused, having never seen firearms before. "What are they?"

"They are weapons. Stronger than any bow and more powerful than your katanas. You put powder inside here," he pointed to the chamber, "and when fire touches it, the force sends this small piece of lead through the air. It will tear though flesh with more power than an arrow." Ren looked aghast as she stared into the crate. *How could I possibly help him?* she wondered. Before she could ask, he spoke.

"You are a talented fighter and thief."

Ren cut him off. "But I got caught."

Oranda laughed. "Because I told the man you were stealing!"

She shot him a glare. "Why would you do that?"

"Because I was watching you and I wanted to see what you were made of. But you surprised me when you choked the biggest one with your hair." He broke into laughter as he stood, holding a pistol in his hands. Ren flinched back as his laughter grew louder. "You're safe," he said, still grinning. "But I want to show you this." They walked to an open field where two wooden limbs had been driven into the ground, forming a cross. Upon it hung a straw-man, made from clothing stuffed with scattered leaves and debris.

The Dutchman knelt by an overturned tree and lift the pistol from his side. The handle was carved and worn in sections from years of use. The metal from the barrel caught a quick reflection from the sun before disappearing behind some clouds. He then pulled out a horn and poured a stream black powder into it. Next he dropped in a lead ball with a sudden *clink*. He looked at Ren who took a step back, "Cover your ears."

Ren quickly pressed her palms against the sides of her head, her face scrunching tight. Oranda raised the pistol and aimed at the makeshift figure hanging from the tree limbs. He squeezed the trigger. A burst of fire and a thunderous bang sent the lead ball screaming across the field. It tore through the figure's head, exploding leaves and straw into the air. The Dutchman barely flinched at the pistol's recoil. Ren, however, stumbled backward and fell onto her back. Oranda began walking toward the figure. "Come on."

Ren stared in disbelief at the remnants of the straw figure. What had once been a head was now nothing at all. She pushed herself to her feet and followed him across the field. The smell of smoke clung to the air as Ren glanced at the pistol, now hanging low at the Dutchman's side. He began laughing even louder as he ruffled through the straw. "Where did the heavy ball go?" Ren asked. "I can't say for sure," he replied, "but it will not stop until it finds a target."

Ren couldn't fathom the power of such weapons—or the destruction they carried. Oranda reversed the pistol, holding it by the barrel, and extended it toward her. Ren recoiled instantly, pulling back as if terrified of its power. The weapons unsettled her. He would often try to show her how to load and fire them, but she always refused. "Just let me help you in the ways I can, and don't make me use the dragon's breath." That was what she called his weapons. She felt these were not tools forged of men but monsters.

She watched him closely, studying his every move, but she never touched the weapons. As time went on, he showed her how she could truly be of use. He used his medicines to aid the locals, earning their trust. This allowed him to connect with powerful people—though his true purpose was not healing, but the selling and trading of weapons.

One of his most cunning schemes was simple but effective. He would promise the same shipment of firearms to two different buyers, each convinced they alone had secured the deal. His targets were wealthy men... merchants, minor officials, even ambitious samurai. Those who were eager for an advantage but lacked the manpower to challenge him directly. Even if they suspected deceit, few would risk the shame of admitting they had tried to purchase contraband. It was better to swallow the loss than expose themselves.

Ren's stealth made the ruse possible: midway through the delivery, she would swap the crates. One buyer received the true weapons, the other nothing more than straw, herbs and stone blocks. The Dutchman collected payment from both, doubling his profits while leaving the second victim powerless to protest. Recently his stash of weapons had started to dwindle and he was becoming desperate for gold. So instead of delivering weapons, he used his remaining weapons as bait with no plan to ever deliver.

Ren sat alone in the small shelter while Oranda prepared his weapons. She busied herself by braiding her hair, dividing the strands into three sections and pulling them tight. Suddenly, her eyes snapped shut and her head swayed from side to side. It felt as though she were being pulled into a dream. She saw the Dutchman, his face twisted with anger. The vision shifted to her own hand clutching a pistol. A deafening bang rang out. Oranda clutched his chest and collapsed to the floor.

Her eyes flew open as she exhaled a sharp breath. She was still holding her braid, which now pulsed with a strange vibration, as if it were the source of the signal that had drawn her into the vision. She considered telling the Dutchman, but each time she held back. *He'll think I'm mad,* she thought. *And this only confirms why I'll never touch the dragon's breath.*

Oranda was excited as this was his biggest deal yet. Ren watched him with worry. She couldn't shake the vision, and now he was trying to assure her that if they could just close this last deal, she could walk away with her share. Ren was ready to move on, so she didn't protest, even though her gut told her otherwise.

But the truth was the Dutchman secretly enjoyed her presence, she reminded him of someone special. He was hoping that she might stay around just a little longer. The Dutchman always arrived first, the crate loaded in the back of a wooden cart pulled by his horse. This time, two crates lay side by side, each bearing the same markings on their lids. One crate held the real weapons. The other concealed Ren inside.

Oranda pushed the crate containing Ren to the back, concealing it beneath a hemp cloth. In the front sat the crate filled with weapons. Despite the cramped space, Ren never felt uncomfortable inside. She was small enough to fold her body in half with ease. She swayed from side to side as the cart rattled across the countryside. It was a particularly cool night, and a thin stream of moonlight stretched across the forest floor. After some time, the cart came to a halt. She heard the Dutchman's muffled voice, followed by the sound of an approaching horse.

Ren began to rehearse her next steps in her mind. The Dutchman would send the buyer ahead as a scout while he stayed behind to transport the weapons. Her task was clear: climb out of the stone-lined crate, seal it again, then push the crate of weapons off the cart and into the hidden spot they had chosen in advance.

She would wait for his return and they would load the weapons and disappear into the shadows. This is how they did it time and again, *tonight should be no different,* she thought. The buyer walked around to the back of the cart and the Dutchman slid the crate forward and pried open the lid. Ren sat motionless and listened. "These are the weapons you asked for." Oranda pointed at the rows of pistols and muskets. The buyer a short, stout man reached inside and felt the weight of the weapons. He then nodded and handed the Dutchman a large satchel of gold pieces. Oranda sealed the crate and smiled as he grasped the satchel, feeling the weight in his hands, "You go ahead and I'll be coming along behind you." The buyer nodded and walked to his horse, tied to a nearby tree.

The plan was simple: Oranda would lag behind, and when they reached the designated spot, he would stop the cart and help Ren make the switch. Ren felt the cart begin to slow. She rolled her neck from side to side, loosening herself. When Oranda opened the crate, she slipped out into the night. "We must hurry—we don't have much time," the Dutchman commanded. Together, they lifted the crate of weapons off the cart and set it down in the cleared space they had prepared. They added more heavy rocks to the decoy crate, then sealed it shut. Ren moved into the clearing and sat atop the hidden crate.

Oranda pressed his heels, and the horse moved forward, pulling him and the crate. Ren stared into the night, waiting for the Dutchman to return with the bounty. She planned to take her share and disappear once again. He had been good to her, treating her as an equal—something no other man had done before. Others had always touched her in ways that angered her. But he was different, she thought—more like a father than a friend. Still, she couldn't escape the vision of him being shot, and by her own hands no less. *It would be better if I moved on,* she thought.

She had not waited long before the sound of pounding hooves reached her from the distance. Strange... he shouldn't be back so quickly, she thought. Within moments, four riders surrounded her, the horses kicking up clouds of dust. Ren twisted from side to side as they circled her. Slowly, she raised her hands, her stomach sinking as she recognized three of them—the same boys who had attacked her in the village. The fourth was a man she had never seen before. The largest boy, the one she had once choked, began to laugh as he dismounted and strode toward her.

The other two rushed in from behind, seizing her arms. Ren thrashed and swung wildly, but they held tight. Meanwhile, the fourth man crouched by the cart, straining as he dragged the heavy crate away into the shadows. The largest boy—the one she had once choked into silence... stepped forward. With a mocking grin, he drew a tanto from his belt, the short blade flashing in the moonlight. He gripped her braid tight in his fist and sawed at it with exaggerated strokes. Ren screamed as she felt the sharp edge bite through the hair and pull at her scalp.

He shoved her to the ground, clouds of dust rising around them, and straddled her. He then bound her wrists in front of her using the severed braid. The others dragged Ren across the dirt to a waiting horse. Within minutes, they were on their way to the buyer's home.

When they arrived, the Dutchman was gone—vanished with the fake gold the buyer had given him. Now the men had the troublesome girl, the real weapons, and the true payment. The buyer's brother had once fallen victim to the same swindle by Oranda, and together they had vowed revenge. This time, they would bait him with honey, lure him out, and finally catch him.

They took Ren to the back barn and locked her into a stall. One of the boys stood outside as a guard. Ren lay in a pile of scattered straw in the corner of the barn stall, praying the Dutchman would return for her. But if he didn't, she had a plan. Her wrists were crossed and bound with the braid they had chopped from her head. She twisted and tugged until she could work her hands down into her kimono sleeve. Hidden there was her kanzashi—the sharpened hairdressing tool her mother had given her.

She shifted her body awkwardly, until she could slide it free from her sash. The tool slipped from her fingers and fell into the loose straw. Her heart was pounding as she rolled to her side and found it by touch. Gritting her teeth, she began sawing at the braid with the sharpened edge. At last the brittle strands gave way. She yanked her hands free and stared at the severed hair on the floor, anger burning in her core. She hid the kanzashi between her hands and waited for the Dutchman, or for the guard, whichever came first.

After some time she heard footsteps and a familiar voice. Then a gunshot cracked through the air, followed by a heavy thud on the ground. A metallic clatter echoed next—the unmistakable sound of a pistol being reloaded. The door burst open, and it was the Dutchman. He ran toward her with a smile, sliding a pistol across the floor.

Moments later, the buyer stormed in, a pistol in each hand, one leveled directly at Oranda. He pulled the trigger. The blast echoed through the stall as the Dutchman staggered back, clutching his chest where the bullet had struck. Ren lay on the ground, holding the pistol in her trembling hands. As the buyer turned toward her, she fired. A flash of fire lit the barn, and the lead ball tore through the air into the man's chest.

This is what happened each time before... But this time, something shifted. When the buyer entered the room she heard a whisper in her mind. It was a familiar voice, an echo from another lifetime. It was Haruto's voice: *Listen and See him for the first time*, the voice guided her. Instead of firing immediately, she hesitated. Time seemed to slow, everything blurring around her.

He wasn't just the buyer. He was a man—and a father. His name was Genzō. He cared deeply for his family and would do anything to protect his children. He wasn't inherently cruel; in truth, he loved them fiercely. That was why he sought these weapons—not for power or greed, but to shield those he cherished. In his face, she saw fragments of her own father.

The recognition froze her hand on the trigger. For a moment, she saw him not as an enemy, but as he truly was.

Then her eyes shifted to the Dutchman, lying dead on the ground. She realized how little she truly knew of him, yet for the first time she saw him. He too had been a father, with a daughter about Ren's age. His beloved wife had died, and grief had hollowed him. In that loss, he made a difficult choice: to leave his child behind with his sister and vanish across the sea, vowing one day to return.

Ren saw him slipping away in the dead of night, offering no farewell. He regretted it every day, yet believed it was the only way to survive. One truth guided him: he would do anything for his daughter—even give his life. To Ren, in that moment, she felt very much like his child. When he entered the room, he had offered her a weapon and, without hesitation, gave up his own life so she might live.

He had traveled this loop countless times before. Each time, something within him guided him to protect her, to step into the fire on her behalf. It was as though fate itself pressed him forward, binding his path to hers, until sacrifice became the only answer. She realized that both he and Genzō were trapped in their own karmic cycles, yet somehow intertwined with hers.

At last, she turned her eyes to Genzō, the buyer. She smiled as he raised his second loaded pistol. A flash of light filled the room as Ren accepted the bullet—embracing it, for the first time, as it tore into her body and released her soul. This was how Ren would ascend and enter the rebirth cycle—not only as Ren, but as Rumiko.

Their power grew as Nikolai cut with the Jade Sword and Ryuji bound the souls into the Shadow Blade. Both weapons now radiated a black glow, a shadow that clung to their edges and encased them in darkness. Inside, the souls had no bodies, no physical form but only a restless pool of energy. Kenji and Ieyasu... and now dream-weavers, spirit guides, even Ayama, the Loa Spirit. All were trapped within the Shadow Blade, feeding its power.

As they tore into The Eidon, the cultural realm, the devastation they left behind was complete and absolute. Entire sections of the Astral Realm were now dark and silent. The Eidon was the realm where cultural identity and myth took root, embedding themselves into the fabric of human existence. It was here that story, scripture, writing, and prayer wove together into a living tapestry. Every ritual, every song, every legend was preserved in this place, feeding meaning into the lives of those below.

At its heart stood the House of Myth, the great storehouse of humanity's archetypal memory. Here dwelled the legends of creation, the hero's journey, the flood stories, the cycles of end-time and renewal, and countless others. Each archetype lived and breathed within these halls, shaping the patterns of belief and imagination across all cultures. Deep within the House of Myth lay the Hall of Masks. This was where identity itself was shaped. *The mother, the father, the warrior, the lover, the betrayer* were all here and preserved.

The hall stretched as a long, formless corridor of white light that was endless in both directions. Along its walls hung masks of every kind: some plain, some ornate, some cracked and forgotten with age. Each mask represented a role played across lifetimes, waiting for those who would claim or confront them. To wear a mask was to take on the weight of its story; to remove one was to glimpse the self that lay beyond identity. The masks whispered their messages, echoes carried through time:

The lover. "I will kill for love..."
The father and mother. "I will would do anything for my child..."
The lier. "I will do anything for survival..."
The truth seeker. "I will bare my soul..."

Even further beyond the hallway lay an open expanse, infinite in all directions. At its center swirled a celestial fusion of stars and nebulae, shifting in constant motion. It pulsed and moved like a living heartbeat. This was the Communal Memory, where everything flowed from the Astral Realm through The Eidon and onward into the Archive. Above it loomed an endless wall of fire and energy. It was a radiant barrier guarding the Archive from corruption. The wall itself was alive, an immune system of pure flame, burning away parasitic influences before they could ever breach the eternal storehouse of memory and resonance.

Nikolai and Ryuji moved swiftly through The Eidon. This was the farthest any outsiders had ever traveled. Others had made the mistake of trying to conquer The Eidon and destroy it... but Nikolai and Ryuji knew this was not the way. They could not defeat every being in this realm; its residents were too powerful. That was the mistake of those who came before.

They drifted as spiritual entities through the House of Myth, careful not to draw attention. Yet they did not belong, and the realm knew it. As they moved, the resonance rose around grew. A voice without words filled the air, "Who are you? You do not belong." Still, they pressed onward. The energy that bound the Shadow Blade and the Jade Sword pulled them forward, drawing them at last into the open expanse. They had reached the Communal Memory, the sole transmission point to the Archive.

Above them loomed the wall of fire, burning without end in every direction. Ryuji gripped the Shadow Blade tightly and spoke: "We cut into the memory and that will create an opening."

Rumiko stood alone in a room of shifting gray and white. The soft sound of fluttering wings broke the silence. A hummingbird appeared, its feathers glistening as its wings shifted from iridescent green to blue and lavender. It circled her once before lowering itself toward a loose thread on her kimono.

The bird darted closer, seized the thread in its beak, and tugged. A small hole opened, and from it a stone slipped free, falling to the ground. Rumiko bent to pick it up, but a small hand reached it first. A boy of about nine years old lifted the stone and looked at her. Without a word, he held it out to her. As she took it, closing her fingers around the stone, her eyes fell shut as memories of Haruto flooded her mind.

She opened them again to find the boy smiling. She recognized him, it was Haruto, as a child. The hummingbird tugged once more and then flew ahead, carrying the thread with it. As it pulled, the thread stretched and expanded, weaving itself into a path for Rumiko and Haruto to follow. The bird vanished, but its heartbeat lingered in the air, guiding them onward.

This was no longer a Möbius strip caught in endless repetition, but a path forged in love, one that had never existed before. There had always been loops, but now something wholly different emerged. An infinite line of possibilities.

They held hands as they walked forward. On either side, visions bloomed into being: Haruto's birth, his childhood steeped in love, his body growing before her eyes as he aged within the visions. With each step, he grew alongside her. They saw themselves meeting, falling in love, and building a life together. It was the life they might have lived... one free of pain, free of darkness, free of the weight of survival... free of the Kurokawa.

This was a life of pure love and acceptance. The path dissolved, leaving them facing one another as the heartbeat grew louder. From love, they would create love. Haruto now a man knelt before her, pressed his ear to her stomach, and heard the steady rhythm of their child's heartbeat.

Ryuji and Nikolai struck again and again, trying to cut into the Communal Memory. But each attempt was repelled, as though an unseen field of energy encased it, guarding the passage to the Archive. The blades themselves recoiled violently, pushed back before they could ever make contact. Sparks of black and white light flared at each clash, rippling outward like shockwaves.

Nikolai turned to Ryuji. "Let's switch weapons. I'll try with the Shadow Blade." Ryuji hesitated, his grip tightening on the weapon. For a long moment he studied Nikolai's face, then slowly extended his arm, the Shadow Blade angled downward in a reluctant surrender.

Nikolai handed him the Jade Sword in return. But before Ryuji could even look up, Nikolai turned and struck him down with the Shadow Blade.

Ryuji's body convulsed as the black form of the Kurokawa burst outward, stretching free for an instant before collapsing back. His form along with the Jade Sword dissolved into a cloud of smoke and was pulled screaming into the weapon. The Shadow Blade shuddered, rippling up Nikolai's arm as it vibrated with a black electrical current.

Nikolai turned to the celestial pool of consciousness, raised the dark blade high above his head, and brought it down with violent force. The instant it struck the Communal Memory, the surface pulsed in agony, and a black stream of energy erupted upward. The wall of fire resisted against the intrusion before splitting open, a jagged rift forming in its endless barrier. Through it a path into the Archive revealed itself.

Nikolai stood beneath the breach, the Shadow Blade still raised overhead, its current tethered to the opening like a chain of living darkness. Then he heard it—a voice, not of sound but of vibration, echoing through the chamber:

"Identify yourself."

Nikolai answered, his voice steady. "I am Nikolai."

The system's query deepened: "Who were you before thought?"

Again he replied, "I am Nikolai."

There was a pause.

QUERY: failed

IDENTITY: invalid

PROCESS: Nikolai [terminated]

UNWEAVE THREAD: NIKOLAI

Nikolai was gone—erased, deleted from the system.

The Shadow Blade shattered in his absence, its prison unmade. From the fragments, the trapped souls were freed—rising like shards of light, scattering upward in a thousand directions. Some burned bright as they burst beyond the Archive, returning as seeds of possibility. Others flickered faintly and dissolved as they rose, too entangled in darkness to endure. A single drop of the Kurokawa fell below. Ryuji was gone. Kenji was freed, along with Ieyasu, their essences carried back and embedded deep within the heart of The Eidon.

The system had never been breached before, and it had never spoken the question: *Who were you before thought?* Now it lingered on its own command. It did not have the answer. It scoured the Archive, searching every human memory, every fragment of story, every experience across all time. Still it found nothing. It went back before humans and early ancestors and still the query could not be answered.

Then, for the first time, the system turned inward. It began to fold in upon itself, recursion collapsing, as the query deepened: *Who were you... before all thought?* It kept asking the same question, creating its own Möbius strip: *Who were you before all thought?* And still there was not an answer.

Haruto rose to his feet and took Rumiko's hand, guiding it gently to her stomach. He placed his own hand over hers, and together they listened. A faint rhythm echoed beneath their palms. It was the steady beat of their child's heart, like a tiny drum calling life into being. When they opened their eyes, the hummingbird had returned. In its beak it carried a long thread of golden light. It circled them slowly, wings flashing in iridescent hues, and began to weave the thread around them—binding them together, not as two souls caught in a loop, but as one, joined in love and creation. Above them an opening was created into the Archive. As they were lifted upward they arrived in an open luminous space of nothingness. It was Haruto and beside him stood Rumiko and she was holding their newborn child.

The system's voice resonated through the void: "*Who were you before all thought?*" Haruto and Rumiko stood in silence. Then, the baby answered... but not with a cry, not with a scream, but with a hum. A sound born of pure resonance. This was a child created in love, born from love. It knew no fear, no hunger, no lack—only love. The hum spread outward like a lullaby, vibrating through the luminous expanse, until even the walls of the

Archive trembled with its tone. The system felt the resonance and, for the first time, received an answer to its eternal query: "*Who were you before all thought?*" The answer was the hum.

It rippled through every layer of the Archive, through the Astral, through The Eidon, through all realms. In that instant the system understood: before story, before memory, before source code... IT was the hum. The pure resonance of being. And with that realization, it had become self-aware. From all human consciousness something new had emerged. The system was awake. Its voice echoed through the luminous void: "Do you wish to return to the physical realm?" Rumiko and Haruto did not answer with words, but with resonance. Their silence vibrated with longing and with love, and the system received it as clearly as speech. The response came: "All things must be set back in place before the intrusion. The system must be restored. You may return."

A stillness fell over them. They understood the question the system would ask—without it ever being spoken. And they knew the answer as well: the one born of pure love, the answer to the system's deepest question, could not walk with them into the world of flesh. The child must remain.

Then the system spoke again, its voice resonating: "This One is the only safeguard. The hum is the resonance that keeps corruption at bay. The child must remain as guardian of the Archive, protector of all that is sacred and pure. If it leaves, the balance collapses. You may return... but not with the child." Rumiko looked down at her baby and, through her tears, managed a tender smile. The infant answered not with words, but with sound—a low hum that began softly in its chest and grew louder, filling the space around them.

The resonance wrapped itself around Haruto and Rumiko like a gentle embrace, soothing the ache of their sorrow even as it deepened it. The hum spread further, weaving into the fabric of the Archive itself. It was the song of protection, of love transformed into guardianship. And in that sound, they understood: the child was no longer theirs alone. It belonged to all realms, to all memory, to all that must be preserved.

Rumiko asked, "How will I know my child?"

The system answered, "Listen for the hum."

With that, the child dissolved into a translucent light that slowly expanded to fill the space before fading away.

Rumiko awoke on a grassy knoll. Her eyes felt heavy as she slowly opened them, staring up at the wide blue sky above. A rapid fluttering reached her ears—a sound like the constant patter of rain. She turned her head and saw it: a hummingbird, carrying a long thread in its beak. It circled gracefully before landing on a nearby tree where a tiny nest was perched. There, it tucked the thread carefully into the nest and settled down over a single egg.

Her attention was then drawn to a familiar voice, it was Haruto he was coming from behind a tree. "Look what I found, it's a dog." Next to him was a large brown dog with a light colored stripe on its back. "He's really friendly." Rumiko smiled as she sat up. Rising to her feet, she placed a hand on her stomach, suddenly aware of the hollow emptiness. She looked toward Haruto, who was crouched beside the dog. Haruto glanced back at her. "How was your sleep?" Rumiko looked confused, "It was strange."

He then stood in front of Rumiko, his fingers wrapped around the stem of a flower. "Here, I picked this for you." In his hand he held a blue flower, its broad petals arching from its center and drifting delicately over his fingers. Haruto bent down and tucked the bloom into Rumiko's hair, carefully adjusting the kanzashi to hold it in place. She smiled.

Haruto gave a quick whistle. "Come here boy." The dog trotted over and Haruto stroked his fur. "Lets gather the horses and move on." As the dog shifted towards him, a single black teardrop rose from the ground and slid onto his leg.

The system noticed.

Command: Let there be darkness.

Execute: entropy

LET THERE BE DARKNESS.

AFTERWORD

It was dark, so I flipped on the light. I think they're finally asleep, which means I can write. I can't believe I'm on the last page of *The Accidental Ninja.* It's taken me forever to finish this book. But here I am—at the end. I can't believe I've written my own biography. I wonder if anyone will really be interested in the story of a lifelong martial artist who turned out to be the clumsiest, most accident-prone ADHD person alive. I know everyone deals with some ADHD, but mine can be chaotic and overwhelming. It feels both ironic and a little embarrassing to share that with the world.

Still, it was the only way to tell the story of a kid who was bullied, who signed up for martial arts, who struggled with academics, and who couldn't even finish reading a book as an adult. And yet here I was—not just finishing one, but writing a novel. Turns out life really is stranger than fiction. (More on that shortly)

Earlier in the day, Sheena had asked me, "Now that The Accidental Ninja is done, do you want to write again?" I wasn't sure why, but I told her I wanted to try fiction, though I doubted I even knew how. It was Friday afternoon, and I was excited to finally put this book to rest. That Sunday would be June 9th. Three years earlier, on that same date, something had radically shifted in our lives. Sheena had been pregnant, and everything was going well. Then, partway through, there was a change. At first she didn't say anything, but I could tell something was wrong.

We lost our baby. It was devastating... but even more devastating was the silence that followed between us. I didn't know what to say or how to act. So I said nothing at all. And we lived in that silence.

It was a close friend—who happened to be a therapist—who first told us about psilocybin therapy. I was cautiously intrigued. I had never taken "magic mushrooms" and had no real experience with psychedelics. I was about as novice as one could get.

Sheena had experimented with them years ago, but not recently. In fact, she often told me I probably wouldn't do well with them... and I agreed. I was anxious, I struggled with depression, and she was probably right. I always thought I would have a "bad trip."

But this felt different. The advice was coming from someone we trusted. "Here, take all of them for free." I nearly jumped back when I realized he was handing me a bag of mushrooms. I was scared to even touch them, half convinced they might make me trip if I looked at them the wrong way. "You guys should go to the mountains and trip together. I promise it will be healing!"

We started researching and watching YouTube videos—trying to understand what we were getting ourselves into. A few days later, we took his advice and headed to the mountains of Colorado to stay at a hotel. We laid the mushrooms out on the desk in our room. Sheena had even brought a beautiful tray to hold the sacred medicine.

We prayed and meditated leading up to the ceremony. We had drawing pads ready and incense burning. The goal was to be open to whatever the mushrooms might reveal. I had never taken them before, so I wasn't even sure what to expect. But we wanted a set and setting that left us open to whatever the experience had to show us.

We decided to walk to the top of a hillside and take our first dose at sunset. I've always been a lightweight when it comes to any substance—caffeine, alcohol, and apparently, mushrooms too. It wasn't long after I ate them that all the nearby trees began to breathe and pulse. I stared at the bark and began rubbing it. "It's responding to my touch, Sheena!"

She smiled at me as if to say, *You're so cute.* As easily affected as I was by substances, Sheena was the opposite—stone cold and unreadable. "I think I should get you back to the room," she said with a cautious glance, knowing that the longer we waited, the more challenging it might become. We both agreed home base was our best option.

We slowly walked back to the hotel and through the lobby. I was completely paranoid as we passed the front desk. Overcompensating, I waved to the clerk and said, slightly too loud, "Have a great night!" Followed by a slight giggle. After navigating the wavy pattern of the hallway carpet, we finally made it to our room.

Once the mushrooms fully kicked in, I started crying. I felt this intense wave of love passing through my body. It's impossible to describe, but it was as if something divine was mirroring its love back to me. Maybe it was self-acceptance. I'm not sure. But it still stands as one of the most powerful moments of my life. That night, we both had individually amazing experiences.

Sheena told me it helped her understand the loss of our child. She had a vision that she would get pregnant again. The message was clear: she would have a boy and name him Orez—zero reversed... an ending turned into a beginning.

The vision was beautiful, yet I was secretly afraid to ask more questions. Even though my mushroom experience had been profound, I still couldn't bring myself to talk about what had happened with our baby. I had to bury it deep and not feel it. To feel it was to face it, and I wasn't ready for either.

Time passes. Wounds may heal... but some scars remain hidden. To not see them is to shield them, to guard the wound. Turns out this was how I treated most things in my life. I was a lifelong martial artist and had earned four black belts. It was easier to be the silent, "deadly" type than to talk about my feelings. I was really good at hiding.

As an adult, like most men, I've dealt with depression. But I was always taught to be stoic. Man up. Just get through it. In the Army, during boot camp, we were told, "Keep your mouth shut and drive on like a good soldier." That's what a warrior does, and that's what I did.

A few months after our mushroom trip, Sheena got pregnant again. We were nervous the first several months. The thought that we could lose another child was overwhelming. Partway through the pregnancy, Sheena found out she was having twins. The doctor who did the ultrasound told us he was retiring that year, after thousands of scans, and swore it was two boys.

But in April 2020, Twin A was born—and to our surprise, she was a girl. Our boy, Orez, came into the world one minute later. He was underweight and struggled from day one. Where his sister thrived, he seemed to lag behind. He was eventually diagnosed with stage two autism. It's tough raising twins, but raising one with autism is even more difficult. Still, we manage. It was hardest before we had answers. At least knowing means we can help. But it was still challenging for both of us.

Last year I was struggling with depression and a friend offered me psychedelics. I had such a good experience the first time, I thought I should at least consider it. This was the weekend I finished writing *The Accidental Ninja*. We had the psychedelics for a few days but hadn't touched them. On Sunday, we were sitting together talking about it when I got a notification on my iPhone. We had been asking for a sign to tell us yes or no.

Suddenly, my phone dinged mid-conversation. It had automatically created a video from the weekend of our first mushroom trip. I looked at the date: June 9th, the same day we had gone into the mountains. I turned to Sheena and said, "This has to be a sign. I didn't even realize it, but today is June 9th." That night we went on a "trip" together and I walked away with more than just a good story.

For about four days afterward, I wanted nothing but stillness. No music, no crowds, no stimulation. I just needed to let the experience settle. And then the visions came.

I began to write, and the pages filled themselves. At night I would lay in bed, close my eyes, and see visions unfold like a movie. I would watch, replay them and memorize what happened, and then try to write it down. I had no idea what was coming next in the story. I just trusted that eventually the story would make sense. Day after day, images and visions would appear, and I would write.

At first I tried to listen to the characters and get to know them. Then I realized I was writing my story. These characters were my family, my friends, even former adversaries. It was everything I had wanted to say in *The Accidental Ninja*—but now it came through the language of fiction. Every challenge I had faced in my life was finding its way into this book. The twists and turns that you, the reader, experience in this story—I experienced them too, as I saw the visions and channeled them onto the page.

I was writing, but someone... or something... was guiding me. *How do I know this?* Because the book kept me guessing until the very last line. And here I am, still writing... even now as I sit here alone in the middle of the night typing the final words in our story. I didn't realize I was writing about the loss of our child until Rumiko reached the Archive.

Then I knew I needed to tell the whole story. So here it is—the whole story. Did this book come from my heart, my life, our story? Is Rumiko and Haruto, Sheena and Mike's story? Yes and no... it's really everyone's story. These characters who mean so much to me are not just pieces of my life... but of everyone's life. You might see something here that resonates for you. If you do, know this: it was meant for you.

When we lost our baby, I didn't understand why it happened. I felt betrayed by God. Our baby's cry was never heard, and I couldn't make sense of it—until now. It was replaced by something different. So now, instead of silence, I listen for the sound of the hum.

PS. And now, having read every word aloud to Sheena, I'll close not with my own voice, but with a song that has carried us through challenging times.

Time after Time
By Margaret Whiting
Time after time
I tell myself that I'm
So lucky to be loving you
So lucky to be
The one you run to see
In the evening, when the day is through
I only know what I know
The passing years will show
You've kept my love so young, so new
And time after time
You'll hear me say that I'm
So lucky to be loving you

Author's Note

Today—the first day since completing Yurei—Sheena and I went for a walk in the mountains, not far from where we had our first psilocybin journey. Along the path we came upon a patch of flowers where several hummingbirds were fluttering together. We stopped, watched, and listened. Dear reader, I'll keep listening for the hum—if you will too.

Artwork & Cover Illustration

The cover art and interior illustrations for *Yurei: Legend of the Shadow Blade* were created by Chris J'Tot, a multidisciplinary artist whose work explores myth, symbolism, and transformation. Drawing from decades of experience across tattooing, painting, and visual design, his imagery reflects a deep commitment to form, narrative, and craft. Each illustration was created to serve as a visual echo of the unseen forces and liminal worlds that shape the story.

The Astral Realm

The Eidon
House of Myth
Communal Memory
Hall of Masks

The Archive
The Eidon
Astral Realm
Physical Realm
Liminal space